In Bed With the Enemy

NATALIE ANDERSON
AIMEE CARSON
TAWNY WEBER

Published in Great Britain 2015
by Mills & Boon, an imprint of Harlequin (UK) Limited,
Eton House, 18-24 Paradise Road, Richmond, Surrey, TW9 1SR

IN BED WITH THE ENEMY © 2015 Harlequin Books S.A.

Dating and Other Dangers, Dare She Kiss & Tell? and *Double Dare* were first published in Great Britain by Harlequin (UK) Limited.

Dating and Other Dangers © 2011 Natalie Anderson
Dare She Kiss & Tell? © 2012 Aimee Carson
Double Dare © 2007 Tawny Weber

ISBN: 978-0-263-25229-3
eBook ISBN: 978-1-474-00408-4

05-0915

Harlequin (UK) Limited's policy is to use papers that are natural, renewable and recyclable products and made from wood grown in sustainable forests. The logging and manufacturing processes conform to the legal environmental regulations of the country of origin.

Printed and bound in Spain
by CPI, Barcelona

DATING AND OTHER DANGERS

BY
NATALIE ANDERSON

To all the fabulous staff at Coffee Culture, Timaru—
who never mind when I sit in my favourite booth for
hours (and hours and hours), and who know not to
give me wifi access until I've done a decent amount of
work... You guys are always so patient and friendly—
thanks heaps for giving my 'office' such great service!

CHAPTER ONE

WOMANBWARNED
Don't be a Doormat!

Sick of bad dates and being taken advantage of? Check the facts on him here first—and don't forget to tune into our latest tips to survive the dating jungle...

***WomanBWarned** thread #1862: Mr 3 Dates and You're Out!*

CaffeineQueen—posted 15:49
Ethan Rush might narrowly avoid screwing someone else at the same time, but he'll screw you over in a way that's worse. He's hot but he knows it—and totally fakes the charm. He'll take you somewhere flash a couple of times, flatter you 'til you can't think, give you the best sex ever. You're so dazzled. But before you know it he's saying goodbye. No explanation—just an "it was fun" note. He has to be setting up the next date while he's kissing off the last because next day he's out with her. He goes from the next to

the next to the next. Don't fall for the irresistible act or try to catch because he'll never commit—3 dates and you're out.

MinnieM—posted 18:23
OMG, I dated him 2 and u r so right—he'll make u feel incredible but he'll never want more than 2 or 3 dates. Then u don't feel incredible. U feel like ur heart's been conned out of u. He's a total usr.

Bella_262—posted 21:38
He took me to this incredible restaurant. It was the most amazing night of my life. But for him? Who knows? All of a sudden it's over. I think he's just after numbers. I was so into him. Now I just feel like an idiot.

CaffeineQueen—posted 07:31
He had what he wanted and he went on his way. The fact that it was so good made it worse. You're left hanging, thinking you're half in love with him. And that there's something really wrong with you.

MinnieM—posted 09:46
I still don't know why he stopped calling. I thought it was going gr8 but no warning and is all over. Got amazing flowers but that really didn't help.

CaffeineQueen—posted 10:22
You got a bunch of flowers too? So did I. Definitely his standard MO. Bet there are heaps of others he's done it to. He's the one with the problem, ladies, not us. Avoid at all costs—don't let him get away with the playboy-rat routine any more!

BENEATH his jeans and tee Ethan's skin burned hot one second and snap-froze the next as he read the website. He'd thought the link embedded in the e-mail his sister had sent would lead to the latest hilarious viral vid.

This wasn't hilarious. This was a horror-fest—all about him.

Mr 3 Dates and You're Out picked up the phone.

'Polly, you made this up,' he rapped, as soon as his sister answered.

'Sadly, no.' Polly sounded half-apologetic, half-teasing. 'You're *internetorious*.'

'But I don't use women.' The defensive instinct was impossible to suppress. 'No more than they use me,' he added when she didn't answer. 'I'm a generous date.' Good restaurant. Good company. Good time—for both parties.

'Generous in what way?' Polly asked. 'They're right. You never go on more than three dates with one woman. And you constantly date. *Constantly*.'

'And that's a problem because…?'

'You're only after one thing.'

'No, I'm not.' He enjoyed the company of women, but he didn't sleep around. 'I don't even go to bed with all of them.'

Polly's disbelieving silence echoed. Great. His own sister didn't believe him. Irritated, he glared at the computer, angered all the more by the petty words some bitter ex-dates had written about him. 'You cannot agree with this. Anyone can say anything they want on the internet. Where's the verification?'

'Well, I know the flowers thing is true.'

Because she was the florist he just about single-handedly kept in business. 'So that makes the rest of it true?'

His sister remained silent. Stupidly, it hurt more than it should—the way a paper cut made your eyes water despite being the smallest of incisions. He grimaced at the stupid cute logo with its blinding bright colours. 'Who does this, anyway? What kind of person sets up a website devoted to letting bitter and twisted women vent their vitriol?'

Hell had no fury, and the scorned woman behind this website must be one manipulative wench. She even had awful tee shirts for sale, so she could make money off the vulnerable and vindictive.

'Forget it, Ethan.' Polly tried to switch topic. 'I shouldn't have sent it to you. You're coming to the christening, right? Alone?'

'Yeah,' Ethan growled. 'So I can shield Mum from Dad's latest. And you were right to send it this to me, but off to believe it.' Eyes glued to the screen, he clicked on another couple of entries and seethed even more. He was on there with all the cheats and creeps—though that assumed that what these women claimed was actually true. He knew for sure *his* thread was fabrication, so he was sceptical. And increasingly furious.

'This is defamation.' The injustice burned. 'The internet might be all about free speech, but this is wrong.'

It was completely wrong. Damaging and dangerous. A site like this shouldn't be allowed. Someone had to do something about it before some guy's life or job was derailed by a bad online reputation.

Ethan Rush never shied from a challenge. And he didn't take *anything* lying down.

Nadia's eyes hurt as she squinted at her inbox. Staying up all night to moderate and update the forum had been such a dumb idea. And she'd had to come up with two new blog topics—which at three in the morning had been next to impossible. Her site had gotten so much bigger than she'd ever dreamed it would—truly fabulous—but it made focusing on the day job difficult. Unfortunately it was the day job that paid the bills. And it was the day job that was going to buy her the life and respect she'd fought for for ever. So she wasn't going to screw it up.

She closed her eyes and took a deep breath. Despite exercising on her way to work, there'd been no endorphin high, and she was going to need something more to get through the next eight hours. But before she could raid the snack machine for an assortment of fatty, sugary, salty, fifty-times-processed, plastic-wrapped rubbish, her phone rang.

'Nadia, I have a gentleman in reception asking for you,' Steffi the receptionist informed her, with an incredibly sparkly intonation.

'Really?' Nadia checked her calendar, but her first appointment wasn't scheduled for an hour. 'Me?'

'You. Apparently no one else will do.'

Really? Nadia didn't think so. He was probably a relentless wannabe recruit and Stef was fobbing him off on her. Millions wanted to work at Hammond Insurance. She knew. She'd fought like a wildcat to get her foot in the door.

'He's pretty insistent. Shall I send him through?'

Oh, yeah—Steffi was totally fobbing off some weirdo on her. 'Okay.' Nadia caved. 'Meeting room five, in three minutes.'

'Fantastic,' Steffi gushed.

Nadia frowned and lowered her voice to whisper into the phone. 'Stef, is everything okay?'

'Sure. Why?'

'You sound a little…puffed.'

'Oh, no.' Steffi laughed too loudly, all her breath seeming to blast down the phone. 'I'm *fine!*'

Uh-huh. Nadia hung up and swivelled her chair. She needed some screen-free time anyway. She picked up one of the recruitment packs and walked to the meeting room.

If he was a wannabe recruit Steffi could have given him an info pack, but some of them were determined to talk to someone beyond Reception. Ah, well, it was a relief to delay starting properly, and she could raid the vending machine on her way back. She got to the meeting room and took up her position behind the desk. She flicked open the pack and prepared herself to deliver the bright smile and the spiel outlining the benefits of this amazing, ancient company, but not allowing too much hope to build in the guy. Hammond only took the best of the best. It took a hell of a lot of hard work to cut it here, and ninety-nine percent of people who applied never got over the threshold.

She looked up as a figure appeared in the doorway. She blinked at the brightness of Steffi's smile. The receptionist was flushed and sparkling, as if she'd had three too many glasses of champagne. She loudly told the person following her, 'Here's meeting room five!' then stepped to the side and Nadia saw the guy himself.

Cue several blinks in quick succession.

So not what she'd expected. She'd been thinking recent graduate—nervous, but bright. Sometimes they were youthfully brash, but they were never this smoothly confident, never this coolly controlled, never this kind of three thousand percent full-grown, red-blooded *man*. Sharp tailored suit, even sharper eyes, and a smile on the face that went with the prime male body. Nadia had never seen anyone with such perfect features in real life—that kind of symmetry was the domain of airbrushed aftershave ads. Only this guy had an edge that was *never* in those ads. No wonder Steffi had morphed into a breathless bimbo. Nadia's lungs squeezed helplessly in sympathy and she couldn't even manage an answering smile, let alone a hello. But the minute Steffi disappeared so did his smile.

A ripple skittered down Nadia's spine and her brain

sharpened. She blinked away the blinding effect of his beauty. He didn't look as if he hoped to score a job at the most prestigious insurance firm in the city. He looked as if he had the world and its riches at his feet already, and could take or leave anything at his leisure. But that edge was there—*simmering*—and something raw was a scant centimetre below his incredibly smooth surface. Something she wasn't sure she wanted to identify.

He paused another moment just inside the doorway, then carefully closed the door behind him. All the while he stared as hard at her as she belatedly realised she was staring at him. Finally he spoke. '*You're* Nadia Keenan?'

She swallowed. 'That surprises you?' she asked, with a coolness that surprised her. She gestured to the seat across the table, because she was going to get a crick in her neck if she had to look that far up for another moment. Yeah, she should have stood, but her legs were as supportive as soggy tissue paper, and somehow she knew revealing weakness in front of this guy wouldn't be a smart idea.

He took the seat, moving his all-muscle, no-fat frame in a too controlled kind of way that made the ripples run even faster across her skin. Apprehension…and something else she *definitely* didn't want to identify. Instead her brain tracked down another avenue. Exactly how had he known to ask for her specifically? Because she was sure now he had—it wasn't Steffi fobbing anyone off. This guy was here for some very precise reason. But she was merely an HR assistant. It wasn't as if her name was listed on the company website. So why her?

Silence sharpened another second. She glanced past him, relieving her strained wide eyes and trying to regulate her pulse back to normal. Two of the walls were windows—the lower half frosted, but the upper part clear. Her clenched muscles eased a smidge. Anyone walking past could see in.

There was no reason to feel isolated—no reason to feel as if the room had been sucked of all its oxygen. There was no reason for those ripples to relentlessly slither back and forth across her skin. And it wasn't exactly fear…it was that something else.

She swallowed again and drew another cooling breath. 'How can I help—?'

'What's the policy on internet use here at Hammond?' he interrupted.

Pressing her lips together, she nudged the recruitment pack on the table between them, avoiding looking at him as she pulled her scattered thoughts together.

'I should imagine it's pretty conservative,' he continued, before she'd collated her answer. 'Pretty conservative establishment all round, is Hammond.'

'Do you have a point, Mr…?' She paused deliberately, still not looking him in the eyes.

'Rush. Ethan Rush,' he said, as smoothly and unselfconsciously as if he were James Bond himself. 'Do you recognise my name?'

'Should I?'

'Yes, I think you should.'

She blinked and pushed the pack again, to buy another moment of thinking time. Except she couldn't really think—she could barely breathe—and her pulse was *pounding*. 'Well, I'm sorry, Mr Rush, you'll have to explain.'

'But you've been warned about me.'

'I have?' Startled, she looked up—and found herself snared in the reddish tint of his brown eyes—the *hardness* of those eyes.

'Yes, on WomanBWarned. Do you know that website, Nadia?'

In less than the micro-second it took for her to gasp, shock had covered her body in goosebumps. Every inch of her skin screamed with sensitivity; every cell was shot with adrenalin. She let another second slide, and as it did she decided to avoid—then feign ignorance. And if that failed she'd deny, deny, deny.

'Was there something you needed today, Mr Rush?'

'Yes, I wanted to be sure about the internet policy here at Hammond, and apparently you're the HR expert on it.' He didn't seem to move, but he was somehow even bigger, filling the room with ferocious energy. 'Tell me,' he said drily, 'does your employer know you run one of the bitchiest, most defamatory sites on the internet?'

Nadia's throat tightened as if a hangman's noose had just been jerked, rendering speech impossible.

'It wouldn't do your little HR role much good if your bosses found out about your hobby, would it? Not when you're sending out these little edicts to all their employees about online protocol. Not in a great position to give advice, are you?'

Nadia firmed her jaw—she resented the "hobby" description.

He pulled a paper from his pocket and unfolded it, placing it in the table. She glanced at the heading, and then back up to his simmering countenance. She didn't need to read more because she'd written most of it. The internal memo on internet access and computer use, explicitly detailing that social networking sites, forums and such, were forbidden. She'd drafted the updated policy before getting it approved by Legal and her supervisors.

'Where did you get that?' And how on earth had he tracked her down?

'I find it so ironic that you deliver seminars to the other employees about protecting their online presence and reputation when you're so vicious in cyberspace yourself.'

'Do you have a point, Mr Rush?' She curled her toes and

tensed her muscles. She wanted to escape but refused to run away. Because she really needed to know what his point was. Despite her hammering heart, she told herself to keep calm. She was safe. She'd never used Hammond computers for her forums and she never would—her job mattered too much.

'What do you think, Nadia? Why am I here?'

She shrugged her shoulders slightly. 'No reason I can think of. Unless you wish to discuss possible employment at Hammond, I don't think we have anything to say to each other.'

He smiled as he surveyed her. Sitting back in his seat, he was now completely at ease, as if he was the one who worked here, and not total stranger who'd just come in off the street. And he was completely gorgeous, in an all-male, all-arrogant way.

Oh, yes—woman be *warned*. She knew his type—too good-looking for his own good. A spoilt playboy who'd been outed as a two/three/four or more timer for sure. And he wasn't happy about it? Too bad.

His eyes compelled her to answer his challenge. Fire burned in them—literally a touch of russet in the cinnamon iris—impossible to ignore.

But she'd damn well try. 'You might be twice my size, but you don't intimidate me. You can take your threatening attitude elsewhere.'

'Threatening?' He laughed. The sound spiked the air with danger. 'I'm not here to threaten, Nadia. I'm here to extract a promise.'

She quickly touched her tongue to the inside of her dry lips.

'The thread about me is defamatory,' he said bluntly.

'Well…' She forced a smile. 'The defence to defamation is truth.'

'That's right,' he agreed.

'So you're saying what's on there *isn't* the truth?'

'That's right.'

She shrugged. 'So prove it.'

Six seconds passed by. Her senses had suddenly grown so acute she could hear the hand of her tiny watch ticking, so she knew exactly.

'You don't think that's the wrong way round Nadia? In a free and just legal system a man is innocent until proven guilty. But in the little world *you've* created he's guilty until proven innocent. You don't see a problem with that?'

She shot him a look designed to wither. 'The men detailed on my site *are* guilty.'

His answering glare was withering and then some. 'You don't accept that it might be open to abuse? You don't think a woman with a vendetta might take advantage of it?'

'A woman with a vendetta? Please—men like you made up that kind of stereotype.'

'So you're *not* a woman who was hurt by some man and seeking payback? That isn't why you set this thing up?'

Her temper flared. 'I set this up so people had access to information. All kinds of information.'

'Because all men are bastards?'

'Information about dating in the modern world,' she corrected. But this conversation was futile. He was never going to understand—clearly his outsize ego was too bruised. 'I don't need to justify myself to you.'

'Oh, I think you do.' He leaned forward. 'I think you need to justify your actions to a lot of people. And why won't you come clean about it? Why hide behind online anonymity? Your employers here don't even know.'

She glanced out of those windows, wishing they were solid walls now. Of course they didn't know. They'd totally disapprove. They stressed online responsibility and reputation—it was what *she* taught every new recruit. And she did not want to jeopardise her job. She'd worked too hard to get it.

'I don't cheat,' he said firmly. 'And I don't swindle naïve girls out of their life savings. So why am I on there?'

'You've obviously hurt someone.' And she'd be reading the thread to find out how, the second she got the chance.

'So where's my right of reply?'

'You can post a rebuttal. You just have to register and log in.'

'What? And give myself an anonymous identity like the shrews on there?' He shook his head. 'I think *you* need to take ownership of the site that you've created. *You* need to take responsibility for the accuracy of the content and for the damage that can ensue from it.'

'In what way has it damaged you?' He struck her as bulletproof.

He paused. 'Reputation is an unquantifiably precious thing.'

She knew that. 'So what do you want?'

He sat back in his seat, the back of his fingers brushing his mouth and jaw. She tried very hard not to follow the movement and focus on that mouth with its full lips. Instead she tried to meet his gaze—except it seemed it had wandered...

She watched, steaming up, as he looked at her mouth, her neck, her chest. She saw the deepening fire in his expression and felt the response inside herself—her muscles shifting as hormones rushed. Beneath her blouse her breasts tightened...

Of course her body would react to just a look from this too handsome playboy stud. Her mating instinct was so *off*.

Slowly his lashes lifted and he captured her gaze with his gleaming one. 'I guess if I have to prove it, then I'll prove it.'

'How are you going to do that?' And why was she suddenly whispering?

'Three dates,' he said, just as softly.

'Pardon?'

'You and I are going to go out on three dates. You're the judge, jury and the executioner, right? So judge me on the facts. I'll prove to you that what's up on your site is untrue.'

She laughed—only one note lower than hysterical. It was preposterous. 'I'm not dating you.'

'It's that or call your lawyers.' His gaze coasted over her again, assessing in the most base way. 'Got lots of money for lawyers, Nadia? No, of course you don't. Otherwise why would you be working as a lowly HR assistant?'

'The users of my forum sign a waiver.' She tried to recover her ground. 'I can't be held responsible for what they put up there.'

'It's so convenient for you to hide behind that rule, isn't it? I think it could be due for a test in court, though.' He smiled sympathetically. 'And it'll take months. All that time off work… Everyone here at work is going to know, Nadia. And your family, friends…' His eyes narrowed. 'They don't know either, do they?' He went for the kill. 'You're going to need good lawyers for a long and expensive time, honey.'

'You're willing to waste that money yourself?' Her stomach churned. He couldn't be serious. Surely he wouldn't do that?

'I don't think it is a waste. Anyway, I *am* a lawyer, I can represent myself.'

Of course he was a lawyer. He was every inch an aggressive, adversarial jerk. Well, he wasn't going to intimidate *her*. She swallowed back the bile burning its way up her throat. 'I'm not taking your thread down. It's freedom of speech.'

'Actually, I don't want you to take it down,' he said thoughtfully. 'Let's face it, once things are out there on the web they're out there for ever. What I want is a retraction.'

'Then you need to contact the woman you slimed, not me.' He didn't need to involve *her* at all. Three dates? It was ridiculous.

'They're anonymous—I don't know who they are.'

They? Oh, how very nice. 'And you can't figure it out because there are so many possibilities?' She widened her eyes in fake surprise. 'Be honest.' She snapped into attack mode. 'What you really want is a suck-up piece, going on about how fabulous you are in bed.'

'You're offering to sleep with me so you can report with accuracy?'

Her face went hot. So did every other part of her body.

'I don't need your approval to know my worth as a lover, Nadia. What I want is an acknowledgement that sometimes people put things up there with a warped perspective. Although what I *really* want is for you to pull the plug on this poisonous swamp of bitterness altogether.'

'That's not going to happen.'

'Being a bitch is that important to you?'

She shrugged. 'If warning other women about jerks who want to use them makes me a bitch, then I'm happy to be considered one. For a long time.'

'So how do you know what they put up is accurate?'

'Why would anyone lie?' It was simple. 'I've already told you these aren't women with a vendetta. These are women who've been hurt really badly.'

'Women like you?'

She froze for a nano-second. 'It isn't personal for me.'

'Like hell it isn't.'

Grimly, she hid her fists beneath the desk and tried to think of a way out. But she was backed into a corner and she knew it. 'Okay, then. You want three dates? Fine. But we go Dutch.'

He winced theatrically, but that didn't hide the satisfaction in his eyes. 'Yeah, you would be that crass.'

'I wouldn't want to feel I owed you anything, Mr Rush. Or that you expected anything from me because you bought me an expensive dinner.'

'Actually, I'm expecting quite a lot from you Nadia.' He smiled with genuine amusement. 'And call me Ethan.'

She stood up and walked to the door, because if she didn't her anger was going to burst out utterly inappropriately. He stood too. She saw him take in her height and glance down to register the height of her heels. She just knew he was mentally calculating the difference if the shoes were off.

'Very dangerous things come in small packages,' she said tightly.

He grinned—the patronising, "amused by the little girl" grin that she'd seen way too many times in her life.

'So do very precious things,' he countered softly.

She didn't see him the rest of the way out. Couldn't. The wave of heat all but blinded her. Half fury, half something else altogether. Oh, yes, he deserved to be on WomanBWarned, even if he wasn't a bona fide candidate. He'd trample hearts without any effort whatsoever.

But not hers. Never, *ever* hers.

CHAPTER TWO

WomanBWarned
Top tips for surviving the dating jungle. What not to do on your first date…

Don't drink—at least not much. Alcohol impairs judgment and you want to make safe, sensible decisions.

Don't be too sexual—if it's a possible relationship you want, not a one night hook-up, then keep a little mystery. You want to be taken seriously.

Don't go on and on about your ex(es) or your ailments or how awful your boss is. Negativity is a downer.

Don't go to the movies—it's a cop-out. You want to get to know the person, not sit next to them in silence for two hours.

Don't try too hard—just relax and be yourself.

ETHAN sprawled on the sofa in his apartment and laughed as he read, his laptop balanced his stomach. Oh, boy! *OlderNWiser*—the online pseudonym for one Nadia

Keenan—really had her rules, didn't she? There were a ton of little blog bits on her site, giving tips for this and that in the dating realm. As if she was some kind of expert.

He *so* didn't think so.

The woman needed a lesson or fifty from a true master. And he knew just how he was going to do it—by taking over her own turf, of course. Fighting fire with fire and all that. Because anyone could set up a blog, right? And fortunately he was partner at a firm that *didn't* have uptight HR princesses like Nadia Keenan. His firm believed in treating adults like adults, and didn't care about what personal things employees decided to put up on the internet. There were no draconian, moralistic guidelines attempting to govern their workers' private lives. So long as it wasn't work-related, and didn't impact negatively on the business, they weren't interested. If the people he did deals with stumbled across it they'd most likely laugh and cheer him on. They were human, with senses of humour.

Yeah, it wasn't because of *his* work that he was bothered by her reputation-shredding website. For him, it was the core injustice of having to prove innocence instead of guilt. That violation of a fundamental legal principle. Okay, there was an element of the personal too. They'd picked on the wrong Rush. Ethan didn't deserve to be slated—it was his father who was the jerk. And Ethan refused to be anything like his father—not fickle, not deceitful, not hurtful. Ethan might play, but he was up-front and honest about it, and always nice to the women whose company he enjoyed. Mind you, he didn't feel like being nice to Nadia Keenan.

He logged onto one of the major blogging sites and thought for a second about a title.

GuysGetWise?

Fantastic—not registered, and his to use.

And his tagline?

Taking on the Dirt-Dishing Dating Divette.

He could do alliteration too, see? And at least he could spell, rather than use basically illiterate abbreviations. The t-crossing, i-dotting legal writer in him detested those. Although admittedly "divette" was his own invention—but she was too itty-bitty to be a true diva. He filled in the little grid detailing "all about this blog"...

Ethan Rush—supposedly "shamed" as Mr 3 Dates and You're Out over on WomanBWarned wants those women to get real and for guys to wise up to the dating reputation dross that's online. Come hang out here, boys, and get clued up to the reality. And get way better dating advice than any you'll read over there...

Because he was so much more of an expert on dating than Ms OlderNWiser, and she was going to know it. He chuckled as he composed his first entry. There was nothing like a direct challenge to get his blood pumping. Grin wolfish, he started typing the beginning...

GuysGetWise: *The chick flick is your friend*

*According to the self-proclaimed guru over at **WomanBWarned**, **OlderNWiser**, going to the movies is a dumb first date destination.*
   Wrong.
   *A cinema is a nice, totally safe environment that can push the defrost button on even the most hardened ice queen—like **OlderNWiser** herself.*
   You can round it out more if you want by going for pizza before, if necessary—NOT the usual cheap delivery, guys. This first time it's got to be gourmet.

Be seen to be making an effort. But, as we all know, there's nothing worse than being stuck at a pricey restaurant with a vacuous woman who has no conversation while waiting hours for two strips of potato, a fifty-pence-sized piece of steak and some weird green oil drizzled in dots on the edge of an oversized white plate. Instead go for pizza to say hi, and then ease off the pressure for a bit.

The movie gives you a couple of hours to settle into each other's company—you're close, but not too intensely focused on each other. Afterwards you've got something to talk about to start you off. And then, once she's started, she won't stop. Babes like to talk— and they will if warmed up. After a movie she'll be in the mindset. So let her share with you.

Immutable dating fact: the more you let her share, the more she'll want to be with you. It's that simple.

You might wince, but the chick flick in particular is your friend. She'll get the warm fuzzy feeling. Go for the one-two punch—the chick flick followed by dessert. She'll be as gooey inside as the chocolate pudding she's spooning in. And, bud, you will benefit from the happy ending hormones she's riding on.

*Brace yourselves and get her to a rom-com, feelgood kissy flick. That's what I'll be doing with Ms **OlderNWiser**. It's the perfect first date softener. And us guys like soft.*

Ethan paused, his fingers hovering above the keyboard, his lips twisting as an evil urge gripped him.

Stay tuned for how to nail her on the second date.

He hit "publish" before he had second thoughts. Hey, he'd said it all along—there was a lot of rubbish out there on the internet. And she'd shredded his rep anyway, right? This was his way of reclaiming his own image. He didn't really give a damn about what the anonymous readers on the ends of the ethernet thought, but he was *not* a cheat—yes, he played, but all the playmates had fun. And he'd get even the world's most uptight woman to appreciate some *fun…*

His blood quickened, but he forced his brain to stay open for duty. He went into the WomanBWarned site and registered—under his own name—and then went to the *Mr 3 Dates and You're Out* thread to comment.

> *EthanRush: Looking for another side to this little story? What happened to balance and verification of information? Neither of those things are apparent on this bitch-fest. So how about a challenge? The woman in WomanBWarned herself—OlderNWiser—has agreed to a series of dates with me, Mr 3 Dates and You're Out. As she's Chief Judge and Executioner around here, she's agreed to give me a fair trial.*
> *Three dates, of course.*
> *She'll play them her way. I'll play them mine.*
> *We'll report back and you can decide—who's the honest one and who's the user?*
> *Who's the victor?*

The comment appeared beneath all the others. He'd well and truly thrown down the gauntlet. What he needed now were some supportive comments to get traffic his way and stack the odds in his favour. Happily, he had some guys who knew him well enough to know his tongue was—partly—in his cheek. Guys liked sport, and he was a team player. His team would get behind him. He put the link on his social networking page, then shut the laptop and closed his eyes.

And then it hit him.

This was *mad*. This wasn't what was supposed to have happened. He was supposed to have gone in there all guns blazing and torn shreds off her. Demand she take down the thread, take down the whole damn site, and totally threaten to sue her.

Okay, he *had* threatened that.

But only after he'd been struck by a far more entertaining idea. The threat had simply been a way to push her into accepting that far more entertaining idea. With her *OlderNWiser* handle he'd figured he'd be facing down some ancient hardened up crone, but in reality she looked like one of the fairies on his three-year-old niece's miniature china teaset. All fine bones and fine features in her heart-shaped face, with her hair tumbling loose and kinking at the ends. And, yes, his thoughts *had* immediately kinked.

He'd have to be careful how he played this, because he refused to end up in a mess. He did charming and nice—never messy. But he'd teach her a lesson—Nadia Keenan was going *down*.

No, *not* sex—there'd be no sliding along sun-kissed limbs, no stroking delicate collarbones, no relentlessly touching 'til she begged for mercy and then screamed her ecstasy in his mouth. No matter how vivid that fantasy was, an even bigger temptation bit. He'd get her hot and twisted and then be a total gentleman. Restraint all the way. And she'd hate him even more than she already did.

He couldn't get over the contradiction—she looked sweet but she savaged people with her vindictive website. Who'd hurt her, and how? She'd said it wasn't personal, but there *had* to have been a guy who'd broken what little heart she had. Her online ID even acknowledged she was *OlderNWiser*.

He flipped the laptop open again, went back to *WomanBWarned* and clicked on the archives link.

To win any game you had to be prepared. You had to understand your opponent's weakness...

Nadia wished Megan was home, but she was in Greece for three weeks, meeting her boyfriend Sam's family, meaning the flat they shared was quiet and empty and totally lacking in advice—the walls weren't answering back.

She pushed aside the clothes-hangers in her wardrobe, desperately searching despite knowing exactly what items were there and that whatever it was she wanted wasn't.

Because she didn't know *what* she wanted and she didn't have the funds to shop.

She had to ace it over Ethan Rush, but he had every angle covered. Good looking, intelligent, loaded—that was obvious from his clothes and his confidence. Everything came easily to him—even her acquiescence to his stupid idea. She had to shake him from his self-satisfied, smug little perch. But how?

She picked up the bag she'd tossed on her bed. Her phone rang just as she got hold of it. Megan—hooray for serendipity.

'What do I wear to a date I don't want to go on?' Nadia asked straight off.

'A date?' Megan's high-pitched amazement was no surprise. 'Why don't you want to go?'

'Because he's a complete jerk who's bullied me into it.'

'Nadia,' Megan scoffed, 'no one bullies you.'

Ten hours ago Nadia would have agreed. 'If I don't date him he says he's going to sue me for defamation and out me as the woman behind WomanBWarned.'

'Don't tell me he's on it?'

'Yeah—has his own thread. *Mr 3 Dates and You're Out.*
Totally smooth snake who's only interested in sex. Moves
on immediately after. Serial dating offender, seriously arrogant. More than one victim has commented.'

'He used *that* to get you to agree to go on a date with
him?'

'Three dates.'

'Three?' Megan started to giggle. 'Oh, he's good.'

'He's not good. He's mad.'

'But he won't waste money suing. Just tell Hammond you
run the site. They won't care. It's in your own hours and on
your own equipment.'

'I worked too hard to get that job. I'm not screwing it
up.' Independence mattered—achievement mattered. Nadia
wasn't failing now, having secured a great flat and a great
job when no one in her family had believed a "little thing"
like her could—or, worse, *should*. They'd thought a big city
was too bad a place for her, so she'd gone to the biggest city
in the country and got employed by one of the biggest, most
traditional-to-a-T firms. That was the only way she could to
prove herself to them—they'd just be baffled by her blog.

'I'm reading the thread. He sounds interesting.' Megan
drew in a long, slow breath. 'Good sex. When did you last
have sex?'

Nadia banged the wardrobe door shut. It was all right for
Megan. She and Sam were still in that honeymoon phase,
so she was getting it at least twice a day. Nadia hadn't had
it twice in the last year. Or two.

'Nadia.' Megan's tone totally changed. 'Did you see his
reply?'

Nadia's blood iced up. 'There wasn't one.' She ran into
the lounge, where her computer dominated the dining table.
Praise be to high-speed broadband, because the thread

loaded in a flash. And it only took a flash to realise what he'd done.

'He's made it public. The dates.' Her throat clogged. 'Why? Everyone is going to know we're going out.' And there was going to be a *victor*? Oh, she'd been right. This was war.

'Well, they know *he* is.' Megan morphed into the voice of calm. 'You've still got your anonymous ID. There's a link to a blog. He has a blog?'

'It's new, and I'm already reading it,' Nadia said grimly, quickly skimming the post and growing all the more aggravated.

But Megan giggled. 'I can't wait for him to "nail" you on the second date.'

'He's a conceited jerk. He's not nailing anything.' Certainly not her. And she certainly wasn't feeling a quiver of excitement at the thought. The quiver was suppressed rage.

'He's good-looking, right?' Megan asked. 'He must be to be this confident.'

'If you like over-sized macho men who think they're it and everything else.' Physical invincibility didn't do their personalities any favours, and she didn't need the over-protectiveness that tended to accompany their delusions of demi-god status.

'He sounds just the ticket.' Megan had pepped up. 'What *are* you going to wear?'

Nadia bit back her growl. She knew Megan wanted her to be as loved-up and happy as she was, but she didn't want to be attractive to Ethan—she wanted armour. Fortunately high-pitched beeps interrupted whatever Megan was saying now.

'I have to go, Meg,' Nadia said quickly. 'I've got another call.' She jabbed the buttons. 'Hello?'

'Nadia.'

From the frying pan to the fire. Just her luck. 'Ethan.' Those infernal goosebumps smothered her skin. She refused to recognise the other instant reaction deep and low in her belly.

'Wednesday night good for you?' No preamble or polite chit chat—but his voice was caramel enough.

Wednesday. Mid-week and only two days away. She needed more prep time. 'Actually, I already have plans for Wednesday,' she lied. She wasn't going to make it easy for him. Not at all.

'Thursday, then?'

'I could do Thursday.'

'I was thinking a movie or something.'

Total fail on the originality front, but she'd get him back—because she'd read his stupid blog. She wasn't going to let him know she'd read it. Damn. She suddenly realised that he would know if he checked his traffic stats and knew her ISP. Which he obviously did—he seemed to know way too much about her internet activity. She quickly took a screenshot and logged out of the site. She'd only check it from wireless hotspots now, at random coffee bars or something.

'That sounds great,' she said with zero enthusiasm. 'Can I choose the movie?'

'Of course.'

She paused. 'How did you get my number?'

'Same way I found out you're the woman behind WomanBWarned. There's a lot of information out there on the internet.'

'But it's secure.'

'Never as secure as you think. I'll pick you up from your place.'

'You know where I live?' Now, *that* was scary.

'Sure.' She could hear his smile. 'On the corner of Bitter and Twisted Street, right?'

'What a shame you won't *get lost*.'

'I don't plan to,' he drawled, in a way that made her shiver more. 'Text me all your details and I'll let you know what time.'

'Oh, I can't wait,' she cooed, just to get the last word in.

She tossed her phone onto the sofa and stared at the words frozen on her huge screen. It was the "divette" that did it. The patronising, belittling, condescending bastard.

Damn it, she *was* going shopping. She wanted to look more than nice. She wanted to look *hot*. So hot he couldn't help but want her and make his one move too many. The possibility was there—she'd seen the flash in his expression when he'd looked her over so boldly in her office today. Definite sparks. And she didn't deny she'd responded on a basic level. But she could control her own reaction while blowing harder on those sparks. Get *him* hot. And then— when he made his move—she'd refuse him. And that would be so incredibly satisfying.

Nadia wasn't conceited, but she didn't underestimate her potential strengths either. She knew she had a little something that intrigued some men. *Little* being the operative word. A lot of guys liked petite women. Funnily enough, it was often the taller guys who liked petite women most. Nadia figured it made them feel all the more manly. Men like that loved to be looked up to. Literally.

Ethan the Arrogant would definitely like being looked up to.

So she'd do the pretty little woman thing and emphasise her femininity. She went back to the WomanBWarned thread and looked at the comments from the women who'd dated him. She was curious to know more—as moderator she could e-mail them and surreptitiously try to get more info. A possibility she'd definitely keep on file. But if what they said was true then a move from Ethan was probably inevitable, no matter what she wore. Sexual conquest was as natural to him as breathing. It wasn't that he was interested in the individual woman—it was the chase that thrilled him. Pure predator.

But she wanted to turn the screws on him as hard as she could, so she had to make herself more attractive prey. Because she was going to be the woman to put him in his place.

CHAPTER THREE

SHE had found the best ever dress. Not evening formal, but floaty, floral and ultra-feminine. A little pricey, but it was worth it. She teamed it with soft ballerina flats rather than strappy heeled sandals, to really highlight the height thing. She normally never wore anything less than two inches outside her front door, but she was prepared to make a few sacrifices for this mission. She left her hair loose, wearing a slim scrunchie as a bracelet in case it got hot on her neck and she wanted to tie some of it back. She had a soft wrap for her shoulders and a dainty little bag hanging from her shoulder. Minimal make-up—mascara, a little eyeliner, and pink-tinted gloss on her lips.

Fresh, feminine, an innocent at large—that was the look she was going for.

As she'd expected, he turned up right on time. When she heard the knock on the door she had an overwhelming urge not to answer, but she flicked her hair back and faked a smile. It died the second she saw him, and anger flared in its stead. How dared the guy be so hot-looking? Staggeringly perfect, in a steely, square-jawed kind of way—not to mention tall and broad and big in terms of presence. Immaculately dressed in casual jeans and a cotton tee that showed off his shoulders and abs, he just didn't seem real. No wonder he thought he could sail through women without a care—it happened all too easily for him to realise otherwise. Her confidence evaporated in the face of his undeniable attractiveness. Who did she think she was kidding? Could she really play with fire this hot?

'I thought we could get some pizza before we go to the movies,' he said. Amusement and satisfaction lurked in his eyes.

She stiffened as she saw the smugness, and her game plan zipped back. The urge to better him overwhelmed her. She'd do it whichever way she could.

'Oh, that would have been great...' She let her voice trail and frowned a little.

'But?' he prompted.

'Well, the thing is, a movie I've been wanting to see for ages is on, and to catch it we need to go straight to the theatre.' She deliberately bit her bottom lip and looked up, up, up at him, with wide, wide eyes. 'Do you mind?' she asked, as softly and breathily as a 1960s screen starlet—she hoped, anyway.

He didn't answer for a long moment, that lurking light of amusement completely snuffed. 'That's...not a problem.' He half turned away. 'Shall we go now, then?'

'Oh, come in for a moment,' she said with a sweet smile, aiming to appear as accommodating as possible. 'I need to get my wrap.'

It was a warm summer night and she *so* didn't need the wrap—she was boiling. But after half an hour in the movies she always ended up freezing, and she had no intention of snuggling next to him for some heat, despite her plan to fire up the flirt between them.

'Thanks.' He sounded surprised. He looked surprised. She glanced back and saw him taking in the bright surroundings. She knew the flat was stylish and welcoming. But he made rooms shrink when he stood in them, and he made both the background and colours fade—so her focus was forced towards him.

'You've got a nice place.'

Nadia picked up the pashmina that she'd artfully draped on the edge of the large, soft sofa. 'You thought I'd live alone in some dreary bedsit?' Like the lonely, bitter spinster he believed she was? She'd known he'd think that, so she'd deliberately put a slide show of pictures from one of her and Megan's riotous trips to France on her computer. What was it with people pigeon-holing her? Her own parents had told her she shouldn't move to London—that the city was too big for her. The only thing that was too big was the price of the rent. But she had a job at a fabulous firm and sharing this place with Megan was worth it.

His smile grew as he watched a few pictures glide across the screen. 'I'm a fast learner, Nadia. And I'm learning to expect the unexpected with you.'

'Really?'

'Sure.' He faced her. 'So let's get going.'

Adrenalin zinged. She followed him out and locked the door. They walked down the path a few metres before he hailed a cab. She was surprised—for some reason she'd thought he'd have a car.

'You don't like to go by cab?' He caught her hesitation as he opened the door.

Truth was, she didn't want to sit in the back with him. It felt intimate—she'd have preferred to be in separate seats, with a drinks holder between them. Sharing this one space made all kinds of inappropriate images flash—namely, snogging in the back seat.

She banished the wild idea, crossed her knees and ankles, and crouched into the corner, firmly telling both her body and her thoughts to settle down. He relaxed across his half, not taking up more than his fair share. But it felt like it. He was angled towards her. She didn't look at him but could feel him willing her to. She sighed and gave in, registering his slight smile.

'You look lovely, by the way,' he said suavely. 'Very beautiful.'

'Thanks,' she said without meaning it. 'You look good too. But you already know that.'

'Well, *you* know you look incredible no matter what you wear.' His smile teased. 'But isn't it nice to be told anyway?'

She just rolled her eyes.

'Compliments don't work for you?' He looked all the more amused.

'Not from you,' she said bluntly—despite it being partly untrue. 'This whole date thing is a really stupid idea, don't you think? I'm not going to believe a word you say because all you want to do is impress me so I'll say you're a great guy and how wrong all those women are.'

'The circumstances don't matter,' he argued calmly. 'I bet you're a tough woman to impress at the best of times.'

'What makes you say that?' She shrank into an even tighter ball.

His gaze locked on her, and she stiffened at the dispassionate, intensely assessing expression.

'I think you live life according to a list of rules,' he said. 'Many lists of rules. Like the first date protocol you posted on your forum. You have rules for everything—like the uptight HR assistant you are. And anyone who doesn't meet those rules is an auto-fail. There's no room for human error in your life.'

'That's not true.' Her life was strewn with human error—mostly her own.

'No?' A faint smile. 'You're saying sometimes you don't follow your own advice?'

'The little advice I offer comes from my own experience. I'd be a fool to repeat my past mistakes.'

He nodded as if she'd confirmed something. 'So you've turned into a coward.'

Nadia's blood heated even more. 'I'm not a coward, but I am cautious. And I'm not going to apologise for that.'

'Yes, but it strikes me you're a very intelligent, capable woman. Maybe you should have more faith in yourself.'

'Oh, please.' He was back to the complimenting already? This was all part of his charm attack.

'Seriously, you should give your instincts free rein—let yourself go.'

'Oh, you would say that,' she said witheringly. 'That's your aim—for women to let down all their defences *in your arms*.' She shook her head. 'So you flatter and listen and smile your charming smile—and wait for the cherries to fall right into your mouth. It's all so damn *false*.'

His jaw dropped, then he shut it again. Had she actually hit home with that one?

'All right then.' He cleared his throat. 'I won't try to impress you.'

She should have felt a spurt of satisfaction, but the wretched thing was he didn't need to *try* to impress. His very existence did that—he was beyond blessed with physical attributes, and had a voice that demanded attention. Even worse, some of what he said was of interest. Okay, compelling. She'd bet he was a brilliant lawyer.

Why was her stupid radar tuned to men filled with maximum virility when the simple presence of such sensual drive meant they couldn't possibly keep it zipped? Giving in to her instincts would have her as easily obtainable as all the other women he'd encountered. So she'd have to fight against them all the harder.

'So tell me about the movie.' He switched to neutral ground.

'I've been meaning to see it for ages.' She hid her smile as she thought of what was in store.

They got to the small independent theatre and were directed to the smallest viewing room. There was only them and one other person at the screening. She'd done a whole five minutes of research to find the worst-sounding movie on in London, and within three minutes of the film rolling she knew she'd succeeded.

It was in French, with subtitles so crooked they were unreadable, and about the tortured lives of an artist, his wife and his lover. And it was torture to watch. Lots of scenes with the artist painting—they literally got to watch paint dry.

After only ten minutes Nadia was beside herself with boredom and hoping Ethan was going as insane as she was. But she wasn't fidgety just because the on-screen action was mind-numbing. She was hyper-aware of him. They were too close in this darkened space. And the worst of it was the film was just over three hours in duration—that was why she'd picked it. But now she had to sit so near to a man who attracted her body as much as he repelled her mind. And three hours was beyond torture.

The artist scratched his thin brush on canvas for another hour or so. Oh, it was so bad—but it would be worth it. Ethan would hate it as much as she did. They'd both come out of it grumpy, and that served him right for thinking he'd "soften" her up with a movie. A chick flick? Hell no.

But wait a second. He was *chuckling*. She'd missed the wonky subtitle on that bit. She glanced sideways to read his expression in the flickering light. It appeared that he was completely absorbed in the movie, while she was almost out of her tree. The frankly useless artist worked for hours, mostly in silence. Occasionally he muttered in French. Hang on, that was *Ethan* muttering something in French—what? She glanced at him. He was smiling again, as if the movie was the most entertaining thing ever. How was watching paint dry even remotely fun?

And then, to her horror, the so thrilling action was finally interrupted—by an incredibly raw sex scene, featuring the artist and his lover. Not graphic, but so passionate and un-controlled she felt like a voyeur. She sat completely still, as every cell burned up, and seriously wanted to escape. She shut her eyes but the sounds haunted her—and images popped into her head. But no longer was it the scrawny artist—no, it was the fit, filled frame of six foot *several* inches Ethan.

Oh, no, no, no—she was not imagining him. And her.

She was *not*.

She was so glad when the guy went back to his paint-ing. Ten minutes of that settled her pulse again. But then there was another sex scene—a way more graphic one. The action was really ramping up now—this time with the wife. Only in the middle of all the puffing and panting Nadia's stomach started rumbling—loud enough to be heard despite the sudden ecstatic shrieks of the woman.

Even though she'd known she was going to refuse Ethan's pizza offer, she hadn't eaten before he arrived—the butter-flies hip-hopping in her stomach had made that impossible. So now she coughed to cover the uncontrollable gurgling sound, but that was somehow worse as the couple on screen kept right on rutting each other. She buried her face in her hand and simply wanted to die. Why hadn't she checked the rating comments on the film and picked up on the high sexual content warning?

'Are you not feeling well?' Ethan asked solicitously—leaning uncomfortably close.

'I'm fine,' she ground out between gritted teeth, quickly glancing up, only to see total laughter glinting in his eyes.

Damn.

Finally the credits rolled—not fast enough—and apparently Ethan was a watch-them-till-the-end man. It wasn't until the lights went on, bright and unforgiving, that he turned and gave her an even higher wattage smile.

'Was it as good as you'd hoped?' he asked.

'Oh, yes,' she lied as she stood and marched out of there. 'So you speak French?' Of all the rotten luck.

'*Mais oui*, of course.' He held the exit door for her. 'Shame you don't, because some of the subtleties were lost in translation, I thought it was a very interesting film.'

'Really?'

'No, it was rubbish.' He let the door slam behind them. 'But that was the point, right?'

So he knew. Of course he knew. No normal person would really want to sit through that film. They'd have to be bribed with a lot of money. Still, it had served him right—right?

'Let's get something to eat,' he said. 'I'm well aware you're as hungry as I am.'

She'd intended to go home as soon as the movie ended. And frankly she had a headache from tension and hunger. She hesitated.

'You've already cut off your nose to spite your face once tonight,' Ethan said blandly. 'Don't do it again.'

In truth she was so hungry she was beyond able to make a decision now anyway. 'Okay.'

'Great.' He hailed a cab. 'My choice this time. I insist.'

It was a French restaurant. No, it was heaven on earth. Because along one wall stood a gleaming glass case filled with the most amazing pastries—cream cakes, custard and fruit tarts and chocolates. Nadia's functionality reduced even more—she couldn't think or speak, only stare while her mouth watered so much she very nearly drooled. She glanced round the rest of the room and despair hit—the place was packed.

'We won't get a table,' she almost wailed.

Ethan looked down at her, the picture of smug calm in the face of her collapse. 'We already have.'

CHAPTER FOUR

NADIA nearly fainted with relief. Ethan put his hand on her lower back, pressing her forward to follow the maitre d'. She jumped—he had to have one of those trick buzzers in his hand, because he'd just about electrocuted her. The shock made her gulp, and she was hit by a single rational thought. Should she really have agreed to this when her pulse pounded an extra thirty beats per minute the closer the guy got?

Low blood sugar meant she had no choice, right? Those pastries looked too damn good. She glanced back at the display case once more before taking her seat. The sight made her giddy and her thoughts turned crazy again. Maybe she could claim some ground in her quest to intrigue him. Didn't guys like girls who displayed healthy appetites? Wasn't there something seductive if you licked off all the cream or something? If she could raise his want level, drop-kicking him later would have more impact. Hell, yes.

'What do you feel like?' he asked.

She hesitated, toying with some really inappropriate replies—but she figured she should stay subtle at this point to get him over the world's worst movie trick. 'I'm going to skip a main and go straight to dessert. Two desserts, actually, if that's okay?'

His face lit up. 'Sure.'

'What about you?' She mirrored his smile.

He rubbed his flat stomach, 'You don't mind if I do savoury while you do sweet?'

'Not at all.'

Total truce. Or so she'd let it appear. At that point she spent some time studying the menu—purely to have a break from looking at him. Too much of that made her go vacant, and she wanted to stay on track.

'They have an excellent wine selection,' he said blandly. 'Would you like some?'

'Not just at the moment, but you go ahead.' Her smaller physique meant she didn't handle wine that well. She generally had it by the thimble, so she wasn't going to be daft enough to have any now. She waited until the sommelier had left to get the bottle Ethan had selected without even consulting the list. 'So how did you get us this table?'

'I sent a message from the cinema—found out what time the film finished when you were in the little girls' room beforehand.'

She sat back as the waiter poured Ethan's wine, bristling at the phrase "little girl". So he'd known he was in for bum-numbing time at the flicks. She flushed—hating being thwarted, hating feeling this hot. She needed to regain her equilibrium and act more grown-up. She looked at the burgundy liquid. 'Maybe I will have some of that too—thanks.' One glass wouldn't make her legless. And, frankly, she was overheated after that marathon movie and hearing Ethan mutter in French and then spinning her mind by bringing her to gastronomic paradise.

He waited while she sipped. 'Is it okay?'

It was fabulous—smooth, incredibly drinkable and soothing. She sat back after ordering, her happiness skyrocketing at knowing divine food was coming soon.

'Feeling better now?' He looked sly.

'Much, thanks.' She sighed. He smiled, and inside so did she—no doubt he thought that if he added sugar and chocolate he'd have her as gooey as he wanted. He was *so* getting a surprise.

'Did you have a nice night last night?' he asked.

Last night? Oh—that's right. She'd told him she was busy. 'I was catching up with some friends.'

'Yeah, you posted a lot of comments last night.' His smile went evil. 'You live more than half your life online.'

She took another sip of wine to bring her internal thermostat back down. 'You've been snooping.'

'It's not snooping when you put it all out there for anyone to read.'

'And you've been a bit active online yourself,' she said, finally broaching it.

'Ah.' He settled more comfortably in his chair. 'You're mad at me for blogging about our dates?'

'Not mad. Surprised. I didn't think you liked the whole public angle. I thought you wanted to protect your privacy and all that.'

'I'm not the one with contrary privacy issues,' he said pointedly. 'This whole thing isn't actually about you and me, Nadia. Did you think we were going to keep it just between us? What would the point of that be?'

'I'm still not sure what the point of any of this is.'

He chuckled. 'Well, right now, the point is some damn good food.'

With perfect timing the waiter set the dishes down— both her desserts at once, as she'd requested. She pounced, spooning in the sweet. Her nerves scrunched with sensation. Oh, there had to be so much butter in this, so much fine sugar, and put together with so much skill in the kitchen. Edible ecstasy.

He hadn't touched his meal, was just watching her reaction. 'I take it it's nice?'

'Nice?' she mini-screeched. 'What kind of a word is *nice*? This is so much better than nice. It's...'

He waited, smile quirking.

'It's indescribable.' She didn't have to fake blatant sensual delight at the dessert. It was genuine and impossible to hide. Frankly, she couldn't get enough of it.

Grinning, he concentrated on his own meal—some meat thing that she really had no interest in. Not when she had the *yum* stuff.

She gave up on trying to converse—not when she had this to concentrate on. She took a bite from each, alternating while panicking about which one she was going to save for the very last bite. The decision was just about impossible. And she was *not* softening towards Ethan in any way whatsoever. She was *not* feeling a ridiculous kind of favour towards him because he'd been clever enough to get them here. She was *not* actually enjoying their conversation and the challenge he embodied.

'What are you thinking about?' he asked eventually. 'You've gone very quiet.'

Well, she couldn't talk when she was so busy inhaling all the cream. But now she was a little sugared up her fighting spirit revived. A divine dessert wasn't going to soften her attitude. 'I'm composing my write-up of this date for my blog.'

Something flickered on his face and he set down his cutlery and pushed his plate away.

'What are *you* going to write about it?' she asked, sweeter than her pastry. 'I'm so looking forward to our next date where you "nail" me.'

'I'm looking forward to that too,' he answered, utterly unabashed.

'My choice for the date, though, isn't it? You wanted to go to the movies for the first.'

'Okay, so what do you want to do?' He conceded surprisingly quickly.

'A day date, I think.' Safe and out in the open, where lots of people would be around. She didn't want to drop-kick him out of touch until the very last date, which meant she was going to have to play the first two just right.

'A *day* date?' Ethan sat back so the waiter could clear their plates.

'Sunday afternoon suit you?' Nadia asked. The sooner it was all over, the better.

'Sure.' He refilled their glasses. 'I'm really looking forward to spending more time with you. You're really good company.'

She suppressed a giggle at his not-quite-hidden sarcasm. Instead she lifted her glass and challenged him. 'I thought you said you weren't going to try to impress me.'

'I guess it's habit.' He shrugged, but let loose that smile.

'You always compliment?'

'Always.' He gazed intently at her. 'And you don't think that's okay.'

'It's not necessarily a bad habit,' she mused. 'But it is if you don't mean what you say.'

'But I do mean it.'

'Always?' She put down her glass and frowned.

'Sure.'

'Really? Don't you sometimes do it because you know it'll make the other person feel good?'

'Is that a bad thing?'

'It is if it's not honest.'

'All right,' he said softly, and leaned across the table. 'You want honesty? Here's some for you—I think you look fantastic in that dress. I think you look really fantastic. I don't want you to. It would be a lot easier if I didn't find you attractive, but *honestly* I think you look…'

'What?'

'It's *indescribable*,' he said roughly. 'Maybe you should feel what you do to me? Can you handle that kind of honesty?'

His hand shot out and grabbed hers, and before she could blink he'd pressed her palm to his chest. Through the cotton she could feel the heat, the fast, rhythmic pounding. Suddenly she could hear it too, thudding in her ears. Her own blood was pumping in time with his. And that wasn't her body's only reaction. She breathed more quickly, shallow. And worst of all was the softening—that warm, melting sensation happening in secret deep inside her. The readying for full possession by a body so much bigger and harder than hers.

She stayed frozen for five seconds too long, until awareness of their surroundings slowly returned. She was stretched across a table in a fine French restaurant, gazing into this guy's gorgeous cinnamon-brown eyes like as if was mesmerised. She was feeling this intense, intimate *thing*…

Then she remembered her rule.

Don't be too sexual.

And this was all about the rules. She swallowed, battling to return to the right regime. But every movement was sexual. Everything about him was sexual. *He* was a complete magnet and he knew it. But she was going to disarm him—be the one piece he couldn't pull.

'Oh, you're good,' she said, forcing coolness into her voice, sliding her hand out from under his and bringing it back to press her fist hard against her belly beneath the table-edge. 'You like to have the women want you, don't you?

Maybe that's the real reason you compliment so much—it's not their need you're filling, it's your own.'

'And you're really good at coming up with fiction.' He sat back, looking a ton cooler than she'd sounded. 'Whereas I prefer *facts*. And I did my research on you.'

'And what *facts* do you think you found out?' Her temperature soared again as anger bubbled.

'You put it all up there yourself. It wasn't hard to find. That very first entry on WomanBWarned.' He leaned forward. 'Rafe Buxton, wasn't it?'

She avoided answering by taking another sip of her wine, her blood drumming in her ears. How dared he bring that up? That was personal.

'What were you thinking, going with a guy called Rafe in the first place? Weren't the alarm bells ringing then?' he asked, refilling her glass when she set it down.

'I'm not discussing this with you,' she snapped. 'You're unable to feel any empathy. All you want to do is push your agenda.'

'Not true,' he said, annoyingly quietly. 'I only want to understand where you're coming from.'

She just glared at him.

'So he was a "virginity collector"?'

Heat blinded her—anger, yes, but incredible embarrassment too. She'd been so stupid, and she really didn't want to relive it. Didn't want to discuss her pathetic sexual past with such a shark. She didn't want him to know it at all, so she had another sip of wine. A big one.

'So your first was a jerk?' He shrugged. 'You don't have to let it colour the rest of your life.'

Oh, she couldn't not answer that. 'What I won't do is let him get away with it. He preys on young women who are getting their first taste of freedom. Finding independence.' A tutor at a university, he dazzled naïve students with his good-looks and charm and intellectual ability—or at least that façade. Once she'd found out the truth she'd seen that those things were cultivated, not innate or truly deep.

'But we all have to make mistakes. That's part of being human.'

'No,' she disagreed. 'There's a difference between making a mistake and being abused.' And Rafe *had* abused her—and several other young women. 'Illusions shouldn't be shattered like that.'

'But everybody has to face reality some time.'

'You think *that's* reality?' She was appalled. 'So there's no such thing as a committed, loving relationship?'

'Happy ever after?' Ethan shook his head. 'No.'

His cynicism hurt, even though it shouldn't have surprised her. But she could acknowledge a portion of truth in his words regarding that painful episode.

'Maybe not at that age,' she conceded. It had been her second year of university. She'd come from a small northern town and she'd been sheltered. Cosseted, really, by overprotective parents and brothers. As a result she'd been gullible and so easily dazzled. 'I wasn't looking for marriage. But there could have been some kindness and some fun. Not just being another number on his list.' Not being anything but an object. It had been a complete game for him. And once he'd had what he wanted—her virginity—he'd gone on to the next. Another virgin. In the very same week.

Megan.

Only neither of them had known about the other. About all the others.

'You wanted some respect?'

'And honesty.' He'd played them both together. And others. And once they'd found out, by talking at night at a party one night, their friendship had been forged. It was the one truly positive thing to have emerged from an otherwise crushing, humiliating situation. And it had led to WomanBWarned.

'You're really into honesty, huh?' Ethan's brown eyes burned darker.

'There can be nothing without honesty.' Certainly not trust. And without trust or honesty or respect there was nothing to support any kind of a relationship.

'But *you're* not honest.' With careful deliberation he struck at her integrity.

'Yes, I am.'

'No.' He shook his head, a wry smile softening the accusation. 'You're not. You hide behind your website. Behind your stature. All wide eyes—like you're this little thing who has no control over the situations you find yourself in.'

Stunned, she stared at him—he was wrong. 'That's not true.' She hated how people perceived her as weak because she was little. She certainly didn't think she was weak herself. She spent her life proving she wasn't. 'I was tricked,' she said. 'But I admit my own responsibility, my own stupidity.'

'So you won't ever be that stupid again. And you're out to prove it with your website.'

Nadia swallowed more wine to hide the mess of emotion inside her. He made it sound so simple. But there was much more to it. It went so much deeper. She stared down at the stem of her glass and breathed in. The oxygen hit, enhancing the flavour of the wine.

'So tell me about working for Hammond. Is it as great as they all say?' He diverted the conversation, his whole tone lighter.

She didn't lighten to match. Too late she realised he was following his game plan— "get them to share". He thought by inviting her to spill her guts to him she'd actually *like* him for it? Even more wrong.

'It's fine. What about your work? Do you enjoy it?' It was his turn to talk. She'd find his weakness and play on that—his rules.

'It's fine.' He echoed her words dismissively.

She looked up, finding his attention intensely focused on her. She couldn't look away from him. Once more the room receded and there was nothing but his fire-filled deep eyes.

Her senses were swimming now—from the sugar, the warmth, the wine. *Not* the company. She shook her head to clear the confusion.

He broke the intensity, smiling at the waiter and signalling for the bill. 'Time for us to depart.'

The cab ride home passed far more quickly than the one they'd taken earlier. This time she wasn't bothered by the seemingly small space they shared in the back, and there was far less space between them now. She still felt the way his heart had pounded against her palm and her own heart beat faster. Exhilaration, anticipation. Because in moments he'd go for the goodnight kiss and she'd do a quick step to the side. She couldn't wait.

He sat quiet, appearing to be deep in thought. She wondered what about. Hot and half floating, she turned towards him to read his expression better.

He glanced down and smiled.

It was like being tossed into an ice-water bath. Shocked, she blinked and looked again. But her first instinct had read it right—there was none of her desired outcome in his eyes now, none of that heat. Her dress, her wide eyes and smile were having no effect. Despite him saying earlier he thought she looked fantastic in the dress. They'd been meaningless words. Because right now he was clearly more amused by her than attracted. She leaned a little closer as the cab turned a corner, but still nothing. Just benign amusement—and withdrawal. She could *feel* him pulling away.

Why? Where was the move? Where was the "best sex" those women had talked about?

The cab pulled over and Ethan got out, paying him off. He glanced and saw her surprised expression. 'I'll see you to your door and then walk.'

'I'm not inviting you in for coffee,' she said, stupidly hurt by his impersonal politeness.

'I'm not expecting that,' he answered, as if he couldn't care less.

And he couldn't, could he? Anger surged again as she realised this guy was totally not interested. Why not? Why wasn't he, when according to all reports he slayed any female who had the misfortune to slide across his path?

He rested his hand on her back as she turned to walk up her path. Anger burned hotter when she felt again the electric effect that one touch had. His hand was all she could feel. Impotent emotion clogged her throat as she blindly stepped forward.

But because she felt that touch so acutely she felt the stroke of his thumb upwards across her spine—a slow, intimate sweep. The smallest of signals.

Oh, thank goodness—there it was. Satisfaction slammed into her. The man couldn't help himself. Finally he was going to go with some of his moves. She walked slowly now, enjoying the thrill of him moving so close behind her, smiling as she imagined her refusal scene. She'd keep it polite tonight, but playful too—to give him the illusion of possible success in the next date or two.

But in reality it was impossible. For sure.

She unlocked her door and flicked the switch just inside so light spilled from the room out onto the path. Then she turned to say goodbye, her smile impossible to contain.

He really was very tall up there, still in the shadows, looking down at her. She could tell he was smiling too—but suddenly she knew it wasn't a lust-fuelled smile. It was that amusement again. Was he laughing at her? Her certainty of success faltered.

'Thanks for an interesting evening, Nadia.' Loaded with irony.

He *was* laughing. She'd been wrong about that touch. He wasn't going to do it—no move, no kiss. There was nothing. She felt piqued. And disappointed. And anger swamped her. She was *not* going to let him go without scoring a point of her own.

'I'll see you Sunday,' he said in farewell.

Just before he turned she grabbed a fistful of his shirt and stood on tiptoe as high as she could.

And pressed her mouth to his.

He froze. Didn't pull away, but didn't respond either. So she worked a little harder, stroking his lower lip with her tongue. A faint response then—the smallest flinch of his muscles. But it was so faint she let go and stepped back, suddenly aware she'd made a massive mistake.

'What was that for?' he asked, somehow closer despite her retreat.

'Curiosity,' she flipped back at him, frantically thinking up her defence. She'd crashed out of the floating feeling now. 'I wanted to know if you're as amazing as they all said.'

She felt his muscles firm even more and he loomed closer still.

'And the verdict?'

'Not as hot as I'd been led to believe.'

'But I thought one of your top tips on first dates was not to get too hot.'

'You were playing by my rules?'

'What? You thought you were playing by mine?' He laughed. She could feel the vibrations in the scarce space between them. 'You really have no idea.'

'Don't patronise me.'

'But, darling, you don't just lean in and stick your tongue down a guy's throat.'

Mortification and the hated goosebumps made her skin—and soul—painfully sensitive. So she covered with mock incredulity. 'Are you giving me kissing advice?'

He was a jerk—she hadn't stuck her tongue down his throat and he knew it.

'A little lesson in seduction, if you like.' He stepped even nearer. 'I think you need it.'

She tried to push him away, but he was a mountain in front of her now—immovable and impassable. Her hands were tiny on his chest, her fingers instinctively curling into the fabric of his shirt.

'To begin, Nadia,' he said softly, and with light sarcasm, 'less is more.'

'Is that right?' she snapped, smarting, tipping her chin high to glare into his eyes, deliberately digging her nails into his skin now.

He leaned closer, resting his hands on the wall behind her as he bent, his words whispering across her face. 'Anticipation is everything—didn't you know?'

'It's only everything if the end result is a disappointment,' she said caustically. 'If the end result was as amazing as it's meant to be, then the anticipation would be forgotten in the heat.'

'Oh, you're wrong.' He smiled. 'You need to live moment by moment.' His head lowered. 'It's much more fun.' He paused, his mouth a millimetre from hers, as he gently instructed, 'You start with lots of soft, teasing touches.'

His lips brushed hers lightly, just once. But the second

she went to snap back at him he did it again. Then again and again and again. Until it was lots—as he'd said. Not deep, hungry kisses, but slivers of rich sensuality that made her open her mouth for more before she'd thought to stop it. Then she couldn't think at all—she only wanted to move closer for more.

But he kept them light, lifting back as she tilted towards him.

'Uh-uh,' he teased. 'You keep it the same—don't go deeper until she's begging.'

With one hand he played her like an instrument, gliding one finger after the other across her neck. Not making music but pleasure, with gentle touches. But she *knew* the strength was there.

And she wanted it.

'You keep doing it, keep touching, until she can't think of anything but more, more, more.' He punctuated the words with teasing kisses—now across her jaw and her cheekbones, trailing lazily across her face, until she turned her head to put her mouth back in his path. Because she hadn't been able to think of anything else for eons now.

Vaguely she understood the extent of his charm and experience—he hypnotised with mere words and the most restrained of touches, influencing her mood and her mind and making her want to move. At first she didn't know how to respond. She didn't want to push him away, but something burned. She didn't want to be his mindless plaything. And then she realised he'd told her how to captivate him right back—with soft, teasing touches.

She unfurled her fingers, pressing them lightly on his chest. She felt his flinch as she did so. Through the cotton shirt she could feel his heat. With the tips of her fingers she smoothed slightly downwards, feeling his abs tighten all the more. Then she went north, spreading until she felt his hard nipples. She circled them and began him kissing back—nibbling at his lips, then pressing teensy, saucy smooches across his slightly stubbled jaw.

She realised he'd frozen. One hand was still pressed on the wall behind her, the other still cupped the back of her neck, but his own kisses had stopped.

Fear flashed—he was about to reject her touch again. But then she heard it. In his roughened breathing, in the rigidity of his body, she recognised the strain of holding back.

She smiled, moved her hands the tiniest bit faster, firmer, kissed more feverishly along his jaw. Little kisses, tormenting little touches. Only trouble was she was tormenting herself just as much—she wanted *more*.

He stopped her retaliation by grabbing her hands and forcing them down behind her back. The sudden manoeuvre thrust her breasts into his chest. Sensation shimmered down her body and on pure reflex she arched her spine, pressing closer against him.

His head came down, his mouth crushing hers. Nothing soft and teasing any more. Her neck stretched painfully as he forced her head back and plundered. He thrust his tongue into her mouth, deep and rhythmic. She sucked on it and she felt the growl, felt him tighten even more. With incredible strength he lifted her, sliding her up between his body and the wall—chest to breast, pelvis to pelvis, hand to hand, mouth to mouth.

He didn't thrust against her—just pressed his hips into hers as hard as possible, pinning her so she could feel *all* those inches. Her senses rioted—screaming with overstimulation while demanding yet more. More skin, more heat. All her instincts were insisting she get closer. She kissed him back as hard and furiously as he kissed her. Rough and hot and reckless. The force of each other's passion merged and grew into something even more powerful between them. Blistering and insane. She shook with the fierceness of her need, aching to cling closer to him. But he still had her hands, so she clung with what she could—her mouth and then her legs. Hooking one around his waist, angling her body so she was more open to his. For a moment it was heaven as she felt him hard against her.

But he tore his mouth away, his hot breath gusting as he groaned, his grip painfully crushing her fingers.

'I'm not going to make it that easy for you, honey,' he said ferociously.

It was torture. It was bliss.

With each ragged breath his chest slammed against her taut nipples.

'I could move this on here and now. Take you to your bed and finish this off. But why the hell should I?' He was furious. 'In the morning you'd be blinded by regrets. You'd convince yourself you'd been used all over again. You'd label me a seducer. Whereas the reality is *you* started this. But *I'm* stopping it.'

Her whole body throbbed, and painfully she lowered her leg from its tight curl around him. She was so sensitised she could feel her blood beating everywhere. He let her go and stepped back. She slid down the wall. She couldn't look up at him. Instead she stared at his hands—bunched into fists at his sides.

'I'm not going to take advantage of a woman who's had one glass of wine too many.'

'I have *not*—' She broke off. Actually, him thinking she was tipsy was the perfect excuse for her incredibly stupid behaviour. Hell, maybe she *was* tipsy. Her head definitely felt cloudy—and her blood was running so quickly in her veins it was dizzying. With only some cake for dinner and then that wine… Yes, that was definitely her problem. And frankly she'd rather he thought she was a cheap drunk rather than this *easy* sober.

Oh, now the regrets poured in. The self-hate. She had been *so* close to being his latest conquest. So damn easy. And he was right, she'd been the one to start it. He hadn't even wanted to start—only she'd pushed his buttons. Deliberately. Because she'd thought she could control it—and him. What a fool she'd been.

He was watching her too closely, knowingly. 'You want to put it down to the wine, Nadia? Would that be convenient for you?'

Oh, it would. But she knew she couldn't. She'd been hot for him from the moment she'd laid eyes on him tonight. And even though she knew he was a jerk she still wanted him. Stupid, *stupid* hormones. 'I'd like you to go now.'

He shook his head. 'You said you were honest. So be honest now and admit that you're attracted to me as much as I am to you.'

She didn't answer. Couldn't. Yeah, here was the most terrible thing: she *was* into him. There was something about him that she really wanted. But this was nothing at all special to him. He hadn't even wanted to kiss her, and only had because she'd started it. Hey, if it was offered on a plate he'd oblige. It was humiliating.

But suddenly he stepped forward, slamming her back against the wall of the house with his big body.

'You know it's true,' he said, low and angry in her ear. 'And now the anticipation is even stronger, right? Because now you know what it's like. How good we'd be.' His head lowered, his lips intoxicatingly close to hers. 'You're going to lie in bed tonight and not sleep a wink because all you'll be able to think about is how much you want me. You'll think about everything you want me to do to you. And what you want to do to me.'

'Yeah, I know *exactly* what I want to do to you.' She tensed and pushed uselessly against his chest. She'd certainly sobered up now. The guy was the most conceited jerk, and she was furious with herself for falling for his façade and his skills—for being pleased that he wanted her when it was no compliment. It wasn't *her* he wanted. It was any woman. It was just that she was the one in front of him now—who'd made it even easier than usual.

'It's not me you should be mad at.' He stepped back, totally misunderstanding her anger. 'Don't forget, Nadia, I've been the perfect gentleman.'

She darted inside and slammed the door, turning the lock with loud, vicious force. Even so, she could hear his chuckle as he walked down the path.

CHAPTER FIVE

NADIA drank three huge glasses of ice-cold water but was still hotter than a Habanero chilli. Her hands shook as she tossed the glass into the sink and she didn't care when it shattered against the stainless steel. She bent her head and berated herself some more. She was furious. And he'd pay. He'd damn well pay for being such a player.

She stalked to her computer and pulled up the WomanBWarned blog, not stopping to think, just letting the words write themselves.

So, as you've read over on the Mr 3 Dates and You're Out thread, the man himself has challenged me to go on three dates with him—so he can prove he's not the use-her and lose-her jerk he's portrayed to be. Interesting idea, don't you think? And what does it tell us about the man himself—conceited, much?

It's the absolute zenith of arrogance that he thinks he can somehow "win me over" in three dates. He is so cocksure of his attractiveness that he thinks he'll prove what a "nice guy" he really is…

But I'm fair, willing to give him the time to try, so I said yes and brought my open mind with me.

So let's talk about the first date—he went with the movie idea. As we know, from his new GuysGetWise blog, he's of the opinion that a movie is a good option—despite reading my view that its not the best first date option. Proof that while the guy might say he wants women to "share", he's not actually listening to what we say or want.

So I selected a three-hour foreign film that totally sucked. I chose it because he wasn't getting any "chick flick, happy ending hormones" from me. Oh, no. In truth my favourite kind of movie is actually a good thriller or a cut-'em-up horror. I like the adrenalin. But why should he get the benefit from the kind of movie I like? Isn't it up to him to give me the buzz—just from his company?

So lesson number one for Mr 3 Dates: you can't stereotype women. We all have different tastes. And guess what? You are not my favourite flavour.

Sure, you're good-looking, but is there anything beneath your pretty surface? Not so far as I can tell. Ladies, let me sum up what I learned about him tonight:

Mr 3 Dates is the kind of guy who tops up your wine glass when you're not looking.

Mr 3 Dates is the kind of guy who thinks a fancy restaurant with beautiful food is all the effort he needs to put in.

Mr 3 Dates is the kind of guy who shrugs off any personal questions as if he's afraid he'll reveal something vulnerable that a woman might use "against" him—like the enemy he sees us as. He's all about the hunt and women are the prey.

Yes, so far, Mr 3 Dates is totally living up to the rep he's been given online. Without doubt he's a player. The ball's in his court to try prove otherwise. My advice to him?

Try harder.

* * *

Ethan read the blog post that had already appeared by the time he'd power-walked the half-hour home. Not that it had dispelled any of the energy cramping his muscles. He went to the cupboard and poured a whisky, knocking it back neat. It burned. But not as much as what she'd written. What? It was his fault she'd been thirstier than a fish? Not for the wine but for his kisses! She hadn't been able to get enough. But had she admitted that? Hell, no. She couldn't face reality at all—certainly couldn't admit to her own responsibility, her own desires. She'd just warp speeded her way back to Planet Nadia.

Well, he was going to get her to face it even if it killed him. Which it might very well do. Sure, he got what she was saying about her ex. The guy was a total user and an absolute jerk. But Ethan wasn't anything like him. He respected women. And what was so wrong with taking her to a nice restaurant? He totally didn't deserve this—and look how conveniently she'd skipped over half the date, the *important* half. Riled beyond the rational, he opened up his own blog and shredded her right back.

Date Number One *is Done.*

So Ms **OlderNWiser** *went out with me tonight. The Date Movie. Now, all's fair in love and war, and as this is war she'd read my blog. So she said no to the pizza first. And no to the chick flick. Instead she made like she was "desperate" to see one of those arty things with subtitles that goes for hours. To my surprise, I found it not bad, but I suspect it's not her usual thing because she got fidgety. And—oh, look—she's written up the date on her blog already. Yeah, not her usual style. She likes horror? How appropriate.*

However, as the flick tonight was in French, it was the perfect segue into one of the best restaurants in the city. I'd texted from the cinema and got us a table before the film even started—lesson for you, guys: always be ready to adapt and recover a date that's going sideways. And, for the record, I'd still recommend the chick flick. Horror is for cowards who are too afraid to face their own personal demons, so they try to get the cathartic effect by riding on other people's nightmares.

Anyway, the restaurant. From her blog you'd think she wasn't that impressed. Maybe not with me, but the food for sure—she orgasmed her way through two desserts. Or maybe she was faking it, because I suspect her tastebuds can't cope with anything more than bland.

Most interestingly, if you go to her What Not To Do on the First Date blogpost, you'll see she has five "don'ts" listed. Guess how many of her own rules she broke tonight, boys?

Yeah. You got it.

All five.

She went to the movies. She drank (and she asked me to fill her glass, by the way). She talked about her ex. She definitely tried too hard—as in tried not to have a good time—but in the end she couldn't resist...

Yeah, I know what you're wondering about most— too sexual?

Well, if making the first move on the first date makes a woman too sexual, then, yeah, she checked that box too.

But let me say this. A gentleman always sees a lady

safely home. A gentleman doesn't take advantage of a lady's indiscretion. A gentleman doesn't kiss and tell.

*Ms **OlderNWiser** however—does she tell?*

Not the truth, it seems.

*And why is that? Well, why should she, when from the convenient anonymity of her online "user" ID, she can launch her attack? I'm named and shamed while Ms **BitterNTwisted**—sorry, Ms OlderNWiser—hides behind her computer screen in safety. Anyone else see the irony in this? It doesn't seem fair that I and several hundred other guys are named, and yet the women on **WomanBWarned** get to preserve their privacy. Am I going to out her? I know you want me to. But I've made a promise and, contrary to what some may think, I do keep my promises.*

*But I know what else you're wondering. Is Ms **OlderNWiser** actually that old and wise? Truthfully, she's not anywhere near as old as you'd think. Nor is she anywhere near as wise as she claims. So, ladies, I'd be very wary of taking the advice of a woman who's too young to have been even part-way round the block. Just thought I'd point that little truth out for you to think about.*

It took ten minutes for Nadia to read all of Ethan's response, because the red haze in front of her eyes blinded her for most of that time. He was out to undermine her completely, to make her anonymity untenable. This whole situation was untenable. With a vicious tug on the cord she pulled the plug straight out of the wall—not caring about the possible damage she could do to her computer. She turned her back on the black screen and stomped to the shower.

Icy, icy water didn't blast away the fever boiling her blood. He'd trumped her at every turn. The worst thing was that most of what he'd written was true—she *had* done all those things. Except she hadn't faked it over the dessert—she'd *thought* about doing that to tease him, but she hadn't needed to. And she *hadn't* teased him. He'd been unmoved. But he'd guessed her intent anyway. He'd *known* she'd wanted to snare his interest. And all he'd been was amused—until she'd goaded him into a purely physical response.

And what was the "indiscretion" he hadn't taken advantage of? The wine, or the way she'd made a move on him? Damn it, three minutes in his arms and she'd *wanted* to be taken advantage of—as wholly and hard as he could. She'd basically been begging for it.

He'd been the one to stop it and say no. Her stupid plan to be the one woman to say no to him had gone in a flick of his eyelashes.

Angry tears slid down her cheeks. Because now she knew she could never win this war against him. Not when she wanted him as she'd never, ever wanted a man before. Not when she was so out of control she was behaving in a way she'd never behaved before. There was some kind of combustion that occurred within her when he was around—pure aggravation and pure lust. So the only way to combat that was never to see him again. The deal was over—it had to be. Not just for her dignity, but her sanity as well.

She'd take down his thread—much as it galled her. But she had to. Because this humiliation of wanting a guy so badly she was shaking with it was worse than anything.

Ethan lay awake most of the night, reliving the date, thinking about the next, laughing aloud as he imagined her response to his blog. She was going to be furious, and he couldn't wait for her to unleash all her hell on him.

Yes, he'd been attracted from the moment he'd laid eyes on her in her office. But when she'd appeared on her doorstep last night? For the first time in his life he'd been speechless. She'd hassled him over his flattery—but in truth all his usual eloquence had disappeared. There'd been no room in his brain for anything but *wow*. Closely followed by *I want*.

And he'd been honest when he'd told her he didn't want to find her attractive. He really didn't. But he so did. And that attraction was increasing every moment he had with her.

She was completely gorgeous—even when she was hamming it up and looking at him with those doe eyes and biting her lip in total tease fashion. Her enjoyment of those desserts hadn't been faked. She'd totally ignored him and lived in the moment, and he'd enjoyed watching her. He'd really like to watch her in the moments when real pleasure claimed her. He wanted to be the one who made it.

But he'd pulled back. He'd had no choice. He'd been able to tell she wasn't used to much wine. He'd known she'd been drinking more only because he made her uncomfortable—a small fact that he'd take some pleasure in. But he wasn't going to take physical pleasure from a woman whose defences were down. He wasn't going to take advantage. He'd figured she wasn't ready to handle the sparks between them. Not yet. He wasn't sure he was ready yet either.

Only she'd turned his expectations upside down again, hadn't she? She'd kissed him with that hot, slick mouth and the slide of her delicious tongue. He'd almost fallen to his knees, pleading for her to stroke that tongue in some other place. So how could he resist teasing her? A few light kisses to twist up the tension and make the game that snippet more interesting.

Hello, heaven. The rushing in his head? The movement of his body? He'd almost lost control completely and screwed her in her front doorway. It would have been so easy. So good. And over too damn quick.

He wanted a bed, a whole night, and her to be willing and ready and uncomplicated. Yeah, there was the rub. This set-up wasn't anything like his usual flings. Already he knew more about her than he knew about his casual dates. And casual was how he preferred it. He kept things simple—yeah, sexual. And fun. Light and easy and a breezy goodbye.

That wasn't going to be possible with Nadia. It was too late already—how could there be light and easy when there was so much antagonism and mistrust?

But the drive to have her want him—*and admit it*—overrode the alarm bells clanging in the back of his brain. Ms OlderNWiser had passion and energy and he wanted it. Oh, yeah, he wanted to be all over her every which way. He wanted to hear her cry, beg and scream for him. To admit that she wanted exactly what he wanted and every bit as badly. Because there'd never been a want as bad as this in all his life, and he was not going to let her deny it.

Early in the morning he rolled out of bed, completely unrefreshed, took a freezing shower to try and wilt the raging erection he'd been crippled with the last twelve or so hours, then went to work and tried to concentrate. But it, like his body, was too hard.

Finally he picked up the phone. He'd watched the comments appear—yeah, some of his cruder team-mates were getting vocal now. He drew a deep breath, discomfort niggling over some of the things they were suggesting he do. Well, he wasn't uncomfortable with the suggestions themselves—hey, he'd been thinking those exact same things and several hundred more—but he didn't like it being out in the public like this. Another comment pinged up—really crass. He turned away from the screen as he waited for her to answer, damn glad her real name wasn't out there in the blogosphere.

'Hammond Insurance. Nadia speaking.'

His fingers clamped the phone harder, responding to that hint of ruthlessness in her voice. The tough lady tone hinted at the tiger within.

'Good morning.' He didn't give his name—knew he didn't need to. She was as alert to him as he was to her.

Yeah—all he got was silence.

'How's your head?' He decided to provoke her. He had a nagging pain in his—a nagging that drilled down the rest of his body too, because it still resented the way he'd ripped away from her last night.

'I'm not going out with you again. The deal's off.'

He'd expected it, but even so her words winched his stiff muscles even tighter. 'You're such a coward,' he said softly.

'No, this is just a waste of time.' She sounded crisp. 'You're everything those women said and then some.'

'Not true.' He sat back in his seat, smiling at her illogicality and her determination to resist the challenge. 'If I was really a user I'd have taken everything you offered last night. And be honest, Nadia, you offered *everything*. But instead I was chivalry incarnate. Shouldn't I get recognition for that?'

'You're the devil incarnate,' she snapped, the ice barely covering her volcanic reaction. 'This whole thing is over.'

'So you're going to identify yourself? You're going to pull your forum?'

'I'll pull your thread. You can do whatever you want. I don't care.'

'You'll risk your job?' He frowned. Was she really going to give in so easily? That didn't sound right. And it was exactly what he didn't want. No way did he want this battle to be over—not now it was getting so interesting.

'Is your thirst for revenge so great you'd see me on the street?'

Ethan tensed. She was calling his bluff—and, no, he wouldn't expose her. He didn't want her to lose her job. He needed some other kind of leverage. Fortunately he figured he had it. 'But you care about your site.' He clicked his computer to refresh the screen. 'Haven't you seen the number of hits on my little blog this morning? And all the comments on yours?'

Nadia buried her head in her hand, closing her eyes, wishing she could close her ears to his charismatic voice—she couldn't halt the response in her bones to the smile she could *hear*.

'Nadia?'

She pressed the phone closer to her ear and sank lower into her seat. Just the way he said her name made her wet. Maybe it was some kind of hormone imbalance or something? Maybe it was because she hadn't had a date or sex or anything remotely romantic for so long? Maybe she'd subconsciously fixated on that one bit of his reputation—the "best sex ever" bit? Okay, not even subconsciously—it was right up there in the forefront of her brain, flashing neon-sign-style.

'Have you seen them?' he asked again.

'No.' For the first time in years she hadn't checked her computer on waking. And now she was at work. The only people in the company who had access to social networking sites on their computers were those in Human Resources, so they could check the online presence of employees and possible recruits—yes, they checked the profiles of applicants, and their posts. They didn't hire people who made fools of themselves or who had loose lips. That meant she could check his page now. She glanced behind her—no one could see her screen. Super-quick she typed in the URL. It only took a moment to load. She gasped—there were over a hundred comments. She read the first few and her lungs froze.

'Isn't that why you run your site, Nadia? To feel important? To be popular? Don't you *want* to get all these hits and all these comments? Isn't this the whole point?'

No, it wasn't. And there were hits and there were *hits*. And there were some really awful hits on there. Personal, derogatory, mortifying comments. As she loaded the second page to read more, another couple were added. She read them. They were getting worse. Nadia's eyes stung and she tried to blink the acid away.

'I hate you for this.' She couldn't keep the emotion out of her voice.

'Doesn't feel nice, does it?' he said, in his hatefully compelling voice.

'You should be moderating the comments.'

'Like you moderate the lies on *your* website?' He chuckled. 'Surely this is the best thing ever? All this extra traffic making the world more aware of your site.'

Nadia didn't answer. She flicked to WomanBWarned and saw the number of comments there—with much nicer, "go-girl", supportive words. She breathed out—they were good, and her hit rate was incredible.

'So it's not over, is it, Nadia?' Ethan purred. 'I don't think there's any going back now. And I'm really looking forward to whatever it is you have planned for our day date.'

Was he, now? Nadia grinned, her confidence and courage streaming back after the "we love your blog" and "take him down" boosts.

'I really don't want another date with you,' she said, lying to them both.

She went back to his blog post and added a comment beneath all the phnaar, phnaar macho innuendo—

Typical boys, you can only think south of the belt buckle.

'You know you don't have a choice. You know you can't resist.'

Her hand froze on the mouse, because he was right and she couldn't think straight. 'In three days' time I'll wake at four in the morning with the perfect plan to take you down eighty pegs.'

'And for now?'

'Kiss my ass.'

'Ask me nicely and I might oblige.'

Nadia responded the only way she could think of. She hung up.

CHAPTER SIX

WomanBWarned:
Progressing to second & third dates...

The day date is the perfect way to get to know each other without the pressure of romantic expectations that can be present in the evening. So it's a good option for early on in your dating relationship. Suggestions for fun day dates:

A picnic in the park

A walk in the local botanic gardens or zoo

Visiting an art gallery

Beachcombing

Something adventurous—paddling a canoe in the park, paintball if you're that way inclined.

But here's a tip—don't choose something that one or other of you is an expert at if the other is a complete novice. No one likes to look a fool.

Also, while it's nice to be getting to know each other, and it's understandable to want to see if he'll integrate well with your friends, go easy. It can be intimidating to be introduced to a ton of strangers who are all sizing you up. And definitely don't introduce him to your family too soon!

* * *

Ethan studied the list and wondered which of those things she was going to inflict on him on Sunday. Actually, he thought it was a damn good idea. The cold light of day would be the perfect place for her to face some undeniable truths—like the sizzle between them. There'd be no wine for her to hide behind.

He sighed and brought up his own stupid blog. He had to write a post, but honestly he didn't know what he was going to say. The number of comments had gone up massively and he felt a buzz. Yeah, he could see the attraction now—it was somehow satisfying to see more and more people were tuning in to his words. Good grief, was he going to turn as narcissistic and ratings-driven as his dad? Uh—no. Because he was about to write himself into a corner.

He typed a title.

Nailing Her on Number 2

Now what? How the hell was he going to get around this one?

*Have to be careful here, boys, because as we know **OlderNWiser** is reading my write-ups—and commenting now too. Welcome, darling—we always appreciate your thoughts. But it means I can't give away too much strategy before the deal.*

Actually, he didn't have any strategy. He was winging it now—going on his gut in these uncharted waters.

What I can tell you is that date number two is the lady's choice and she's opted for a "day date"—I think this is her thinking she'll escape the nailing.

*But I guess that depends on what it is you all think
I'll be nailing.*

*I may be a bloke, but I'm not that crude. Not
always.*

Yeah, right. It was all he could think about. All he
wanted, wanted, wanted.

*What I'm talking about here is not the physical, I'm
talking the emotional. The intent. What you want to
nail on date number two is her interest. Get her intrigued and soon enough you'll get anything else you
might care to want.*

So how do you nail her interest?

*You tease out her curiosity, and with that you trap
her. Tease and trap, boys. Give them a little mystery,
a little reticent man, and then let them think they can
be the one to figure you out…*

Ethan had been right. Nadia couldn't sleep. Couldn't stop
thinking about him and her and what she shouldn't do with
him if she were going to remain a sane, sensible woman. But
she wanted to, and in just a few short days it had become a
complete obsession.

Yeah, she knew she was obsessive—she got these great
ideas and ran after them with all her energy. Some ideas
were great—some were rubbish. Ethan Rush wasn't a great
idea. Did she really want to risk herself with him? She
leaned back in her big comfy chair and stared at his taunting words on the screen while the ones he'd whispered to
her replayed round and round in her head—that she should
live *moment by moment* and not be a *coward*. And on top
of that temptation he planned to "tease and trap" her? Oh,
he already had. She was so interested already. He had all

the benefit of his beautiful body and the charm that he'd
honed with years of experience. And he was clearly smart.
Very smart. She liked that in a guy too. But she snorted at
the last line—she didn't want to figure him out. She just
wanted to jump his bones.

Only she *was* being a coward. For what was the risk
here? What was it she was so afraid of? A broken heart?
She laughed at the ridiculousness—there was no way her
heart was at risk with Ethan Rush.

Suddenly she saw she'd been thinking about this all the
wrong way. Full of fear about being used, hating herself for
coming so close to being just another of his easy conquests.
She didn't want to be the passive victim.

So then she shouldn't be passive, right? She should be
the one in charge. She should do what she wanted to do—
control the situation and her response to it. Sure—live in
the "moment", be brave, be the boss.

This wasn't just about the notches on his bedpost—what
about her own bedpost? Why shouldn't she carve in a beautiful mark to remind her of an incredible sensual experience? Why shouldn't she enjoy the rush that was Ethan?

She wanted, and there was nothing wrong with
wanting.

And he wasn't completely indifferent. Yes, his response
had been instinctive—she knew that. The guy had a high
sex-drive. That was okay—because for sure they weren't
talking relationship. They were talking hook-up. She just
had to be sure she understood what it was she wanted.

Rafe's intentions had not been honourable. She'd been
expecting something different from that relationship. She'd
wanted more. She didn't want more from Ethan. She just
wanted his body, his expertise, to feel some more of the
way he'd made her feel.

Wasn't she worth it? Didn't she deserve to experience

that kind of sizzling animal passion? Why couldn't *she* use instead of being the one who was used? It wasn't as if it was ever going to bother him. He wasn't sensitive enough to get hurt. If she let go of her old 'happy ever after" expectation and just went with "what feels right now" she'd be fine.

She giggled at her thoughts, mocking the way her brain could work, twisting and turning to justify something simply because she wanted it so badly. But she deserved some fun and he'd be good. And then it would be over—this bubble of obsession would be burst.

But what of her original aim? Could she still teach him a lesson? She was under no illusions that he'd fall for her if she slept with him, but surely she could still execute a flick-off somehow? She'd figure something out...

The immediate problem was that he was resisting the heat between them. Even though she knew he'd been turned on the other night, he'd stopped. She was going to have to subvert his mission to prove himself a nice date. She was going to have to make his physical instincts overrule his intellectual intentions.

She was going to have to provoke him into action.

Saturday morning Ethan snatched up his phone when he read the caller display. 'Hello, darling. Ready to do date two?'

'I might be ready by tomorrow. Can you wait that long?'

Ethan's brows shot up. So did another part of him. He hadn't expected her to purr quite like that. He stretched back in his bed and enjoyed listening as she continued softly.

'I've checked the forecast and it looks good. So we can meet there.'

'Where?' he asked.

'Hyde Park. By the Serpentine.'

'Going public?' he noted.

'And in broad daylight.'

He could hear the smile in her voice. It made him smile all over.

'Coward,' he mocked.

'Not at all. But…' Her voice trailed. 'You need to dress for action.'

'What kind of action?' He couldn't suppress his physical reaction to the way she'd tossed out that little *double entendre* so carelessly.

'Something you can move in.'

'Okay.' He couldn't move for the anticipation making him rigid now. He tossed the phone away and breathed deep to relax. Hell, he had to get out of bed and do something to release some energy. She was definitely taking him for a walk in the park, like on her list—too damn tame. But perhaps that was her point.

The next afternoon couldn't come soon enough for Ethan. He forced himself to walk rather than run there. The sun beat hot on his back and people were at the park in their masses. Ice-cream vendors were doing a roaring trade. He wanted them all to clear off. He wanted to be alone with her.

He loitered by the water, on edge, wondering if she was going to stand him up. His edges sharpened. If she did, he was damn well going to make her pay—somehow.

A roaring sound behind him grew louder, and just as he turned something crashed into him. A lithe body. A very hot one. His hands automatically shot out to steady her.

She blinked and smiled up at him. 'Sorry I'm late.'

He kept his hands on her narrow waist. 'Not a problem.'

She was taller. He glanced down. She was wearing

rollerblades. Oh, man. A sexy roller-chick image flashed in his head. He blinked it away and checked out the reality. Nope—not minuscule hotpants, but black leggings and a tee shirt.

Good grief—she was wearing exercise clothes. Workout gear to a date. She'd meant that kind of action.

'Thanks for making such an effort,' he said drily. 'This is what you have planned for us?' Fricking rollerblading round the park? He really didn't think so.

She looked coy. 'Aren't you game?'

'Weeeeell…' he drawled, deliberately keeping hold of her. 'According to your website you shouldn't do something on a day date if one person is an expert at and the other is a novice.' He was not putting on any damn skates.

'But you told me I shouldn't live my life by all those rules.' She did her wide-eyed innocent look. 'I'm just taking your advice.'

'You're being a bitch.'

Her smile blossomed. 'Or is it that you're a coward?'

He let her go then, and stalked over to a cart where there was a guy renting out skates. Nadia, of course, had her own—not the ancient, shonky-looking ones the rental dude had displayed. Ethan glanced at her. Her feet were so small that even in the ridiculous boots with wheels on they still looked tiny. Whereas *he'd* be doing a Bigfoot impersonation. But then he checked over the rentals again and gave a muttered word of thanks before turning to her, totally satisfied. 'Sadly they don't have skates in my size.'

'He has skates in all sizes.' Nadia pushed past him to check out the range.

'I have big feet.'

She turned and looked down at his feet. He watched the pink deepening in her cheeks as she looked—*slowly*—back up his body. He knew she was wondering whether another body part measured up.

Of course it did.

'Oh.' She looked flustered. 'Um…so what do you want to do?'

Ethan grinned. He knew exactly what he wanted to do—but he wasn't going to. 'My flat isn't far. I have a bike there. We could grab it and come back. You skate—I bike. Then we can get an ice-cream and sit on the grass, yeah?'

She shrugged. 'Okay, that sounds like a plan.'

Ethan strode out while she skated just in front of him, circling back when she got too far ahead. Actually, her exercise gear was growing on him. He liked watching the slide of her thighs as she took each stroke. The leggings and little tee emphasised her compact body and cute butt. She was slim, but still had curves. He liked the light flush building in her cheeks—it made her eyes sparkle more than ever.

'You skate a lot?' he asked.

'I skate to work every day.'

'What?' He stopped on the footpath and waited for her to come back to him. 'To *work*?'

'Yeah.' She looked surprised at his amazement. 'And home every night. It's only forty minutes each way.'

'In the filthy London traffic and across the middle of Hyde Park? What time do you go in the morning?'

'I don't know. Seven or so. Shower and change at work. Have breakfast at my desk. It works well.'

'All year—in *winter*?'

'Well, not if it's raining.'

'But it's dark and you're alone. Or do you have a skate buddy or something?'

She looked at him as if he was mad. He *was* mad. 'No skate buddy.'

'You shouldn't do it.' Some primal feeling had built in him. 'It's not safe.'

'Oh, please—you think it's dangerous?'

'It *is* dangerous. The park is big. Any weirdo or creep could drag you off, and that would be that.'

'Here's the thing, Ethan.' She skated up to him. 'When I'm on wheels, I'm *fast*.'

'Oh, really?' He *wasn't* being distracted by her flirting.

'You know, in my experience—'

'Vast as it is,' he interpolated sarcastically.

'Yes.' She sent him a slayer look. 'There are two kinds of men—protective and predatory. I'd never have expected you to step into the former category.' She put a light hand on his chest. 'I don't need a protector, Ethan.'

'You want to be hunted?' His attempt to ignore the flirt failed. 'Are you sure that's what you want?'

'Well, I definitely don't need someone who thinks a little thing like me shouldn't wander down the main road without a bodyguard.'

'Because you can take care of yourself?' He folded his arms across his chest to hide how tense she had him, and looked down at her the way he knew she hated.

'That's right,' she purred, but he knew her claws were out.

He smiled. Oh, she was begging to be taught a lesson. 'You really think you could get away from a guy like me—if I set my mind to it.'

'Absolutely.'

'Prove it, then. Let me get twenty paces ahead, and then you try and skate by me. Let's see if you're really fast enough.'

Excitement kindled in her eyes, turning the emerald

jewels into bright, liquid fire. 'All right, then. You go ahead.'

He walked backwards so he didn't break eye contact as he moved away from her. She waited, hands on hips in total defiance, as he stepped further away. But she had no idea what she was in for. He'd been on the first fifteen at school and at university. He knew how to tackle.

Twenty paces out, he turned away from her, every sense attuned. His hearing was especially acute, waiting for the rhythmic sound of her skates on the concrete. There it was—the strikes getting faster and louder as she neared. He stepped up his own pace, breaking into a run. As she drew abreast of him he put on an extra burst of speed.

He wasn't stupid—this was a narrow stretch of path and she had to stay on the smooth surface to maintain her speed. So he blockaded—pushing her nearer the edge as she tried to pass. And just as her energy spurted he scooped one arm around her waist, half lifting her as he ran that bit faster, further to the side, until they both fell to the grass. Full body tackle. Relentless in his pursuit, he rolled so he was on top of her, clamping her arm between their bodies, completely stopping her escape. He cupped one hand over her mouth and held down her free arm with the other while he adjusted his position to trap her legs between his.

She shivered violently beneath him. His muscles locked tighter in response.

'Gotcha,' he ground out through teeth clenched in masculine victory. 'No one's come to your rescue, Nadia.' His words slurred as all his predatory instincts celebrated, shutting down his brain and firing up his body. He kept his hand over her mouth. Tried not to enjoy having her at his mercy too much. But he failed on that one.

Beneath his tense bicep, her breasts rose and fell quickly.

'It's the middle of the damn day and you're mine to do what I want with. In the morning, when you skate through here, there are even fewer passers-by. You'd have no chance.'

He felt the ripple in her body again, watched the green in her eyes deepen, some emotion welling up in her. But it wasn't fear.

Oh, hell.

It swamped him too, obliterating all those intentions. He tried to hold on…meaning to prove that point. But he couldn't remember what the point had been now… He knew what he wanted, but he was not going to—not going to…

He lifted his hand and quickly kissed her—hard.

And he groaned as quick became long and slow. He dived into the sensations—the hungry, soft mouth, the sweet slide of her tongue. His brain shut down completely as he was immersed in searing, delicious heat. For ever and a bit later he lifted his head and looked at her. Her tee had rucked up a bit when he'd tumbled her down, baring her midriff. Now he ran a single finger just above the snug waistband of her black leggings, loving the satin feel of her smooth warm skin. Loving the catch of her breath even more.

He watched her reaction—the increase in her pulse, the liquidity of her eyes—and went bolder still, firmly pressing the palm of his hand against her belly, feeling the response ripple through her. Oh, man, she had fire.

He slid his hand beneath that waistband and watched her mouth open in a silent *oh*. For a brief moment her eyes closed as he went lower, brazenly sliding his fingers right down into her pants.

Her whole body spasmed.

He paused, breathing hard as he felt her instinctive rocking up to meet his hand. She wanted him.

'Don't be too pleased with yourself,' she panted, defiant to the end. 'I'm always hot after I exercise.'

'Oh, very hot.' He delved deeper. Slow, exploratory strokes that he quickened when he felt how incredibly hot she was. Hot and wet and uncontrollably arching her hips to ride his touch.

She shrugged, but she had that drugged look. 'It makes me more orgasmic.'

Ooooookay. 'My touching you?' He leaned closer to catch her breathless whisper.

'No...'

'No?' He half laughed, half groaned as he massaged her wet heat, sliding his fingers deep and thumbing her sweet spot. 'How close are you?'

'Not...that close.'

He barely caught her answer she was so breathless. Ethan exulted in the fire escalating within her, flicked his fingers that bit faster. And incredibly, awesomely, that was all it took.

Her head arched back violently, her eyes closing as she clamped hot and tight, suddenly releasing hard and fast, a strangled moan slipping from her full lips.

'Did you just come?' Astounded, he had to ask to be sure. 'I hardly did anything.'

And he was so excited he was about to make a fool of himself.

'Like I said,' she panted, opening her eyes—they glittered so bright they revealed nothing. 'Exercise makes me more orgasmic. You know—the blood was already pumping.'

Oh, he wanted pumping. He wanted pumping right now. Only he was stuck in the middle of a public park and he had no chance of getting what he wanted in the next five minutes. His jaw ached because his teeth were clenched so hard.

But he had to clarify her outrageous statement. 'So you're saying it wasn't really me? That it was the *exercise*?'

Her shoulders lifted lazily.

He laughed, delighted with the appearance of her inner ball-breaker. She was totally angling to emasculate him. 'So five minutes of skating got you to screaming point? Wow. That's a good tip to know. You meant it when you said the wheels made you fast.'

All he could see were green jewel eyes, a lazy smile and lightly flushed cheeks. She even let out a little sigh of satisfaction as she muttered, 'Yes.'

Oh, he didn't believe her. He focused, reading every tiny little sign. Understanding her was suddenly everything. Her tongue flicked, quickly dampening the corner of her mouth. She lowered her lashes, hiding her dawning reaction.

Unadulterated challenge and nothing but.

Reluctantly he slid his fingers from their newfound favourite home and lifted them to his lips. He leaned over her, pressing his aching erection right between her upper thighs, not caring if he squashed her for this one second—to get his point across.

Her eyes widened, glazing over again, her breathing hitching to almost hysterical. Yeah, she liked it. And he loved how much she liked it.

'You think you're going to teach me a lesson?' he taunted softly. 'Trouble is, you're not satisfied yet, darling. You and I both know that was just the warm-up.'

CHAPTER SEVEN

NADIA didn't know what she wanted first, second or third. It was worse than when she hadn't eaten for a few hours. Decision-making was completely beyond her. So was prioritising. She didn't want to move, but she was desperate to. She didn't want Ethan to lift his gloriously heavy body from hers, but she wanted him to hurry so they could get somewhere private. She wanted him to go on top, go underneath, go down. She wanted him so many ways she couldn't think, breathe or speak for the anticipation.

Yes, now she knew just how good the guy was. Some of it was the packaging, some of it was chemical, but most of it was attitude and skill. He had every right to be the cocksure dude he was. And which was more important to Nadia right now—deflating his ego or having the time of her life?

Time of her life. Hands down.

Maybe he felt it—the moment of pure surrender, the subtle relaxation of her body as she gave in. Maybe the desperation was all too obvious in her expression. But he smiled and lifted away from her. Maintaining blatant, blistering eye contact as he extended a hand to haul her up.

She awkwardly walked the few paces across the grass to get back to the path, her thighs so wobbly she doubted she could skate any more. But some kind of muscle memory locked in. Some last shred of dignity—the need to mask how completely shattered she'd been by those few moments in the grass and pretend some more it had all just been the exercise. As she began to recover a little co-ordination he started to jog. She skated faster to keep up.

'We'll continue with the plan and go get my bike,' he said, sounding too damn unruffled and making her doubt everything again—especially that hungry stare he'd subjected her to as he'd pressed her into the grass.

She concentrated hard on the concrete path, not wanting him to see how disappointing his words were. She was gutted that they hadn't done everything right there and then. Had he recovered his reason now? Was he going to go back to being the gentleman—not the rogue who always took what he wanted without giving a damn?

She really wanted him to take what he wanted. She wanted to *be* what he wanted. She skated as her energy returned to comic book superhero levels—courtesy of frustration. As she sped up, so did he, until they were moving swiftly out of the park, down the paths, easily avoiding the pedestrians—as if they really did have some kind of superhuman co-ordination and speed.

She glanced at him, absorbed the effortless grace of his big body in motion. He was fit—surprisingly fast for someone so tall. And maybe it wasn't so effortless—because as she looked closer she saw his fists clenched so tight his knuckles were white, his big biceps more defined than ever. Anticipation sent adrenalin licking through her veins again.

His hand suddenly closed on her upper arm, and he gave a sharp tug so she veered off course, spinning in a half-circle and colliding against him. His other hand caught her round the waist, pressing her chest and belly to his and keeping her there.

'We're here.' He lifted her, keeping her clamped to him, and jogged up the three steps to the main door, wincing as the toe of her boot accidentally connected with his shin. She was too puffed, too turned on, to apologise. At the top he lowered her, releasing her arm to reach behind her. His other hand kept her pushed hard into his hot body. She heard a series of beeps, figured he'd pushed a security code into the pad next to the big door. Sure enough, she heard a click as it unlocked.

'Can you manage the carpet with your skates?' He didn't wait for an answer, just pushed her so she rolled in backwards.

The door slammed shut behind him.

He stopped on the first-floor landing and pulled out a key. 'Hot again after that exercise?' he asked, dripping with innuendo.

Oh, yeah—as if it was the exercise warming her up. What a liar she was. She'd been hot for days, since that kiss after the movies. It was *all* him. But while she wasn't about to deflate his ego this minute, she wasn't going to puff it up even more either.

'Not hot enough,' she said bluntly, and slid past him onto the wooden floor of his apartment, gliding down the hall and into the main room. It was a big apartment—tasteful. Not that she took in many details.

She heard the door shut and his fast pace. His hands caught her hips and drew her back against him, his mouth hot on the side of her neck. She instantly angled her head so he could access more skin. Her skates propelled her forward, away.

He growled as he pulled her back against him and nudged his leg between hers. 'It's like a teen fantasy. Your legs literally slide apart.'

For him they did. They would even without the wheels.

He shaped her body, cupping her breasts and then sliding down her stomach. She loved the size and firmness of his hands. Her breathing escalated—fast, shallow—and she shamelessly leaned back against him, encouraging him to continue the hot trail of kisses over her skin.

'I wasn't going to do this,' he muttered, furiously nuzzling into her neck.

'You could always stop,' she taunted, pressing her butt harder against his erection.

'You know that's not possible.' He groaned, gliding hard and firm down the length of her body, pressing pleasure into her skin and deeper into her muscles. 'You sure you can handle the hurt?' he asked roughly.

'Is there going to be hurt?'

'I didn't think there was usually. But people have been at pains to point out to me that I'm wrong on that. So I think it's only fair to warn you.'

Amused by his flash of conscience, she teased him some more with her body. 'Who's to say it'll be me who feels the hurt?'

'You're the one with the venomous website.'

'I've already been warned, Ethan. Don't worry.'

He lifted the hem of her tee shirt and she instantly lifted her arms to let him take it right off. But as he released his hold on her she glided forward again.

He swore in annoyance and then simply pushed her forward some more, until she crashed into the back of a leather armchair. Her feet couldn't move further forward now—and he was in place firmly behind her. She bent at the waist so she could feel his hard length pressing closer to her core. She reached into the cup of her bra and pulled out the condom she'd hidden there, passed it back to him.

He grunted. 'A woman who knows what she wants. Full of surprises, aren't you?'

With barely leashed ferocity he undid her bra and held each strap in his hands—using it like a bridle to control how far she could lean to and from him.

And she wanted to be ridden. 'Harder,' she moaned, thrills shivering along every vein.

He pulled tighter, flattening her breasts against the cotton, her nipples sensitive against the material. He teased with his hips. Round and round, pressing hard and close and then away again, while he kissed from across from one shoulder to the next, stopping to nibble at her neck and her upper back. Her breathing shortened, keeping rhythm with the circling motion of his pelvis against her. She was going to come again, and he was still fully clothed.

Not okay. She wanted him inside her.

She rocked harder, faster, circling her hips back against him, wanting to stir him beyond restraint so they'd strip and screw right now—now, *now*. Suddenly he picked her up and started walking across the lounge back towards the hall. She struggled so much he dropped her, and her feet went out from under her. She crashed onto her hands and butt.

'What's wrong?' He thudded to his knees beside her.

'I don't want to see the notches on your bed.' She scrambled to get on all fours. 'I'd rather be out here on the floor.'

'I haven't slept with nearly as many women as you seem to think,' he spat back, equally furious, his hand shooting out to grasp her wrist. 'And so what, anyway? Isn't it now that matters? I'm not sleeping with anyone else right now. I'm *not* going to do that to you.'

'I still don't want to see your room,' she growled. 'I just want to…to…' Her lungs jerked so hard she could hardly speak.

'You just want a quick shag—is that it?'

'Now,' she said bluntly.

'Well, we're getting rid of the skates first.'

'Fine.'

He fought with one while she worked on the other, until with heavy thuds he tossed them both over his shoulder and in one smooth movement pulled her beneath him as he rolled over her. She liked that he was fearless about being on top of her. She liked how much he weighed her down.

'That's what you want, isn't it?' He grinned evilly down at her. 'Like to be dominated, darling?'

'Watch your step, Ethan. You're more vulnerable that you realise.'

'You think?'

She ran a nail down the side of his neck while she slipped her other hand between them. She cupped his balls though his shorts and squeezed ever so slightly. He flinched and rose on all fours astride her, suddenly smiling—even though she knew he was as angry at her as he was turned on.

He yanked the dangling bra free from her body and then with two hands pulled her black leggings down, revealing her knickers.

He slid them halfway down her body and stared at the plain white panties.

'Cotton Lycra.' She tried not to sound too apologetic. 'Comfortable for exercise.'

'Indeed,' he said. 'And nice and stretchy.' He grasped them, pulling them to the side, and very gently blew warm air over her. 'Something very tantalising about it.' He let the material cover her again and pressed his open mouth against the cotton.

She'd just about burst out of her skin at the luscious breath, and now the wet heat of him through the cotton was absolute torture.

'Damn it, Ethan,' she groaned. 'You make me mad. You make me laugh.' She banged her head back on the floor, arching as he licked her through the cotton. 'You drive me crazy.'

'Well, that's totally fair.' He switched to sucking and twisting his tongue into the cotton. 'You do the same to me.'

She shook her head frantically. But it didn't matter now—too late. She cried out through clenched teeth and contracting muscles as she came again.

She opened her eyes to see Ethan's satisfied smile as he stripped the last of her clothes from her body and then stripped himself. He dealt with the condom and then looked up, his brows flickering when he saw she was watching avidly.

'What shall we do now?' he asked innocently.

'I've orgasmed twice already,' she said bluntly. 'I just want you.'

He hesitated. She could feel his tension as this time he carefully took the bulk of his weight on his elbows. He gently probed her with his thick erection.

She shivered, all the goosebumps back. 'Girth is good, Ethan.'

He laughed and kissed her. 'You could use that as another website. GirthIsGood.'

'Yeah?' She rocked sinuously beneath him, wanting him to close those last few inches. 'I've got a better one.'

'Mmm?' He kept up the tease, still not penetrating.

'Pump. Now. Please.'

'Okay.' But still he didn't. Instead he bent and with a wide mouth sucked hard at her nipple while stroking with his tongue, his hand cupping its twin so it didn't feel neglected. Something else felt neglected.

Breathlessly she tightened her grip on him, jerking him up by the hair. 'Do me or die,' she ordered.

'Oh, that's nice.'

But she'd won. She saw the flare of his nostrils, the narrowing of his gaze as his focus centred.

He pushed forward. Hard.

She moaned—a low, wild sound that came from deep in her chest—and he paused. She could feel his heart thumping. She inhaled deep, then sighed and smiled. 'Good, good, good,' she muttered. 'Now give me more.'

'Demanding,' he choked. 'So demanding.'

'You like it.'

'I do.'

'So why have you stopped?'

'I like it too much.'

'Ethan…'

'Will you give me a break?' he snapped. 'I move an inch now and I'll come, and I don't want to come just yet. I don't want this to be over that soon.' He exhaled sharply, closed his eyes on her, his whole expression creasing into a frown of agony and need, frustration and determination.

'Oh…' She all but came again herself. Thrilled. She didn't want it to end yet either, but she wanted him to feel as ecstatic as her—as desperate.

'It's not funny.' He moved out of her.

'What are you doing?' She growled her disappointment.

He frowned right back at her. 'It's okay for you to be fast. It's not okay for me to be fast,' he gritted. 'I don't want either of us to end up frustrated.'

He sat back and rearranged her, pushing her legs further apart, and then moved forward again, stopping to suck her some more before sliding his length deep inside and causing those mini-convulsions in her again.

'How hard?' he asked, the strain audible.

'Rough as you can.'

'Oh—' He swore crudely and swiftly left her again, rising to his knees and rubbing his hands over his face as he inhaled huge gulps of air.

She sat up and stared, amazed to see him struggling so much. 'Are you worried about your reputation, Ethan?'

Didn't he know he'd already given her the best sexual experience of her life? Or did he think she had orgasms in public parks every day of the week?

'No.' He glared at her. 'But I'm not completely in control of myself with you.'

'And you usually are?'

He grunted.

She smiled, crazily pleased that he was having a hard time coping with how turned on he was. 'Well, I don't care about control,' she said quietly. 'I just want you inside me.'

'What you say to me,' he said through even more tightly clenched teeth, 'does not help.'

'You want me to shut up?'

He looked at her for a long time and then suddenly smiled, the tension in his face altering from strained to wicked—but still edgy. Had he won whatever battle it was he was having with himself? 'Yeah—why don't you just come and take what you want?'

'All right.' She rose to her knees and crawled the half-metre to sit astride him.

He lifted his face to look her in the eye. She saw the mix of molten fury and desire as she rocked herself over the tip of his erection a few times. She'd known it would be good, but she hadn't expected this kind of blistering, on-the-edge passion. Equal parts anger and hunger and helpless humour.

She put her hands on his shoulders, her fingers spread wide, but still not big enough to curl right around them. That didn't matter. She could use them as leverage anyway. And she pushed down hard as she took him in to his hilt.

His hands were pressed hard into the floor, and she pushed harder on him as she lifted her hips and ground back down. The sensation was outrageously awesome as she slid up off him and then slammed back down. Slow and deep and again and again.

He said nothing. Nor did she. But she felt the way he was forcing his breathing to stay regular. She smiled, watching him watching her breasts sway with her rhythm. She touched them, cupping them in her hands and presenting her taut nipples to his lips.

His hands lifted, tight on her thighs, and he tasted—as she wanted. She laughed, drunk on the excitement of seeing him so desperate for her.

His hands suddenly tangled in her hair, pulling her closer, his tongue rampaging into her mouth, not letting her go and giving no respite from the ferocious, powerful kisses. She half moaned, half hummed with ecstasy into his mouth as he started thrusting up to meet her—making the ride even more incredible.

The thrill rolled in on unstoppable waves, crashing over her, tossing her into a pleasure-filled place that was so captivating she alternately held her breath and then gasped for relief as they ground closer and closer again. And then she could no longer move, no longer control the ride. Her senses, her sanity crumbled under the onslaught of pure, unbearable ecstasy. His arms tightened as she quivered and then shuddered in the throes of an orgasm like no other.

As it ebbed he moved, flipping her over, crushing her beneath him. And pounded. Sliding further and harder into her heat. She clamped on him, arched up every time to pull him closer still and not let him go. With every surge of friction she was driven back to the brink. She cried out helplessly—wanting a rest but desperate for more. His breathing rasped in her ears, melding with her own broken entreaties as she chanted his name again and again. They were way past the boundaries of civility, burning now with raw, instinctive need. Blinded by sensations, beyond reason, just desperate and aching and frantic for final fulfilment.

Nothing had ever felt as amazing as him driving into her with such magnificent masculinity. Nothing could ever surpass this moment. He lifted her higher and higher with his ferocious force, filling her with power and strength and pure, sweet joy.

Her scream cracked as it became too much to bear. He reared up, grinding forward in one last, fierce long thrust, roaring his own satisfaction, tossing her body once more into convulsions of rapture and her mind into blank bliss.

Even though she could see again, she kept her eyes shut, flinging her arm over her eyes to hide awhile longer. He was close by, still half on top of her, but he'd tumbled slightly to the side so he didn't crush her. So she could breathe.

But she couldn't. Her heart galloped. She felt the vibrations of his heart thudding too, and his harsh breathing as they both fought to recover as fast as possible.

She didn't think she'd ever recover. Her whole body throbbed. Sweat slid. Her lips were so well used she was almost bruised.

An aftershock made her tremble uncontrollably. She felt his body flinch in response—and hold for a moment. But his tension didn't ease. And hers grew all the more.

Silently he took his weight on his hands and withdrew from her body.

'Excuse me a minute,' he muttered.

She didn't answer, didn't move as she listened to his footsteps recede. Then she peeped past her elbow. Empty room. Quickly she sat up and reached for her tee shirt, slipped it down as best she could. Her panties were wet and cold. Most of her was wet and cold—all heat sucked away by some giant invisible vacuum cleaner the moment he'd left the room.

Yeah, whoever it was who reckoned that sex dispelled tension was wrong. Because it was so much worse now. And not just tension—terror. What the hell had she been thinking? Rising panic sent her pulse frantic, threatening to burst her eardrums.

She struggled to her feet, stuffed her knickers into a rollerblade boot and tried to descrunch her leggings enough to be able to pull them back on. Hell, she had to get out of there as fast as possible—no way could she hold herself together if she got close to him some more. No wonder those woman wanted to warn others—he was unbelievable, and all she wanted was every bit of him, every star in the whole fantasy dream.

'Regretting it already?'

She looked up, Ethan was on the edge of the room, watching her uncoordinated movements with a towel slung round his hips and a frown on his face.

'You know *you* were the one grinding on my hand in the middle of a public park.' He stepped closer.

Her pulse went supersonic. She was shocked by his bluntness. She couldn't bear to look at his darkened eyes, or his sculpted, glistening torso, so she looked at the floor and tried to get back to decent. 'You put your hand in my pants in the first place.'

'I was merely pointing out how vulnerable you are.'

'You couldn't resist touching.'

'Because you were gagging for it.'

She stumbled as she tried to yank her leggings up, hopping on one foot with no dignity left whatsoever. She gave in. 'Yes, you live up to your reputation Ethan. You must be feeling very satisfied.'

'Absolutely not.'

Nonplussed, she shut up and sent him a wary glance. He looked grim.

'Don't you dare insinuate that I took advantage of you,' he said, his temper clearly fraying as badly as hers.

But she had to play it very cool, very sophisticated, and hide the fact her heart was still beating louder than a jackhammer and about to burst out of her mouth. 'I wasn't going to. You know I wanted it, Ethan. And I enjoyed it.' She shrugged as if it had all been nothing. 'And now I should get going.'

'Because you've had what you wanted?' he said bitterly. 'So what? You're going to go home and write about it?'

She froze, abandoning the hunt for her bra. She'd hadn't given a thought to the damn blogs and their little online war. This was nothing to do with that—this had been so much *more* to her than she'd realised even two hours ago.

The frown thundered across his brow as he obviously took her hesitation as affirmation of guilt.

'Don't write it,' he said.

Nadia turned away from him and picked up her rollerblades, knowing she'd just found the way to end it with him. To escape completely. 'But its popularity is skyrocketing.'

'It's that important to you?'

'Yes, my website is very important to me. This was just a fling.'

'You're going to detail it, then?'

'No.'

'So you're going to fabricate what you put on there?'

He thought she was going to embroider on all this? He had to be joking. She turned back to glare at him. 'Are you setting me up?'

'So little trust, Nadia,' he said coolly. 'When you just let me right inside you.'

Yeah, that had been utter madness. 'I'm keeping on writing.'

'Then so am I.'

She swallowed. 'It'll be my perspective. Honest.' And with zero detail.

He leaned back on the arm of the chair, hands gripping the towel. 'So you're going to say you seduced me?'

'Is that what you think happened?'

'You made all the moves, honey.'

Well, not quite. But she knew what he meant. She'd given the green light. 'Only because you goaded me into it.'

'So you still don't want to take responsibility? When are you going to be honest and admit that I don't use women? That I have fun with women who are as up for it as I am. Women. Like. *You.*'

Yeah, she was one of the masses now, wasn't she? And as pulled under his spell as they'd all been. 'Not all women realise you're only up for "fun". That's why they've all flocked to warn others about you.'

'I don't cheat, Nadia. I don't ever offer them anything.'

'You do. You just don't realise it.' He offered the sun and stars and the moon and all the excitement in the universe. And then he left a big black hole.

His eyes darkened. 'So what? Unconsciously somehow I'm a jerk? Is it my fault they weave some kind of fantasy after one round of sex?'

That was a mistake she refused to make. And to avoid it she had to get out of here and away from him right now. She would not be thinking about him ever again. Not seeing him ever again. How had she ever thought she could get away with sleeping with him and come out unscathed? 'It's all about expectation. Do you make it clear from the beginning that it's only three dates?'

'I did with you.'

'You know this situation is different. This is a total fabrication. You and I would never have met ordinarily.'

He stood and the towel dropped from his hips. She closed her eyes. When she opened them again his shorts were back on and she could breathe.

'I bet you don't usually say, Hey, let's go out a couple of times, maybe fool around and then let it fizzle,' she said rawly.

'I don't know it's going to fizzle.'

'And yet it always does.' Like *hell* he was actually hunting for something more.

'I make it clear I'm not looking for anything serious.' He pulled his shirt on with vicious movements, trying to justify the unjustifiable. 'I don't like complications.'

'Why is that, exactly?'

'Because I don't like scenes like this. Why are women always so complicated?'

'All humans are complicated, Ethan. Even you.'

'I'm not. I have very simple needs.'

'All basic instinct?' she asked. 'You just haven't grown up yet. You don't want to deal with whatever it is that makes you such a commitment-phobe.' She tried to stuff her foot into a boot and realised something was in the way. She put her hand in instead and pulled out her damn knickers. She looped her hand through one leg of them and bent to pull the boot on.

He swore. 'What do you think you're doing?'

'What does it look like?'

'You're not going to skate home,' he spat. 'Absolutely not.'

'Fine.' She ditched the boot effort and stood upright again. 'I'll get a cab.'

'I'm driving you.' As barefoot as she, he snatched up his keys from the floor and stomped to the door.

Silently she followed.

He had a car as flash as his apartment and didn't need directions, so the trip was fast, the conversation nil.

'We have one more date.' Scathingly he broke the pulsing atmosphere as he pulled in front of her house. 'Friday suit you?'

Never in a million years. As far as she was concerned this whole mess was over. She was getting out of it *now*. 'I can't do Friday,' she said, just as snappily. 'I have another date.'

'Oh, you do?'

'Well, this isn't exclusive or anything, Ethan,' she lied, cauterising her heart with her burning, words. 'Do we really have to suffer through another date?'

'Oh, yeah, those screams were real *sufferance*, Nadia.'

He'd gone sceptical and she didn't blame him. But she wanted this to be over. She didn't want to have three dates and be out. It would be two and she was through. No more. Kicking him to the kerb now was the only way to ensure he'd never want to hear from her again. And then she could get over this massive, massive mistake. So, with a calculated, completely fabricated indifference, she got out of the car and walked. She clutched her blades to her chest to hold in her huge hurt heart.

'So you've had all you wanted? It was just curiosity driving you?' Ethan called after her from the open car window.

She could hear the sarcasm—and the scorn. She kept walking, hating herself more than he hated her.

'Hey, Nadia, who just used who?'

CHAPTER EIGHT

ETHAN shoved his foot on the accelerator and the wheels screeched as he shot away from the kerb. He hated complicated, and this was beyond that. This was a mess. And why? Ordinarily he wouldn't mind at all about a date coming to its conclusion. But this hadn't been the usual flirty goodbye—this had been cold, sudden and frankly vicious.

Yes, he liked sex. He liked it and he'd had a lot of it. But he'd never had sex like that before. Not so intense and angry and hot and funny all at the same time. He'd never before been so hot he almost hadn't made it. Not so on the edge and up in the stratosphere—so good his guts were still twisted. And all he wanted right now was more. With her.

He'd not intended it to happen. Before the date this afternoon he'd been determined to play it easy—tease but don't take. That was the whole point of this damn deal anyway. Oh, of course he'd wanted to—but he'd thought he had a little more self-control. Clearly he didn't.

He got back to his flat and stalked to the shower to cool off. He was confronted by his massive bath, overflowing with bursting bubbles, and water all over the floor. Yeah—he'd turned the taps on before, gone back out to the lounge to scoop her up and put her in it with him so they could have lazy, floating, spa sex to recover. Only she'd been back in her tee and desperate to get away from him, spitting insults.

Her fury completely unjustified when he had *not* scorned her. Quite the reverse.

Furiously he mopped up the mess and took a shower. Stewed over the last hour. So she'd had what she wanted and apparently she didn't want it again. Didn't want anything else. Didn't give a damn. Hell, she couldn't have spelt it out more clearly—all she'd wanted was a quick shag on the floor.

By rights that should be nothing for him to get upset about—wasn't that exactly the uncomplicated kind of hook-up he enjoyed? So why the hell was he feeling so bitter and twisted?

Because he wanted more. He wanted her again—now. But he also wanted to spar some more, and alternately laugh with it. He totally got off on the challenges she threw his way. He liked just being near her almost as much as he liked being in her. He shivered, his skin going goosefleshy despite the fact he was now standing under a jet of hot water. He crashed out of the shower, shrugged into some clothes and went to make coffee, still feeling cold despite the warmth of the late afternoon. Sick. That was the problem. Summer flu or something. That was the reason for the whole body ache.

Nadia hid in her house—blinds down like a bat avoiding the last of the sunlight. She dreaded Ethan's next blog post. How honest was he going to be? And how honest was *she* going to be? She couldn't regret having sex with him, but it had been reckless and no way could she do it again—despite the itch already spreading in her veins.

She clicked "refresh" on his blog for the forty thousandth time. It was official. She now had OCD. But still there was nothing. Blog silence. She showered and slipped into one of the "limited edition"—five hundred had been the minimum order—WomanBWarned tee shirts she'd had printed, and that were now stacked in a box tower in the corner of her room. She'd sold four. But that was a start, right?

Ugh. She turned her back on them and hurried back to the lounge to check his blog again. Then, when there was nothing, her e-mail. There were several posts to the forum that she should respond to. Later.

She opened a message from Megan, which included a picture of her sailing around some idyllic Greek isle with Sam.

> *OMG, we (and the rest of the planet) are so ablog over your war with the Ethan guy—too funny. You've so got to put him in his place. He sounds hot, tho— he's a possible if it weren't for the ego, right? So who cares about the ego? Just have some fun!*

Um, yeah, she'd tried that. Succeeded too—until the doubts had needled in only seconds after her multiple-orgasmic warmth had started to fade. As for putting him in his place—yeah, right. She was going to. But the wish to do that had receded—there were other things she wanted now. Like to know more about him.

She curled her feet up beneath her in her big, comfy swivel chair and stared at the font he'd chosen for his GuysGetWise banner. It, like the rest of him, told her nothing. What more did she know of him after two dates? Even now she'd had sex with him did she really know him any better? Oh, sure, she knew he was quick-witted, that he had a wickedly infectious laugh, and that when he looked at her she felt like the most captivating woman on the planet—but beyond that?

Frowning, she leaned over her keyboard. She clicked into her own blog and started typing.

The Day Date

Okay, I admit it, as I did on the first date—I broke a couple of my own rules. Last time it worked against me. This time I hoped it would help me get one up on him. But it didn't—if anything it backfired completely. So take heed of those tips, girls. They're there for good reason.

In fairness—and I am trying to be fair here—Ethan is a nice guy. He makes an effort, he's generous and, yes, he knows how to make a woman feel good. He's courteous, he's chivalrous, he's protective. Oh, and he can talk flirt'n'dirt like no one else on earth.

Yet there's so much that you just don't get to know. He'll get intimate physically, if that's something you want. But emotionally?

That's a total no-go. I know as little of anything meaningful about him as I did before date one.

In my last post I questioned whether there was anything beneath that charming, handsome surface of his. But now I ask why is he so determined to hide whatever there may be?

Is it his way of maintaining his "mystery"? Because, if so, then hats off to him—because curiosity is a thing that will hook a woman. Yeah, his tease and trap plan works. But then he still doesn't share anything about himself, his family, what he cares about. And for most women sharing bodies isn't enough.

So what is it he's afraid to reveal? Maybe it's just that there really is nothing there. He's simply superficial. So he limits the length of the game because he knows his own limitations—and that if you go for anything more than three dates, you're going to know it too.

* * *

Ethan stared at her blog, the churning lava of his temper boiling ever closer to eruption. A reaction that he knew was more extreme than her words warranted—for had she fabricated? Had she kissed and told?

No. That was honesty he was reading, and she'd been honest and open in a surprisingly discreet way. Some hints that really only he would pick up. There was no denial of what had happened, but no blow-by-blow account either. He guessed she'd neither confirm nor deny when her blog followers asked the inevitable "did you do him?" question. Which was exactly how he'd respond when his readers asked him.

She'd done okay with her write-up. But still he hated every word. Most especially that "Ethan is a nice guy" bit. Ugh—nice. What kind of a word was *nice*? It was ironic that he'd always tried to be *nice* and now he was it seemed as flavoursome as dishwater. He didn't want to be so average, as if he was some loser she had to be kind to. He didn't need her generous, not-particularly-moved judgement, thanks.

And, while she admitted a smidgeon of responsibility, she still laid too much at *his* door. What was the crap about not knowing anything more about him? She couldn't blame that on him. Date one she'd been too busy talking about herself—which admittedly he'd engineered. Date two she hadn't asked. She'd just got out of there as fast as she could. She hadn't so much as glanced round his apartment, hadn't asked about his work or life or anything. She'd screwed, then scarpered. So how was her not getting to know him more a result of him "hiding"? What was it she wanted to know, exactly? Should he draw up a list of his favourite things? His most happy memory? It was rubbish. If she'd wanted to get to know him then she should have stuck around and spent more time with him.

He knocked back his coffee in one gulp—and got the bitter bits at the bottom. Grimacing, he stabbed the keyboard.

Was Date Number 2 Nailed?

With that pathetic start, he stopped. He really didn't want to answer it. Didn't know how he could without admitting what had happened—which he really didn't want to do. He didn't kiss and tell. Right to his bones he now regretted the whole online blog thing. It was such a stupid idea, and it had dumped him into something he didn't quite know how to climb out of. But he couldn't just delete the thing because he refused to let it be over with her. And the three dates deal was the one way he could catch her again. Yes, he wanted to catch her one more time. Catch her and blow her mind. So he had to respond now.

Tease and trap—mission accomplished.

*A surprisingly honest **OlderNWiser** even says it herself: the technique works. But she also points out the major flaw—it's only successful for a limited time.*

Sure, I accept that. But it begs the question for how long do you want to trap? Catch and release is the aim of the game for many men. And, let's face it, lots of women love the chase and to be caught too, and are happy to go onto another game with another guy after. Therein is the excitement, the thrill. It all depends on what you're looking for, and so long as you're looking for the same things then no problem, right? It's pretty obvious with most guys.

Guess it's up to the ladies to be honest about what

they're looking for. In my experience they're often not, and then the guy gets the blame for the broken heart when in fact it was the girl who decided to play with the matches in the first place. Think on that, all you sweethearts out there.

Ms OlderNWiser debates my level of superficiality vs. depth. I'd challenge her definition of superficiality—'cos, honey, I'm not going to sit around pontificating about politics or religion on a date. Where's the fun in that?

But we have one more date to go, so let's see what that brings. Clearly it's time to put her in touch with my "sensitive" side. But I'm not giving away any secrets pre-date. We'll do it first and then I'll report back. I can tell you it's my choice for the date, and it is going to be nothing like what she expects.

Ethan watched the cursor flash, unhappy with what he'd written but unable to come up with anything better. He was still too steamed. She wanted to know more about him? He'd let her learn a few things, for sure, and he knew exactly how to throw her into it. He laughed at the evilness of his idea—but she'd asked for it, after all. The almighty great pain in the neck was that it couldn't happen for a week. He pressed "publish" then shoved away from his desk, suddenly furious that it was so many damn days away. Still, maybe that gave him a chance to get his hot-for-her hormones back under control. Damn it, maybe he'd go out on another date himself on Friday night. She'd said this wasn't exclusive. He could go and have some real fun with someone less trouble. He'd head to his favourite bar with the boys and see what action he could chase out.

His guts twisted painfully again, and the bitter coffee

taste still burnt his tongue. Yeah, he was definitely suffering some sort of flu when the thought of hitting the scene made him feel sick.

Monday, Tuesday and Wednesday were the longest days Nadia had ever lived through. Nothing had rattled her nerves, sleep and appetite like this. Not even discovering her perfect boyfriend actually made a hobby of conning the virginity out of as many young uni students as he could—as he had her. Nope, not even that had had her as distracted or on edge as this.

She was awake more than half each night, watching the comments coming in to the blogs. It was horrific. She was so, so glad of her anonymity, and hated the fact his name was out there—even though most of the comments on his blog were bigging him up as "the man". The speculation was rife—and also right—and several comments were crass. Interestingly there hadn't been a word from the women who'd posted on the original thread. It surprised her— she'd have thought they'd be interested and amused by the challenge.

She even surreptitiously checked at work—totally fixated. She struggled to stop herself refreshing both their blogs every other minute. Most of the time she managed, but one in ten she didn't. Nothing more appeared online directly from Ethan. He didn't comment on the comments. Nor did she any more. But she was waiting. Nothing, she now knew, was as bad as waiting. He'd said they were going to do date three, yet he hadn't contacted her about it. So she was waiting, waiting, waiting. Jumping every time the phone went or her e-mail pinged, sitting on her hands to stop herself calling him. So much for never seeing him again, for getting over her fatal attraction to him. Instead she wanted to apologise for being such a cow when he'd dropped her home—wanted to suck back that bitter end to the afternoon. Only she really didn't think he'd care all that much. He just wanted to win. It was still all a game to him.

And then it happened—her mobile rang, with his number on the display. Sweat bubbled from every pore and she gulped a breath which didn't help. Her lungs and brain still shut down as excitement overrode everything. All she had in her head was the stupid hope that her voice wouldn't hit squeak territory when she said hi.

Of course it did.

Panic shot high as she waited to hear what he had to say—except she could only hear her pounding heart.

'About our next date,' he said slowly.

'You still want to do another?' she blurted.

There was a pause. Nadia closed her eyes and winced at her unintentional *entendre*. She really had to learn not to jump in on him.

'Did you think I'd let you off that easily, Nadia? A deal is a deal. Or are you backing out?'

'No. We can do the last *date*.' She spelt it out, giving him no cause to think she meant something *else*.

'I know you're already seeing someone on Friday, but can you do Saturday?'

'Yes.' She didn't correct her lie, but didn't try to play any more games by putting him off again either. This was purely about survival now. Of course if she really wanted to survive she should just say no, but she couldn't say no to him—the beating of her blood just wasn't going to let her.

'Afternoon,' he said calmly.

'Another day date?' Heat filled her face as she thought of the last one. The scent of the grass suddenly hit her, along with the remembered sensation of him pressing her into it.

'Kind of. But there won't be any exercise this time. You

need to wear something a little more formal. That dress you wore to the movies would be good.'

She swallowed. No exercise, huh? His oh-so-casual attitude sharpened her antagonism. He *so* wasn't dictating her wardrobe to her. 'I can do a little more formal.'

'Great. Then I'll pick you up at one.'

'Okay. See you then.'

He rang off without saying goodbye. It made concentrating on work the rest of the day impossible. Well, not impossible, but it was extremely annoying that she had to be there and not at home so she could obsess.

She went out for a walk and bought an ice-cream—to cool herself down on the inside. Gave herself a headache by eating it too quickly. She really had to pull herself together. She was *not* going to ruin her reputation at work because of some guy she was going to see only once more. She had to get a grip. Self-pep-talked up, she went back to the office and sat down and worked overtime, losing herself in the tasks and not once going back online.

In the evening at home she texted Megan for support. He wanted a little more formal? She was going to need some help with that. Formal for day-time wasn't that easy to pull.

Def wear dress but hair down not up. Help yourself to anything in my wardrobe.

Saturday morning she followed Megan's advice, plaiting just a narrow section of hair near the front and then clipping it back. She totally wished she could borrow some of Meg's amazing shoes—except she'd have to stuff tissue into the toes to fit them, and that just wouldn't be a good look. She put a little more make-up on than usual—mainly to hide the signs of sleeplessness under her eyes.

Right on one o'clock she opened the door, and with a brain-draining combination of nerves, excitement and foreign shyness looked at him. Neither spoke. The moment of silence went on so long she started to panic.

'Is this not okay?' Totally husky rather squeaky this time.

'No, it's okay.' He cleared his throat at the same time she did. 'You look great.'

He was smart-casual too, and she was glad she'd gone with the little gilt heels and the silver dress. But she was melting into a puddle—awkwardness was the only thing that saved her. She wanted to apologise, she wanted to beg, she wanted to start over. She wanted so many things that were impossible.

He had his car, held the door for her to get in. She didn't look at him.

'Change the music if you want,' he said as he pulled out into the traffic.

Actually, she liked this band and their loudness. The car smelt nice—it smelt like him. 'Where are we going?'

'Oh, you know I like to preserve a little mystery,' he answered too smoothly.

She glanced at him, but he was looking hard at the road ahead and she wasn't inclined to try and start the conversation again. Nor was he—so somehow forty minutes rolled by in silent, screaming tension.

Eventually they cruised into one of those cute home counties villages—all quaint and expensive. And then he pulled into the driveway of one stunning country home. There were little pink balloons on the gate, and a line-up of flash European cars parked along the street.

Nadia's tension couldn't stay silent now. What the hell were they coming to? She slowly got out of the car and followed him to a beautiful doorway. Through the windows of the house she saw people in pretty party dress milling—and she knew.

'This is some kind of family occasion, isn't it?' Appalled, she slowly climbed the steps up to the door. All the needing-to-apologise feeling fled.

'My niece's christening, yes.'

'I can't be here.' She saw the amusement on his face and her temper flared. 'This isn't the place for you to play your manipulating games.'

'Oh? That's fine coming from you—the mistress of manipulation. Treat me mean, keep me keen—is that what you were doing?'

There was only one bit of that sentence she registered. Dumbfounded, she gazed up at him. 'You're still keen?'

'Why?' Roughly his hands snaked around her waist and he yanked her against him right there on the doorstep. 'You still want me?'

One hand slid lower, firmly curving around her butt. Through the thin shiny dress his heat burned. Her instant tremor was obvious to them both. And suddenly she felt like crying. She was tired of feeling this desperate for him. 'I wasn't playing games with you.' Oh, she sounded pathetic—and pleading.

'The hell you weren't.' His intense gaze stripped her completely.

And she was pleading now. He was vibrating too—with annoyance, and something else. Something every ounce of her wanted to believe was desire. She gazed up at him, too thrilled by the close contact to realise what she was revealing to him—too hot to care. All she wanted was this contact to become closer still.

She heard his breath catch, watched immobile as his head angled and slowly lowered, his sensual lips coming towards hers. Her own breath caught then, while her heart thundered. She tilted her chin, wanting the kiss so badly. His hands tightened, sending more pleasure shocks along her nerves. She liked feeling the strength of him.

But suddenly he looked up. Too late she registered that the door beside them had opened.

Not releasing her from his tight embrace, Ethan suddenly flashed a totally different sort of smile. 'Hello, Mother.'

CHAPTER NINE

'ETHAN! It's you.' The woman sounded stunned. 'You and...'

Nadia flinched, felt his muscles spasm too. Suddenly it registered that she was resting all her weight against him. But she couldn't pull away. The steel band across her back—i.e. his arm—wouldn't let her. Desperately she licked her lips, so she could manage a smile, and turned her head to face the one woman she'd never, ever expected to meet.

'Ethan?' Another voice, and then two other, younger women materialised to flank his mother's sides.

'Mother, meet Nadia. Nadia, this is my mother, Victoria, and my two sisters Jessica and Polly.' The mocking amusement in his voice was apparent, but it didn't chase the surprise off all their faces.

Nadia wished he'd let her go so she could run away to a small dank cave. But he still held her far, far too closely. She shook her head slightly to dispel her fuzzed vision—only the situation dived drastically when she saw his family clearly. Ethan the Gorgeous just *would* have two glamorous, swan-like sisters and a model-of-class-and-refinement kind of mother.

'How lovely to meet you.' Polly swapped a look with her sister. 'See—this is why I had to pick up Mother, instead of Ethan.'

'Well, it wasn't like *you* were going to bring a date.' Ethan said, still not releasing Nadia from the inappropriate clinch.

'We didn't expect you to either,' Polly snapped back. It took five crucifying silent seconds for her to realise the her gaffe before she blustered with a sheepish smile, 'Of course it's wonderful you could be here, Nadia. You have *no idea* how thrilled were are to meet you.'

Nadia kept digging her fingers into his shirt, trying to push him away, but the man-mountain wasn't moving. She could feel the slow, deep rise and fall of his chest against her cheek—completely tantalising and scattering her focus. 'Oh, thank you so much,' she babbled to cover her confusion and embarrassment. 'I'm so sorry to be here unexpectedly. I hope it's no trouble. I really don't want to intrude…' She stumbled over the words and felt her flush deepening. 'I can—'

'Come right in.' Ethan suddenly moved, turning and pushing her slightly ahead of him with firm hands on her upper arms.

The three women stepped back into the house. Nadia walked past them and kept walking to the nearest corner—quite a distance in the stunning large atrium she found herself in. Ethan kept pace.

'I'm not staying here,' she hissed, facing him.

'You have to now.' He grinned down at her, looking too relaxed all of a sudden. 'This way you can get to know more about me—my family and my history and all those fascinating, irrelevant things women want to know. I'm sure my sisters would love to fill you in on a few facts.'

Oh, so *this* was his way of showing her more about himself? She shook her head—he was unbelievable, and now she was stuck here, with no wheels to get away. Of course her curiosity was ravenous…and he knew it.

From the stunned look on his mother's and his sisters' faces she figured him bringing a date wasn't an everyday occurrence. But she knew not to read any significance into it—this was all about their little war.

'This is so impolite,' she told him, hoping for a last minute escape.

'There was me thinking you were an expert at being impolite.'

She swallowed that, then fired right back. 'You were the one keeping us in that shocking clinch on the step.'

His grin broadened back to wicked. 'It would have been much more of a shock if I'd let you go and they'd seen how hard I was.'

Nadia flushed, both mortified and melting again. 'You really think it's okay for me to be here?' She gazed up at his laughing façade and saw the shadows lurking in the back of them.

'As long as you don't get too close to me again while there are people around,' he murmured.

'There's a little service at the church down the road in a few minutes, and then it's back here for afternoon tea on the lawn.' Polly crossed the atrium and interrupted them.

'Oh.' Nadia smiled through her breathlessness. 'Is there anything I can do to help?'

Ethan laughed. 'Jess and Polly have this thing planned with military precision. You can just be decorative, like me. Is *he* here?' That last to his sister.

Polly nodded with a helpless sort of shrug. 'But alone.'

Nadia didn't miss the look that flashed between the two of them. Who were they talking about?

'Hey, I haven't had a chance to say congratulations on the latest league tables,' Polly added suddenly. 'Most billable hours, biggest revenue earner in the year to date. Way to—'

'Don't try to impress her, Polly,' Ethan interrupted drily. 'She sees through to my "internetorious" nature.'

Polly's eyes widened and she looked flustered. 'I wasn't thinking of Nadia. I was thinking you should tell *him*.'

Ethan just grunted.

Polly sighed and turned the sheepish smile on Nadia again. 'Come on, we'd better get going.'

The church was only a few minutes away, and all the guests walked in a festive procession. Nadia walked near the front, with Ethan still keeping a courteous hand at her back. She wished he wouldn't. It made her skin there sing—while the rest of her yearned for more of his touch. Deep in her belly the urge for payback burned, but increasingly she doubted she had the skill to play these games with Ethan. She didn't really know the rules.

To keep herself on track she focused on watching the little girl at the very front, the one all dressed up in a pretty pink confection and bouncing around as if she was on a sugar high.

'That's Isabella, Jess's eldest.' So Ethan was watching her too.

It seemed everyone else was watching *them*. As they stood circling the font during the service, she caught several people looking at her and at Ethan, and at the way he now held her hand tightly—not from affection, but so she couldn't inch away from where he stood too close. Near the back of the group there was a gaggle of beautiful women in beautiful dresses, and they all had hungry features when they looked at Ethan. Even those women obviously in a couple glanced at them too often, curiosity bright in their eyes. Nadia felt more midget-like than ever, and dreaded the tea party to follow. She suspected she was in for some unsubtle grilling. And she was right.

'Meet Nadia.'

Over and over again he introduced her, never once applying any description to her name—no *my date*, Nadia, no *my friend*, Nadia, no *bitch queen*, Nadia—and of course no one there was impolite enough to ask. Yes, he was a master at preserving the mystery. She met uncles, aunts, cousins, family friends, an endless stream of people involved in Ethan's life. And she was too acutely aware of his presence at her side to be able to learn anything much.

'I'll get you another drink,' he murmured, relieving her of her empty champagne glass. 'We'll switch to lemonade now, huh? Wouldn't want you getting too hot from the wine.'

She ignored the wicked look he threw her, too nervous about being left alone to face questions to be able to rise to the banter. She turned towards the garden, hoping to avoid everyone, and followed a path between billowing roses, reaching out to touch some of the soft, perfect petals.

'Beautiful, aren't they?'

Nadia glanced up. From the other side of a crimson rose-laden bush, an older man held out a glass of champagne to her. To her surprise she recognised the smooth voice—but not his face. She took the glass he offered with a slight smile and rummaged round her useless mind. 'Yes, they are.'

'I like that one best—*Grüss an Tepliz*.' He pointed to the red ones and added with a smile. 'My name's Matthew.'

Of course, she had it now—Matthew Rush. He was a veteran political correspondent. She'd heard him do hundreds of interviews on the radio in the morning, when her parents had been listening as they'd got ready for work. She'd been "shushed" so many times for talking during this guy's reports. Matthew *Rush*—so in what way was he related to Ethan?

'I'm Nadia.' She smiled and took the tiniest sip from her glass. Ethan had actually been right in knowing she didn't want more, but she wanted to be polite. 'I like these.'

Matthew nodded. 'Good choice. *Souvenir de la Malmaison*. Polly planted them for Jess a couple of years ago. She did a great job.'

'Yes, they're amazing.' Nadia walked further into the display.

'This one has an incredible scent.' Matthew touched a bush smothered in milky blooms. *'Madame Alfred Carrière.'*

'Nadia.'

Nadia turned at the sharp interruption. Ethan stood at the beginning of the grassy path. She could feel the waves of hostility from here. She snatched a quick glance at the man by her side. But Matthew Rush wasn't giving anything away.

'Ethan,' he said calmly.

'Dad.' Ethan clipped the iciest answer back.

Nadia couldn't have broken the huge, gaping silence even if she tried. Matthew Rush was Ethan's *dad*?

Finally Ethan turned to her and spoke, his voice betraying a roughness that his father's polished-for-radio tones never would. 'I'll show you the boathouse. Jess has just had it redecorated.'

'Okay—great.' She nodded and walked, sending Matthew a smile for farewell, completely confused as to why Ethan had suddenly turned into the ice man.

'I didn't know Matthew Rush is your father,' she said, just for something to say.

He didn't answer—just kept walking until they were both out of earshot and view of the other guests, until they were in front of the cute restored wooden boathouse. Only then did he turn and face her.

Nadia swallowed when she saw his expression—tight, pale, too controlled. He was angry. Angrier than the day he'd stormed in to see her at work and threatened to sue her.

So angry she felt adrenalin surge into every cell, preparing her to *fight*. Except she didn't know about what.

'He's pretty famous,' she added, still confused. 'I've heard so many of his reports.' He'd written a book too, if she remembered right. And now the interviewer himself got interviewed.

'Yeah, you and he would hit it off. You have a lot in common. The need to make yourself important. To be heard by a lot of people. To be recognised.' Ethan almost snarled.

Okay, she knew she was missing something major, but he didn't need to go off at her. 'There's a flaw in your analysis, Ethan.' She wasn't going to let him get away with insults just because he'd been hit by a freak bad mood. 'Your father seeks fame under his own name. I'm anonymous. WomanBWarned isn't about me—it's about making a difference. I'm not taking advantage of my relationships to make a name for myself. In fact *you're* the one who put our dates out there for everyone to read.'

He glared at her. She watched closely for the steam to start shooting from his ears.

'Maybe *you're* like your father,' she said blandly. 'Wanting to be popular.'

Colour flooded into his cheeks. 'I'm nothing like him.'

'Really?' His vehemence intrigued her. 'Why? What's he like?'

'Isn't it obvious?' he snapped. 'Hell, how do you think it makes me feel to see him hitting on the girl I brought here?'

'*What?*' Nadia gaped. Then giggled. A lot. 'Ethan, he wasn't hitting on me. We were talking about the roses.'

But Ethan wasn't seeing the funny side. Ethan was glowering all the more. 'I've known the guy a whole lot longer than you. I've seen that look before.'

She shook her head—the idea was outlandish. 'You've had too much champagne in the sun. You're seeing things.' But her humour died when he still didn't lighten up. He really thought his own father had been flirting with her? That she'd go along with that? 'You know, it's completely insulting of you to think that I'd—'

'I know *you* wouldn't,' he snapped. 'But he would.'

Nadia thought about it. She hadn't seen Matthew up at the front near Ethan's mum during the christening. She hadn't seen Ethan talk to him. There'd been some veiled comment from Polly when they'd arrived—about who'd been going to bring their mum, about whether "he" was here. And "him" being here alone had been major enough for Polly to point it out. She didn't need a psychology degree to figure his parents had split—and that it wasn't amicable. And that there'd probably been adultery issues. Yeah, now she thought about it, some *would* think Matthew was suave. She'd just thought he was old.

She nibbled the inside of her lip and tried not to stare at how uncomfortable Ethan looked. Fiercely defensive, but vulnerable, he turned away from her. She melted, and the desire to reassure him rose—she wished she understood what scar it was that had just been ripped open. 'Ethan, your father was nothing but charming to me.'

'Yeah, he's always charming to women.'

Nadia half smiled and answered softly, 'So are you.'

Sharply he faced her, but said nothing. Slowly the blaze in his eyes died out, leaving a hint of something like hurt. And he just looked at her. And the longer he looked, the more that hint of hurt seemed to grow. She didn't understand why.

His lips parted, she heard the indrawn breath, and she waited, her own breath bated.

Piercing shrieks made them jump three feet apart.

'Ethan, can you help me?' Jessica hurried towards them, struggling to carry a very red-faced, wriggling toddler. 'Bella's having a meltdown, I need to feed the baby and Tom needs to entertain the guests—and Polly's working hard to keep Mother away from Father.'

'Sure—give her to me.' All calm, Ethan reached out for the wailing child.

'I'm so sorry to interrupt.' Jess looked apologetically at Nadia. 'What must you think of us?'

Nadia didn't know what to think.

'She's just feeling out of sorts.' Jess looked panicky as Bella geared up for another bellow.

'She's not the only one,' Ethan muttered, getting his niece out of his sister's earshot. 'How good are you at entertaining little kids?' He looked desperately at Nadia.

'Hopeless,' she whispered, but she followed. They by-passed the guests and circled wide back to the house. By the time they got inside the girl's wails had lessened as her Uncle Ethan spoke quietly to her.

Nadia opened the door that Ethan pointed to, stepped in after him, and then closed it again. A music room. And Ethan was at the baby grand piano.

'You have to stop crying because you have to help me play,' he told the child. 'You know I can't play without your help.'

Bella sat on his knee, he put his hands on the keys, and she put her hands on top of his. It was obviously a game that had been played many times before. She was smiling now. So was Ethan. He started, got four bars into a really stodgy sort of grade three piece. Nadia bit her lips to stop laughing—it was sweet, really—and suddenly realised she was falling deeper into complete 'like' with a guy she'd been so sure was a shark.

But then Bella interrupted. 'No, no. Not that one. The other one.'

'You're sure about that?'

Nadia recognised the teasing tone in Ethan's words. She saw Bella did too. So this was part of a shared joke—a routine that had to be adhered to.

He started to play again, and Nadia was stunned into immobility. Despite the burden of a little person on his knee he played magnificently. Notes thundered as his fingers crashed over the keys. Bella glowed with excitement as her hands rode fast on his. A massive, loud passionate piece from Rachmaninov, huge and echoing and—hell, she'd had no idea Ethan could play so well.

'Play it again?' Bella asked, even though the last note hadn't stopped vibrating round the room.

Ethan groaned and turned to spot Nadia. 'Come and sit beside us. We can't play again unless you do.'

Reading the look on the girl's face, Nadia moved quickly.

Ethan laughed as she did and shuffled along the seat to make room. 'Do you play?'

'Not that good stuff. I was stuck with Mozart. My hands are too small to cope with any of the great romantics.'

'Not so bad to be stuck with Mozart.' He cuddled the little girl closer. 'Play some now.'

His mood had been restored even more than the child's. He was back to smiling and charming and gorgeous, and Nadia was floored. 'I'm not as good as you, and I haven't played in a really long time.'

'I disagree with the former but am well aware of the latter.'

She looked balefully at him. 'Do you think along those lines all the time?'

'Around you? Absolutely.'

'Play, play, play,' Bella interrupted petulantly, completely missing the undertones.

'Yeah, Nadia,' Ethan said slyly. 'Play.'

She sighed, hiding her smile, and put her hands in position. It really had been a while. But years and years of practice couldn't be completely forgotten. After a few bars she began to enjoy it, giggling when she stumbled over the odd passage, but soon getting the feel for it again, losing track of time as she worked through her favourite piece. A quiet one—not the kind of rollercoaster ride of emotion up and down the stave that Ethan had crashed through.

'Keep playing,' he whispered in her ear.

She glanced sideways and saw Bella was fast asleep in his arms. Amusement warmed her. Oh, to be a kid again and fall asleep at the flick of a switch. He carefully edged off the stool. Nadia did as he'd asked and kept playing the soft sonata, turning her head a couple of times to see Ethan carefully putting his niece on the sofa near the big fireplace. He glanced at her and mouthed 'keep playing' again.

She nodded, glad to turn back so she wouldn't have to go like goo inside, seeing him be so tender. She started the piece for a third time, even more gently, waiting for the word that it was okay to stop.

There wasn't a word. There was touch. Hands—large hands—cupped her shoulders and then slid down the length of her arms to her hands. She bent her head and stopped playing.

'I think you play beautifully,' he whispered softly, his cheek brushing against hers.

She only had to turn a fraction to kiss him.

'We'd better get back out there,' he said, as if it was the last thing he wanted to do.

'Of course.' It was the last thing she wanted to do too.

They tiptoed out of the room, closing the door on the

calm inside. She paused, not wanting to go back to the lawn. He stood still too, looking at her.

'Nadia…'

She knew he wanted to kiss her. And she wanted to kiss him. No games this time—just because it would feel so good. So right. But something was stopping him, and Nadia didn't know what.

'Where is she?' Jess appeared in the hall.

Ethan turned away and answered. The relief on Jess's face revealed the stress she'd been feeling. Ethan put his arm along his sister's shoulder and teased, 'Soothing irritable girls is my speciality.'

Nadia didn't know if that was a coded message to her or not. But the fact was she didn't want to be soothed. She wanted to be stirred.

Ethan chatted to his sister for a few minutes more, but the second Jess wandered away to mingle, Ethan's teasing façade dropped and he looked plain tired. No wonder. She'd just seen how hard he worked to be the charming guy who held it together for the women in his family even when he was at the very end of his own patience. But he'd masked it, protectively cared for Bella—and Jess—a gently wicked joker who'd made them feel better. But right now he looked like the one who needed help to feel better. She wished he'd talk to her. But why would he open up to his opponent in this stupid fight of theirs? She knew he was mortified by his mistake about his father, and she didn't want to embarrass him more, but there was something there and she wanted to know.

'I'd never have thought you'd play the piano like that,' she said to lighten the atmosphere. 'You look too rugby.'

He managed a grin. 'The girls had to learn. I got sent along too. They never liked it enough to practise.'

'But you did?'

He nodded briefly. 'Let's get out of here.'

People were departing, so it wasn't as if they were the first to leave, but Nadia was glad they weren't going to be the last.

'You outdid yourself, Jess. Again.' Ethan gave his sister another hug.

'Thank you very much,' Nadia said to Jess. 'It was the most beautiful afternoon tea I've ever seen. Everything was so perfect.' She wasn't lying. The décor, the food, the style of it all had been amazing.

Jess smiled at her. So did Polly.

'It would be really nice to see you again some time, Nadia,' Polly called after them.

With an uncomfortable ache in her heart Nadia kept walking to his car and pretended she hadn't heard. She couldn't face another forty minutes of silence on the drive back so she went for light, safe conversation.

'So tell me about your work. All those billable hours, huh? Are you prosecution or defence?'

Ethan gripped the steering wheel even tighter. Oh, hell, he really hadn't told her anything—and he grimaced about telling her now. He didn't do the save-the-innocent barrister act, and if she really was all about 'making a difference' then she was going to be disappointed. Still, he was used to that—right? His dad had never got over his decision to go corporate rather than chasing after the Queen's Counsel dream, despite the fact Ethan earned more now than he'd ever have done in chambers. But for his father it was all about public prestige. For Nadia it was that higher purpose thing—which meant she was going to be even more sceptical than his dad.

'I'm not a barrister,' he said heavily. 'I don't go to court and present arguments to a judge.'

'Oh? What do you do, then?'

'Corporate.' His discomfort was stupid, because his job was unbelievably competitive. 'I'm an aviation specialist.'

She frowned. 'Aviation?'

Yeah, there wasn't that much adulation in that. 'As in big deals between big airlines and aircraft manufacturers. Leasing and financing and stuff.'

'And that's law?'

'They need legal advice to do the deals—so, yes.'

'Oh.'

'It's very interesting.' Hell, did he sound desperate for approval or what? But he loved it. Wouldn't work crazy hours if he didn't.

'I'm sure.'

'It's more interesting than HR.' Totally defensive now.

'Well, that wouldn't be hard.' She laughed suddenly. 'So, does that mean you get to go for rides in flash private planes?'

'The question everyone asks.' He rolled his eyes. 'I expected more from you. Sometimes—not often.'

'But you like planes?'

'Always have. I like flying.'

'*Can* you?'

'I have my pilot's licence.' And he sky-dived. He liked the rush of that.

'Oh, that's cool. So you really love it?'

'Yeah, I do.' Finally the grin broke out of him. 'Going to work is fun. But it's not what people think of when you tell them you're a lawyer.'

'Who cares?' she said. 'You work in a field you love. You're lucky. Your parents must be proud.'

Ethan sent her a sideways look, but she was smiling ahead at the road, all innocence. Yeah, right. She was fishing, but he wasn't biting. Because, no, his father *wasn't* proud.

'You mean you don't love HR? But you get to make people miserable, right?' He teased his way out of answering.

'Very funny.'

'So why did you get into it if it's not floating your boat?'

'I wanted a job in a big firm. All big firms need HR people.'

'Why big?'

'The usual reasons—money, security.'

'Yeah, but bigger isn't always better.'

'You're wrong.' She shook her head. 'It was nice meeting your family.'

Nice—great. That awful word again. And she couldn't possibly think it had been nice. She was back to fishing. Apprehension slithered down his spine. Inviting her into his life this way had been crazy. How was she going to report back to her web-witches? He figured he'd be in for a caning. But had she seen his family's vulnerability? Did she even care? What about Bella? Those moments by the piano that had filled him with pleasure before now made him wince. Did Nadia think he was superficial enough to have orchestrated that? She was so untrusting she probably did. He wanted to skip this as the third date. They should do something else. But that would mean seeing her again—and that seemed like a really dumb idea. This wasn't the game it had been, and it sure as hell wasn't uncomplicated.

As he pulled up outside her flat he knew he had to address it. 'Please don't write about today in your blog.' Annoyed at how husky he sounded, he spoke faster, more harshly. 'I don't want all that out there. Not Dad. And I didn't set that up with Bella to prove anything to you. Can't—?'

'Do you think I don't know that?' she interrupted, her voice shrill. 'Do you really think I'd mention any of that?'

He was silent.

In the confines of his car her anger reverberated. Her outrage. Her hurt.

'What kind of a person do you think I am?' she asked, totally wounded. 'You haven't gotten to know *me* at all, have you? You haven't listened to anything I've told you.' She leapt out of the car and ran up her path.

Ethan stared after her—hating himself even more than he had that moment almost two hours ago. He'd felt sick when he'd seen his father talking to Nadia. He'd seen the look. It was how *he* looked at her—as if she was some delicate morsel to be devoured. Nadia had been wrong. Or maybe she'd been right and it was just that Ethan was so paranoid about his father he couldn't see straight.

Either way it didn't matter, because the revelation was still clear and still true. He'd always said he was nothing like his father, but Nadia had said differently. And he *was* the same—every bit the same selfish, insensitive jerk. He'd just proved it.

He swore and leaped out of the car.

'Nadia!' He grabbed the front door handle so she couldn't open it and get away from him. But she didn't turn around. A slender, silver fairy-woman stood in front of him—one he wanted to pull back against him and keep her there. He ached for the hot, sweet relief to be found with her.

He bent his head, lightly brushing his lips in her hair, hoping she couldn't feel it as he breathed in her scent. 'I'm sorry.'

'It doesn't matter.'

'It does.' He felt her trembling.

'I don't blame you for thinking I'd do that,' she said softly.

But he should have known she wouldn't. Deep down he had. Nadia, with her big green eyes and her sweetheart-shaped face, wasn't in this world to hurt people. Now Nadia herself was hurt—and it was his fault.

'I wish you'd talk to me,' she whispered.

'And tell you what?' His blood chilled. There wasn't anything to say. 'Don't think you know anything more about me just because you've met my messed-up family.'

'But wasn't that the point?'

He clenched his teeth. The original point had been to make her uncomfortable. Only it had backfired completely, and he was the one feeling tortured and embarrassed and angry.

'How you act around them tells me a lot.' Her voice wobbled.

He shook his head. 'It doesn't.' She knew nothing—because he'd only realised a couple of things himself this very moment. He gripped the door handle even harder, physically fighting the urge to take her into his arms.

'You're not the carefree guy you make yourself out to be. You're more sensitive than that. You care about them.'

It was so ironic that now she thought she was seeing some good in him, when he was realising just how little there actually was. 'You don't know anything, Nadia.'

She'd been right. He did hide what was beneath his surface—because underneath lurked the same kind of indifference that his father had. Indifference to relationships, commitment, marriage. Sure, he had passion for his career, but none for the burden of family and responsibility—and certainly not a woman's happiness. So he wasn't going to get into a relationship and hurt someone over and over, like his father had his mother. And Nadia was a relationship girl through and through—romantic, idealistic, a little bruised and misguided, but soft-hearted still for all that. And, for whatever warped reason, those qualities were endearing her all the more to him. But it was dangerous for her, because he would never be the right guy. Which meant he had to walk *now*.

He breathed deep to try and push out the pain cutting into his heart, but it was a mistake. Her scent curled tighter around him. Her proximity was tantalising—her soft, warm limbs and passion were so close. She didn't move. Her head was bent as she waited in silence—for what? The inevitable? He had to rebel against that.

He released the handle and pushed the door so it swung open. She stepped inside. Not following her was the hardest thing he'd ever done in his life.

It was so unfair that doing something right felt so wrong.

CHAPTER TEN

NADIA stared at the blank form on her screen. For a long
time. Then she clicked in the corner to close it. Three days
later and she still hadn't posted anything online. That was
for ever. Her hit rate would start to slide. Already people
were commenting and asking questions. Questions she
didn't want to answer.

Her mobile rang. She picked it up and checked the screen;
the number was withheld which meant it wasn't him. Her
heart accelerated anyway. 'Hello?'

'You haven't updated your blog.'

Okay—it was him. 'Neither have you.' She managed a
light answer. There'd been no posts—no comments, e-mails,
texts or phone calls either in the last three days. That was
for ever and *ever*. The only thing stopping her from going
insane was the thought that he hadn't sent her the flick-off
flowers yet, like the women on the original *3 Dates and
You're Out* thread said he did. Then again, he probably
didn't feel the need to keep her sweet. They'd done the three
dates. It was all over and out.

'A gentleman always lets the lady go first.'

'I'm not ready to write it yet.' Nadia turned away from
her screen, screwed her eyes shut as she boldly went down
the road she'd been fantasising about for the last three eter-
nally long days and nights. 'There's a problem.'

'What kind of problem?'

She pressed her hand on her chest to stop her heart beating out of it, and blurted the words she'd rehearsed too many times to be natural. 'I can't say those claims are wrong when one major aspect is completely right.'

'What aspect's that?'

'That it's three dates and you're out. You're totally doing that to me.'

She heard the whistle of indrawn breath from his end of the phone. 'You want a fourth? You want us to go out again?'

Oh, she wanted way more than that. But right now she'd take what she could get. 'I just can't see how I can refute what those women say when we've only gone for three.'

'But you're planning to refute some other things?'

He didn't sound as pleased about that as she'd thought he would. Truthfully, she didn't want to write another word on it.

'Nadia, you know what'll happen if we meet up again.'

She waited, nibbling her lip so hard it hurt.

He cleared his throat. 'Is that something you're willing to risk?'

'Life's no fun without a little risk.' She bit harder, waiting for his reply, her nerves teetering on a cliff-edge.

'Well, there's risky and there's reckless. I told myself not to see you again.'

'Well, you don't have to.' She held her breath, held back the hurt. And waited.

For ever.

'But I think I do,' he said on a groan. 'Let's go out for dinner. We've not done the traditional date, have we? Only I'm out of town for a few days. Can you do Friday?'

'Sure.' Friday was months away. 'Where are you?'

'In Germany, trying not to think about you.'

'Are you succeeding?'

'Well, I'm calling you now, so I guess not.'

Her whole body curled into a smile. Noise broke up the line—talking in the background got louder.

'I have to go.' His voice came and went. 'You'd better put something on the blog. You'll lose people.'

'So had you.'

'I don't have time. I'll see you Friday.'

Nadia hung up and turned to her computer, determined to get some work done now.

The next morning she went back onto his blog to see if he'd put anything up. Nothing. But she noticed some of the worst comments had been taken down, and there was a note from Ethan to say that he'd be approving the comments before they got posted from now on. It seemed he'd suffered an attack of gallantry. Or was it just that he was worried about what his work colleagues would say? No, she guessed he didn't really give a damn about what other people thought of him, considering what he'd put out there. Which made her wonder more about why he'd hunted her down as the creator of WomanBWarned—what was it that had bothered him so much?

Underneath that arrogant playboy attitude Ethan really was a nice guy. He liked women, and he treated them well when he was with them. He just didn't want true intimacy or a relationship. The smoking remains of his parents' relationship had to be the cause of his reluctance. Whatever had happened had put him off committing, and he and his father were clearly at war. Which meant all she'd ever be was another one of those women he'd had a fling with. Except she had just got to date four—the final frontier. And, yes, deep inside that very stupid part of her wanted so much more. He was so easy to fall for.

The days didn't pass fast enough. She went shopping. She

went for a manicure. She went indoor speed-skating to burn energy and make her tired enough to sleep. It didn't work. So by the time Friday night rolled around she was ready too early and beside herself with anticipation. She practised yogic breathing and waited. Waited some more. Tried not to look at her watch every ten seconds. Only made it to fifteen once and got so mad with herself she took her watch off. She had her fab new dress, matching fingernails and toenails—the bits in between buffed and polished too.

But time ticked on and on and there was no knock at the door. The summer sun set and Nadia sat frozen in her chair.

Finally her phone beeped. A text message. She knew what it was before she even looked at it. He didn't even have the decency to talk to her. Tears tumbled and she was so glad Megan was still away and not there to see her humiliation. She couldn't bear to admit what a fool she was. According to the text he'd been delayed at work and missed his flight. He was on a later one and wouldn't get in until it was too late for dinner.

She totally didn't believe him. He just didn't want to do dinner at all. He never had. She'd just pushed him into something he didn't want to do and he was trying to get out of it lightly—like always.

Ethan had been trying to forget her. They'd done the three dates, so he could think about something else for five minutes now. He could find some other woman attractive. He could do nothing but work for fifty-six hours straight.

He'd only managed the last one.

He checked his phone again. Still no reply. He didn't want to call and speak to her because she wasn't going to be in a mood to listen to him. He hated letting her down. He hated how complicated this had become—but he *had* to see her again. His body wasn't letting him do otherwise, nor would his brain. She was all he could think about. All he wanted. So he'd make his apology in person. He'd make it up to her in person. But that wasn't going to help in the next few hours. He quickly punched in another number.

'Polly, I need a favour. Big favour. You've got to take your best ever bunch of flowers to Nadia.'

'Oh, Ethan,' she wailed at him. 'We liked her.'

Ethan gritted his teeth. 'So do I. So send the damn things, will you? And say I'm sorry on the card.'

'Sorry for what?'

'None of your business. But get them to her now.'

'So it isn't over?'

'It will be if you don't get them organised.'

'Okay.'

The doorbell rang. Nadia saw herself in the hall mirror as she went to answer it and swore at her panda eyes. Still, at this time of night it could only be a telecoms salesperson or something—so what did it matter.

It was a courier. He handed her the biggest bunch of flowers she'd ever seen.

Nadia took them without a word and slammed the door. The card was typed in an old-fashioned typewriter font.

I'm sorry.

She tossed the flowers on the table and tore the note in two, then three, and chucked the bits like pity party confetti.

How had he managed to get them out at this hour? Florists didn't work this late. He must have planned the whole thing hours ago. *Days* ago. In fact she now figured he'd totally set her up. She'd been the one to suggest another date. He'd got her in the palm of his hand just as he'd wanted and now he'd crushed her.

Her eyes were drawn back to the bright mass of blooms. Yes, they were beautiful, but she hated them. The flick-off flowers. Just as the women on WomanBWarned had said. She wiped away more scalding tears and sniffed. Why had she been so stupid as to expect anything else?

There she'd been, actually feeling something like sorry for him—trying to figure out why he avoided everything: emotional intimacy, relationships, conflict. Thinking she understood more after seeing his family the other day. But he'd so taken her for the fool she was. He was an all out jerk with not a shred of sensitivity. And right now he was laughing at her something awful.

Furious, she had to do something—anything—to feel better. And that didn't include talking to honeymoon-happy Megan. She didn't want anyone she knew to know what an idiot she'd been. But she had to vent to someone. She went into her WomanBWarned admin database and hunted. Ten minutes later she'd fired off e-mails to the other women who'd posted on the original thread. She wasn't going to put this up on the internet, but she was *so* having a private rant with them. She'd bond with others who bore the wounds— the humiliation—of being an Ethan Rush conquest. She'd snarl and moan and gnash her teeth, but not with anyone she knew.

First she just asked if they were who she thought they were, and what other info they wanted to share.

She glared at the flowers, tempted to put them in the rubbish, but she put them in Megan's room instead. Marching back, she clicked 'send/receive' ten times on her e-mail but nothing landed. She stalked to the bathroom and ran a super-hot shower, getting rid of the hair product and the panda eyes and the floral scent of her favourite perfume. She yanked on one of her WomanBWarned tee shirts and some boxers. Not that she was going to bed—sleep was impossible now. Instead she did a final check on the forums and stepped away from the computer. She'd hear the ping of e-mails from the computer if those sisters replied. There was only one thing left to do. Drink wine and watch movies. Horrors—a corpse-fest, with scary music and evil, evil monsters. She'd work her way through the all the *Nightmares on Elm Street*. To put things into perspective.

She'd watched a ton of gory numbers with her brother and initially she'd been stoic through them so as not to be the 'scared little girl' he'd expected. Now she just plain liked them. Things could be so much scarier and worse than real life. And she'd eat eye-watering chilli with it—to terrify her tastebuds too. Provide an extreme sensory experience to overwhelm the extreme agony inside.

She was twenty minutes into the third instalment when her doorbell buzzed again. Way too late for a salesman this time. Or anyone. Nerves fluttered and she paused the movie, telling herself not be scared by something Hollywood had invented. Just because it was almost two in the morning it didn't mean there was going to be a disfigured guy with knives for fingers on the other side of the door.

She opened it a fraction, and then let it swing wide.

'What are you doing here?' The strangest cocktail of feelings flooded through her—a heady mix of disbelief, relief, pleasure and uncertainty.

'I just got into Gatwick.'

'You really were stuck on a plane?'

'You didn't believe me?' His bag thudded at his feet. 'I knew you wouldn't. That's why I got Polly to send the flowers. But you still didn't reply.'

'I figured if you were in a plane you wouldn't get a text anyway.'

'No, you just don't believe me. Or trust me. Or—'

'Or what?' Her defensiveness reared. 'You sent me "see ya later' flowers.'

He frowned. 'The note was supposed to say I'm sorry.'

'It did.'

He closed his eyes and breathed deep. 'Okay, I shouldn't have come here now. It's late and we're both grumpy.' He picked up his bag.

'No.' Recovering from the shock, she grabbed his arm. 'You look shattered. Come in and have a coffee or something.'

She'd so go for the 'or something', but he really did look shattered—unshaven, red-rimmed eyes, crumpled clothes, pale.

He didn't move, even though she was using most of her weight to tug his arm. 'You didn't make other plans when I cancelled?'

'Sure I did.' She tugged harder. 'I've got movies loaded and a huge amount of ice-cream.'

He stepped in, the thinnest gleam piercing the dullness of his eyes. 'So there isn't anyone else on your sofa?'

'Is that what you were worried about?' She dropped his arm. 'That's what you're checking up on?'

'You told me this wasn't exclusive.'

'What did you expect me to say?' She shut the door behind him. 'I have some pride, you know.'

'I'm well aware of that.' He finally cracked a grin. 'So what's the movie?'

'A horror.'

'I hate horrors. They make me feel sick.'

'I'll hold your hand in the scary bits, if you like.'

Ethan managed another smile, but he was seriously out on his feet. He shouldn't have come, but somehow when he'd got into the cab at the airport, hers had been the address he'd given. Now he was here the tiredness had hit him—right when he didn't want it to. But, oddly, it was relief wiping out the last scrap of energy—relief at seeing her wide green eyes fill with the sparkle of promise, pleasure, desire.

Her sofa was fantastically big and he sank into it. He wanted her, but he couldn't even move. Could hardly keep his eyes open. Everything overwhelmed him.

'I didn't sleep,' he mumbled.

'You spent the whole time awake?'

'Lots of work.' And that was true. They'd worked crazy long hours to close the deal. And in the few short hours he'd had to catch some ZZZs, all he'd done was toss and turn and think about Nadia. The more he tried not to, the more he had. In the end he'd decided to see her again and get her out of his system. Somehow.

'You mean you were in German lap-dancing bars twenty-four-seven.'

He laughed. It turned into a groan because the energy required was too much. 'I'm sorry. I'm rubbish company. I'm too tired.' He should go home. He didn't want to. Nor did he want to let her down any more—and he was already.

'Shut up,' she said, sounding bored. 'I'm watching the movie.'

As if to prove it, she turned the volume up a notch.

Even though his eyes were closed he grinned, loving the way she was being so nice to him—in her fashion. He just needed a short snooze and then he'd be all over her. Oh, he so would.

'Ethan?'

Nadia stared down at him in amazement. He'd hooked his legs up on the sofa, his feet dangling off the end, and he'd lain down, using her lap as his pillow. Which was nice. And frustrating. Because now he didn't answer. How could anyone fall asleep during a horror film? In less than three minutes?

She lifted her hand and tentatively stroked his jaw with the tips of her fingers, enjoying the rough stubble. Ethan Rush was an exhausted man. She sat back, scrunching a little deeper into the sofa so his 'pillow' was smoother.

An hour later the film had finished and she still wasn't remotely sleepy. Nor had she watched much of the movie. No, she'd been completely tragic and watched him sleep—the rhythmic rise and fall of his chest, the long lashes shadowing his cheek. She was absurdly pleased he didn't snore—it wasn't as if that was relevant. It wasn't as if she was going to spend the rest of her nights sleeping beside him. Even so, she was happy. And concerned. Because he was going to get a crick in his neck if he stayed like that much longer.

She stroked his temple, loving being able to touch him so intimately. He didn't stir, so she bent forward and whispered in his ear. 'Ethan, wake up. You're going to get so uncomfortable.'

Okay, *she* was uncomfortable. It wasn't that his lying on her like this hurt, but it was hot. All she wanted was for him to wake up and play. But he was blissfully asleep and she couldn't bring herself to try harder to rouse him—especially because doubt niggled that he might not want what she wanted when he woke.

She changed the TV to a music station and lowered the volume. She rested her head on the big cushions and stroked his head, trying to match her breathing to his so she'd get to be as calm and rested as he was.

'Nadia?'

'Mmm?' Nadia sighed, lost in a really great dream.

'Nadia?'

She roused, realising that the voice was real and very

amused and very near. She looked down at the heavy, warm weight in her lap.

'This is good.' He smiled. The flickering light from the TV made his eyes twinkle too. 'What are we doing here?'

'You were too heavy to move to bed.'

'You wanted me in your bed?' He shifted, rolling to face towards her tummy.

Her muscles weakened. 'Uh...um...'

'I've missed you.' His words were muffled, but still she heard the rawness. He pressed his face close to her, sliding his hands up her thighs, under the loose cotton of her boxer shorts.

Nadia shivered, half trying to suppress her tremoring nerves, but her body had lit with the lightest of touches and those few words. His hands caressed, and she couldn't help relaxing, slightly spreading her knees wider so his fingers slid higher still. She swallowed, barely able to control her breathing, high on anticipation. Oh, she wanted his touch there—all the way there.

For a moment there was nothing else—just fingertips caressing skin, slowly taking the path already on fire for him. He suddenly lifted his head and looked around the room behind them.

'What is it?' She looked up to see what was catching his attention.

'I'm looking for the treadmill,' he teased. 'You must have been exercising while I was sleeping. Your blood is pumping hot.'

In lifting his head up he'd made way for his fingers to surf even higher—which she guessed was the whole point. So Nadia just spread her legs wider.

'You've been lying with your head in my lap for the last

five hours.' Her panting mutter wasn't as saucy as she'd intended. 'I'm on fire.'

'Oh, so it's *me* making you this hot?' He lay down on her again. 'You like me this close?'

She smiled back—oh, *so* saucy now. 'I'd like it better if you were awake and I was naked.'

'Well, I am awake—but you don't need to be naked.' His touches went further, softer, teasing. One hand went north, sliding under her shirt, cupping her breasts, stroking her hard nipples. 'No bra, no knickers,' he groaned.

'Boxers are knickers,' she argued vaguely.

'Loose,' he murmured happily, his fingers pressing more firmly.

She pressed her head back on the sofa, closing her eyes and lifting her face to the ceiling. Her body was so hungry for him—all slippery and hot, welcoming the slide of his fingers, the rub of his thumb. She bit on her lip and suddenly pressed her knees close, trapping his hand as waves of pleasure contracted her muscles. It hit quick, hard, and it wasn't enough.

'Making you come is the ultimate turn-on,' he muttered as he sat up. 'And it's so damn easy.'

Uh, yeah... Struggling to regain her breath, Nadia felt embarrassment rise. It was only easy because she was so insanely attracted to him. It was humiliating.

But then she noticed he was now standing, and basically ripping off his clothes.

'What *are* you wearing?' he asked.

Her humiliation faded as she heard how he snapped the question, saw how his hands were shaking as he fought to get a handful of condoms from his pocket. So he'd been prepared to come and see her?

She knelt up on the sofa and enjoyed the show. Her body was even warmer than before. The man had muscles—everywhere—and they were all bunched. He glared at her tee shirt again. Had he only just noticed what it said?

'It's really offensive. Take it off.' His jeans thudded to the floor. 'Off, off, *off*,' he demanded.

But before she could argue he issued another order.

'Stand on the sofa.'

Nadia blinked. 'Is this because I'm short?'

A muffled curse as he moved—fast, effortlessly—lifting her so she stood in front of him on the sofa. 'No,' he said curtly, whisking her tee shirt over her head and then her boxers to her ankles. 'This is because I want to kiss you here.' He licked her nipple and then sucked it into his mouth. 'And then here.' He moved, kissing down her sternum to her stomach.

'Okay.' Oh, more than okay. Oh, yes, yes, *yes*.

Between kisses he laughed—low, sexy—making her melt all the more. His hands dropped to her thighs and he pushed them apart. She shifted her feet to please him—only he kept pushing, and pushing, until she was standing with her feet as far apart as they would go. There was something about being bossed by him that was delicious. Her body was all soft and lax and malleable, while his was all hard and strong and ready to fire, and she couldn't wait to find out how he was planning to do it.

So she stood on the sofa, her hands on his shoulders, while he stood before her, his feet on the floor. She could look him right in the eye—and his eyes were smiling. So she smiled too. His big hands held her thighs hard, keeping them wide but also giving her support. A good thing because when he suddenly thrust—all the way in—her knees buckled. She hooked her hands tighter round his neck and held on for sweet mercy. But there was no mercy—he was big, and his movements were powerful, relentless, and awesomely good.

Nadia moaned, loving the completion, the friction as their bodies slid—locking and unlocking. She thrust with him, their position incredibly decadent and abandoned, and she relished the hedonism. Every movement hit better than the last, so in seconds she was breathless and barely coping with the surging sensations. His pelvic bone ground against hers, rubbing deliciously against her bliss button, sending her faster still towards break-point. Her so-sensitive breasts were flattened against his solid chest—more fantastic friction.

But the thing short-circuiting her completely was the way they stood nose to nose and eye to eye. Unbearably intimate. He kissed her—little teasing kisses broken by the occasional lush, deep one. She could see his passion, the raw, unbridled desire. It was so intense she had to close her eyes against it. She couldn't believe that all the fiery want in his gaze was for her.

'Look at me,' he growled. 'Let me see.' As he spoke he maintained his rhythm, driving her, knowing exactly what he was doing—how close she was. How moved she was—how much she wanted him. How good he made her feel—how much more he made her want.

And that was what he wanted—she knew. He wanted to see her hit orgasm. He wanted to miss nothing. He wanted all her secret wishes—and to know that he was the one who'd fulfilled them. And just that thought—that frightening, exhilarating thought—made her come all the quicker. Because it was *him* doing this to her.

Her body tautened, then convulsed as the waves tumbled over her—so powerful that for an instant she was scared. But then it was too good to think of anything but how incredible it was. She didn't know if she cried out—all she could hear was the hiss of his satisfaction, the grit of his teeth as he held her through the rapturous storm and forced himself to stay that half-step behind her.

She sucked breaths in harder, unable to recover as he thrust more forcefully. She threaded her fingers through his hair, holding him so he couldn't look away from her either. She half laughed, mostly cried with sensual delight, as she saw the signs of unbearable strain in his face—the clenched muscles, the veins popping in his neck, the pained, desperate look in eyes that suddenly widened, but were blinded as it swamped him.

'Oh, yes,' she sobbed. Her blood pulsed—in her lips, in her most intimate nerve centre—as the sight and feel of him, so tortured by her, sent her back to the pinnacle of ecstasy.

His movements went wild. His body jerked as he lost the fight against holding off. He shouted—a raw, masculine response—as release surged and the moment of ultimate pleasure was his. All she could do then was cling.

His hands shifted, clasping round her middle, and he held on to her tightly, his forehead pressing into her shoulder. She felt his harsh, ragged breathing gusting down her sweat-soaked skin. Her own breathing was irregular, her brain dizzy. Her legs were completely wobbly. So did was her heart.

'Are you going to let me go?' she asked, her voice woefully small.

'No.' With sheer brute strength he lifted her, sliding one hand under her legs so he could carry her more comfortably. Dexterously, between his third and fourth fingers, he scooped up another condom packet that had fallen on the edge of the sofa. 'Which is your room?'

She directed him, and he walked with ridiculous ease. He placed her on the bed, but immediately followed with a smooth lunge. Taking the bulk of his weight on his elbows, he pressed his lower half firmly on hers—so she couldn't escape.

'Oh,' she said, needing to strive for some kind of control in this shattering situation. 'You want to be dominant?'

'No,' he breathed.

Nadia's voice failed as she saw his burnt brown eyes had refilled with that passionate fire. He bent his head and kissed the last remaining brain cell out of her. His tongue swept into her mouth in gliding strokes, over and over, while his hands framed her face, holding her up to him—open. Yeah right he didn't want to be dominant.

By the time he'd finished she was uncontrollably rocking her hips, grinding against him in a way that was desperate and hungry and unbelievably happy, running her hands up and down his slick, muscular back. He looked down with smug satisfaction as she panted and writhed beneath him.

His low whisper positively purred. 'You're not running out on me again.'

CHAPTER ELEVEN

LIGHT blasted through the window and Nadia sighed, reluctantly admitting to consciousness—because now she had to face the music. She rolled over. He was awake, propped up on a pillow, book in hand—looking totally at home.

'What are you reading?' She tried to act normal, but her croaky voice let her down.

He showed her the cover. 'Found it on your shelf. It's quite good.'

Groaning, she reached down beside the bed for her phone. She had to check Megan and Sam's arrival time. She was panicking that she had their arrival time wrong and it was a.m., not p.m. The last thing she wanted was for them to walk in on her and Ethan like this. Megan would read too much into it. Nadia was having a hard enough time stopping herself from doing that.

'What are you doing?' His voice had a slightly rough inflection too—so he wasn't *that* engrossed in the book…

'Updating my profile,' she lied.

'Of course you are,' he said drily. 'What are you saying?'

She tossed the phone away, satisfied her flatmate wouldn't be arriving for another ten hours or so. 'Nothing.'

He theatrically mirrored her action, tossing the book

away and faced her. The sheet slipped to reveal his broad, bronzed, way too hot, chest. 'So, Nadia, what do we do now?'

She had no idea. She'd bluff. 'Shower?'

It was a good idea. Forty minutes later there was so much steam in the bathroom the extractor fan failed. The trip switch went when it was overworked, and it was totally overworked now.

'Damn thing.' Nadia pushed her wet hair out of her face and hunted for the stool to stand on so she could fix it.

With a grin Ethan nudged her out of the way, reached up and did it for her.

She glared at him. 'Don't treat me like some incompetent little girl.'

'I'm not.' He chuckled and held her still way too easily. 'Don't project your hang-ups onto me.'

'I'm not.' She wriggled, vainly trying to escape. 'But people see me and think I'm some doll who can't manage anything on my own.'

'Honey, I'm aware of all you can manage.' His hands slipped into soft places. 'But isn't it nice to have help sometimes?'

'I don't want to be patronised. I can manage just fine alone.'

'So you won't admit to any physical limitations? But you have some, Nadia, and that's not a bad thing.'

'I refuse to be limited,' she argued. 'I can and will do anything. My parents didn't want me to move to the city— never believed I'd get a job in a big firm like Hammond. But while I may not have the size, I *do* have the smarts.'

'And you prove your power even more with your stabbing words on the internet?' He shook his head reproachfully. 'Why does it matter so much?

'You've not spent your whole life fighting the assumption

that you're not as capable as the rest of the population because you're short.'

'Yeah, but proving your capability doesn't have to mean all by yourself. You know, *some* things you have to have a partner for.' He picked her up and demonstrated just how much stronger he was—and what a 'partner' could do.

'It's not fair,' she moaned.

'Life isn't fair. Yes, I'm physically stronger than you—but there are benefits to that. Benefits you enjoy.'

She knew he was teasing, to turn her flash of anger into amusement. And it was working—because he was so right. 'Oh, really?' Her protest sounded as pathetic to her ears as it must be to his. Secretly she loved his size and strength. It was as if she'd been programmed to seek out the biggest piece of masculinity she could and cling to him. And Ethan was certainly that.

'It turns you on when I press you deep into the bed,' he muttered, kissing her neck. 'You like being lifted by me like this just as much as I like lifting you. But even big guys like me have vulnerabilities, you know. Everybody does.'

'Oh, you do?' She suspected he actually did. She just wished she knew and understood them. 'Tell me more.'

'And give you power over me?' He chuckled. 'Never.'

'You don't think I have power over you already?' She aimed to tease him back.

Their gaze met and held. And held some more.

'Why don't you find out?' he invited eventually, wickedness flaring in his eyes.

Yeah, he always brought it back to sex, didn't he? Any time the conversation got a little too close to the bone, too personal, too emotionally intimate for him, he kissed or teased his way out of it.

But right this second she was happy to let him away with it.

An hour later Ethan took another quick shower, and wandered out towel-clad to find her in front of her computer, busily tapping away. He pulled up a chair next to her and unashamedly watched her work.

'It's a pretty impressive machine.' The screen was huge.

'Yeah.' She wrinkled her nose. 'Cost a bomb.'

She was going through the million e-mails that had landed last night, checking all the comments that had been posted on WomenBWarned were okay, answering queries and direct messages. She was incredibly organised. There were tonnes of folders, the titles of which amused him—especially the 'Feedback—Excellent' and the 'Feedback—Awful' ones.

'Which one has more messages in it?' he asked, pointing to them.

'Which do you think?' She laughed, standing to answer the ringing phone. 'Oh, hi Megan…'

Ethan tuned out of her phone conversation as he read the e-mail that was next up to be sorted.

Can you please, please, please put together a Top Ten list of the worst cheats ever on WBW? Or, even better, could we vote for them? I have THE guy to take it out on…he so deserves to be front page, number one…

Great—another scorned and furious harpy. Shaking his head, Ethan resisted the urge to hit 'delete' and instead pulled the message into the 'suggestions' folder, as Nadia had done with the previous one on a similar theme. Then he started reading the next e-mail.

*I wanted to tell you how much I appreciate **WomanBWarned**. Not because I think all guys are* *scum, like the guy I dated, but because there's a place out there where someone listens and I can read about other women's experiences and talk to someone in privacy about what happened. And it was rape. For so long I didn't know if I could call it that—if it was my own fault or what. But it wasn't. I didn't do anything wrong. He did. I've never told anyone in my real life, but I have a voice on here and you listen. It helps.*

Nadia's arm reached past him to the mouse and the e-mail was pulled into a folder. 'Some of the messages aren't on the public forum,' she said quietly. 'There are some private threads.'

'Of course.' He leaned away from the screen and realised he'd been holding his breath for some unknown reason. He pushed the stale air from his lungs. 'That's awful.'

'Yeah.' Nadia sat beside him again.

'How do you know what to say to someone who's been through that?'

She clicked through a couple more e-mails. 'It's not so much about offering answers. I mean, what answers can there be? There's no cute line anyone can say to fix that. But I can give what she says—space and a place to have a voice. I link to lots of resources, and there are other women who've been through similar experiences who speak up. I'm not a counsellor. I guess I facilitate. But, yeah—' she looked glum '—some women deal with way worse than a stupid virginity collector.'

That was true. But what had happened to Nadia had also been horrible. And if Ethan ever came across Rafe Buxton in real life he'd have to be forcibly restrained from doing violence to the bastard. But if he did punch the guy out Nadia would probably commit some form of violence on *him*—she was so determined to take care of herself and not have any help or protection. Especially not from a big guy like him. As if that was the worst thing ever. But he couldn't stop that need rising in him—that *caring*.

Oh, hell. Ethan glanced at her profile and took in the shadows under her eyes. He knew she needed some recovery time and all of a sudden so did he—but it wasn't physical rest he needed, more mental and emotional. He didn't know what to think about anything any more.

'I should probably get going.' Contrarily, he instantly hoped she'd tell him to stay.

'Okay.' She nodded and kept focusing hard on the screen. 'My flatmate gets back tonight, and we've got a big catch-up planned.'

'Yeah, of course,' he said, battling disappointment and failing. He glanced briefly at the message she was reading.

Do you think weakness can be inherited? Because I'm worried it can. For years my mum stayed with my dad, even though he cheated on her. I swore I'd never be like her—stupid enough to put up with it. But here I am and my boyfriend has cheated on me and I don't want him to leave—

Ethan pushed away from the table, found his clothes, and went to her bedroom. He didn't want to know what Nadia's response to that one would be. Did being the son of a slimeball make you a slimeball too?

'Ethan?' Nadia stood in the doorway.

Ethan bent and pulled on his shoes, concentrating on his laces. 'My dad cheated on my mum all the time. Eventually he ran off with one of his "assistants". Then he cheated on her too. Every relationship he has, ends with him cheating.

But Jess has married, and Tom is the last guy on this earth who'd do that. You should e-mail that woman and tell her. It's not some hereditary thing. Patterns don't have to repeat like that.' Not for Jess, or Polly. And not for him—because he'd made the decision to be different. Only now he didn't know if he'd been any better—if he *could* ever be any better.

Nadia blinked. 'Okay.' She took a step into the room. 'When did they divorce?'

Ethan straightened and walked back out to the lounge, picked up his bag. 'I was fourteen. It was a relief.' He wished his mother had thrown Matthew out sooner.

'Why—?'

'Nadia, I don't want to talk about it.' What did she want to know? How he'd heard his mother's tears late at night for years? How he and Jess and Polly had tried to get their father's attention and never could compete with the bright young bimbos at the studio? How Ethan had worked so hard to make his mum smile?

'I know that.' Nadia looked him square in the eye. 'But maybe you should.'

He almost smiled. But he said nothing. She really didn't want to hear his sob story. He couldn't think of a bigger turn-off. He was so much better at making her smile.

She walked with him to the door to see him off. 'Bye,' she said. 'It was…'

'Don't say *nice*.' His feelings were even more mixed-up. 'Have fun with your flatmate tonight,' he said.

'I will.' She smiled, but he could see she was biting back questions.

He didn't want to go, but she had her own friends and her own life and it was busy. So busy there wasn't as much room in it for him as he suddenly wanted. She put so much of herself into her work, her forum, her friends… So what?

Now he was feeling jealous of those things? Clearly he needed more sleep.

When they'd finally sated themselves in the small hours last night, she'd curled into a little ball and slept like the dead. He'd woken too early and waited for ages, willing her to wake up, but it had taken so long he'd had to find something to read to keep himself from bothering her. He hadn't wanted to disturb her when she looked so tired.

And he didn't want to bother her now. Much.

He bent and kissed her. The way her lips clung made him feel better. Yeah, the sex was good. And that was all he wanted, right?

Well, no. Not any more.

Dissatisfied, Ethan walked home alone. He worked for a while. Spoke to a few mates. Decided on a quiet Saturday night in—the first in ages. And he spent it in front of his computer.

Megan lounged on the sofa looking like a totally pampered cat. 'It was the best three weeks of my life,' she purred. 'The absolute best.'

Nadia laughed—three weeks sailing round the Greek Islands with a lover wouldn't be bad, would it?

'So tell me about yours?' Now Megan looked completely feline—and sly.

Nadia had tried hard to keep Megan talking about herself, but Megan wasn't being denied any longer. She had her iPad on her lap, and was scrolling through the nightmare that was Ethan's blog.

'Did you know he's put up another message?'

'He has?' Nadia's heart raced. She'd hoped they were just going to forget about the blogs. She'd been gearing up to delete hers. But there it was.

* * *

Okay, so we're behind on the date reporting. And I'm not going to report because the reality is a whole lot more complicated than this "he said/she said" forum. I just want to pass this message on to the women out there who are reading. You want a clue into the male psyche?

Here it is.

Utterly unlike the sharing need of the female, we guys don't like to emote or analyse. Guys like action. So let us act. Let us be guys. Let us do the things we like to do for a woman.

Well, what did *that* mean?

'Are you up for sharing, Nadia?' Megan asked, her sly tone gone quiet. And curious.

Nadia shook her head. She'd already shared way too much of herself these last twenty-four hours—with him.

CHAPTER TWELVE

HE DIDN'T call on Sunday. Or text or e-mail or make any more comments on his blog. So she didn't either. Which wasn't to say she didn't obsess over him any time she didn't have her thoughts on a tight rein. And she worked late, late, *late* on her site.

Too early Monday morning Megan called up the stairs. 'Nadia, there's someone at the door for you.'

At seven? She went down, not trusting the wicked expression on Megan's face.

But when she got to the door she understood. Ethan, looking dynamite in casual, a combo of relaxed and confident. He all but knocked her out.

'What are you doing here?' she managed to ask.

'I thought I'd see you to your work today.'

She stared at the shiny new mountain bike beside him, still astounded to see him. 'But your work is nearer here than mine.'

'Well, I need more exercise than you.' His eyes twinkled.

'You're not serious?'

'Completely.'

Nadia's eyes narrowed. He was here, but not for the right reason. She became aware of Megan, unsubtly hunting for something in the lounge, so she could check out Ethan some more. 'I'll just get my bag.'

Nadia backed into the house, drawing the door almost fully closed behind her.

'Oh, Nadia.' Megan stood with arms crossed, foot tapping, and a smile wider than Australia. 'Nadia, Nadia, Nadia.'

'No matter what you hear in the next ten minutes, do not come outside—okay?' she instructed her friend.

Megan's eyes widened. 'Okay.'

Nadia ran to finish getting ready. She rammed her feet into her skates and skated out through the door, banging it behind her. She met his bright-eyed gaze as she did up the clip on her helmet. He'd turned the bike around and was astride, ready to push off.

Nadia moved up beside him—and then pulled her surprise.

The most horrendous, ear-splitting screeching sound suddenly deafened them.

'What the hell is that?' Ethan shouted, looking around.

Nadia pointed to the little black rectangle tucked into her waistband.

'It's a scream in a can,' she shouted back. 'I just pull this cord and it makes this god-awful noise. So I don't need a bodyguard to get to work safely, Ethan. I can take care of myself.'

'That's not why I'm here,' he bellowed.

She silenced the screamer and stared at him, not letting him away with it.

He sighed. 'Okay, that's a little bit of why I'm here.'

'You don't need to be here for that at all.' She waited, brows lifted.

His mouth shut—firm—and didn't open for several seconds. And then he blew her away.

'Look, why do you insist on pigeon-holing guys?' he demanded. 'What's with the protective/predator split—why can't I feel a bit of both? I'm quite sure you can take care of yourself, Nadia. But even if you had a black belt in karate and carried a bazooka I'd still have this random concern. It makes me feel better to be with you in the park early in the morning, okay? And what's wrong with that? Look, I'm not going to stop you from doing anything—I doubt I could. But why can't it be fun to do things together? Why do you have to prove yourself all on your own all the damn time?' He paused to swear—pithy and powerful. 'Honestly, the main reason I'm here right now is because I wanted to spend some time with you, and this is one way of sneaking in an extra half-hour. Is that a crime?'

'No.' Winded, Nadia moved forward on her skates so he couldn't see her ridiculously huge smile and her basically heaving bosom. 'That's just fine.'

But she couldn't resist glancing back—and catching his rueful, *gorgeous* smile.

It was a fantastically clear morning. She'd always loved skating. She loved how free and fast it made her feel. But skating alongside Ethan was even more of a rush. He was so right—being together made for much more fun. And he wasn't here to stop her, or because he thought she couldn't do this on her own—he actually acknowledged that she could. He was being with her right now for the pleasure of it. Adrenalin and anticipation coiled together, spinning through her veins, sending her pulse racing and her happiness meter to the sky. Because he was right. Together side-by-side like this was fantastic.

Ethan pedalled quickly, amazed at just how fast she was. And how hot. She had the leggings on, and a cute singlet top, helmet and wrist protectors. He really shouldn't be turned on by that get-up. But he was.

He'd stayed away yesterday and hated every second of the day. So now he was giving in to the nagging, all-encompassing urge to be near her. Only with her this close the urge was crippling. He wanted her more than he'd ever wanted anyone or anything, and he wanted her this instant. And he wanted more from himself—he wanted to *be* more—but he didn't know how and he hated it. Where had his carefree, walk-away attitude gone?

'I'm going to have a heart attack, exercising with you,' he muttered when they finally got to her workplace. He rested his bike against the side of the building and put his hands on his hips, trying to get his rioting body back under control. 'You have a shower in there?'

'Yes,' she said, taking off her helmet and shaking her hair loose.

'Strangers allowed?' he rasped, hormones even more wayward now.

'No.' She bit her lip and looked disappointed.

He was devastated.

But an impish look crossed her face and she leaned close to whisper in the most torturous way. 'Have you got anything with you?'

Ethan thought for a second, and his heart crashed. How could he have been so stupid as not to have a condom on him? But he'd not done this with the intention of getting some. But of course it was all he wanted right now.

Bizarrely, her expression lit up even more as she registered his dismay. 'There's a restroom in the foyer.'

So? What was the point of that when they couldn't do what he so badly wanted to do? But he followed. Couldn't *not* follow. It was so early there was no one in Reception, only a guard on the outside door, and he didn't blink when Ethan followed Nadia into the building. She went straight to a little room. Once he'd ducked in she locked the door and stepped up to him, pushing him back against it.

'You can't get back on your bike like this.' She grinned, her hands moving fast on his fly.

'Don't worry about it. I'm okay,' he said roughly. His body screamed its argument against his words. 'Really, you don't have to—'

Oh. Oh. Oh.

His heart stopped as she dropped before him and dived straight to party central. Everything—save that one organ—shut down. He shuddered at the hot, soft drag and pull of her mouth. Then the *not* so soft drag and pull. Her hands moved firmly—one on his shaft and the other teasing his balls. His body pounded, threatening to burst out of its skin. He ran his hands through her hair—silky and long and sweet-smelling. His head clunked hard against the door, his vision blanking out as internal sensation soared.

He should have known she'd be as passionate and whole-hearted in her efforts here as she was in every other aspect of her life. She put everything she had into everything she did—and her effort and ability totally outweighed her stature. She was a dynamo. Just being around her jolted him to life. And right now he felt more alive, more intense, more focused on one person than he ever had. Vitality streamed through his system—and unstoppable, massive force.

'Nadia,' he gritted, desperately trying to warn her. 'Nadia, *please*—'

But she ignored him, and then it was just too late. He groaned as scalding pleasure coursed through his veins, powering out of him into her hot embrace.

He hauled her up and crushed her body to his, her face into his chest, only relaxing long moments later when it occurred to him that she mightn't be able to breathe. He just wanted to hold her and absorb the zest for life that vibrated from the depths of her body. His heart thundered, slamming against the wall of his chest as if it had grown too big to be hemmed in there. Speech or anything like it was impossible. And it wasn't because of the sex. That was the really dumbfounding thing. That was the thing terrifying his tongue into knots.

Eventually she wriggled out of his arms and brushed her hair back from her face, her cheeks flushed. He stared at her, barely functioning enough to zip his pants again.

'I'd better go get changed.' She looked meaningfully at the door he was still slumped against.

'I want to see you later.' Clumsy and stupid, his words all slurred together.

'Megan will be at Sam's tonight.' The colour in her cheeks deepened.

'Great.' Then he'd be at her house.

Ten minutes later, after a cold shower, Nadia sat at her desk, phoned Megan, and told her to stay at Sam's and not come back until she'd sounded the all-clear.

By Thursday she still hadn't given her friend the signal. Ethan accompanied her home every night—and ravaged her the moment she turned the key in the lock. Once they actually got to her bedroom. Once they stumbled to the sofa again. Once he simply slammed them against the door. Later they threw together scrappy dinners, put a movie on. They'd debated and eventually agreed on action flicks—not too gory, but not dull either. They rarely got through the screenings without an intimate intermission. Between the movies, the food, and the mad, fiery sex they worked—him on his laptop, her on the computer. Until he tried to entice her to bed—to *sleep*.

'You work too much.' He stood behind her chair and wrapped his arms around her, preventing her from typing.

'You can't keep this up.' He must have felt her stiffen because he laughed and quickly corrected himself. 'Okay, I know you *can*, but it's not healthy for anyone. Most people don't do two full-time jobs at once.'

'I know,' she muttered, conceding her tiredness only because she knew he truly did believe she *could* manage. 'But I want to.'

'Is it necessary, though? Can't you ditch Hammond and just do the forum?'

'I don't really see how. And I *want* to work at Hammond. I want them to see me succeed there.'

'Nadia, you'd succeed at anything—and anyone who knows you *must* know that.'

Oh, that out-and-out statement of support so totally deserved a reward. She spun in her chair, looked up at him and smiled wickedly. 'Let's go to bed.'

But as the days passed she refused to think beyond each moment with Ethan. Surprisingly her work days flew because she threw herself into them—keeping her thoughts on that tight leash. And every second outside the office she was with him. She knew she needn't fear he was seeing anyone else as Rafe had. There simply wasn't the time. And she knew he was loyal. She'd witnessed that with his family. But she wasn't family. So she didn't talk to him about what they were doing—didn't want to hear his literally non-committal answer. His avoidance of any emotionally personal conversation. She knew she was in trouble. This was physical for him—only about the sensational sex they shared. But no matter how much they did it, the need in her didn't lessen. It worsened. And her case of "like" for him was worsening too—teetering dangerously close to that other L-word.

So her anxiety ratcheted up, and the gaping, aching hole inside her chest widened. Worse, the feeling of ecstasy didn't last as long as it had, so more and more frequently she turned back to him for the fix. She wanted more. She wanted so much *more*.

Come Friday, her nerves were fraying from sheer exhaustion—and emotional uncertainty weakened what little grip she had left. She'd had a couple of coffees and some sugar to get her through work, but seriously she was hanging out for the close of day.

But then her boss, and *his* boss, called her in for a meeting—and told her to shut the door. Nadia shot a querying look at her line manager, but he wasn't meeting her eyes. Lumps of ice infiltrated her veins, chilling her system at warp speed. Something was wrong.

'We've been going through the records for the last couple of weeks.' Her boss's boss did the talking. 'The computer records.'

Nasty-tasting spit filled her mouth. She swallowed, but it didn't go away.

'Nadia, we know you've been accessing websites that are unrelated to work. Social networks, group forums.'

'It was only a couple of times. Very quick.' Only when Ethan had rung and she'd tried to get out of the dates. Only when she'd needed to see if he'd responded… Only lots.

Her superiors were silent.

'So I'm getting a warning?' she asked, hoping for the best, her cheeks flaming hot enough to fry an egg.

'Nadia, there was content of an explicit nature on those forums.'

They'd read them. No wonder her boss wasn't looking at her. All those comments people had left on Ethan's blog. And she knew what it meant—gross misconduct. Instant dismissal.

'So you're firing me?' Her voice was thin, as if she couldn't believe it.

But inside she could. She knew that that was exactly what

they were about to do. But she couldn't let it happen. She couldn't lose her reputation—everything she'd worked so hard to achieve—*the* job at *the* company in *the* biggest city. Something no one in her family had done or ever believed *she* could do.

But even as she opened her mouth to argue, they forestalled her.

'I'm sorry, Nadia. You know we have no choice.'

She did. She'd drafted the damn policy herself.

'Nadia, how could you be so careless?' Her line manager said once they'd got out into the corridor. 'You *know* there's zero tolerance—especially for…things of that nature.'

'I know.' Nadia wiped her clammy hands down the sides of her skirt. 'It's my own fault.'

But it wasn't. It was his fault. All *his* fault. Ethan and his web war and his crass friends.

She left the building only an hour later. Took a cab with her pathetic little box of personal effects. She'd lasted less than six months. If she didn't get another job she wouldn't be able to pay her rent. Megan was going to move out soon anyway—Nadia just knew it. Megan and Sam were so together and so serious and so happy.

And what was Nadia doing? Screwing around with a jerk who didn't give a damn about anything other than having a bit of fun. She and he weren't *together*, they weren't serious, and Nadia most certainly wasn't happy. Her career was finished, and so was her fling.

She sent him a text.

Don't bother meeting me at work. I've left early.

Her phone rang three seconds later.

'Are you okay? Why have you left early?' he asked the second she answered.

'It wasn't my choice,' she snarled into the phone.

'What?'

'I've just been sacked.'

'What?'

'Gross misconduct. For accessing inappropriate material on the internet. Your blog.'

There was a silence. Then, 'Where are you?'

'Home. I don't want to see you.'

But he'd already hung up.

Twenty minutes later he was pounding on her door and calling for her to let him in. She unlocked the door and glared at him. He pushed past her. She saw him glance at her box of belongings from Hammond.

'Nadia…' His tone was too warm—trying too hard to soothe.

And the thing was she *did* want soothing. Her anger dropped the second she saw him and she wanted a hug. She wanted him to tell her it didn't matter, that it was all going to be okay. She wanted him to tell her he cared.

But she was terrified he wasn't going to. 'I don't want to see you right now.' She was hot, shaking, mortified that she wanted his support so badly and sure she wasn't going to get it.

'You're blaming me?' The soothing bit dropped from his voice.

'Who else?'

'Oh, I don't know.' He faced her, and to her utter incredulity he was *smiling*. 'How about yourself?'

Her stupid eyes flooded with acid tears that burned and made them water all the more. She turned her back on him quickly to hide them.

'Nadia—'

His hands settled on her shoulders and she quickly moved forward out of reach. 'I *hate* you.'

'You don't hate *me*.' She could still hear his smile. 'You hate how much you want me.'

She gasped. So, what? It was only *her* wanting *him* that much? That was exactly what she'd been afraid of. 'You're the most arrogant prick I've ever met.' Even if he was right.

'Nadia.' He walked towards her, his eyes hot enough to melt Antarctica.

She stood her ground and snarled, 'You think you'll make it all better with sex? You think that'll make everything okay? Have a quick screw and then be gone? That's your whole attitude, isn't it?' It was on that level that he saw everything and tried to fix everything.

And, yes, she wanted him, but she didn't want just that from him. All the uncertainty and stress of the week compounded, multiplied, and made everything in her vision wobble like just-set jelly.

'No.' He stopped and sighed. 'I just don't think this is the calamity you think it is.'

'Not the calamity—?' Her jaw dropped. 'It's a catastrophe. You've messed up my life completely. I hope you're satisfied.'

'Nadia, be honest,' he said drily. 'You weren't into that job anyway. You were only there to prove to everyone you could get a job at a firm like that—because you were dumb enough to think people didn't think you were capable of it.' The sensual invitation in his demeanour dropped, and suddenly he looked all serious. 'The fact is your heart has never been in it. You resent the time you have to be there. You give it your best—because you're incapable of giving anything less—but there are a million things you'd rather be doing. It's just that you're too chicken to do them. You're scared of failing. That's why you wouldn't ever identity yourself on WomanBWarned. You're a coward.'

She couldn't believe he didn't get how devastating this was. She couldn't believe he didn't acknowledge his own responsibility for this mess and its seriousness. She wanted him to feel the hurt she was feeling. She wanted him to be sorry and show her he cared for her in a way other than sexual. But he didn't. Hell, she *did* need protection— from herself, for being as naïve as the kid people sometimes mistook her for. For hoping there was more to their relationship.

'*You're* calling *me* a coward?' she yelled at him. 'You— the guy who *never* takes any risks? You only ever sail in easy waters—avoiding real conflict by keeping any relationship on a sexual footing and never going any deeper.' She snatched a breath and charged full scorn ahead. 'You don't date anyone long enough to get to know them. You don't invest anything. Certainly you don't build trust and *talk* to anyone. Then you skip on to find someone else, ensuring you've left things easy with the last lover. My website hit-rate matters to me, but it's nothing on what *you* need from your followers in real life. You send flick-off flowers so those women are left half in love with you and wondering what the hell is wrong with them.'

'Nothing's wrong with them,' he shouted back at her. 'But I told you I don't want complications or scenes.'

'Or commitment.' She said the one word he never had. 'So you escape before it can arise. You hide behind superficial charm. You don't *want* to care. You're as bad as your dad.'

'I'm not,' he roared. 'I don't cheat—'

'But you *hurt* people,' she interrupted furiously. 'You *have*.' He was now.

'You think I don't know that?' His voice rose even more. 'You think I haven't realised a few new things in this last week? Give me some credit, Nadia.'

'Why? When you can't even admit that I'm in a mess and that you're partly responsible? When all you can offer is a quick frolic like that's a Band-Aid to fix everything? Yes, I stuffed up—but so did you. And you still are.'

He lifted his hands, shaking them in frustration. 'What do you want from me? I'm here, aren't I? I've been here all week. Doesn't that count for something?'

'What have you been here for, Ethan?' Panting, she fought back the weak tears as she challenged him. 'What have you been here *for*?'

'Well, what have *you* been taking?' he sneered. 'You can't get enough of what I've been offering.'

She shook her head. 'I was stupid enough to try it your way. To throw caution to the wind—'

'You're crippled by caution,' he shouted over the top of her. 'It's so easy for you to believe the worst of me, isn't it? Because you're so untrusting. But the person you trust least is yourself.'

'Yeah? Well, what about you? Who do *you* trust? You say guys don't like to share—but that's the most pathetic excuse, and what little you offer isn't enough. So your father's a bastard? Why not open up and get over it? You're the one who needs to vent the bad stuff out.'

'Oh, like you have? Like you've *so* moved on from having some guy screw you over? Yeah, Nadia—you're so whole and healthy you've decided you won't ever need anyone or anything. You can't even let yourself rely on someone else to reach up and flick a switch for you.'

At that Nadia hurled the worst she could at him. 'At least I *care* about the things and the people in my life. I don't want to be like you. I don't want to skim through, not feeling anything other than a cheap thrill every now and then.' She'd lost everything over something that to him was *nothing*.

He stood very still, staring at her with eyes that had darkened from brown to black. 'So all we've been is a cheap thrill?'

'At best,' she snapped, hurt into hyperbole and the denial of her own deeply precious feelings. 'And all I want now is for you to get out of my life and stay out of it.'

CHAPTER THIRTEEN

The point of this blog was for guys to get wise. Of course the guy who really needed to wise up was this one. Ladies, you can celebrate—Mr 3 Dates and You're Out has got what was coming to him.
  She's ended it with me. And it's hell.

ETHAN stared at the black characters on the screen so long his eyes hurt. Okay, the rest of him hurt too. His life had never sucked so much as it did right now—and right now he couldn't see a way to make it better. He'd been in uncharted waters with Nadia—from the moment he'd met her she'd been everything unexpected. It had been as awful and infuriating as it had wonderful. And it had only grown all the more wonderful. And awful.

She hadn't got the message he'd left on the blog the other day—about letting his actions speak. Instead she'd misread his actions, and he guessed he couldn't blame her for that when he'd been too afraid to verbalise them even to himself. He'd never felt this way about anyone before, and he was feeling his way blind. But he'd been trying, damn it—wanting to do more and be more and go further with her than he ever had with another woman. He'd he spent every moment he could with her—wasn't that caring? What more did she want? This wasn't a hook-up for him. It was so much more than sex.

But not, apparently, for her. For her this *was* merely a cheap thrill. Yet she'd said she wanted to care—she *did* care about things—so passionately his own blood burned in response to equal hers. So why couldn't she care about *him*? Was he that unlikeable? That unlovable?

Well, yeah, at heart that was what he was most afraid of. That she'd gotten to know more about him in the last few days and he wasn't enough—like she'd said in her blog. There was nothing but superficial charm that faded.

Since his teens he'd worked so hard to ensure no one else would ever leave him—being a charming, entertaining brother and son. Being a super-nice date for women—women he'd left before they left him. He'd worried that if he wasn't the charming nice guy no one would want to know what was underneath.

With Nadia nothing had followed the usual pattern. They'd been playing a stupid game, flaming their antagonism and attraction, and it had come to matter more than everything else in his life. But old habits died hard, and when he'd been confronted with her looking that pale, her green eyes watering, his instinct had been to hold her and make her smile however he could. And he knew how much Nadia enjoyed his touch. So maybe he'd come on too teasing? Maybe he should have offered a no-thrills hug? But when she'd rejected him so furiously he'd been cut to the quick and retaliated right back. Too hard. Telling her the things he thought with zero subtlety or cushioning. And she'd responded in kind—couldn't have made it clearer.

For the first time Ethan had been dumped by a woman. And it hurt way worse than he'd ever thought it could because he'd offered so much more to her than to anyone.

He'd been trying to give her himself—in his own time. But it seemed that was so little she hadn't even realised.

He looked at the words he'd typed into the computer—they mocked him with their uselessness. There was no point in writing anything. She wasn't ever going to believe him—*in* him.

Once, twice, a hundred times, he slowly depressed the "delete" button.

Nadia curled in her chair, hugging her knees to her chest, staring at the screen and the blogs Ethan had posted to tease the hell out of her only a week ago. There was nothing new and there was no point looking. No wonder the good feeling had been fading faster—there had been no emotional foundation. At least not from him. Her doubts had only grown as the days had passed, and she'd been right to feel them. Now she knew she wasn't one to have flings. She couldn't "use" anyone like that. She only ended up used herself. Just as she'd been with Rafe. She *couldn't* trust her own judgement.

She heard the ping of e-mails landing and toggled the screen. A few messages on WomanBWarned that she skimmed—then she shot her feet to the floor and leaned close to the screen. Sandwiched between the usual comments were two e-mails that sent adrenalin shrieking down her veins.

CaffeineQueen and a couple of messages later *MinnieM*—two of the women who'd posted on the original thread. They'd finally replied to the e-mail she'd sent the night she'd thought Ethan had stood her up. She hesitated, heart battering her ribs. She held her breath and clicked the first.

Total disappointment. There was only a repetition of the same spiel that she'd first put up on the thread—no more detail, no more comment. Nadia frowned and opened the other one.

Same deal. Still, what had she expected? To feel some kind of kinship with these women? She stared for a moment, absently looking at the details at the top—the time it was sent, the date, the name and address…

Wait a minute…

Nadia flicked back to the first e-mail from *CaffeineQueen*. A cold, wet feeling slithered down her spine. She checked *MinnieM*. Then checked again in case she'd made a mistake. But no.

While both e-mails had different names, the actual e-mail address in the pointed brackets was the same.

Two online identities and domains traced back to one e-mail address. One woman.

Nadia's skin prickled. Tears sprang as the ramifications clanged round her bruised body. So simple. So awful. She'd been so stupid.

She thought back to that very first, fraught meeting she'd had with Ethan, when he'd suggested that her site was open to abuse, to someone taking advantage of it. He'd been right. And she'd been wrong. So very, very wrong.

And all she'd done since was yell at him. Blame him. Hurt him. And why? Because she'd been upset that he didn't care about her the way she'd come to care for him so quickly?

Well, that was her problem. Not his. And he didn't deserve to have borne her fury. Most likely he didn't deserve this other woman's fury either. Oh, hell. She had to tell him. She had to make it up to him.

And she had to do it now.

With three clicks of his mouse Ethan deleted his entire blog. He hated that she'd lost her job. He'd never intended that she be hurt like this. Yes, he'd wanted to teach her a lesson—but not total her life. And instead of him teaching her anything, she'd made him question everything about *his* life—and he didn't like the answers he was coming up with. All he wanted now was to get her back. She was already lodged in his heart and there was no getting her out of there. He'd never had to get a woman back before—until now he'd never wanted to.

Somehow he figured flowers weren't going to cut it. He was just going to have to become the kind of man she wanted. A man with depth. A man not afraid to take risks— the risk of commitment. A man not afraid to open up and talk.

Well, he'd take a risk now—put his neck on the block for her to take a swing at again.

He banged on her door. It wasn't that late. Knowing her, she'd be awake.

A woman answered, but not the one he wanted. 'You're Megan.' The flatmate.

She didn't look surprised to see him. But she didn't smile. 'She's not here.'

His stomach dropped. 'Where is she?'

'Gone to see you.'

'Oh.' He stiffened to stop from sagging. He'd gone that boneless. 'My place?'

He hardly noticed her nod. He was running back down the path to catch the cab that had already gone part-way down the street, telling the driver to floor it once he was inside.

Nadia was hovering on the footpath outside his place. He didn't know if she'd knocked already or not, but she looked about to run, so he grabbed her hand and made use of his superior strength. Only the physical pressure wasn't necessary—she walked beside him, even walked in ahead of him, slipping her hand free as she did so.

It wasn't until they were both inside and he was standing between her and the door that he said anything. His internal organs were working overtime to process the anxiety swamping his system—because she didn't look good. 'Are you okay?'

'I'm sorry to bother you,' she answered, like an automaton. 'Do you have a minute?'

'What's happened?'

He really needed to know. *Now*. Because she clearly wasn't here to get back with him. She looked as if her world had fallen apart—all pale and shivery and scared.

She bit her lip. 'I did some research. I should have done it sooner.' A tear trickled over.

'What research?' He forced himself to stand back—not to swamp her in his arms as he ached to. This time he had to *listen* and then *talk*.

'I e-mailed the women who'd posted on your thread.'

He froze, dropping his eyes from her to the floor as he absorbed that. *So* not what he'd expected.

'It was when I thought you'd stood me up and I was mad with you,' she said quickly.

'And they wrote back?' He measured his breathing—and his reply.

'*She* did.' Nadia's voice cracked. 'It was only one woman. She'd made up another log-in. I checked and found she'd done all the others too. I think she made it up.'

Ethan still couldn't look at her, because seeing Nadia this cut up tore him apart. If he snuck even another glance he'd be over there and stuffing things up again.

'So you were right.' She spoke so softly he hardly heard her words—but he heard the heartbreak.

He shoved his hands in his pockets, feeling more sorry for her than he did for himself.

'How many others are on there, making up rubbish?' she asked, not seeming to expect an answer because she went straight on, her distress becoming more audible. 'I really believed in it. I really did.'

'I know.'

'I'm so sorry, Ethan. I've already shut down the thread. I'm going to shut down the whole site—I just need to give the members some warning.'

She was broken.

Only a couple of weeks ago he'd have been punching the air and yahooing about the site being pulled. Laughing. He'd never felt less like laughing.

'I don't want you to shut it down.' She really was an idealist, wasn't she? Believing in the best of people—except for "men like him", of course. Believing she could make a difference. And she could—she really, really could. But being such an idealist meant she could also be crushed—as she was now. 'Don't shut it down.'

'I have to. This makes it worthless.'

'No, it doesn't. You can't kill all that effort. I saw some of those e-mails. And there were so many other e-mails in those folders. You help people. Just because one woman abused your system it doesn't mean you should ditch all the others by shutting down the site. Just like the fact that one guy took advantage of you in the past shouldn't put you off all the rest.' He *really* didn't want her to be put off.

'But it was you she hurt. It was *you*.'

'And that makes it worse?' His whisper was as soft as hers.

'Yes.'

His heart beat unbearably fast, and his eyes stung as if wind had blown sand in them. But he jammed his hands deeper into his pockets, determined to be *honest* and open up to her. 'Nadia, what's on that thread about me is right.'

'No, it's not.'

'It *is* true,' he argued, aching inside. 'I guess that's really why it bothered me so much when I first saw it.' He looked up at her. 'Whether I actually went out with that woman I don't know. But what she said was right—I was shallow. I was arrogant. I played—' He broke off and laughed painfully. 'And what you said earlier was even more true. I thought I had it together. My life was settled and easy. And empty. I love my job, but I shied away from relationships because they were too much work. I didn't want to be like Dad and neglect a woman by spending all my time at work, or cheat. I told myself I was okay because I dated only one at a time. Always nice, never arguing. But really I was just like him. Knowing how to take advantage. Not having the fibre or the soul to commit. I *used* those women. I was shallow to think that everyone was having a good time and no one was being hurt.'

He couldn't look her in the eyes now, couldn't face the condemnation he deserved. 'But you want to know the real pathetic truth, Nadia? You want to know why I didn't go for more than three dates? Because I didn't want to be hurt. You know, he walked out and I still wonder why. Why didn't he want us? Why hasn't anything I've done been enough to get his affection or attention? I know it shouldn't matter. I know it's his loss—but I still feel it. And I hate that rejection. I hate that it matters so much. I don't want to feel it again. I don't want to let anyone have that power over me,' he mumbled. 'But then I met you, and I've had it so wrong. You make me want so many things I never thought I'd want.'

Nadia moved three paces towards him, desperately wanting to touch him but too scared because he still stood so defensively—all shut away and retreating from her. 'Ethan—'

'Please don't come near me. If I touch you now I won't tell you all the things I need to tell you. I'm sorry, okay? I'm sorry.'

But he didn't need to be. 'Ethan, you're nothing like your father.' She tried to swallow the burning lump in her throat so she could speak clearly. 'You're a fantastic son and brother and uncle. You're loyal, you're dependable—there for them when they need you. You know just how to make them smile and feel better. You bring sunshine to their world and that's such a skill. That's not superficial. I'm sorry I said you were. Because you're not. You care too, Ethan.'

He still stared hard at the floor. 'But I've never cared about anyone the way I care about you.' His voice dropped to almost inaudible. 'I've never wanted a woman the way I want you.'

Her breathing ratcheted. The goosebumps of old feathered across her skin. She couldn't move.

'You're the most passionate person I've ever met. And I'm don't mean sex.' Beneath his tee shirt his biceps flexed. Then he lifted his head and drilled those fiery eyes right though her. 'Whatever it is you take on, you pour everything you can into it. Yes, you make the odd mistake—but so what? You also achieve amazing things. I love the energy you have for *everything* you do in life. I want to be like that.' His hands jerked out of his pockets as he suddenly strode towards her. 'But sometimes it seems like you don't need anyone or anything. You're so determined to get out there and achieve it all on your own.'

Was that what he thought? Her heart wrung—he was so wrong.

'But you *do* need people.' He bent, grasping her upper

arms. 'And you *want* to be valued. You want to be loved, and you should be—just for you.'

She didn't bother trying to hide the tears slipping down her cheeks. She just wiped them with uselessly wet fingers.

'You *are* valued, Nadia. You *are* loved.' His voice dropped to a whisper. '*I* love you.'

'You don't.' He couldn't. He just couldn't.

He looked distressed and his fingers tightened. 'Please believe in me. In us. In yourself. I know there's courage in you, Nadia. Please trust me.'

'But I've been such a bitch. You can't possibly like me when I've been so horrible.'

The desperate pinch in his features lessened. So did the pressure on her arms. 'Well, I've been a jerk too.' A smile flashed then. 'And, yeah, there've been a couple of seconds when I didn't *like* you—but I absolutely love you and I always will.'

It was a mountain blocking her throat now, so she couldn't speak at all. She couldn't actually think. There was just amazement and disbelief and relief and the sweetest warm feeling trickling through her.

'WomanBWarned does a lot of good things. Put in a few more checks and balances, Nadia. Make it better. Don't destroy it. And let me *help* you—not because I don't think you can do it on your own, but because I *care*. Let me be beside you, cheering all the way.'

She smiled, the block in her throat melting. 'You don't want to be involved in WomanBWarned.'

'Yes, I do—because it matters to you and I can see what it could be.' He sighed. 'It doesn't matter what any of those people think about me...' He hesitated, looking almost shy as he muttered, 'All that matters is what *you* think of me.'

A rainbow burst in her chest, flooding her with colour

and warmth and light—and, yes, *courage*. Real genuine courage to go for what she truly wanted. 'Ethan, I think the world of you.' She stretched up on tiptoe as if she could make him believe her if she was closer. 'You're the sunshine, the air—you're everything to me. I love you.'

He smiled, but in his eyes there was still a scared look. 'Really?'

'It shouldn't be so hard to believe.' She ran her fingers down the hard planes of his chest. 'Let me prove it to you.'

He covered her hand with his and stopped its journey down his flinching abs. 'I don't want to think we're just about sex. I mean, it's the best *ever* with you, but there's more to us than—'

'I know that.' She put her fingers over his mouth. 'Take me to bed, please, Ethan—and *make love* with me.'

Still he hesitated. 'I thought you didn't want to…'

His bedroom. She remembered now—she'd been such a bitch she'd refused to go into his room last time she was here. 'Those women are a part of your past,' Nadia said. 'I might not like it that much, but I do accept it. Just like you're willing to accept WomanBWarned.'

'You know I'm only interested in one woman now,' he said seriously. 'And there weren't really that many notches.' His eyes suddenly danced. 'And last week I got a new bed anyway. I thought I'd turn over a new bedspread.'

'Instead of a new leaf?'

'Yeah.' He held her closer still. 'And it's so much better than I'd ever have believed.'

'So I'm going to be the first in your new bed?' she teased.

'And the last.'

He hoisted her up and she wound her legs round his waist. He moved quickly. They stripped quickly. But when they lay down they both intuitively slowed. It was love-making at its simplest—face-to-face, arms entwined. The moment of completion was sublime. She clamped her legs together, locking him inside her. He kissed her deeply so they were as close and connected as possible, taking up only the narrowest space in the super-size bed.

'I love you,' he whispered again.

She answered him over and over, until ecstasy hit and sent her to paradise. Clinging to him tightly, she took him with her. She rested on him after, coasting her hand down his chest, joyously free to caress him as she pleased. And she was *so* pleased—so in love.

'Let's go on a date.' She lifted her head, energised by a resurgence of elation. 'We could go dancing—I'd love to dance with you.'

'No. I'm not ever going on a date with you again. Not ever.'

She stared down at him, her breath catching.

'Neither of us are in the dating scene, okay?' he said intently. 'We're in a *relationship*.'

'A what?'

'You heard.' He grinned—although it was a little short on his usual confidence and heavier on self-consciousness. 'You're the woman I want to be with. The only woman. Whatever it takes, Nadia. Even—' he breathed deep '—commitment.'

She clapped a hand over her mouth to hide her giggle of incredulity—and of delight—because there was no doubting his sincerity.

He grabbed her wrist and pulled it back so he could see her smile and kiss it. 'You and I both knew the minute we laid eyes on each other that we were going to end up in bed together,' he said huskily. 'Now we're just staying there the rest of our lives.'

'In bed?'

He rolled his eyes. 'And you accuse *me* of wanting only one thing?' But he nudged his hips up, pressing between her thighs and proving that he, too, still wanted *that* as much as ever.

Nadia reached her arms round him and hugged him as close as she could, amazed to discover that she could feel so happy. It surged and swamped and then radiated out of her. It couldn't be contained. He gave her the confidence, the certainty she craved—not just with his actions, but now with words too. His actions had been telling her for days what she'd been too chicken to believe. He'd been there for her. He'd wanted her, challenged her as much as helped her, made her laugh as much as he'd made her mad, and she loved him more passionately than she'd ever thought possible. With him, her heart was infinitely huge.

And finally she could truly believe—he was strong, supportive, sexy and *hers*.

'I won't let you down, Nadia,' he whispered, his expression filled with pure liquid promise.

'I know.' She framed his face between her palms. 'I won't let you down either. It's going to be fun.'

He smiled, his face as handsomely charming as ever, and full of inner emotion. 'It's going to be for ever.'

WomanBWise!

*I'm Nadia Keenan—formerly **OlderNWiser** on **WomanBWarned**. I know we've been counting down to our whole new look for a few weeks now, and I'm so thrilled to be able to unveil it today!*

First up—you've noticed the change in name, right?

I know my old ID said I was wiser—fact was, I

*wasn't. I'm still not. There's so much I have to learn…
We all do, right? But we can get there together…*

So, welcome to the launch of **WomanBWise**. *I hope
you like the new format, I think it's pretty easy to
navigate your way round. We've incorporated several
of your suggestions from our "feedback frenzy", and
we've added in a few new ideas of our own. There
are a couple more boxes to fill in when you register,
but we think it's worth the extra five seconds. And
remember your privacy is important to us. We don't
share your personal info with any third parties.*

*Some exciting new features include our online
shop—you can get our too-cute tee shirts, and we
also have a very nifty personal alarm that's little
enough to conceal in the tiniest of evening bags—or,
even better, on yourself. And if you're a girl who likes
bubbles at a party, be sure to pick up one of our cute
bottle stops that fits onto your mini-bottle. You sip
through a straw so there's no chance of your drink
being spiked. It fits soda and juice bottles too and,
again, will tuck into your purse super-easy.*

*Our personal safety items aren't about being para-
noid, but about being prepared when you get your
party shoes on. We're all about making smart, strong,
safe choices. And we're about building a sisterhood
that supports. Mr 3 Dates and You're Out was right—
we women do love to share. And so we should—the
good as well as the bad!*

*Yes, there's a new section for your best date des-
tination ideas, and a section for success stories—
there's one up there already. You might have read
about them before…they had a little blog war going
for a while there ;)*

Dating, dancing, going to dinner and meeting

new people should be a fun and positive experience. But sometimes it doesn't work out. Sometimes bad stuff happens. So let's listen, clue each other in, and learn—so we can move forward and maybe make fewer mistakes…

And as you all begged for it, there will be a regular blog from Mr 3 Dates—our man from the dark side. I know how popular his views are with you all!

Meanwhile, he and I are now up to date number 128. Yes, I know its only three months since our first dreadful movie date, but we've been having a few two-date days. Actually, Ethan insists we're no longer dating, but that we're in a relationship. He's given me a diamond to try to prove it.

But we are dating—because how can I run a dating divas support centre if I'm not dating?

Oh okay—to settle his nerves, I confess online, in public and unreservedly, that I'll be dating him the rest of my life…

Which just goes to show that even the burnt-by-boys girl and the scared-to-settle guy can get over it when they meet the right one for them…

So get out there, get dating, and have some safe, sexy fun. If fate has her way you'll find your one when you least expect it. But, no matter what, remember that we're all here to help, listen and laugh along the way—and we'll be wise women together!

Love, Nadia.

DARE SHE KISS & TELL?

BY
AIMEE CARSON

The summer she turned eleven, **Aimee Carson** left the children's section of the library and entered an aisle full of Mills & Boon® novels. She promptly pulled out a book, sat on the floor, and read the entire story. It has been a love affair that has lasted for over thirty years. Despite a fantastic job working part-time as a physician in the Alaskan Bush (think *Northern Exposure* and *ER*, minus the beautiful mountains and George Clooney), she also enjoys being at home in the gorgeous Black Hills of South Dakota, riding her dirt bike with her three wonderful kids and beyond patient husband. But, whether she's at home or at work, every morning is spent creating the stories she loves so much. Her motto? Life is too short to do anything less than what you absolutely love. She counts herself lucky to have two jobs she adores, and incredibly blessed to be a part of Mills & Boon's family of talented authors.

To my dog, Akiko,
who is really just a cat incognito.
Thanks for the entertaining attitude.

CHAPTER ONE

Arms crossed, legs braced shoulder width apart, Hunter Philips stood in the Green Room at Miami's WTDU TV station and studied the woman on the monitor, mentally preparing for the upcoming clash. On screen Carly Wolfe smiled at the talk-show host and the audience. The little troublemaker was prettier than he'd imagined, with long, glossy brown hair pulled forward over one shoulder and elegant legs crossed. Her leopard print slip dress was flirty and seductively short, matching a pair of killer heels. An outfit perfect for the host's live midnight show, but mostly for visually seducing a guy into a stupor of compliance. Every man in the viewing area with a functioning libido was quite likely licking their TV screen about now.

Clearly smitten, the blond talk-show host leaned back in his chair, his mahogany desk catty-corner to the leather love seat where Carly Wolfe sat. "I enjoyed your daily blog accounts of your…shall we say…" Brian O'Connor's smile grew bigger "…*creative* attempts to obtain Hunter Philips's comment before running your story in the *Miami Insider*. Owning a network security consultant business must leave him little time for the press."

Her smile was warm and genuine. "I was told he's a very busy man."

"How many times did you contact him?"

"I called his secretary six times." The woman laced her fingers, hooking them at the end of her knee, and sent the host a delightfully mischievous look. "Seven if you count my attempt to hire his company to help with my social networking security settings."

The wave of laughter from the audience blended with the host's chuckle. He was clearly charmed by his guest, and Hunter's lips twisted in a humorless smile. Carly Wolfe's fun-loving nature had the audience firmly twined around her delicate pinky finger, which meant Hunter was in some serious trouble.

"I don't know for sure," Brian O'Connor said, oozing the easy sarcasm that made him so popular with the heavily sought-after twenty-to-thirty-five-year-old demographic, "but I imagine Hunter Philips's company usually deals with more complicated accounts than simple social networking settings."

A playful twinkle appeared in her gaze. "That's the impression I got from his secretary."

Hunter stared at Carly's captivating amber-colored eyes and creamy skin, his body appreciating the entire package. Physical attraction he'd learned to ignore, but these last few weeks he'd grown intrigued and amused as Carly Wolfe's attempts to get his comment had proved increasingly more ingenious. Unfortunately the sassy sex appeal and the spirited sense of fun was an irresistible combination.

No doubt she'd learned to use her charms to her advantage.

Despite the need to pace, the urge to *move*, Hunter remained still, mentally running through his options for handling the journalist as he assessed her on the monitor. Years ago he'd undergone extensive training, learning how to wait patiently and ignore the chaotic pump of adrenaline surging through his body—no matter the danger. And what did it say about the sad state of his life when danger now came in the form of a pretty reporter?

Hunter forced himself to listen as the host went on.

"Ms. Wolfe," Brian O'Connor said. "For those few Miamians who haven't read your article, tell us about the program Hunter Philips created that has you so upset with him."

"It's a break-up app called 'The Ditchinator,'" she said. There was a second ripple of laughter from the audience, and Hunter's lips twisted wryly. Leave it to Pete Booker, his partner, to choose an insulting name. "Voicemail, text messages, even email," she went on. "We've all been dumped coldheartedly before." She turned to the audience with an inviting smile that called for solidarity among the rejected. "Am I right?"

A rousing round of applause and whistles broke out from the crowd, and Hunter grimaced. His reason for designing apps on the side was to fight his growing restlessness—an uneasy edginess he couldn't explain—*not* to bring about a potential PR problem for his company. Especially with a program he'd created eight years ago during a moment of weakness. He never should have given his partner the go-ahead to rework the idea.

Forcing his attention back to the monitor, Hunter listened as the host addressed Carly. "Are you still interested in speaking with Mr. Philips?"

"I'm *more* than interested, Brian," Carly Wolfe said. "I'm dying to talk to him—if only for a minute." She turned her winning expression toward the audience, and her beguiling charm reached through the television screen and tugged hard on Hunter's libido. "What do you guys think?" she said. "Should I keep pursuing Mr. Philips to hear what he has to say for himself?"

It was clear from the whoops and cheers that the audience was ready to string Hunter up, and his muscles tightened with tension, like rubber bands stretched to the max.

Long ago he'd been secretly tried, convicted, before being

metaphorically hung for being the bad guy—all thanks to another beautiful reporter who had needed her story. This time he had every intention of fighting back…with any means necessary.

"Mr. Philips?" a crew member said as he entered the room. "You're on in one minute."

With the announcement of a commercial break, Carly relaxed in the love seat arranged diagonally to the host. She hoped Hunter Philips was watching the show and saw that the audience was as fired up about his insulting app as she was.

She was no stranger to humiliation—was becoming quite the expert, in fact. And who *hadn't* experienced an impersonal break-up these days? But the memory of Jeremy's insensitive Ditchinator message boiled Carly's blood. If he'd simply broken it off with a quick text message she would have been over him in about forty-eight hours. Okay, probably less. The way she'd learned Thomas had dumped her—via a newspaper article and, worse, to save his financial bottom line—had been a theme park ride of embarrassment, minus the thrills and fun. The Ditchinator took the experience in a different direction. It was heartless, for sure. But the worst part? It was so…so…*flippant*.

And just how horrendous would it have been if she'd actually been in *love*?

There was no way she was going to let the elusive Hunter Philips remain in the shadows, raking in money at other people's painful expense.

The commercial break over, the host said, "We were lucky to receive a surprise phone call today. Ms. Wolfe, you're about to get your wish."

Carly froze, a strong sense of foreboding and inevitability curling in her chest, and she forgot to breathe as the host went on.

"Ladies and gentlemen, please welcome to the show the creator of The Ditchinator—Mr. Hunter Philips."

An electric flash zapped Carly's every nerve, leaving her body numb. *Great.* After chasing Hunter Philips for weeks, he'd trumped her maneuvers by turning up when she was most unprepared. Crafty little devil.

Stunned, and irritatingly impressed by his move, Carly felt her heart hammer, and she forced herself to breathe as the man appeared, heading toward her amid the audience's applause. He wore dark pants and a classy black, long-sleeved knit shirt that hugged a chest too delicious to contemplate. Talk about feeling unprepared. Delectable torsos could definitely prove to be a distraction.

His dark hair was short on the sides, with just the right amount of thickness on top. His tall frame, replete with lean muscle, moved with a sinewy grace that exuded a lethal readiness—conjuring images of a night prowler poised to pounce.

Carly had the distinct impression she was the target.

Brian O'Connor stood as the man strode toward the couch and the two shook hands across the desk. The applause died down as Hunter Philips sat on the love seat beside her. The leather cushion dipped slightly…and Carly's stomach along with it.

The host said, "So, Mr. Philips—"

"Hunter."

The man's voice was smooth, yet with an underlying core of steel that triggered Carly's internal alarms, confirming that this was not a man to treat lightly. But after all the stunts she'd pulled, well…it was too late to back down now.

"Hunter," the host repeated. "Miami has been following Ms. Wolfe's blog updates as she tried several unusual techniques to get you to comment before she ran her column, and I'd like to know what you thought of her attempts."

Hunter Philips shifted in the seat to face her, his intense

iced-blue eyes landing on Carly. A static energy bristled along her nerves, paralyzing her. A classic "deer meets headlights" moment.

Hunter's smile was slight. Secretive. "I was disappointed we couldn't accept your social networking job. It sounded fascinating," he said dryly. "And sadly," he went on, "I wasn't able to use the *Star Trek* convention tickets you sent as an enticement to accept your offer."

An amused murmur moved through the audience—most likely because Hunter Philips was so far from the stereotype to attend such a function it was laughable.

Which was probably why Brian O'Connor was chuckling as well. "Thoughtful gift."

Hunter Philips studied Carly, his brow crinkling mockingly. "It would have been even better if I were a fan of the franchise," he said, his nerve-racking gaze pinning her down.

Mentally she shook herself from her stupor. *Now's your chance, Carly. Just keep it cool. Keep it easy-breezy. And for God's sake, whatever you do, don't let your emotions get the best of you again.*

She tried for her standard disarming smile, the kind that usually won people over, holding out little hope that it would sway this darkly dangerous man next to her. "Sci-fi isn't your thing?"

"I prefer mysteries and thrillers…"

"I'm sure you do." He was mysterious, all right. "I'll keep your genre preference in mind next time."

His lips curled at one corner, more in warning than humor. "There won't be a next time."

"Pity." Those watchful eyes made the hair at her neck prickle, but she refused to back down from his gaze. "Even though chasing your comment ultimately proved fruitless, it was still fun."

The host chuckled. "I liked the story of when you tried to deliver a singing candy-gram."

"That didn't even get me past Security," Carly said wryly.

Hunter lifted an eyebrow at her, even as he addressed the host. "My favorite was when she applied online for a position at my company."

Despite her nerves, and the smoldering anger she was beginning to feel building inside her, she tried injecting a little more false charm into her smile. "I'd hoped a job interview would at least get me personal contact."

"Personal contact is good," Brian O'Connor commented slyly.

Hunter's gaze grazed purposefully across her lips—setting off a firestorm of confusion in her body—before returning to her eyes. "I can see how Ms. Wolfe's charms would be more effective in person."

Carly's heart contracted, and her anger climbed higher as comprehension dawned. He wasn't simply checking her out; he was accusing her of flirting with intent. And the warning in his gaze made it clear he was less than amused. But engaging others came naturally to her. She liked people. Especially *interesting* people. And the fascinating Hunter Philips was overqualified for the title.

"Well…" She struggled to keep her irritation from showing. "While *you* specialize in avoidance, I'm much better at one-on-one."

"Yes." His tone held an intriguing combination of both accusation and sensual suggestion, setting her every cell thrumming. "I imagine you are."

Her lips flattened. If she was going to be accused of using flirting as a tool, she might as well give him her best shot. She leaned a tad closer and crossed her legs in his direction, her dress creeping higher on her thigh as planned. "And you?" she said, as innocently as she could.

His glance at her legs was quick but hair-raising, followed by a look that acknowledged both her attributes and her attempt to throw him off. In contrast to the wild knocking in her chest, he was cool and collected as he went on. "It depends on who the other 'one' is."

She wasn't sure if he was truly attracted to her or not. If he was, he clearly could control himself.

"I'm good with a face-to-face with someone I find intriguing and clever," he went on. She got the impression he was referring to her. And yet somehow…it wasn't a compliment. "The encrypted résumé you sent to my office was interesting and creative. The simple substitution cipher you used was easy to decode, but still…" a barely perceptible nod in her direction "…it was a genius touch that ensured it got passed directly to me."

"As one who seems overly keen on protecting information," she said with a pointed look, "I thought you'd appreciate the effort."

"I did." His tiny smile screamed *Caution! Trouble ahead!* and his words made it clear why. "Though my silence on the matter should have been response enough."

"A simple 'no comment' would have sufficed."

"I doubt you would have settled for that." His powerful gaze gave her the impression he knew her every thought. An impression made even more annoying by the fact that he was right—she wouldn't have been satisfied with that easy get-out. "And since I declined your offer of a meeting," he went on, "I'm returning the secret decoder ring you sent as a gift."

As another twitter of amusement moved through the studio audience, Hunter reached into his pants pocket and then held out the tiny object, his gaze on hers. For a moment she detected a faint light in his eyes. Despite everything, he *had* been amused by her attempts to meet with him.

Stunned, she stared at him blankly.

Hunter patiently continued to hold out the ring and said dryly, "I half expected you to show up and request membership at the boxing gym I use."

He almost sounded disappointed she hadn't.

Feeling more confident, she smiled and held out her hand for the gag gift. "If I'd known you frequented such a facility I'd—" He placed the ring in her palm, warm fingers brushing her skin, and the electric current upped her prickly awareness of him by a billion watts. Her traitorous voice turned a tad husky. "I'd have been there."

"I suspect you would have," he murmured.

Carly had the feeling the man was noticing, cataloguing and storing away every detail about her. To what dark purpose she had no idea. The thought sent an illicit shimmer of excitement down her spine. Trapped in his gaze, Carly struggled for a response, but Brian O'Connor spared her the effort, announcing they were cutting to commercial.

During the break, Hunter leaned closer. "Why are you chasing me down, Ms. Wolfe?"

The confidential conversation emboldened her, and she lifted her chin. "To get you to publically admit your mean-spirited app sucks."

He cocked his head in caution. "You'll be waiting a long time."

She ignored his response. "Eventually—" her smile held zero warmth "—I'm going to get you to pull it off the market so no one else has to suffer."

"I'm curious…" His lethally secretive smile returned. "How much of your body will you expose for your cause?"

Clearly he was trying to get her riled. She fought to maintain her cool. "Which parts would prove most effective?"

"I'm open to suggestions."

"My middle finger, perhaps?"

"I prefer rounder…" his eyes skimmed her breasts, leaving

her sizzling "…softer parts." His gaze returned to her lips. "Though your sharp tongue holds a certain appeal."

She considered sticking her tongue out at him until his eyes returned to hers—seemingly unaffected, still unerringly focused, and full of a dangerous warning that left her breathless.

Fortunately the host announced the end of the commercial. Desperate for oxygen, and a break from Hunter's maddening effect on her body, she tore her gaze from him back to Brian O'Connor as he addressed her.

"Now that you have Hunter's attention," the host said, "what would you like to say?"

Go to hell came to mind. Unfortunately this wasn't cable— no swearing allowed.

But if she couldn't speak her mind, she could at least get him to face the music—off-key notes and all. "On behalf of all those affected, I'd like to thank you personally for the creation of The Ditchinator and the message it sends: 'It's over, babe.'" In keeping with their interaction to date, she lifted an eyebrow that was outwardly flirtatious but heavy with biting subtext. "You're quite the poet."

"You're easily impressed."

"It must have taken you hours to compose."

Hunter looked as if he wanted to smile. Whether despite her insult or because of it she wasn't sure. "Only a few seconds, actually. But at least it's short and to the point."

"Oh, it's *extremely* pointy, all right," she said. She twisted on the love seat to face her opponent more directly, refusing to let him get an outward rise out of her. "But what makes the experience *super*-fun is the bulk email the Ditchinator sends, notifying friends and social network followers that you're now single and available." Her smile turned overly sweet. "Nice feature."

"I thought so," he said, as if she was being serious. But

Hunter Philips was the sort of man who didn't miss a thing, not with that disturbingly calculated gaze that bored into hers.

"It certainly is a time-saver," the host said, clearly trying to rejoin the discussion.

Hunter's intense focus remained on Carly. "I admire efficiency."

"I'm sure you do," she said.

"It's a fast-paced world we live in," Hunter returned.

"Perhaps too fast," she said, aware they were still shutting Brian O'Connor out. Hunter wasn't playing nice with the host. She doubted he *ever* played nice. And she was too engrossed in this visual and verbal duel to care.

"Care to hear my favorite feature of your app?" She threw her arm across the back of the couch and leaned closer. His woodsy scent filled her senses. "The extensive list of songs to choose from to accompany the message."

The host chimed in. "The one I'd hate to be on the receiving end of is Tchaikovsky's *Nutcracker*," he said with an exaggerated shiver, clearly for the benefit of an amused audience.

She looked past Hunter to address Brian O'Connor, her tone laden with sarcasm. "Mr. Philips *is* very clever, isn't he?" Her eyes crash-landed back on Mr. Ditchinator.

"Hunter," the man insisted, his gaze trained on her. "And *your* ex-boyfriend's choice of songs?"

"It was an extra-special title. 'How Can I Miss You When You Won't Go Away?'"

Though the audience gasped and snickered, Hunter Philips didn't register the musical slight, and Brian O'Connor said, "Obscure. But effectively rude."

"Which leaves me curious as to why Ms. Wolfe is using her column in the *Miami Insider* to target me," Hunter said.

Hunter faced Carly again. Though braced for the impact, she felt the force of his gaze to her core.

"You don't seem particularly angry at the man who sent you the message," he said smoothly. "Your ex-boyfriend."

"We hadn't been together long," she said. "We weren't seriously involved."

His eyes held hers as he tipped his head. "I find that hard to believe."

"Why?"

"'Hell hath no fury' and all…"

Suddenly she realized he'd turned the tables and the attack was now on *her*. Subtle, so as to not raise the crowd's ire, but there nonetheless. The insinuation increased the tension in the air until it was almost palpable, and their host remained silent, no doubt enjoying the show they were providing.

But Carly let Hunter know with a small smile that she was on to his game. "This isn't a scorned woman's vendetta."

"You haven't flipped the coin from love to hate?" Hunter said.

"Love is one emotion I've yet to experience," she said. Although she'd come close once.

"I'm sorry to hear that."

"Oh?" She feigned surprise. "Does that lessen the fun of your app for you?"

He was clearly biting back a smile. "Not at all."

"Or is it entertaining simply to use your program to dump all your girlfriends?"

"I don't sleep around," he said.

Her brow bunched at his tone. Was he implying *she* did?

"I'm more…" He paused, as if searching for the right word. But she knew it was all for show. "*Prudent* in my choices."

If her lips pressed any tighter at the obvious dig they would merge into one.

The light in his eyes was maddening. "Nor am I vindictive when it ends."

She longed to knock the coolly lethal, amused look from

his face as he continued to bait her. "Trust me," she said. "*If* I'd wanted vengeance against my ex, I would have taken it out on him—not you."

"So why the need to lay your break-up at my feet?"

"It wasn't getting ditched that bothered me." Heart pounding under his scrutiny, she barely restrained the anger that begged to be unleashed. She held his gaze. "It was the method in which he chose to do it. And *you* created the app."

"Yes, I did," he said smoothly.

Her irritation rose. Damn it, his response was so deviously *agreeable*. His simple, matter-of-fact confirmation knocked her accusation to the ground, leaving it less effective. And he *knew* it. "My boyfriend was simply an insensitive coward. You, however," Carly said, her voice low, hoping for a loss of his tight control when faced with the brutal truth, "are exploiting people's callous treatment of others simply to make money."

The worst of the worst. A bottom-feeder, as far as Carly was concerned.

There was no flicker of emotion in Hunter's cool, hard gaze—just like Thomas after he'd dumped her to save himself. Hunter's I'm-in-control smile was infuriating. And right now he was the poster boy for every unpleasant break-up she'd ever experienced.

"Unfortunately," he said, "human nature is what it is." He paused before going on, a single brow arching higher. "Perhaps the problem is you're too naive."

Resentment burned her belly, because she'd heard that before—from the two men who had mattered most. Hunter Philips was a member of the same heartless club as her father and Thomas—where ruthlessness ruled, money was king and success came before all else.

Her sizzling fuse grew shorter, the spark drawing closer to her heart, and words poured out unchecked. "That's a rotten excuse for fueling man's sprint toward the death of human decency."

The words lingered in the stunned silence that followed, and Carly cringed.

Just perfect, Carly. A nice over-the-top histrionic retort, implying you're a crazy lady.

She'd let her emotions get the best of her...again. *Jeez,* hadn't she learned anything in the last three years?

Hunter's relaxed posture remained in place. His eyes were communicating one thing: her wild words were exactly what the infuriating man had planned. "Are you saying I'm responsible for the downfall of human decency?" The lines in his brow grew deeper. "Because that's a pretty heavy accusation for one frivolously insignificant app," he said, and then he turned his small smile toward the audience, drawing them in. "If I'd known how important it was when I designed it, I would have paid more attention."

A ripple of amusement moved through the crowd, and she knew her role in the show had just gone from lighthearted arts and entertainment reporter to bitter, jilted ex—with a generous dose of crazy.

Hunter returned his gaze to her, and frustration tightened its fist on her heart. There was such a feeling of...of...*incompleteness* about it. He'd swooped in, deciphered her like the easy read she was, and figured out just which buttons to push. He was more than an unusually cool, good-looking computer expert—his demeanor was a killer mix of cunning arctic fox and dangerous black panther. Obviously this was no simple network security consultant.

So why had Hunter designed such a personal app? The facts didn't square with the self-controlled man she'd just engaged in a battle of wits. Carly coming in last, of course.

"Unfortunately we're running out of time," the host said, disappointment in his voice.

Hunter's gaze remained locked with Carly's—a gut-twisting, heart-pounding moment of communication from victor…to loser.

"Too bad we can't come back again," she said provocatively, and held Hunter's gaze, hurling daggers meant to penetrate his steely armor, but sure they were being deflected with ease. "I'd love to hear what inspired the creation of The Ditchinator."

For the first time a hard glint flickered in his eyes—a look so stony she had to force herself not to flinch.

The host saved the day. "I would too." He turned to the audience. "Would you like to hear the story?" The audience went wild, and Brian O'Connor became Carly's newest BFF. "You up for it, Carly?"

"Definitely." She turned her attention back to Hunter, her tone silky, as it always was when she tried to control her anger. "But I'm sure Mr. Philips is too busy to participate." Although he hadn't moved, was as coolly collected as ever—God, she wished she had his control—he had to be mentally squirming as he searched for a way out. The thought was much more satisfying than near-miss daggers, but her fun ended when he shocked her with his answer.

"I'm game if you're game," Hunter said.

CHAPTER TWO

A SECOND show. Why had he agreed to a second show?

After a brief conversation with Brian O'Connor's producer, Hunter strode toward the TV station exit, ignoring the corridor walls filled with photos of previous guests as he homed in on the glass door at the end. He'd set himself a task, achieved his goal and won. Carly Wolfe had fought the good fight, but her anger had gotten the better of her. So Hunter should be walking away in triumph. Done. The issue behind him.

But when the talk-show host had mentioned returning, Hunter had looked at Carly's amber-colored eyes that had sparkled with challenge, the high cheekbones flushed with irritation, and he'd hesitated. Her quick-fire responses laced with biting sarcasm were entertaining. And when she'd flashed him her delightfully unique blend of charm-and-slash smile, daring him to a second go around, he'd been driven completely off course. What man wouldn't be captivated by the winningly wily Carly Wolfe—especially after her cheeky crossing-of-beautiful-bared-legs attempt to trip up his focus?

He wasn't worried he'd lose their second round of verbal tag, or that he'd succumb to her allure, because touching her was out of the question. The sexy firebrand was a problem, but one he could comfortably control—because he'd lived with a pretty reporter once, and to say it hadn't ended well was a gross understatement…

There was no better education than a negative outcome. Although with Carly around the view was admittedly five-star.

He heard Carly say his name, interrupting his thoughts, and looked to his left, appreciating her lovely face as she fell into step beside him.

Heels tapping on the wood floor, she struggled to keep up. "Interesting how you were too busy to give me five minutes of your time." The smile on her face didn't come anywhere near her eyes. For one insane moment he missed the genuine warmth she'd exuded early in the show. A warmth that had ended the moment he sat down beside her. "Yet here you are, going out of your way to come on this program, Mr. Philips."

"Hunter," he said, ignoring her enticing citrus scent.

She shot him a you-can't-be-serious look and stretched those beautiful legs, clearly determined to match his stride. "Why do you keep insisting on the use of your first name? To pretend you have a heart?"

Biting back a smile, he trained his gaze on the exit door, feeling a touch of guilt for enjoying her reaction and her struggle to keep pace with him. "You're just mad you lost."

"All I wanted from you was a few minutes of your time, but for weeks you were too busy. Yet you turn up here and then agree to a *second* show." Her tone was a mix of irritation, confusion and curiosity, as if she truly wanted an answer to the burning question. "Why?"

"Maybe you charmed me into it."

"Aphrodite herself couldn't charm *you* into going against your will," she said as she continued walking beside him. "So why *now*?

"The time suited."

She stopped in front of him, forcing him to come to a halt or plow her over. "Saturday at midnight?" Her tone radiated disbelief. "But you must be exhausted after spending the week protecting your big-name clients from sophisticated hackers and designing those heart-warming apps." Apparently she couldn't resist another dig. "I do hope you're well compensated."

Keeping a straight face was hard. "The money is excellent."

He could tell his response ticked her off even more. The slight flattening of her full lips was a dead giveaway. But eight years ago he'd painstakingly begun the process of rebuilding his life. The main benefits of the business he'd started were financial, and he wasn't about to apologize to anyone for that.

"The real question is…" She stepped closer and the crackling electricity was back, heating him up and breaking his train of thought in a disturbing way. "How much has your humiliating app made you?"

"Less than you'd think."

"I'd settle for less than I'd hoped."

He tipped his head. "And how much would that be?"

She planted a hand on a hip that displayed just the right amount of curve. "How far below zero can you count?"

This time he didn't hold back the small smile as she tried to restrain her anger. "Depends on the incentive," he said, feeling an irresistible need to bait her further. "You can try hiking your dress higher again and see how low I can go."

At the mention of her previous maneuver she didn't flinch or seem sorry—which for some reason pleased him.

"What would be the point?" she said, and her smile leaned more toward sarcasm than humor. "You aren't the type to get distracted by a little leg, are you?"

He couldn't afford to get distracted. Getting used by a woman twice in one decade would qualify him for a lifetime achievement award for stupidity. However, his body was taking notice of Carly in every way possible. Despite the years of practice, this time, with this particular woman, he struggled to seize the wayward responses and enclose them in steel even as he appreciated the sun-kissed skin, the silky brown hair and the slip-dress-covered figure built to inspire a man's imagination.

She leaned closer, as if to get his full attention. Which was ironic, seeing as how he was struggling *not* to notice everything about her. "I'm still waiting on an answer," she said.

"To which question?" he said. "If I'm susceptible to a woman openly flirting to gain an advantage or whether I have a heart?"

"I'm certain you don't have a heart," she said, and he recognized the silky tone she adopted when anger sparkled in her eyes. "But you know what else I think?"

Hunter stared at Carly. The bold challenge in her face reminded him of how far she'd gone to hunt him down. He'd pulled his punches tonight, because anything more would have agitated a crowd that was already against him. But right now they were alone, so he wrapped his tone in his usual steel. "What do you think?"

Her lids widened slightly, as if she was having second thoughts. Her words proved otherwise. "I think you're a soulless, cold-hearted bastard whose only concern is the bottom line," she said. "The very sort of man I can't stand."

He dropped his voice to dangerous levels. "In that case you shouldn't have dared me to come back."

Her chin hiked a touch higher. "It was a last-minute decision."

"Having trouble controlling your impulses?"

Her chest hitched faster, as if she were fighting to control her anger. "I have no regrets."

"Not yet, anyway."

"I suspect your reasons for appearing tonight were less

about convenience and more about the free advertising for your heartless app."

His pause was slight, but meaningful. "But I wouldn't be here if it wasn't for you."

He was certain she was smart enough to decode his message.

A message that must have infuriated her more, as her eyes narrowed. "If you benefit financially because of tonight, you should send me flowers to show your gratitude."

The thought brought his first genuine smile. "Perhaps I will."

The muscles around her beautiful mouth tensed, as if she were biting her cheek to keep from spilling a retort. "Orchids, not roses," she said. "I like a bouquet that's original."

She crossed her arms, framing her breasts and tripping up his thoughts. Hunter wasn't sure if it was intentional or not.

"I'm easily bored," she said.

As he stared at his lovely adversary, her face radiating a mix of amusing sass, honest exasperation and barely caged antagonism, he realized why he'd agreed to come back. It wasn't just his inexplicable restlessness of late. Despite the threat she posed, he was enjoying their duel. In truth, he was in danger of liking her—and, with all his money, it was one of the few things in life he couldn't afford to do.

He passed around her, heading for the exit. "I'll keep your floral preferences in mind."

Late Monday afternoon Hunter weaved his way through the crowded, opulent lobby of SunCare Bank. His cell phone rang and, recognizing the number, he answered without a hello. "I just finished delivering the SunCare proposal. I thought you were going to try and make it?"

"*You* have smooth negotiating skills," his partner said. "*I'm* lousy with clients."

"Perhaps because you expect everyone to speak fluent binary code."

"It's the language of the future, my friend," Pete Booker said. "And I might have crummy people skills, but I'm brilliant at debugging our cross-platform encryption software. Which I finished in record time, so round of applause for me."

Hunter suppressed the grin. His friend, a former whiz kid and quintessential technogeek—the stereotype Carly Wolfe had clearly been expecting—hated meetings of any kind. And while Hunter had a healthy ego, was comfortable with his skills as an expert at cyber security, "mathematical genius" didn't even touch Booker's capabilities. Unfortunately what Mother Nature had bestowed on Booker in brains she'd short-changed him in the social graces, leaving Hunter the front man for their business. Still, theirs was a formidable team, and there was no one Hunter trusted more.

"But I didn't call for applause," Booker said. "I called to tell you we've got trouble."

Familiar with his friend's love for conspiracy plots, Hunter maintained his role as the straight man. "More trouble than those secret silent black helicopters?"

"Chuckle on, Hunt. Cuz when Big Brother comes to haul you away, you won't be."

"I promise I'll stop laughing then," Hunter said dryly.

"Do you want to hear my news or not?"

"Only if it's about another sighting of Elvis."

"Not even close," Booker said. "It's about Carly Wolfe."

At the mention of the delightfully charming menace, Hunter frowned as he pushed through the revolving bank door and was dumped out onto the bustling, skyscraper-lined sidewalk. "Go on."

"As per your suggestion I did a little research and found out her dad is William Wolfe, founder and owner of Wolfe Broadcasting. You know—the one that owns numerous media outlets throughout the country." Booker paused as if to emphasize what came next. "Including WTDU TV station."

Hunter stopped short, instantly alert, and people on the sidewalk continued to stream around him. He hadn't completely recovered from his mental tango with the lovely Carly Wolfe. But the little troublemaker suddenly had the potential of being a much *bigger* troublemaker than he'd originally thought. "The station that airs Brian O'Connor's show," he said slowly.

"One and the same," his partner said.

Hunter forced the breath from his body in a slow, smooth motion, fighting the odd feeling of disappointment. So far he'd thought Carly Wolfe had been blatantly frank about all that she'd pulled. Her moves had been amusing because she was so upfront in her attempts to get what she wanted from him. Unlike his ex, whose manipulations had all been done behind his back. And while there were clearly no rules to the game he and Carly were engaged in, there was a sort of unwritten gentleman's agreement—if she'd been a man, that was, which she most clearly wasn't.

In Hunter's mind Carly had crossed the line into unfair play. Because she *hadn't* had to charm her way onto the show—a thought Hunter had found intensely amusing. No, she'd just picked up the phone and called her father. Making her more of a user than a wily charmer. The disappointment dug deeper.

"The second show is the least of our problems," Booker said seriously. "With that kind of connection she could maintain this public fight forever. Enough to eventually hurt the business."

Hunter's cheek twitched with tension. Firewell, Inc. wasn't just about money and success. It was about redefining himself after his old life had been stolen from him. The pause was long as Hunter grappled with the news.

"I hope you have a plan," Booker went on. "Cuz I'll be damned if I know what to do next."

As usual, the weight of responsibility sat hard on Hunter's shoulders, and his fingers gripped the phone. But eight years ago Booker had stuck by Hunter when no one else had, believing in him when most had doubted his honor. On that truth alone Hunter's business, his success—even the contentment he'd eventually found in his new life—*none* of it would have been possible without the loyalty of his friend.

Hunter forced his fingers to loosen their grip on his phone. "I'll take care of it."

He didn't know how, but it was going to start with a discussion with Ms. Carly Wolfe.

After an unsuccessful attempt to find Carly Wolfe at her office—followed by a successful discussion with a Gothically dressed coworker of hers—two hours after Booker's call Hunter drove through a rundown neighborhood lined with derelict warehouses. What was Carly thinking of, doing an interview *here*? It was far from the upscale, trendy end of Miami, and the moment he'd turned into the questionable section of town his senses had gone on alert.

Hunter pulled in front of the metal building that corresponded with the address he'd been given, parking behind a blue Mini Cooper that looked pretty new, and completely out of place. He turned off his car and spied Carly coming up the alley bisecting a pair of ramshackle warehouses. Her attention was on her cell phone conversation.

His moment of triumph was replaced by an uneasy wariness as two twenty-something males exited a warehouse door behind her, following Carly. Both looked big enough to play defensive end for a professional football team. With sweatshirt hoods covering their heads, shoulders hunched, and hands shoved into their pockets, their posture was either in defense against the unusually chilly air…or because they were hiding something.

Their steps cocky and full of purpose, the menacing-looking duo called after her, their intent clearly on Carly, and Hunter's senses rocketed from his usual tensely cautious state straight to Defcon One: battle is imminent.

Sonofabitch.

Pushing all thoughts of confrontation with Carly aside, heart pumping with the old familiar adrenaline of a pending threat, Hunter reached for his glove compartment.

"Abby," Carly said into her cellular, plugging her other ear as she tried to hear over the garbled reception and the city noises echoing along the graffiti-covered alley. "Slow down. I can't understand a word you're saying."

"He came by the office, asking where you were." Abby's voice was low and ominous. "Things are about to get ugly."

Carly grinned at the doomsday prediction. Abby, Carly's beloved Gothic friend, colleague—and perpetual pessimist—never failed to disappoint. Despite Abby's predictions that it would end with Carly being bound, gagged and stuffed in the trunk of a car, the interview Carly had just finished with the two graffiti artists had gone better than expected. Outwardly they might resemble your basic gangsters, but their raw artistic talent had blown her away.

"*Who* came by?" Carly said.

"Hunter Philips."

Carly stumbled slightly, and her heart sputtered to a stop before resuming at twice its normal rate. Gripping her phone, she tried to focus beyond the noisy traffic and a distant call from someone, somewhere. "What did you say to him?"

"Sorry, Carly," Abby said with a moan. "I told him where you were. It's just, well…he caught me by surprise. And he's so…so…"

"I know," Carly said as she puffed out a breath, sparing her friend the impossible task.

"Exactly," Abby said, leaving Carly relieved his beyond-description effect wasn't just on her.

He was too edgy and guarded to be a charming playboy. Too chillingly in control to play the bad boy. Beyond the iced stare he was criminally beautiful, with a dangerous appeal that was so flippin' fascinating Carly had had a hard time focusing on her morning's dull assignment about a new nightclub. Another earth-shattering story to add to a gripping portfolio filled with articles on the latest club, gallery or silliest hottest trend. But who could concentrate when there was someone like the enigmatic Hunter Philips filling her thoughts?

Tonight, hopefully she could keep her mind off Hunter by slaving away on her piece about the graffiti artists. *Another* in-depth profile article her boss probably wouldn't publish.

With a sigh, Carly said, "Thanks for the warning, Abby."

"Be careful, okay?" Abby said.

Carly reassured her she would and signed off, still so caught up in her attempt *not* to think about Hunter Philips that she didn't notice the man who stepped in front of her, failing to adjust her stride. She smacked into a solid chest, triggering an adrenaline surge that shot her nervous system straight to nuclear meltdown...until she looked up at Hunter Philips's face and the whole hot mess got a gazillion times worse.

While her heart added additional force to its already impressive velocity, Hunter put an arm about her waist, pulled her around, and plastered her to his side. Carly's senses were immediately barraged with several competing sensations at once.

Hunter's frosty slate-blue eyes were trained on the two men she'd interviewed. There was an utterly steely look in

Hunter's face. His lean, well-muscled—and protective—body was pressed against hers. And beneath his sophisticated hip-length leather jacket a hard object at his waist dug into her flank.

Alarms clanged in Carly's head. She was aware she should recognize the article biting into her, but she couldn't place it.

Hunter's words reeked with cool authority as he addressed the men. "I think you two should take off," he said, looking ready, able and more than willing to fight if need be.

Thad, one of her interviewees, took a step closer, his bad attitude reflected in his tone as he spoke to Hunter. "Who asked for your opinion?"

Wary readiness oozed from Hunter's every pore. The two beefy young men looked as if they'd been in a brawl or two, or maybe fifty, but Hunter's low voice remained smooth, without the tiniest hint of fear. In truth, Carly got the impression he was almost enjoying himself.

"No one asked," Hunter said, with an undeniably dangerous edge to his tone. "But I'm giving my opinion anyway."

Thad bristled, but Marcus, his graffiti-painting partner in crime, glanced at Hunter uneasily, as if sensing the new arrival wasn't someone to mess with.

"Ease up, man. We're good," Marcus said to Hunter as he grabbed his friend by the sweatshirt and pulled him back a step. "We just wanted to tell Carly she left her recorder."

"Yeah," the other replied with an even worse attitude. "And we ain't asking for *your* help."

Carly's stomach tipped under the tension of this testosterone-fest run amok, but the vicious surge of flight-or-fight response had finally ebbed, leaving communication possible.

"Hunter, back *off*. This is Thad and Marcus," she said, nodding at each in turn. "I just finished interviewing them."

Hunter looked down at her, his expression confirming that he thought she'd just crawled out of the deep end of crazy.

She held out her hand toward Thad, waiting for her digital recorder. Clearly she was more distracted than she'd thought.

Thad, still glaring at Hunter, began to remove his hand from his pocket, and Hunter's body instantly, *reflexively*, coiled protectively tighter. Damn, did the man *ever* ease up? The hard object at his left hip bit deeper into her flank, reminding her of its presence.

What the hell *was* that?

But focusing wasn't easy with the feel of his body pressed against her, the smell of his woodsy cologne, and his hand curved around her hip.

As Thad placed the recorder in her hand, Carly said, "I'll call next week to set up a time to finish."

After a nod at Carly, Thad tossed Hunter a venomous look, and the two friends headed back down the alley toward the side door to the warehouse.

After a few seconds of watching them go, Hunter said, "You can't be serious?"

"About what?"

"Interviewing them."

"Why not?" Carly looked up at him, not sure if she wanted to kick his butt for insulting her tetchy interviewees or kiss him for taking them on while thinking they were a threat to her. Even with the touchy situation resolved, not a single one of his tensed muscles had relaxed—as if he didn't quite trust it wouldn't turn ugly. Of course, *her* senses were still very much in tune with every inch of his body.

And there were a lot of inches. All of them hard.

Her shoulder was jammed against a solid chest. The arm wrapped around her waist held his lean hip to hers, and his long, powerfully built thigh pressed against her leg. This was no laid-back, artsy type—her usual preference. There wasn't a single soft spot on him. Every part was honed to perfection. And if his demeanor during a perceived threat was any indication, in a pinch his body could be used as a weapon...

With a clarity that smacked her system into heretofore unknown heart-rates, the identity of the object digging into her side suddenly became known. Ignoring the mutinous thrill, she whispered fiercely, "Is that a *gun* at your hip?"

It was a rhetorical question, because she knew the answer. How was she supposed to stop obsessing about the man when he showed up going all action-hero on her? And just which side of the law was he on?

Without blinking, he stared at her for a long moment, as if searching for the right way to respond. And then his lips twitched. "Perhaps I'm just happy to see you."

After a split second of stunned adjustment, she rolled her eyes at the ridiculously old joke. "Only if there's something seriously wrong with your anatomy." A spark of amusement briefly lit his eyes, and she knew a comeback was forthcoming. "And forget trying to weasel your way out of my question by assuring me that there is nothing wrong with your anatomy."

His amused tone was intentionally bland. "There's nothing wrong with my anatomy."

She knew that all too well, but she was also perfectly capable of admiring masculine beauty without succumbing to the appreciation. And she hoped to heaven Hunter wouldn't wind up being the exception, because his ultra-cool aura wrapped in hard-edged alertness provided a kind of excitement no man had before. Ever.

Just remember what happened the last time you found a man intriguing and fell victim to your emotions, Carly.

She wouldn't let her fascination sway her again. She *couldn't* let her fascination sway her again. Her career was only just now recovering.

"Who *are* you?" She pulled herself from his grasp and

turned to face him, ignoring her crushing disappointment at the loss of his touch. "And don't tell me you're a simple network security consultant because by the end of that show I knew you were more. And today proves my instincts right."

He looked down at her with the intense focus that always set her on guard. "What else do your instincts tell you?" he said.

That she'd never met anyone like the enigmatic Hunter Philips. That no man had ever intrigued her so thoroughly. But mostly that he was a force to be reckoned with.

"That you could have taken those two guys down with your bare hands," she said, staring up at him, knowing in her heart it was true.

After a long pause with no response from Hunter she debated her next move. She was dying for a visual confirmation of the object that adorned his hip, and there was only one ploy she could think of to accomplish her goal. He was decidedly more dangerous than she'd originally believed, which meant she should pass on the plan. Her palms were growing damp at the thought.

Don't do it, Carly. Don't do it.

Oh...what the hell.

Tamping down her nerves, she stepped even closer, his nearness providing her with a forbidden adrenaline rush. "I think you could have taken them on bare-handed without so much as wrinkling your clothes." She began circling him slowly, not having to work hard at the sensual tone. "Not a mark on your pressed white shirt..." As she rounded his side his alert gaze followed her with a keen interest that prickled her skin. Sweat pricked between her breasts. "Not a crease in your dark pants..." She ignored his probing, assessing eyes, afraid she'd lose her nerve. "Or the classy black leather jacket..."

Heart thumping harder, she stopped in front of him and

began to run her fingers down the edge of his sleek coat, as if to feel the material. What would he do when she tried to take a look?

"Am I right?" Fingers on his lapel, she risked a glance at those oh-so observant eyes, now lit with awareness, and an exhilarating rush skittered up her spine. "Would you have delivered two right hooks and emerged victorious and wrinkle-free?" Tense with anticipation, she began to lift the edge of his coat to get a peek at his hip.

Brow creased in subdued humor, Hunter pulled his jacket back in place, blocking her view. "Maybe."

Good God, he was a tease.

She dropped her hand to her side, the disappointment intense. Damn. The more she learned, the more captivating he became—and the more she wanted to uncover.

In light of everything, an interesting possibility suddenly dawned bright. She narrowed her eyes. "Are you a former crook?" Her answer came in the form of a quizzical eyebrow. "You know…" She tipped her head curiously. "One of those high-tech, illegal hacker guys who gets caught, serves his time, and then starts a security firm helping businesses protect themselves from people like them."

Hunter leaned back against the graffiti-plastered alley wall, crossing his arms. He seemed entertained by the question. Truthfully, he seemed entertained by the entire situation. And he appeared intent on driving her crazy by not answering, along with goading her every chance he got.

"What does your gut say?" he said.

"My *gut* says there is more to you than meets the eye." Carly crossed the pavement and turned to lean a shoulder against the metal wall beside him, close enough to get his attention. Hopefully his *full* attention, without compromising her own.

She had to hike her chin to meet his gaze. Flirting with a

man your own height was so much easier. Flirting with a guy when you weren't sure which side of the law he fell on…?

She lifted a brow. "Are you going to answer my question?" Not one of those beautifully wrought muscles moved. His ready-for-anything aura was undeniably fascinating. "For all I know you're a threat I should run screaming in the other direction to avoid."

Her statement finally triggered his response. "I'm not a threat," he said.

"Then why are you packing a—?"

"I used to work for the FBI."

She bunched her brow, disturbed that her interest hadn't been quelled. And neither had his electrifying effect on her. She'd hoped that learning the truth would put the kibosh on it. Help her focus again. She should have known better.

"And why is an ex-FBI agent chasing me down?" she said.

He shifted to face her, his imposing presence no less intimidating after the truth. Just like love and hate, lawmen and criminals were just the flipside of the same dangerous coin. He said, "To ask how long you plan to use your family connections to harass me."

Stunned, she tried not to gape as a flush washed through her body. Use her family connections? Apparently he was under the mistaken impression her father was an asset to her. And any discussions regarding her dad were bound to get intensely uncomfortable.

She hiked her chin, glad her excuse was real. "Unfortunately I don't have time for a discussion. I have another interview to get to."

His previously amused expression had crossed into decidedly *un*-amused territory, making him more intimidating than before. Apparently he had no intention of letting her go so easily, and her heart sank as her attempt at escape was nixed.

"In that case," he said, "I'll tag along."

CHAPTER THREE

HUNTER sat in the back row of the old theater, empty save Carly, sitting beside him, the crew, and the three naked men on stage, dancing and singing Shakespeare to an electric guitar. *"Hamlet, The Musical!"* was unique enough, and he supposed nudity added that extra edge needed in a town as jaded as Miami. But if there was a god, and s/he was benevolent, this would end soon and he could get back to his regularly scheduled confrontation.

He shifted in his seat uncomfortably and whispered, "When are you supposed to interview Hamlet?"

Carly whispered back, "As soon as the dress rehearsal is over."

He stared at the three actors, bereft of clothing. "They still call it that?"

"They have to do a run-through in costume. Or, in this case, in the nude."

Hunter flinched as one of the male actors twirled across the stage, his male parts a victim to centrifugal forces. "This goes beyond nudity," he muttered.

Her voice held more than a hint of humor. "Wednesday I'm interviewing a participant in the Pink Flamingo's annual drag queen pageant, if you want to accompany me there as well."

He shot her a skeptical look. "What kind of reporter are you, anyway?"

"A lifestyle journalist. I do arts and entertainment pieces."

On stage, the actors formed a brief chorus line, and the image of the three naked gentlemen doing a cancan almost caused Hunter to throw in the towel and leave. "You're a little liberal with your definition of entertainment," he said dryly.

Carly leaned closer, her fresh scent teasing him, her amused voice almost…hopeful. "Are you feeling uncomfortable with the play?"

He stared down at her, not knowing which was worse: the intentionally flirty vibe emanating from her beautiful face or the monstrous scene on stage. One sight scorched his vision, and the other could leave him scarred for life.

She was a manipulator who used her charms at will, yet a part of him was impressed with her courage. A person had to be either stupid or brave to enter that alley in such a dangerous section of town. Initially he'd thought she was the first, but it was evident now that it was the second. And that hint of seduction beneath her pretense of assessing his clothes— all to get a look at his gun—had both tickled him and turned him on when it should have ticked him off. He was dismayed to realize he'd crossed the line. He *liked* her.

An unfortunate complication.

"No. I'm not uncomfortable with the play," he lied, convinced she was hoping the outlandish musical would get him to bolt. But he had no intention of leaving without finishing their discussion. Like her or not, he would protect his interests. He turned his focus to the stage, hoping he had the fortitude to stick it out. "I will, however, admit I'm more comfortable in the back alley of a crime-infested neighborhood."

"Two artistic gangsters are preferable to three actors?"

"They are when they wear clothes."

"I suppose it makes it easier to hide their weapons if they're hostile," she said, obviously amused he'd misinterpreted the men's intent.

"At least I have a concealed weapons permit. I doubt those two did. And I'm ninety-nine percent positive they were carrying," he said. Then he nodded in the direction of the stage. "That's a pretty hostile sight right there."

"Just promise me you won't shoot the actors."

"My Glock is back in the glove compartment." He risked a glance at the stage, wincing at an eyeful of a bouncing Hamlet dancing a Scottish jig. "Though I *am* tempted to retrieve it."

"I never knew network security consulting was so dangerous it required a weapon," she said.

Though her words were laced with her usual dry sarcasm, genuine curiosity radiated from her face, giving her amber eyes a warm glow, and the thrum of attraction settled deeper in his gut. Up until he'd pulled her against him in the alley she'd been just another beautiful woman he could ignore. After experiencing the dip at her waist and the soft curves firsthand, he was less confident. Since Mandy, and with the demands at Firewell, Inc., his relationships had been few and far between. Brief, superficial and uncomplicated worked best.

And it didn't get any more complicated than Carly Wolfe.

Awareness burned through him, reaffirming that his vow not to touch her again was vital.

He pushed it all aside, and said, "My day is typically weapon-free. The Glock is only in my car because I visited the firing range before work."

She shot him a look that went beyond mere curiosity. "Keeping up those skills, huh?"

Hunter's stomach lurched and he turned to stare at the stage, grateful the increase in volume of the music gave him a reprieve from responding. His weekly trips to the firing range were unnecessary, but he couldn't seem to let go of the last routine he'd maintained since he'd been forced to leave the FBI, leaving a massive hole in his life.

The sharp ache resurfaced and his jaw clenched. He enjoyed what he did now, but lately he'd been chafing at the monotony…

Carly must have decided he refused to respond to her indirect question. "Why did you leave the FBI?" she asked.

He turned to study her face. Though she was clearly digging for information, the genuine warmth he'd seen on the TV monitor that first day was back. What would she say if he told her part of the truth? There were bad parts he could share, and there were worse parts he could never divulge. In an effort to protect sensitive information the FBI had kept their investigation of him private. Outside of Mandy's newspaper article about the case he'd been working on, no other information had been made available to the public.

"Off the record?" he said.

She hesitated longer than he would have liked. "Off the record."

"I was stripped of my security clearance and put on administrative leave without pay."

A shocked silence followed, filled with awful music, until she said, "Why?"

"I was working on a case that involved a group of hackers that specialized in acquiring credit card numbers. A branch of Russian organized crime was laundering their money." He took a moment to steel himself for the words that followed. "I was accused of leaking information to the mob."

The pause was painful as she stared at him, wide-eyed. "And did you?"

The words punched hard, his stomach drawing tight with anger. He'd seen the doubt in his colleagues' expressions. The questions in their eyes. Outside of his parents and Pete Booker, no one had believed the truth—not a hundred percent, anyway. Not even after he'd been cleared. So why should *she*? But somehow her doubt took a larger chunk from his already ragged pride, and left him dangerously close to the edge. He leaned closer, and a flicker of desire swept through her eyes. For some reason the thought of a payback appealed. And there was no greater payback than refusing to answer a nosy woman's question.

"What do you think?" he said.

Carly hardly knew him, and had no reason to believe in his honor. But for one terrible moment he realized he was holding his breath, hoping she would.

"I don't know," she said softly, the tone doing little to ease the doubt in her eyes. "Why don't you tell me?"

The seconds that ticked by felt like minutes to Carly, and she held her breath as she waited for Hunter's response. The news about his past had dumped a truckload of fuel on an already burning fire of curiosity, but the impassive look on Hunter's face—so close to hers it was difficult to concentrate—revealed nothing.

And then his eyes flickered with an emotion that came and went too quickly to identify. Finally Hunter leaned back in his seat, but there was a coiled energy simmering beneath the falsely relaxed air. "I think I'll let you draw your own conclusions."

Carly stared at Hunter, quietly sucking in a breath. Damn, the man was determined to drive her down crazy lane. "What eventually happened?"

"The matter was investigated and dropped for lack of evidence," he said evenly. "After that I left the force voluntarily."

From the tone in his voice it was obvious he was done with the discussion. But his response didn't make it clear if the charges against him were accurate, but couldn't be proved, or if they were false. The truth lay buried beneath the impossible-to-ruffle gaze, and her mind kept drifting back to the hard, lethally cool look on his face in the alley.

She cleared her throat, trying to ease the tension. "Being ex-FBI must have helped your business."

He shot her a pointed look. "As much as having William Wolfe for a father has helped *your* career."

The statement was like an elbow-jab to the gut, and Carly's stomach folded protectively into a knot. Her dad was her least favorite subject, and she wished the Shakespeare-singing and dancing men in the buff *had* driven Hunter away. Clearly he didn't scare easily. The next few minutes were going to be rough.

Remember the mantra, Carly. Cool. Easy-breezy.

"It didn't help as much as you'd think," she said lightly. "My dad always insisted I make it on my own." Which she had confidently set out to do, back when she'd believed hard work alone was enough. "When I landed my first job at one of his California papers no one learned who my father was until a year later."

He studied her face, as if surprised. "That must have caused a few ripples."

"My boss was certainly nicer after he found out."

Or he *had* been nice up until she'd made an iffy decision and scandal had rocked her world—both personally and professionally. And, true to his word, her father had never intervened on her behalf...not even when she'd needed his help the most.

The pain sliced like a freshly whetted knife, and Carly clutched her armrest and stared at the stage, grateful the music was loud as Hamlet belted out his monologue, bareassed and lifting Yorick's skull further skyward with every high note. Her father's approval had always felt unattainable. But if she earned her current boss's confidence, and a little leeway to choose her stories again, she'd regain a bit of the dignity she'd lost after her mistake.

"California is a long way away," Hunter said when the

music died down. "Your dad must have been happy you were hired on at the *Miami Insider* and moved back to town."

Carly bit back a bark of humorless laughter, staring at the stage. "You would think so," she said. "But you'd be wrong. My father thinks a weekly online paper will fail. He's convinced I made a disastrous career move."

Or, more accurately, a *second* disastrous career move. As always, his lack of confidence in her rankled. But after his prediction she wouldn't leave even if the *Miami Insider* did take a nosedive at perilous speeds. She was hell-bent on proving her dad wrong.

"As a matter of fact—" Carly sent Hunter a wry smile "—he's probably eagerly waiting for the paper to fold just so he can be proved right."

Hunter narrowed his eyes skeptically. "You're saying your father had nothing to do with you winding up on Brian O'Connor's show?"

This time there was no holding back the harsh laugh. The suggestion was so absurd it hurt. "My father would never show me that kind of favoritism."

"Seems a big coincidence we ended up at the very station your father owns."

"He had nothing to do with it. I contacted the producer of the show—"

"Who wouldn't have given you the time of day if not for the family name."

She wasn't so foolish as to deny it. "Okay, so that part is true." Having the last name Wolfe had to be good for something, because the parental aspect wasn't so hot. "But Brian O'Connor is a fan of my column and was on board with the idea from the start."

"On board for what?" he asked dryly. "Ganging up on me?"

She blew out an exasperated breath. "You handled us as

easily as you handled Thad and Marcus. And you know," she said, fed up with the entire conversation as she twisted in her seat to face him, "I asked to come on Brian's show simply to state my beef with your app. *You* weren't even supposed to be there."

His brow creased with suppressed amusement even as his eyes remained unyielding. "Too bad for you I showed up."

Carly's lips pressed flat as she remembered how he'd goaded her into losing her temper. Was that his intention now?

His intense gaze was relentless as he went on. "I want you to end this public dispute."

"Well, I want you to admit The Ditchinator sucks."

"Fine. I admit it."

She shook her head. "Not good enough. Which is why I'm so pleased you agreed to a second show." She sent him her best winning smile—the one that flirted at the possibility for more. "You can go on air to admit it sucks *and* share the inspiration behind your app."

He leaned close again, a spark of awareness in his gaze that sabotaged her smooth-talking abilities. "I won't do either," he murmured silkily.

Desire constricted her throat, making breathing difficult. She knew he was attracted to her, and God knew he thrilled her like no one had before. She could never mix business with pleasure again, but a part of her longed to know if she could ever get him to act on his attraction. "Well, then, you'd best be on your guard, Mr. Philips."

His gaze dropped to her lips. "Hunter."

Awareness pricking her skin and scrambling her brain, she repeated obediently, "Hunter."

"With you around, I'm always on my guard." His lips curled at one end. "On guard against your sharp sarcasm. The cutting words. The arsenal of charm. And…" his gaze dropped to her legs this time, kicking up her body's response, and then lifted to meet her eyes "…the intentional flash of a little more thigh."

"Come this second show I'm going to pull out all the stops to use that charm and get the history behind your app."

The hard light in his gaze set her body on fire, and his secretive smile sent a shiver up her spine as he said, "There isn't a dress short enough to pull that off."

She bit back the genuine smile that threatened. "Is that a challenge?"

"There *is* no challenge." The light in his eyes grew brighter. "I will, however, take the opportunity to beat you again at your own game."

Despite herself, she let out a quiet laugh. The man might be tightly controlled, but she sensed a playful side in him. One he kept carefully in check, only allowing it to surface occasionally to tease and provoke her. "I'll accept that as the dare that it is. So how about this?" she said. "If I manage to get the answer out of you, I win. And if you can resist me…" She sent him her most charming smile—the one that had always worked up until she'd met him. "You win."

"What's the prize?" he said softly.

Danger and desire intertwined again, leaving her body with a now familiar unsettling attraction that was uniquely his. She was traversing a very narrow line—one so thin it could double as the edge of a knife. And it was hard to focus over her heart's incessant thumping. "I haven't decided on the prize yet."

"Okay, but I expect you to keep the contest fair."

"What does that entail?"

"Leveling the playing field," he said. "No more capitalizing on your father's name as a resource. Which means outside our second show any and all Wolfe Broadcasting media outlets are off-limits in your effort to publically harass me into cooperation." The man gazed at her, his eyes no less intense in the dim light, the hint of humor dwarfed by the thread of steel in his tone. "And no more below-the-belt punches."

Intrigued, she hiked her eyebrow a little higher. "What are you going to do if I break the rules? Fit me with a pair of concrete shoes?" She leaned closer, trying to be heard over the music and desperately ignoring the sensual lips mere inches from hers. "Send me an ankle bracelet attached to an anchor and take me for a boat ride out on the Atlantic?"

His gaze was dangerously daring, lit with humor, and infused with an undeniable heat. The combination provided an edgy thrill and a sense of the unknown that shouldn't have had her so captivated.

Jeez, Carly. You really are your own worst enemy.

His smile morphed from mysterious to killer. "I'll think of something."

"Carly, you know you're heading straight for disaster, right?" Abby—doubting Thomasina friend that she was—shot Carly a worried frown as she clomped across the parking lot towards the Pink Flamingo bar. The heels of Abby's hip-length leather boots were more clunk than spike, and her black leather dress with its flipped-up collar screamed *undead.* "After your blog today, Hunter Philips is gonna be seriously annoyed."

"Why?" Irritation welled for the umpteenth time that day, and Carly frowned. "The Ditchinator just hit the top ten list for app sales."

"Yeah, and *you* just used your blog and your sarcastic wit to share your opinion about that." Abby shot her a sideways look. "Creating quite a furor, I should add."

Carly battled the bothersome regret trying to worm its way in. "It was a couple of rogue comments that started the trouble."

Abby let out a snort. "I've met Hunter, remember?" She began to weave through the noisy crowd toward the front door. "And I doubt he's gonna care *who* started the trouble. He's only gonna remember where it happened."

True. Because Abby's attire might conjure images of vampires, but who wound up resembling the real bloodsucker today? Carly Wolfe, daughter of the notorious William Wolfe, the ruthless man who put results before all else.

Even his own daughter.

She pushed the bitter memory aside and concentrated on the guilt that had been trying to hijack her all day. When a few of the blog commenters had taken up the virtual vitriolic pitchfork and called for Hunter's blood Carly's heart had sunk. *She* had no problem with tossing a few, or twenty, truth-filled sarcastic jabs in his direction, but the vicious turn of the comments had been awful.

But it was done. Time for the pesky little guilt gnats to swarm around someone else.

Carly followed her friend into the old bar. In anticipation of its fifth annual drag queen pageant every inch was packed, from the scuffed wooden floor to the sea of tables and the long bar lining the wall, crowded with patrons of all ages and walks of life. Instantly her tension eased. It was the perfect place to put today behind her.

But Abby clearly wasn't on board. "I'm worried about you, Carly." Hardcore and gloomy on the outside, creamy sensitive filling on the inside, Abby went on. "Hunter Philips is trouble."

Let me count the ways, Carly thought as she trailed Abby through the crowd. He was irritatingly sexy, intriguingly mysterious and possibly criminal, just for starters. "I just want to interview last year's pageant winner and forget about today, okay?"

"Good luck with that," Abby said as she came to a halt,

and Carly almost plowed into her back as she continued. "Because *he* might have something to say about your plans."

Her throat suddenly tight, Carly peeked around Abby. Her gaze landed on Hunter, leaning against the bar. She let out a groan.

Her day had officially gone from bad to worse.

From across the room, his frosty gaze slid to hers, landed, and claimed her attention—something the man excelled at. Her body vibrated and her heart thumped louder than the subdued music pulsing through the speakers hanging from the ceiling.

"What are you gonna do?" Abby said, staring at Hunter.

Nerves scrambling for cover beneath the force of his gaze, Carly said, "I'm thinking."

From his position at the bar Hunter stared at Carly, disappointed in himself. Even after today's blog posts, he couldn't help but appreciate the miniskirt hugging legs that had taunted him during the first show. The hot pink blouse left her shoulders bare. And her sleek brown hair was loosely pulled back, displaying the elegant curve of her neck.

"Now that she's here," Booker said from beside him, breaking Hunter's mental listing of her attributes, "are you going to go over there?"

"No." Elbow on the bar counter, Hunter kept his gaze on Carly as he answered his friend. "I'm going to make her come to me."

"How do you know she will?"

Despite today's online disaster, despite everything this troublemaker had put him through, Hunter's lips tipped up at one end. "She won't be able to help herself."

"Does she have a problem with impulse control?" Booker said dryly.

Memories of her crossing her legs on that first show and

circling him in the alley brought a faint smile to Hunter's face. "You might say that." His gaze lingered on the pretty reporter—a frustratingly fascinating mix of good humor, determination, moments of genuine warmth…and the occasional sultry come-hither vibe. "Impulse control is especially difficult when her curiosity gets the better of her or she's backed into a corner."

"Dude, she's backing *us* into a corner. After her post today my secretary fielded no less than ten calls from clients asking about the negative publicity." Booker's eyes narrowed in suspicion. "I still say the worst of those comments came from blog trolls planted by our competition."

"I think our business competitors have better things to do with their time," Hunter said, suppressing a smile, and then he eyed the lovely Carly Wolfe again. "But it's definitely time to forgo the defensive and embrace the offensive." Something he hadn't done in a very long time.

An unexpected anticipation surged, and eagerness permeated Hunter's every cell with the old familiar thrill of the chase. He was looking forward to carrying out his plan…

CHAPTER FOUR

CAUGHT in Hunter's intense stare, Carly felt her stomach rock with nerves as she ran through all her options. Leave. Stay and ignore him. Or choose confrontation.

His leather jacket was sleekly urbane, not Harley-riding-belt-and-spike. Paired with dress pants and a tailored blue shirt left open at the throat, he looked movie star classily casual. And this time when he'd tracked her down he wasn't alone. Next to Hunter a gangly man slouched unceremoniously against the counter. Despite the crowded room, apprehension skittered up her spine at the thought of facing Hunter after today's debacle. He was clearly here to see her, and ignoring him would only prolong the agony.

Because how could she interview last year's winner and enjoy herself with him assessing her from afar, producing the goosebumpy awareness he always generated?

"Let's just get this over with," she finally said to Abby.

Carly forced her feet in his direction, her nerves stretching tighter with every step. As she drew near, she managed a bright smile.

"Mr. Philips." She stopped in front of the two men. "Amazing how I keep running into you. If I'd known you were coming I would have worn a shorter skirt."

"Pity I didn't call you ahead."

"This doesn't seem like a place you'd usually hang out," Carly said. "Are you here to compete in the pageant?"

Hunter's gaze swept across the room and landed on a contestant—a drag queen sporting a figure-hugging miniskirt and a pair of killer wedge shoes even Carly would be afraid to wear lest she break an ankle. "My collection of miniskirts isn't up to the task," he said dryly. A second participant joined the first, sporting a Marilyn Manson look made of red latex. Hunter turned his iced blue eyes back on Carly. "Interesting job you have."

"I'm trying to convince my boss to expand my column to include interesting community members." Her smile grew bigger as she stepped closer. "Today I proposed I do a story on you. She said no, but I think once she watches our second show she'll change her mind." Ignoring his disconcertingly alert eyes, she leaned close, hoping to get a rise out of him. "I don't think she'll be able to resist the fascinating Hunter Philips."

His cool demeanor didn't budge. "Unfortunately she'll have to."

Carly stared at him. Was he furiously irate, mildly fuming or calmly annoyed at her for her blog post today? Damn it, she shouldn't care. All she wanted was to interview last year's drag queen winner, move past the ridiculous remorse and get her confident mojo back.

"If you're so eager for my company you could just ask me out," she said. "Instead you keep hunting me down." She finally tore her gaze from Hunter to his scraggy brown-haired friend, eyeing him curiously. He wore a gaming T-shirt emblazoned with the words 'Carpe Noctem'—Seize the Night— well-worn jeans, and ratty athletic shoes. "And this time you brought backup too. How very FBI of you."

Hunter ignored her quip and nodded at Abby, as if he remembered her, before training his eyes on Carly. "Abby,

Carly—meet Pete Booker," he said, tipping his head in his friend's direction. "Conspiracy theorist, computer genius, and—" he held Carly's gaze as that secretive smile appeared "—my business partner."

Unwanted remorse bloomed bigger in Carly's gut as polite greetings were exchanged around her. Great, now she was looking at *two* reasons to feel guilty. Pete was cute, in a boyish kind of way that defied his description. Juxtaposed with the coiled, darker edges of his partner, he appeared downright innocent. And both men were looking at her with veiled accusation.

"I suppose your presence tonight is in response to the discussion on my blog," she said.

"Discussion? The dialogue after your post was more like a…" Hunter's voice died out, and he looked to his partner as if he needed help.

Carly knew very well he didn't.

"Firing line?" Pete suggested helpfully.

"Bloodbath," Hunter said.

"Or maybe a feeding frenzy?" his partner went on.

Hunter said, "Better still—"

"No need to go at it all night, boys," Carly said dryly. She blinked back the wave of regret that had swelled the moment they'd started their repartee, but a small resigned sigh still escaped. "That wasn't my intent."

Despite the surrounding chatter, the electrically charged atmosphere popped. Two pairs of eyes were trained on her. Carly was only concerned with one set. Hunter's.

"What *was* your intent?" Hunter's voice was deceptively soft, with the same steely tone as when he'd faced the threat in the alley. "To lose our bet?" he said.

Her smile grew tight. "I'm sure the money your app is now making will make up for today's below-the-belt punch."

"Except *now* I'm getting called by every journalist in

town," he said, and then he lifted a brow with the first hint of amusement of the evening. "And it's not my fault your efforts have shot the app sales to number ten."

"Eight," she said.

He hiked a brow. "Even better."

Oh, he knew the number. Carly's lips flattened, which made maintaining her fake smile difficult. "I should probably thank you for the flowers you sent me today, expressing your appreciation." When the delivery boy had dropped the bouquet off at work, there had been no way Carly could receive the smugly sent flowers without retaliating via her blog. "But I won't."

Hunter's eyes lit with full-on humor now. "I hope the orchid and miniature bamboo arrangement I sent was unique enough for you."

Her mouth tightened. He *would* remember her words and get it just right. Just like he'd remembered her mention of tonight's pageant. Boy, he was the first man in her life to really muck with her mojo. Carly's lips compressed further, practically blocking bloodflow now, but she managed to bite out, "They were beautiful too."

As Carly maintained Hunter's gaze the tension blanketing their small foursome reached a smothering capacity until Abby broke the spell.

"Hey," Abby said, "you two are killing my end-of-the-workday happy place." With a less than happy frown on her black-lipsticked mouth, Abby turned to Pete Booker. "I'm going to enjoy a drink at a table that just opened up. You can join me if you want. And when you say no could you at least send the message via The Ditchinator to *abby_smiles@gmail.com?*" With that, Abby headed toward the empty table.

"Uh…" An awkward expression crept up the brown-haired man's face, and his gaze shifted from the back of Carly's creature-of-the-night friend to Hunter, and then to Carly. Most likely he was trying to decide which was worse—sharing a drink with a pessimistic lady simply dressed like a vampire or the two people who were actually going for each other's throats. "Excuse me," he said, and then headed off to join Abby.

Hunter watched the two with curious interest. "She doesn't bite, does she?"

"Trust me," Carly said, maneuvering into the empty spot at the bar left by Hunter's partner. "She's all doom-and-gloom bark on the outside and no bite on the inside."

"Does she write for the lifestyle section too?"

"No. She's an investigative reporter. Me…" Carly gave a slight shrug. "I find people more interesting than facts."

"Like the renowned photojournalist turned California State Senator Thomas Weaver?"

The name cuffed her on the cheek with all the force of a full-on slap, and Carly's face burned. "You've been checking up on me again."

"You haven't left me any choice." His face had an expression she'd never seen before: curiosity. "The news media speculated you fell for the senator and gave him a free pass in your article. Is it true?"

Guilt and humiliation resurfaced, and she curled her nails against her palm. She hadn't completely fallen under Thomas Weaver's spell, as accused, but she'd cared about him. Had her actions been unethical? Technically, no. Her story had been done and published *before* they'd gotten involved. Inappropriate? Probably. Stupid? Most definitely. Because she should have avoided even the appearance of a conflict of interest. Something William Wolfe, founder and CEO of Wolfe News, Broadcasting—procreator and father of Carly Wolfe, The Disappointment—never let his daughter forget.

"I didn't fall in love." She hiked her chin. "It was closer

to a very intense like." He tipped his head in humor, and she went on. "And I didn't give him a free pass."

"I didn't think so."

She was surprised and pleased he believed her, but the feeling of validation ended when his enigmatic smile returned.

"Did you sleep with him before or after you got his story?" he said.

Her angry retort was cut off when someone squeezed into the space behind her, pressing her forward...and against Hunter's hip. A firestorm of messages bombarded her: heat, steel and a hard-edged awareness. A faint flicker of eyelids was Hunter's only reaction.

"And I wonder..." His voice was low, controlled, the scent of his woodsy cologne subtle. "If I slept with you, would you drop your little vendetta?"

Along with anger, a fierce thrill seared her veins. All from a suggestive comment meant to provoke. Despite his words, she knew he was too self-controlled to follow through on his suggestion. God help her if he ever did. She struggled to maintain a bland tone. "Depends on how good you are."

"Compared to who?"

"Everyone else."

His intense gaze held a hint of amusement. "Hopefully that's not as many as the number of stories you've written."

"Did you come tonight to insult me?"

Someone bumped Carly from behind, pushing her more firmly against Hunter, and he cupped the back of her shoulder to steady her. Every blood vessel in her body grew thick, the blood forced to pulse in jetstream fashion. His hand was warm and seductively smooth, free from calluses that would snag her skin during a caress.

"I didn't come to insult you," he said, staring down at her, his eyes lit with definite humor now. Was he amused by her attempt to continue breathing despite their contact? "That's your MO, not mine," he said.

Carly stared up at Hunter's sensual mouth, the square cut jaw, and eyes that were either icy fire or fiery ice. Carly wasn't sure which. Her voice was strained. "Then why are you here?"

"I came to give you fair warning," he said.

All sorts of warnings were ringing in her head. Professional ones. Personal ones...

She knew she should reply, but the sizzling feel of his palm cradling her from behind was fascinatingly protective and yet unyieldingly hard at the same time. She finally pushed the words past her tight throat. "Fair warning?" A repeat of his last two words was all she could manage.

Brilliant. Now you sound like a stupid, mindless parrot.

His gaze scanned her face. "Maybe putting you on notice is a better description."

Her mind spun. On notice about what? That her body was turning traitor? Trumped by her own libido. *Damn.* As if she wasn't already privy to that disturbing piece of news. She stared up at him, fascinated by the restrained, coiled stillness of the body pressed against hers. Outside an electrifying gaze alive with awareness, and a hard chest that slowly rose and fell—a marked contrast to her increasingly shorter gasps—he didn't move. No swooping in for a kiss, pushing his advantage.

And a very small part of her was...disappointed.

"Notice?" she said, dismayed she was down to single-word responses.

Hunter leaned forward to speak at her ear, his voice low, her pulse pounding.

"You started this war, Carly." The shimmer of his breath on her cheek sent a fresh wave of hot prickles down her back. "I just hope you're ready for the fight."

Without warning he turned and headed off, leaving Carly reeling in the aftermath. And with the sinking feeling he'd just become infinitely more dangerous.

Saturday night, Hunter turned into the WTDU TV station's parking garage, dark save the lights hanging from the concrete beams overhead. He pulled into a space, turned off his car, and sat back in the leather seat, settling in to wait. He'd shown up early with the plan of catching Carly before she entered the studio for the show.

The thought of seeing her again wound Hunter's insides tight. He struggled with the now familiar combination of distrust, amusement, and ever-growing attraction. In the theater, her fascination with his past had been unmistakable…even as she'd questioned his relationship with the mob.

His lips twisted wryly. Carly Wolfe was an unusual woman. With her around, boredom was certainly no longer an issue. At first it had been easy to write her off as nothing more than a vindictive, publicity-driven journalist. But he'd seen her remorse over the results of her blog. He'd thought her outraged innocence during the first show was an act, but this confident, modern woman had a kernel of naivety at her core. He was beginning to realize she truly believed in what she was doing. Worse, her zest for the unusual—and unfortunately for her *job*—made her all the more attractive. He couldn't remember the last time he'd felt so passionately about something.

Before his ex had gotten her story and left? Before he'd been forced out of the FBI? The memories still felt like a vacuum, threatening to suck him down. Unfortunately there was no telling what Carly would say on the show about his app, or in an attempt to learn the inspiration behind its creation…

His insides churned at the memory. But that had been eight years ago, and some things were best forgotten. He'd been stripped of his gullibility, so he needed to do what he did best. Focus. Concentrate. And protect what was his.

The problem he'd been mulling over the last few days was how to throw Carly Wolfe off her game. She was too quick to be bested during the most heated of banter, and she had no qualms about using every weapon at her disposal. Unfortunately she was also getting harder and harder to provoke.

Drumming his fingers on the steering wheel, he remembered the mute look on her face when they'd collided at the bar. For a moment her confidence had wavered, and the confused, dumbfounded expression that had followed had been the most telling of all. Apparently the wily Ms. Wolfe was as susceptible to their attraction as she'd hoped *he'd* be.

She might be a beautiful woman, and hot enough to melt the deepest winter chill, but he hadn't suffered at the hands of his ex without taking away a few hard-earned lessons. Attraction, the electric pull between them, was something he was certain he could control. And to date it was also the only thing that had truly shattered Carly's sassy confidence.

If he had to go toe-to-toe with her on the talk show, then he was going to utilize his every advantage. If he upped his game and started *truly* coming on to her he might throw her off kilter—at least enough to keep the loaded banter, and the *questions*, under his control.

Pleasure sluiced down his spine, heating vital parts, as he contemplated pursuing the lovely Carly Wolfe. But hot on its heels was the vague impression that what he was about to do was reminiscent of the stunt his ex had pulled.

Doubt fisted in his stomach—and then he saw Carly's Mini Cooper pull into the garage and park. She exited her car, and instead of fresh and flirty tonight she was dressed to kill—namely, to kill him. And any qualms he'd had regarding his strategy died.

Her silver-sequined halter top sparkled in the light, her

tiny skirt exposed fabulous legs, and the expanse of tan skin on display was truly impressive as she headed his way. Heart pumping appreciatively in response, now looking forward to his plan, Hunter slid out of his car, shutting the door behind him. The slam echoed in the concrete garage, capturing Carly's attention. And when she caught his gaze, she froze.

Yes, he was going to enjoy besting Carly Wolfe at her own game.

Surprise, intense caution and awareness hit Carly at the sight of Hunter leaning against his car, hands in his pockets. Given his parting words to her Wednesday night, the twirl of excitement in her belly was totally inappropriate—because she couldn't afford to be less than her best.

His tone was smooth, low. "You ready for another show?"

The comment was drenched in undertones, conjuring memories of the bar, but Carly ignored the hot curl of awareness. "Interesting choice of attire for a fight." She stepped closer, taking in his exquisitely cut black suit. The white dress shirt, minus a tie and open at the collar, gave him the perfect blend of elegant evening attire with a casual attitude. "Tonight could get messy," she said. "I hope you're wearing a bulletproof vest beneath that expensive outfit."

His mouth didn't smile, but his eyes did. "I suspect it *will* get messy."

The unknown promise in his gaze left her a little uneasy, and a whole lot disturbed. What trick did he have up his sleeve? The question had haunted her since his warning at the bar, and her heart thumped as all sorts of possibilities flitted through her head.

Just don't go getting all flustered when he flashes those cool blue eyes in your direction, Carly.

"Unfortunately I left my Kevlar-coated vest at home," he said.

She resumed her walk in his direction. "Too bad for you."

"Will you be slaying me with your words or your gaze?"

"Both." She came to a stop in front of him and leaned back against the car parked beside his. "Maybe white wasn't an appropriate choice of a shirt for you," she said with a smile she hoped looked confident. "Bloodstains being so hard to remove and all."

"I know. I had to throw away the one I wore the day of your blog."

"Are we still discussing that?"

"With one difference," he said.

"Which is?"

"At first I thought you'd enjoyed the bloodbath." His gaze held hers. "But after our discussion at the bar I realized I was wrong." He tipped his head, his eyes focused intently on her. "I think the potential for such a vindictive backlash against me never crossed your mind."

It hadn't. Then again, Thomas cutting her loose to save himself had come as a shock too. But that hadn't been nearly as devastating as her father's silence when she'd needed his support.

She stared up at Hunter as she fought the depressing memories, her heart beating a little bit harder. "You know, a part of me hates that you're right. But a part of me is proud too. Yes, I'd expected a healthy online debate, not a mean-spirited, vindictive slug-fest." She crossed her arms. "But if being naive means I reserve negative judgment until I've been proven wrong, it's a label I'm willing to live with."

"The trouble with your approach is that you experience a whole lot of bad."

"The trouble with your cynical view is you miss out on a whole lot of good."

He studied her for a moment, as if considering her words, and then his forehead crinkled in suppressed amusement.

"Maybe the answer to that particular dilemma lies in whether the water in the glass at the midway mark is worth drinking or not." He paused before going on, his voice a fraction lower, bordering on...*husky.* "And how thirsty you are."

The way he was looking at her made her sit up and take notice—even more than she had when she'd first laid eyes on his casually elegant self. He seemed different. She couldn't put her finger on how, except his demeanor was less distant than usual. More approachable. With a faint hint of sensual promise that left her on edge. And she realized since his fateful words at their last meeting she'd expected him to arrive tonight with all his metaphorical guns blazing. Instead, there was a distinct suggestion of something infinitely more subtle, almost...seductive.

Worry and desire slithered up her limbs, and she tucked her hands behind her back, hoping to quiet her damp palms and now fidgety fingers.

His secretive smile was small but instantaneous. "I'm making you nervous."

It wasn't a question, and that fact alone made the tension worse. How could she prepare for a fight when she had no idea what his plans were? But a part of her knew, and her heart tripped faster at the thought even as she grew disgusted with her inability to control the excitement. A heated flush filled her body. "Was reading body language part of your training, Mr. Agent Man?"

"*Ex*-Agent Man," he corrected.

She tipped her head, giving the words consideration as she slowly shook her head. "There's nothing ex about you. You have a very natural way with your understated powers of intimidation."

"I don't believe in bullying people. I'm just very sure of the choices I make in life. If that intimidates others..." He gave a slight shrug.

She hiked a brow meaningfully. "You're very sure of *all* your choices?"

He stared at her as if the question had hit home, his face momentarily doubtful, but then he seemed to recover. "Reading people is a skill I still use every day. Interpreting body language is useful while pitching a proposal to a potential client. It can help you tailor your presentation to make the most impact."

"That must give you an advantage over your techie competition."

"And others."

Did he mean her? He took a step forward. His eyes zeroed in on her face, and her stomach tightened into a smaller knot. Which conveniently made navigating its trip to her toes easier.

"Take you, for instance," he said.

Unfortunately right now she was wishing he would, but she pushed the mutinous thought aside as he went on.

"Placing your hands behind your back is a sign you're hiding something and on your guard," he said. "Advantage point…mine."

He leaned closer, his gaze too close for comfort as he scanned her face.

"You're breathing faster than usual, you have small beads of sweat on your upper lip, and your pupils are dilated."

She suspected he was right, because her eyes were so busy trying to take in every aspect of his handsome face that they were straining mightily—refusing to miss a thing. Every sharp plane, every angular edge was heightened in the play of shadow in the light.

He said, "Advantage to me again. Because it either denotes anxiety…" the loaded pause killed her "…or desire."

Her body sizzled with heat, yet she succeeded in sounding as cool as he did. "Mr. Philips, is this a lawman's way of coming on to a woman?"

"Ex-lawman." His lips tipped into a lopsided grin that was the most delicious Hunter smile to date. "And I'm just being observant," he went on smoothly.

A wave of heat left goosebumps on her arms. Her skin resembled a cobblestoned street.

No doubt he could see those too.

"Maybe I should remind you that women don't sweat." She cocked her head when he opened his mouth to respond. "And I don't like the term 'glow' either," she said.

"What do you prefer?"

"I prefer incandescence."

Before she could react, Hunter reached up and placed a finger at the corner of her mouth. Eyes wide, Carly stared up at him as he slowly stroked the skin above her lip…curling her toes as he went. A feat she would have sworn was a myth until this very moment, but her toenails were busy trying to dig a hole into her high heels. Hunter's finger dipped lightly into the groove bisecting the middle of her mouth, slicking away the few dots of sweat that were immediately replaced by others. Her heart pumped overly heated blood that surely had her glowing by now.

Damn him, he was right. She was drowning in both anxiety *and* desire. Her breaths came in short, tight increments that sounded embarrassingly like small gasps. As she stared up at him Carly's mind ran through every reason—and there were many—why she should step away. Despite her previous attempts at flirting Hunter had hung back, watching her with cool eyes, a hands-off attitude, and that emotional wall that was always present. Only a fool would believe he'd suddenly changed his mind. And William Wolfe hadn't raised a fool.

So why was she standing here, frozen like an idiot? She knew very well this was part of some master plan he'd cooked up. Had the partners at Firewell Inc. met, given the matter consideration and then voted unanimously to muck with her mind?

His eyes crinkled in muted humor. Clearly enjoying his effect on her, Hunter said, "You're definitely incandescent now."

Paralyzed by the sensual havoc he created, breathing was all she could manage as he cupped her jaw and finally placed his mouth on hers. Carly's heart thumped in her chest as her body concentrated on the hand on her face, and the lips that slanted softly, yet insistently, over hers. The rest of his body remained disengaged. Only his warm palm and warmer mouth were involved. With just enough restrained heat to melt her tenuous reserve. Until she was kissing him back, her mind whirling from the barrage of emotions.

Doubt. Distrust. And a whole lot of desire.

Being the dominant one of the three, desire seized her in its grasp, and Carly placed her palms on his chest, frustrated by the distance. Longing to feel the hard length of his body again. Why didn't he pull her closer? Even worse, why was she mad that he didn't?

She pulled her mouth from his, her breathing labored, and stared up at the slate-blue eyes. "You're holding back, G-Man." The need to feel more was driving her on, despite the embarrassing knowledge the whole thing was a ploy. "That's no way to seduce a woman."

"Maybe my goal was to frustrate, not seduce."

Desire still pulsed through her body, but her mouth went flat, the moisture left from his lips momentarily disrupting her thoughts. "Score one for the former FBI agent and his tactics," she said, as lightly as she could.

But now she was doubly annoyed. At him for being so damn honest it forced her to confront just how caught up in the moment she'd been, and how easy it was for him to maintain his distance. That emotional wall was just as frustrating when it was a sensual one. But mostly she was annoyed at herself, for knowing all of the above and *still* being so turned on she could barely think beyond the feel of his smooth shirt, the hard plane of muscle beneath her hand.

Gazes locked, she pressed on his chest. "Your mission was a success." If he wanted to resist her efforts he didn't let on, allowing her to push him back until she'd trapped him against his car.

"Feeling frustrated already?" he said.

In every way imaginable. "Very."

"Now you know how it feels."

Why was she so ticked about his control? She ignored the crippling doubt, beat back the voice that kept telling her to walk away…and popped open the top button of his shirt. Her beef with this closed-off, enigmatic man went beyond his heartless app, now including his ability to arouse her with so little effort. And why *him*—the man whose story she sought?

It's just lust, Carly. Show him you're not afraid. Leave him shaking.

Rationalization complete, unable to wait any longer, she lifted up on her tiptoes and took his mouth, pressing his lips open with hers. Hunter didn't resist, meeting her pursuit—at this level, at least—with a rasp of his silken tongue against hers. A heated ache throbbed between her legs and she finished unbuttoning his shirt enough to slide her hands inside. Mouths melding, breath mingling, the moment lingered as Carly enjoyed the crisp hair on his chest, the firm muscle. And while the kiss seared her to the core Hunter continued to hold her with nothing more than his hand at her jaw. Palms stroking his delicious torso, desperate for more, she pressed her hips to his, to the hard thighs…and other harder parts.

Firing her imagination. Leaving her knees shaky.

Hunter pulled his mouth away and without a word, his

piercing gaze on hers, rolled to his left, trapping her between his car and his unyielding length. Bringing new meaning to the term *lethal weapon*. His well-honed physique triggered all sorts of wicked fantasies. With the shift of position she'd expected, *hoped*, for more. But Hunter simply cupped her jaw with two palms instead of one, brought his mouth down, and began to kiss her with a reserve that left her shaking with frustration even as his tongue tasted hers. His grip on her face was self-controlled, yet sensual. Demanding, yet with a protective air that reminded her of being clasped to his side in the alley.

The sound of a car motor echoed along the concrete walls of the parking garage, growing closer, and Carly pulled her mouth away. She fisted her hands against his chest as she tried to catch her breath before it became humiliatingly obvious that he'd been so successful at reaching his goal.

He had everything to gain—her distraction—and she had everything to lose—like her objectivity about a possible story. Her pride. Her job. *Again.* Even potentially…her heart.

And that was something she'd never lost before.

The rough hair, warm skin and hard muscle beneath her fists were tempting, and she longed to spread her fingers to recapture as much of the sensation as she could.

She forced her hands down to her sides. "I guess I made a mistake."

The sound of the engine drew closer, and Hunter turned his back to the oncoming vehicle, casually leaning a shoulder against his car. "Your continued fixation on The Ditchinator?" he said, his gaze on her face as he fixed his buttons.

"No. I meant I suspect I'm the one that came unprepared. All your shooting range practice has come in handy." She pressed her lips together, tasting him, feeling the lingering heat of his kiss. "With your deadly aim I could really use that bulletproof vest."

A dark look flickered across his face. "Don't bother. It won't work," he said softly, his smile bordering on bitter as he reached the last button. "Some things cut worse than a bullet."

CHAPTER FIVE

"WELCOME back, Carly and Hunter," Brian O'Connor said.

The studio applause finally died as Hunter sank into the love seat next to Carly. Was he remembering wrong or was this a different leather couch? It felt smaller. Shorter. And his position next to Carly was close enough for him to smell her citrusy scent. His body still wound tight, he hummed with vibrant energy from their seductive encounter. A planned attack, actually. He hoped the effort to fluster Carly had worked. Unfortunately it had definitely distracted him as well.

"You two have become quite an item," the blond talk-show host said with a smile as he sat back at his desk. "I'll be the first to admit I enjoy a good debate."

Hunter bit back the urge to laugh and threw one arm across the back of the couch, mindful of Carly's nearly naked shoulder just inches from his fingertips. After tonight's kiss, "debate" was quite the understatement. He kept his eyes on Carly. "Ms. Wolfe is a worthy opponent."

"As is Mr. Philips," Carly said. With a hike of a brow, she shot the host one of her charming smiles before turning her loaded gaze back to Hunter. "I'm learning a lot about the art of war."

The message was hardly subtle, and the memory of their kiss twined its way around his libido and breathed it back to life. If it had ever died in the first place. When Carly had gone on the offensive during their encounter it had taken all he had to keep the moment in check. He should have known she'd fight back, but he shouldn't have enjoyed it so much.

"What have you learned?" Hunter said dryly. "That war is won in the attack tactics?"

"More like it's lost in a failure of the defensive," she said.

Was she referring to herself? Or him? Ironically, it applied to them both.

"If your offensive is strong enough," he said, "the defensive becomes irrelevant."

Her tone was a touch too silky for comfort. "You should know."

He eyed Carly levelly, struggling to maintain his composed demeanor, but his gaze was probably hotter than it should be. He sincerely hoped Carly was the only one to notice. "You're fairly skilled in aggressive tactics yourself."

Carly shifted in Hunter's direction, eyes twinkling with mischief as she crossed her long legs in his direction. Legs that screamed for verification that they were as smooth as they looked. So why hadn't he seized the opportunity when he'd had the chance? His gaze lingered a moment on her limbs before returning to hers, and the sparkle in Carly's eyes turned to delighted amusement mixed with a smoky awareness that was difficult to ignore. Hunter tried anyway.

"Aggressive tactics?" she echoed with an overly innocent smile. "Are you referring to my blog on Wednesday?"

She knew full well he wasn't.

"What else?" he said.

The sassy lady simply held his gaze and said nothing. But, much to Hunter's delight, her lips twitched—as if she was itching to laugh.

"Speaking of Carly's blog," Brian O'Connor said, interrupting Hunter's train of thought. "You did take a pretty good beating, Hunter."

Impatience swelled. He'd forgotten about the host. Hunter suppressed a frown, annoyed at his lack of concentration in the presence of this beautiful woman. And at the need to defend himself *again*. Not only that—this time he'd positioned himself within touching range of the sexy little troublemaker...

His insides coiled tight, the memory of kissing Carly barreling over his usual ability to remain calm. It had been hotter than he'd expected. More dangerous than he'd anticipated even after factoring in her looks and sultry ways.

The blond talk-show host grinned at Hunter. "Carly's Clan had some not so nice nicknames for you."

Despite everything, Hunter had to bite back a smile at the term. "'Carly's Clan' certainly did. And a good number of them can't be shared with your audience. Most of the commenters' choices of names aren't repeatable on TV." He turned his focus back to Carly. "But among the most creative ones I was called were reprobate—"

"Fitting," Carly interjected swiftly.

With a small smile, Hunter kept talking. "Degenerate—"

"Ditto," Carly went on.

"And a rake," Hunter finished.

"Rake?" Brian O'Connor said with a chuckle, beating Carly to the comment punch. "Who uses that word in this day and age?"

Carly's smile was genuine as the two stared at Hunter, making him feel as if he was on trial. "I don't know, Brian," she said. "But it doesn't quite suit the man, does it? Rake sounds far too..." She sent Hunter an *I'm-so-cute* smile and tipped her head. "Too romantic," she finished, and Hunter appreciated the playful look she flashed him as she went on. "I suspect Mr. Philips is a bit too cut and dried for the term."

The host chuckled and said, "You don't think he's a romantic?"

Carly rested her arm on the back of the couch. Their forearms were now lightly touching, the tips of their fingers each brushing the other's elbow—briefly breaking Hunter's focus. Carly's sparkling gaze remained on his.

"You mean beyond Mr. Philips's efficiently designed app? The one he uses to *gently* tell a woman it's over?" A murmur of amusement moved through the crowd. Despite the dig, Hunter's lips twitched. "I'm sure I have no idea," Carly finished.

But her eyes told him she did, and Hunter fought the smile that threatened.

"Speaking of The Ditchinator," Brian O'Connor said. "Today it moved to number five on the top sellers list. Carly has vowed to keep up the pressure until you discontinue the app. She's also mentioned she'd like to hear about the inspiration behind the idea. In fact all of Miami is interested." He leveled a pointed look at Hunter. "Care to share your thoughts?"

"Discontinuing the app isn't in my plans at this time," Hunter said truthfully, deliberately ignoring the mention of the story behind its creation. That was one truth he had no intention of sharing.

Clearly delighted, the host said, "Can I interest you in returning in a few weeks to discuss how you're holding up against Carly's campaign?"

Hunter glanced at Carly, who looked as if she wanted to laugh, and he could no longer restrain the smile. Since Carly Wolfe had entered his life tedium was certainly no longer a threat. In fact the excitement might very well do him in. But the thought of the two of them being through after tonight left him feeling disappointed.

"I'll accept the offer to return if Carly does." Hunter shot Carly a meaningful look. "Though I'm sure Ms. Wolfe will eventually tire of her game."

"Of course I accept." Her eyes on Hunter, Carly's tone was a heady mix of amusement, arousal…and a hint of resigned irritation. "And I guarantee I won't grow tired."

A slight pause ensued, and Hunter appreciated the mixture of emotions in her eyes—until the host interrupted.

"That's right," Brian O'Connor said with a chuckle. "Tenaciousness runs in the family genes. Carly's father is *the* William Wolfe, of Wolfe Broadcasting."

Even though they were barely touching, Hunter felt the instant tension in Carly at the host's words, and the light in her eyes dimmed a touch. As if she was preparing for the upcoming discussion to turn ugly. From his proximity, it was obvious the charming smile she was aiming at Brian was now forced.

"Just to be clear," Brian said, turning to address the audience, "there is no behind-the-scenes monkey business going on. Mr. Wolfe has never been involved in our decision to have Carly on the show." He held up his hands on display. "No screws have been applied to either mine or my producer's thumbs…" He hesitated with impeccable comedic timing. "Or to any other parts of our anatomy."

When the crowd's murmur of laughter faded Carly spoke, her smile bright, her tone light—but Hunter knew it wasn't genuine. "Anyone who's worked with my father is familiar with his strict business policy, Brian. He would never apply thumbscrews on anyone's behalf." She hesitated, her smile growing bigger, but the heart was gone. "Not even his daughter's."

Hunter's brow bunched in surprise. It was the second time

she'd said something to that effect, and he mulled over the development as the host chatted about William Wolfe's current media holdings with Carly. She remained outwardly relaxed, her demeanor easy, but the tension in her body was palpable. And though the host's comments were lighthearted, with every mention of her media magnate father her laughter grew more and more hollow. The audience was clearly oblivious, but the host *had* to sense her discomfort.

It grew worse when Brian said, "In his younger days as a newspaper reporter William Wolfe was famous for his dogged pursuit of a story. He was ruthless, even, in digging up the dirt on secret pasts and shady politicians. Your pitbull-like pursuit of Hunter, here, is reminiscent of your father."

Behind his arm, Hunter felt Carly's fingers grip the back of the couch tight even as he watched her face lose a trace of its color. "We are a lot alike," she said warily.

"I imagine your dad is pretty proud?" the host said, his smile not as warm as it should have been.

Clarity hit Hunter hard. Brian O'Connor clearly *knew* about Carly's dealings with State Senator Thomas Weaver. And the host was using that knowledge to his advantage—targeting Carly. Hunter's chest slowly constricted with anger even as he fought the emotion.

It's not your problem.

His mind scrolled through every reason he shouldn't get involved. She'd brought public scrutiny on herself, was targeting *him* using her popular blog. But the biggest reason by far? He'd traded in his need to be the good guy a long time ago. In the end his commitment to Truth, Honor and Justice—and all those other values worthy of capitalization—and his tendency to protect others…*none* of it had saved him.

"But the real question is…" Brian's grin radiated a double meaning for those close enough to see. "Just *how far* will Carly Wolfe go to get her story?"

The stunned look on Carly's face slammed Hunter in the gut.

Sonofabitch.

Carly stared at Brian O'Connor as her blood seeped lower, her chest clenched so tight it made breathing impossible. Damn, damn and double damn. The host had done some digging and learned about the Thomas Weaver Affair. Humiliation, regret and pain blended in her veins, concocting a potent mix that burned as it traveled.

Blinking back the emotion, she struggled for a lighthearted, suitably glib comment. But somehow she didn't think she could spin being accused of sleeping with a man for his story, or being fired from one of her father's newspapers, in a positive light.

She was good, but she wasn't *that* good.

Carly opened her mouth, struggling for something to say, but Hunter stopped her with a discreet touch of his fingers on her elbow. A protective, reassuring gesture. His posture remained relaxed, but the hint of coiled readiness always simmering beneath his demeanor was wound tighter than usual. It had been hard enough to calmly sit there after their kiss—wondering if he'd been affected at all, aware of him on every level. Now the icy blue eyes directed at their host were positively lethal, and a back-off attitude exuded from his every pore.

Hunter said, "What father wouldn't be proud of Carly, Brian?"

"My point exactly," the host replied, clearly refusing to back down. Both men were smiling, but the undercurrents were fierce. "She inherited the Wolfe tenacity. Wednesday's blog post proves that much. The uproar afterwards must have made you angry."

The host was clearly looking for more conflict—probably in an attempt to boost his ratings.

There was a brief pause before Hunter said, his voice smooth, "Not in the least."

Carly stared at Hunter. The fact she knew that to be a lie made the statement even more outrageous.

Brian O'Connor hesitated, momentarily looking stumped, and then he narrowed his eyes slightly at Hunter, as if sensing an opportunity. "Since it didn't bother you, perhaps you'd also be willing to share the story behind The Ditchinator?"

"Absolutely," Hunter said.

Carly's heart stumbled in her chest, and Brian O'Connor's eyes zeroed in on Hunter like a laser. The switch in his focus wasn't lost on Carly. Everything Hunter did was deliberate, and now was no exception. He'd purposefully placed himself between the host and Carly.

Protecting her…again.

The host's smile was clearly self-serving. "We'd all love to hear how your app got its start."

Hunter's ultra-cool demeanor and hard-edged alertness didn't diminish as he settled deeper into the couch, as if getting comfortable before beginning his tale. "It began where all good break-up apps begin, Brian." The secretive smile was back, and Hunter's control was firmly in place. "It started when I got dumped by the woman I loved."

Late Sunday evening, fingers curled around the leather rim of a newly purchased cowboy hat, Carly stood just inside the upscale boxing gym, empty save the two men in the ring. Hunter lightly bobbed and weaved in a circle around his opponent, his face obscured by protective headgear. His movements were light. Graceful. And the sheen of sweat on his naked torso only added to the moment of pure masculine beauty. His chest was nice to touch, but the visual was a sight she might never recover from.

She loved a well-dressed man, and Hunter knew how to play that card well. But he wore the silk shorts and athletic shoes with ease too. Hunter's sparring partner was heavier, but Hunter had the advantage of speed, agility and a calculatingly cunning patience. With every swing of his opponent's arm Hunter ducked, his reflexes lightning-quick. With a sharp jab, his fist snapped against his opponent's headgear. The two circled, ducked, successfully landed hits, and the dance continued. It was Hunter in his most elemental form. And it was magnificent.

Focus, Carly. Just focus.

She sucked in a breath, trying to concentrate on the task at hand. Since Hunter's startling on-air confession and his abrupt departure when the show was over she'd been struggling to make sense of it all. She felt stunned. Dazed. Never had she met a man with such a conflicting mass of mixed messages. When the going had gotten rough, her father had remained silent. Thomas, her boyfriend, had cut her loose to save himself. Yet Hunter, the man she was at odds with, had sacrificed his privacy to protect her.

In the ring, the two men finished, a double fist-bump signaling the end of a well-matched round. Hunter's opponent ducked between the ropes, hopped off the platform, and headed past her toward the front office, nodding on his way by. Seemingly oblivious to her presence, Hunter pulled off his headgear and picked up a towel draped in the corner, using it to wipe his face.

Gathering her courage, she took a deep breath, inhaling the smell of leather tinged with a hint of sweat. "I brought you a gift." White cowboy hat in hand, she approached the ring. Hunter slowly turned to face her, the hair on his forehead damp, sexily mussed from the headgear. As she drew closer, he leaned on the top rope, looking down at her.

"How did you find me?" he said.

"You told me the first day we met you belonged to a boxing gym. It wasn't hard to figure out which one." She held the hat in his direction. "This is for you."

He glanced at her offering. "You got the truth. You won the bet," he said. "No need to give me a consolation prize."

"It's not a consolation prize."

"Then what is it?"

"It's a simple thank-you gift." She stepped forward to the edge of the ring, the hat still extended up in his direction. "You asked me before if I believed you were falsely accused of leaking information. Now I can say unequivocally that I do." His expression was careful, his blue eyes cautious. He didn't respond, or take the hat, but behind his guarded look she saw the truth—even if he wouldn't confirm it out loud. She stared up at him and dropped her arm, asking the question that had been haunting her since his actions on the show. "Why did you do it?"

She knew the answer, but she wanted to hear it from Hunter. After all his talk about his business, his priorities, and the rest of the rubbish he'd said he believed in, his good deed proved otherwise.

"It seemed like a good way to get you off my back," he said simply.

Twenty-four hours ago she would have believed him. Now she shook her head. "Liar," she said. "That's not why you offered up your confession."

If you could call it that. His account of his break-up had been sweet and simple—laced with a no-nonsense attitude and summed up in a mere four words. He'd loved. He'd lost. But even as he'd coolly stated the facts Carly had sensed the part that he wasn't sharing. He'd fooled the audience, even the host, but Carly had seen in his eyes what the others hadn't. A part of him was *still* recovering, and the fact that he'd offered up the truth, all in the name of saving her, had been humbling.

When he didn't respond, she said, "You didn't give many details about your break-up, but it was good enough to distract the host." Several heartbeats passed, still with no reply, so she went on. "You did it to draw Brian O'Connor off my case, didn't you?"

The enigmatic smile returned. The ever-elusive look in his eyes was going to drive her to insanity—which, at this point, would essentially constitute circling the crazy block. Because she'd already arrived there courtesy of the lovely sight of a shirtless Hunter.

He bent over, stepped between the ropes and hopped down, landing in front of her. "Maybe," he said as he took the hat.

"Cut it out, Mystery Man." She propped a hand on her hip, doing her best to ignore the beautiful chest on display, the lean torso replete with muscle. "I'm getting you all figured out. You were falsely accused of leaking information and went on to start a company dedicated to helping people protect theirs. I think that's a great story. One that the public would be interested in hearing."

The look he shot her was sharp. "My life really isn't that interesting." And then, as if declaring an end to the issue, he turned and headed for the locker room.

Carly followed, heels clicking on the wood floor. "We obviously have different definitions of the word."

"Aren't you tired of me yet?"

"Not even close."

Hunter kept walking, his back to her. "Are you planning on joining me in the shower?"

"If I have to."

Hunter pivoted on his heel and Carly stopped short. For the first time his expression was a mix of curiosity, amusement, and a whole load of impatience. "Do you ever *stop* being the reporter?"

"No," she said, the answer easy. "I can't stop being who I am any more than you can." She crossed her arms, feeling the truth of her words. "I'm a journalist at heart. It's not just my nature, it's my *passion*. Just like being the white-hat-wearing protector is yours, despite the fact you quit the FBI." Even as she said the words she knew the truth. One way or another he must have felt he had no option. Carly dropped her voice an octave. "You were cleared, so why *did* you leave?"

A shadow crossed his face, and the silence that stretched between them was loud—until Hunter finally said, "That nosy nature of yours must have gotten you into a lot of trouble during your life."

"That's not an answer."

"It was simply time to move on."

Carly let her expression say it all. "I'd bet my brand-new Mini Cooper you didn't *want* to leave."

The moment lasted forever as he stared at her, and when he spoke his words surprised her. "The day before we were scheduled to take our first vacation together I came home and found Mandy had packed up her stuff and gone." He paused, as if letting her adjust to the change in topic. "I had an engagement ring in my pocket."

At the words *engagement ring* Carly's heart constricted so tight it was hard for it to keep pumping. It wasn't the answer to the question she'd asked, and his attempt to distract her was obvious, but she could no more change the subject back than she could stop asking questions. He'd cranked up her curiosity, exceeding her lifetime limit to the max.

Cowboy hat in hand, he leaned back against the door leading to the locker room. "After three months of living together it was to be our first trip, and I started with dinner plans at a restaurant she'd always wanted to try. It was too expensive for a government man on a government salary, but I figured it was worth it," he went on. "Because a guy only gets married once."

Once. The assumption brought the threat of tears, burning her eyes, surprising her. When Hunter Philips made a promise, he kept it.

"When I called Mandy from work to tell her where I was taking her she must have guessed what was coming." He shrugged his shoulders. "I suppose it was easier to say no by leaving than refuse me to my face."

She blinked back the sting in her eyes. No one should be dumped in a way so cowardly and cruel—especially when he'd been about to make the ultimate commitment. "What did you do?"

His voice was easy, smooth, but the words hit hard. "I got drunk and stayed that way."

It was hardly the response she'd expected.

He tipped his head, his cool eyes steadily holding hers. "After a week-long alcohol binge that probably should have killed me, Booker finally showed up, dragged me off the couch, and shoved me in a shower with my clothes on." Face composed, he folded his arms, hat dangling from his fingers. A faint smile of memory crossed his face. "It's all a little fuzzy, but I remember yelling at him to turn off the faucet." He cut her a dry look. "Unlike Florida, the middle of a Chicago winter means the water is frigid. But Booker just held me under the spray, and I was too drunk to push back."

The reedy stature and little-boy face of Hunter's friend made the whole thing hard to picture. Not with the physical state Hunter maintained. "I can't imagine your partner effectively fighting you back."

"Like I said," he said. "I was plastered out of my mind and my coordination was bad. Of course alcohol does have the advantage of being an excellent anesthetic as well." There was a slight pause, and he hiked a self-mocking brow. "The only problem was it kept wearing off."

Though his face was composed, his gaze calm, his tone said it all.

"What happened after the cold shower?" she said.

"I sobered up enough to get into dry clothes and sat shivering on the couch, yelling at Booker to get out. He wouldn't leave." He looked at Carly, his words matter-of-fact. But his face reflected a moment that was clearly seared in his memory, earning Pete Booker the title of faithful friend for life—till death did they part. "After about an hour of angry silence from me, Booker told me I needed to stop letting Mandy's defection get to me and start doing something productive, like fight back," he said, steadily holding her gaze.

The next step was easy to guess. "And that's when The Ditchinator was born."

"To keep me busy."

"And get back at Mandy?"

"An outlet for my frustrations." A rueful smile curled on his lips. "Booker helped me work on the program. It was originally designed for email. When vacation time was over and I had to go back to work he showed up at the end of each day and we kept adding features, making it more elaborate. We spent a month on the songs alone, each trying to outdo the other by finding the best tune to go with the message." The tension in his body eased a bit. "Every time I slipped back into my black funk Booker would find another song title that made me laugh. Soon we had so many we decided to list them all as options."

There was a long pause as Carly stared at him, sensing there was more to the story that he wasn't sharing.

"And now that the app is so popular you're laughing all the way to the bank."

"Trust me," he said wryly, a brief shadow crossing his face, "no laughing is involved." He cocked his head, his expression easing a touch. "But I'll take the money, nonetheless."

There was a long pause as they stared at each other. In some small way it must provide him with a satisfying sense of comeuppance. No wonder he refused to take it off the market. But this wasn't the time to discuss her thoughts on that subject again.

Hunter unfolded his arms, providing a better view of his delicious chest. "That's it, Carly." His eyebrow arced higher. "Now you know enough of the gritty details to satisfy even *your* inquisitive nature." He looked down at the white hat in his hand before lifting his gaze to hers, his tone reflecting that he was done with the conversation. "I appreciate the gift, but it's time to call it a night."

Though his expression was still coolly collected, his eyes sizzled with a teasing heat that set her heart racing as he went on. "Unless you're really going to follow me into the shower…" He paused, letting her fill in the blank, and then turned and pushed through the door.

And as it slowly closed in her face she stared at the sign. Men's Locker Room. Body on fire, she bit her lip with a frown. Damn him for being the action-hero defender, an honorable guy who was impossible not to like. Damn him for being so darkly guarded, inflaming her curiosity with his secretive air. And damn him for his well-honed chest paired with an unflappable composure—for provoking her with his teasing words and the sexy look in his eyes…and then walking away.

Heart pounding, she let a full minute tick by as she tried to decide what to do next.

Go home now, Carly. You're done.

But what would happen if she finally called his bluff? She longed to know what he'd do if she challenged him on his sizzling words paired with a frustrating reserve. If she pushed him, would he finally lose a little of that control?

Let it go, Carly. You're done.

She bit her lower lip, staring at the locker room sign, the distinct feeling of *un*doneness leaving her feet stuck to the floor, unwilling to leave. Several agonizing moments passed, but ultimately her curiosity was her undoing. Lips pressed in a determined line, the whisper of desire growing louder, Carly pushed open the door and stepped inside.

CHAPTER SIX

AT THE back of the locker room Hunter pulled out his duffel bag and shut the locker harder than he'd planned. The slam of the metal door echoed off the sea of pristine white tile. Mind churning, he set his bag on one of several long wooden benches, burning with a mix of emotions caused by reliving old memories. And by dealing with the beautiful, *determined* Carly Wolfe.

Annoyed with himself, he pulled out his towel and clean clothes, tossing them all on the bench. After shedding his clothes and shoes, he entered one of the shower stalls separated by chest-high tiled walls.

The sting of hot water felt good, easing his aching muscles and a bit of his tension as he shampooed his hair. He wished the soap could wash the troublesome journalist from his life as easily.

When the sound of footsteps came, Hunter glanced over the wall of the shower stall. Carly appeared, rounding the last row of lockers. Hunter's heart pumped hard and his hands stilled in his soapy hair.

As if she belonged in the male domain, she came closer and stopped on the other side of the low wall. The partition was just high enough to block her view of the lower part of his body. A part that was responding to her presence, her bold maneuver, and leaving his every cell crackling with electricity.

Which brought him to the main reason he'd agreed to go back on the show again. He couldn't lie to himself anymore. He'd duped himself into thinking it was all about his boredom with a job that left him unsatisfied. He could no longer deny the *biggest* reason he was unable to walk away from her—despite all the reasons he should.

Desire. Want. *Need.*

A longing so intense it was disturbing.

And he didn't want her here, testing his ability to keep the lessons of the past in mind. Proving that with every outrageous move by Carly Wolfe those lessons were getting harder and harder to remember.

Frustrated, Hunter stuck his head under the shower, rinsing out the rest of the shampoo. His gut tensed as he debated what to do with the woman who was driving him insane. Wishing she'd leave. Ignoring the small part of him that was hoping she wouldn't.

Finished, he turned his back to the spray, careful to keep his tone level. "Are you here just to watch or to seduce a story out of me?"

Her lips tightened at his slur. "As I recall, it was you who came on to me in the parking garage."

Despite everything, a wry smile crept up his face. He wasn't particularly proud of that moment, but it had certainly been memorable. And having her just a short wall away from his naked body wasn't making this conversation easy. His blood was enthusiastically lining up on its way to a part of him that was paying close attention. *Very* close attention. "I'm not even sure it was effective."

"Oh, it was effective." She propped her hand on her hip. "And if I turned the tables and tried the tactic on you? Would it work too?"

The question lit the fire that he'd fought so hard to keep banked. The sound of water hitting tile filled the room as he debated how to respond. For some reason he couldn't stop pushing her. Testing her. "Depends on how good you are." He nodded in the direction of the condom machine on the wall, multiple Kama Sutra pictures displayed on its front. "And how many of those positions you're familiar with."

Carly glanced at the dispenser, her eyelids flickering briefly in surprise at the images. It took a moment for her to respond. "I'm familiar with the first and the third." She turned to meet his gaze again, her tone dry. "Number five is physically impossible." After a pause, the sassy confidence was fully back in place and she stepped closer, folding her arms on the tile wall, eyes lit with challenge. "But I'm willing to try number four with you."

Heat surged, and he fought the smile. He knew what the little minx was up to, and he felt a punishing need to see if she would actually follow through. Almost as strong as the punishing need coursing through his body now. "Here?" He lifted a brow. "Now?"

For the first time her gaze dropped below his waist. "Why wait?"

If he got any harder he'd crack. "It's your call," he said, and counted out the pounding heartbeats.

Her pink tongue touched her lips, either in nerves or anticipation—or both—and her breaths came faster. "Got any quarters for the machine?"

"Side pocket of my gym bag."

Hunter waited, wanting to see just how far the bold woman would go. Knowing that this time pulling back would be impossible...

Heart thumping from their exchange and intense longing, Carly glanced at the condom dispenser again, conflicted.

She wasn't supposed to be here—not when she'd been trying to convince her boss to let her do a story on Hunter. She'd been refused each time, but sleeping with him now would still be stupid. Massively stupid. Yet, despite that knowledge, she was still torn between what she should do—which was retreat from the challenge—and what she wanted to do…

She cut her gaze to Hunter, forcing herself *not* to inspect the entire package again and risk a total meltdown. Arms crossed, water sluicing down his back, he regarded her with more than just desire in those slate-blue eyes. As always, there was a watchful waiting, an electric awareness that measured her every reaction. She'd never been involved with a man capable of exhibiting such restraint and self-control. And yet, even though he lived behind walls, the man had willingly stepped between her and a speeding emotional bullet.

The memory snagged at her heart, because it was something Thomas had never attempted to do. Instead, when his success had been threatened, he'd dumped her via the *Bricklin Daily Sentinel*. No warning. No phone call. Just her in her PJs, with a cup of coffee on a beautiful Sunday morning, and an article about what was next for the candidate running for California State Senate. Apparently her boyfriend's backup plan had been to feed her to the wolves—despite his vow to stick by her through the scandal.

And then, of course, there was her father's emotional desertion…

The painful memories robbed her of her breath even as the irony tightened her lips into a thin smile. How lame did it make her that she was so grateful that someone had finally stood up for her? Someone who wasn't even family or involved with her in a relationship. No, it was the guy she'd challenged to a very public duel.

What would it be like to make love to Hunter? She'd had her fair share of boyfriends, and was no stranger to sexual attraction, but she'd always been a little disappointed by how quickly it faded. How bored she became. Of course she'd never known anyone quite like the sexy, intense, white-hat-wearing Hunter Philips.

Don't do it, Carly. Don't do it! It's only lust.

But it wasn't really. It was much more complicated than that. And still, despite the fact she shouldn't, a part of her had to finish what she'd started.

Gathering her courage, she crossed to the gym bag, fished out some quarters and headed for the machine, not stopping to think about her plan any further. Fingers clumsy with desire—and a generous dose of nerves—she struggled with the mechanism but couldn't get the knob to twist. She smacked it in frustration.

Okay, so maybe the lust and nerves were a little stronger than usual.

"Let me." A wet hand rested on her left hip as an arm reached around her on the right, and a sensual longing swept through her so strong her knees almost gave way. Her mind froze, chanting out the change in circumstances.

Hunter. Naked. An embrace, of sorts, from behind. From Hunter.

Naked.

Breath fanning her temple, a damp heat emanating from his body, he turned the knob, his movements calm, collected. A condom dropped into the tray with a promising thunk. Carly turned her back to the wall beside the dispenser, examining his naked body. It was still a glorious sight, made much more devastating by his proximity. The lean, well-muscled chest peppered with dark hair. The taut abdomen and the long, powerful thighs. The straining erection.

Even now he seemed so sure of himself. So cool. Deliberate.

His eyes bored into hers. "Will we need more than one?"

With her body's current state of arousal she might not survive the first round. But there was no need to let him know how he affected her. Mouth dry, fingers shaky, she lifted her blouse over her head and tossed it aside. "It all hinges on your stamina."

He nodded at the machine and its display of graphic diagrams. "I choose the second go around."

Heart galloping nervously, she held his gaze as she removed her bra. "Just as long as it's not number five."

He inserted a second quarter into the machine. Eyes on hers, his gaze lit with a mix of humor, bone-melting desire and blatant challenge, he slowly twisted the knob. He *had* to know every crank was bringing her closer to the edge. "How about a modified version?" he said.

The mechanism caught, and a second thunk occurred.

Carly's insides twisted. Their relentless game of cat and mouse was leaving her coiled tight, never knowing which way was up. Or who had the upper hand. If either of them did.

"What if your sparring partner walks in on us?" she said.

His enigmatic smile returned as he pressed her against the wall. The tile was cold against her already over-heated skin. "Let's just hope he doesn't," he murmured as he lowered his head.

The moment his lips touched hers Carly responded eagerly. He pressed her mouth open, his tongue taking hers. The soul-drugging kiss pushed what little reason she had aside as his hands made quick work of her jeans and her panties, pushing them to the floor. Hunter sought the warm flesh between her legs, teasing her until she trembled, slick against his fingers. Her body's ready response was so quick it was almost embarrassing.

It's only lust, Carly.

Carly pulled her mouth a fraction from his, surprised her

voice was so unsteady. "I thought I was supposed to be seducing you."

His mouth moved to her neck, his fingers making her body sing, and he said, "You'll get your turn."

Hunter pressed well-placed, open-mouthed kisses on her shoulder, tasting her on his way to her breast. Her skin tingled in the wake.

Struggling to get the words out, she said, "Just remember—" His lips landed on a puckered tip, searing her nerves, and she arched against him. She closed her eyes and went on. "You promised two rounds."

One hand on her hip, the other between her legs, he drove her insane, his mouth traveling down her abdomen with intent. His words whispered across her belly. "When did I do that?"

"You bought a second condom." Her voice was weak. "That's an implied promise, isn't it?"

"Guess we'll find out."

She hoped they would, but she was too immersed in mind-bending pleasure to tell him.

Fire licked her veins, incinerating her every thought as his mouth crossed her hip on the way to her inner thigh. Carly instinctively spread her legs a little more, a welcoming gesture, and Hunter took full advantage of the invitation, replacing the teasing fingers with his mouth.

Her heart imploded, sensual forces gripping her hard. With a sharp hiss, Carly dropped her head back. His lips, teeth and tongue worked their spell on her body. So focused. His movements deliberate. Skilled. Strategically planned for maximum pleasure. Until Carly was shaking, the nape of her neck damp with sweat.

As his lips drove her closer to the sun, Hunter slid his hands up her belly to cup her breasts. His thumbs circled the tips, and solar touchdown became a near certainty. Back pressed against the cool tile, her body suffused with heat, Carly gripped his shoulders, her thighs trembling. Eyes closed, she gasped for breath. Flames of desire climbed higher, blinding her with white-hot light. Until Carly's body finally launched fully into the inferno. The orgasm consumed her, fanning out in a fireball of pleasure, and she called out Hunter's name.

As her cry echoed off the tile, Hunter stood and took in Carly's flushed face. Her eyes were closed, hair damp at her temples. The quiet was broken by the harsh sounds coming from Carly's throat, her chest heaving as she struggled to catch her breath.

The moment she'd entered the shower room, deep down he'd known where it would lead, despite his attempts to drive her away. And with the risk she posed to the peace he'd achieved with his past, thwarting her attempt to run the show had seemed necessary, her bold moves, her gutsy nature captivating him like no other.

Which was why pushing her up against the wall and taking charge had been so important.

Eyes still closed, her voice steady despite the breathless quality, Carly said, "Does that count as a round?"

"I was just getting you warmed up."

"Well done, you," she said softly. She lifted her lids, her gaze meeting his. "Now…" she slid her arms around his neck, her eyes dark with desire "…take me to the bench."

Hunter's heart thumped hard. Take-charge Carly was back, and need coiled tightly in his groin, choking off any hope of refusing her anything. Blocking all thoughts of the past. The beautifully outrageous, never-backs-down woman created fires within him he might never be able to extinguish.

The surge of alarm he felt at the thought wasn't enough

to change his mind, but it made his voice harsh. "Grab both condoms," he said, and she complied.

Hunter lifted her, and she wrapped her legs around his waist. As he carried her across the room the head of his shaft nudged the wet warmth between her legs, teasing him with its proximity. Taunting him with its readiness. Everything about her tested his restraint. She arched against him, pressing him closer, clearly wanting him inside. He straddled the wooden bench, one foot on either side, and sat on his towel with Carly on his lap, her legs draped around him. Gritting his teeth, fighting the need to thrust deep, he began to lean her back.

But was stopped by her hand on his chest.

Carly's voice was low, determined. "My turn. My choice." Gaze locked with his, she said, "So lie down, Mystery Man." His muscles tensed, but he let her press him back, coming to a stop when his elbows rested on the bench. Refusing to concede any more ground. She tipped her head seductively. "I want to see how long it takes for you to come unglued."

Hunter's lungs constricted as pleasure, anticipation and uneasiness wrapped around his chest, their position on the bench bringing reality home. Outside the frequency and duration of his relationships he hadn't noticed the subtle shift in his sexual life since he'd been played, like his tendency to gravitate toward women who were fairly passive.

Until right now, until Carly, he hadn't realized just how much he'd lost with his choices.

Heart pumping, agitated, Hunter stared up at her amber eyes. Her glossy brown hair fanned across her breasts, and he was incredibly turned on not only by her dominant posture as she straddled his lap but also by her aggressive moves. Despite his troubled thoughts, desire was the clear winner, made obvious by the fact he was so hot he was ready to burst. It all got worse when she cupped his face, lowered her head, and kissed him with a potency that seared him from the inside out, slanting her mouth across his.

Lips and tongues engaged in a duel, she dragged her nails down his chest, scraping the flat nipples, and a groan escaped him. In response, Carly gently began to move her hips, rubbing her slick center along his hard length. Sweat beaded at his temples as he fought the urge to take over. The sensual moment went on, lingering, driving him mad, until she tore her mouth away, sat up and opened a foil packet. When she grasped his erection his blood sang, and his every cell urged her to hurry as she rolled the condom on. With the look of a woman who knew what she wanted, she positioned herself over him and he arched up to meet her, going deep.

"Hunter," Carly groaned, her eyes flaring wide with shock and delight. And then her lids fluttered closed, as if the strength of her desire surprised her as much as his pleasure at her boldness did him.

But that hardly seemed possible.

She splayed her hands on his chest and began to rock her hips, nails digging into his flesh as she arched her back, angling to absorb more of him. He met her thrust for thrust. Eyes closed, cheeks flushed, her mouth parted, she—without hesitation or apology—slowly drove him higher. Pushed him further. Giving him what he craved. All the fire and sultry passion that had turned his head from day one was present in her movements.

Backing him closer to a line he didn't want to cross.

Rocking his hips in time with hers, bench hard against his elbows, he clenched his fists, slipping further under her spell with every painfully pleasurable moment. Her soft body, her citrusy scent and her relentless, no-holds-barred attitude gained more ground, stretching his reserve. Dragging him closer to the edge.

As if she sensed his waning restraint, Carly tunneled her

fingers into his hair and brought her mouth back down, devouring him. Desire shot through his veins, carrying the compelling need to the far reaches of his body. Drowning in the intensely disturbing feeling, he knew he should take over to preserve his sanity. The fact that he couldn't, *wouldn't*, made him angry with himself. Even as she consumed him, increasing the pace. Her mouth and hips greedy. Demanding he give up everything.

Carly dropped her hands to his buttocks and shifted, taking him deeper between her legs.

And he lost a little more of his hard-won control.

Carly lifted her lips a fraction, her gaze burning into his as she whispered wicked words that feathered across his mouth, her voice mesmerizing as she slowly pushed him back until he lay flat on the bench. She leaned over him, relentless as she made love to him from above. Her sweet smell, her softness and her seductive ways were threatening to undo him. His abdomen tensed. His sweat-slicked skin was damp against the wood bench as he fought the exquisite sensation of being immersed. Surrounded. Holding on by a thread.

Carly's moans grew more frequent. More urgent. And Hunter slid deeper, losing more of himself with every passing moment as Carly drew him closer to the flame. And then Carly cried out and her nails dug deep into his skin.

Like a bolt of lightning his control cracked, incinerating him in a blinding flash even as his mind went blank, engulfed by the terrible pleasure. He arched his neck and wrapped his arms around her waist, pumping his hips wildly. Bucking hard. His need desperate and dangerous. Almost destructive. With a harsh groan, Hunter clutched Carly closer as his muscles burned, tensed and coiled ever tighter. And when the pressure became so fierce he thought it would destroy him it snapped, releasing him with a force that shot him into oblivion.

CHAPTER SEVEN

"CARLY."

The lilting female voice cut through the murmur of guests in formal wear in the posh, expansive living room of William Wolfe's home. From the doorway leading to the back corridor—her only means of an easy escape—Carly spied the wife of the CFO of Wolfe Broadcasting approaching. Though she was pushing seventy, through the magic of expensive surgery Elaine Bennett's face had a mask-like look that defied designation.

For a moment Carly was a teensy bit jealous, because she felt as if she'd aged ten years in the week since she'd last seen Hunter, walking away from her at the gym.

Elaine Bennett's beaded black evening dress glittered in the light as she approached. "Your father must be so happy you're here."

Ignoring the urge to contradict her, Carly submitted to an air kiss from the woman. "Mrs. Bennett, you look lovely."

The woman eyed her with the critical affection of one who had known Carly since she was five, and when the lady lifted a perfectly plucked brow Carly knew it would be followed by a carefully targeted reproof. "Since you moved back to Miami we hardly see you. Your father isn't getting any younger, you know," Mrs. Bennett said, almost as if aging was a sin. "You shouldn't be such a stranger, Carly."

Nerves stretched tight, Carly murmured a noncommittal response and took a fortifying sip of her champagne as she watched Mrs. Bennett return to the other guests, dreading the thought of a run-in with her father. Their relationship had always been tenuous, at best, but since the Thomas Weaver Affair it had been as fragile as Abby's good humor.

She wouldn't have accepted her father's invitation—except *not* coming would suggest she was too ashamed to show. Or, worse, paint her as petulant. The elegant party was in honor of Brian O'Connor, not her—God forbid her father should ever celebrate his daughter. No, it was Brian O'Connor who had delivered a surge in ratings with the shocking history behind Hunter Philips's app—a scoop that had been avidly sought by others. The host had even secured a third show, which was now being hyped in the media as guaranteed to be a monumental success. And there was nothing William Wolfe admired more than success.

Hence his strained relationship with his disappointing failure of a daughter.

Carly gripped her champagne flute, refusing to let old emotions from her teenage years drag her down. She'd make her appearance, hold her head high and prove to her father she wasn't ashamed of her life, avoiding any one-on-one conversations. Because, after six sketchy nights of sleep, unable to keep her mind off of making love to Hunter, she didn't have the energy for a confrontation tonight.

She scanned the growing crowd, spying Brian O'Connor schmoozing with her father, and tension snaked between her shoulders. She longed for the appearance of a few naked actors, Harley-riders or drag queens—anything to liven up the party and get her mind off her current train of thought.

And then, as if the powers that be had heard her wish, Hunter entered the room, wearing a beautiful tuxedo. Her heart did a double take and her mind slipped back to the moment her world had collided with a new reality...

Stunned, Carly had clung to Hunter after they'd made love, pulse pounding, chest heaving. She wasn't quite sure what had happened, only that her body had been taken to heights that normally would require rocket fuel—and her ability to recover from the event had been greatly impaired by the knowledge of how aggressive she'd been. She'd wanted him, and had no regrets, but she'd all but hunted him down and backed him into a corner. So it had been hard to maintain that easy-breezy attitude when it was over. Especially when Hunter had retreated behind his wall.

He'd been coolly polite but decidedly detached as they'd spent an awkward few minutes getting dressed, the silence in the locker room consuming every available oxygen molecule. Carly had considered asking why he'd bothered obtaining a second condom, but her chance had ended when Hunter, ever the protector, had escorted her to her car and calmly walked away without a backward glance.

But right now he was headed in her direction.

Shoulder propped against the doorjamb, she gripped her clutch purse, smoothing a damp palm down the silk of her crimson spaghetti-strap dress. A dress that showed off way more leg than it should. At least she was appropriately attired.

Pushing aside the nerves, she said, "Mr. Philips—"

"Hunter."

His demeanor was *über*-cool, untouched, his gaze as sharply alert as ever—a far cry from the man who'd briefly come unhinged in her arms. He eyed her over his glass as he sipped his champagne, the absurdity of her use of his last name radiating from his gaze.

"Nice house," he said, nodding at the lavishly furnished living room, the moonless night obscuring its view of the Atlantic.

"Don't let it fool you." Her gaze swept across the imported tile and Brazilian cherrywood walls that gave off a warm, welcoming glow, carefully designed by an interior decorator with the blessing of her father. "It was decorated for effect," she went on dryly. "To create the illusion of warmth and comfort."

They spent a few tension-filled seconds staring at one another, until Hunter's gaze roamed down her body, lingering briefly on her legs, and a surge of remembered desire suffused her in heat. By the collected look on his face she knew it was a deliberate act.

His hint of a smile didn't quite reach his eyes. "Any number of things can be faked in this day and age."

His tone set her on edge, and she gripped the champagne flute hard. "For example?"

His eyes scanned the crowd of people and paused on Mrs. Bennett. "Youth."

Despite her amusement, the strained air prevented a smile. "Caring?" she said, forcing herself to hold his gaze. "Compassion?"

His words came out deceptively soft, his focus intense. "Or an orgasm."

The statement hit hard, leaving a trail of popping electrical energy as it settled deeper in her brain. She tried to decide which was worse: him thinking she was a reckless fool or that her participation had all been an act.

Stunned, she stared at him. What had started as a game that day in the alley had led to something that now felt deadly serious—a grave threat to her sanity, her peace of mind and her heart. And the tightrope of emotional peril she was crossing with Hunter was one she'd never attempted before. Toss in an intensely hot sexual experience and—well, a girl was bound to feel a little unnerved. Because there was nothing more beautiful than Hunter Philips coming unglued. Of course, getting him there had taken a Herculean effort. He'd resisted her to the bitter end. And as soon as it was over the wall had returned. So what did that say about his opinion of her?

Her stomach twisted, and she fought the urge to retreat down the hall to safety.

Keep it light, Carly. Keep it easy.

She cleared her throat, rallying her mojo. "I can't begin to tell you how crushed I'll be if you confess you faked your way through Sunday night."

The words briefly cut through the tension, easing the intensity in Hunter's eyes a touch. "That's where women hold a distinct advantage over men."

"Since that often isn't the case, I'll take it where I can."

His gaze dropped to her legs, his brow creased in humor. "I'm quite sure you will."

Struggling for her usual self-assurance, she leaned her back against the doorjamb. "You're just jealous I had visual confirmation you were very turned on." She sent him the best charming smile she could, given the circumstances. "Helped, of course, by the fact that you leave evidence behind when you fire off your...bullets."

He smiled. "You're not jealous of my weapon, are you?"

"No gun-envy here." She took a step closer and got a whiff of his cologne, bringing sensual memories of the locker room, and her tone turned huskier than she'd planned. "But you should teach me how to shoot yours."

His body grew still and heat flared in his eyes. His tone matched his gaze. "That could be arranged." His voice lowered to a rumble that was a mix of potent desire and distrust. "Would you approach that with pretend enthusiasm? Or would it be real?"

He clearly wasn't comfortable with her motivation in the locker room. But the truth was too painful, cut too close to her heart, to share. What was she supposed to say? That she'd never had anyone come to her rescue before? That she'd been the damsel in distress in the past, but no knight in shining armor had ever risked anything to ride to her defense? Her profound appreciation of his gesture of protection was so enormous it was pathetic. Almost needy.

And she was a confident woman. She shouldn't have been so desperate to conquer this man's reserve. It wasn't as if it proved he cared about her in any way. Or felt she was worthy of his on-air sacrifice…

Her breath hitched, but she pushed away the thought and steadily met his gaze. "Are you questioning the integrity of my responses?"

"Maybe."

She placed a hand on her hip. "Were my moans not authentic enough?"

"The moans seemed genuine."

"Were my groans lacking in honesty?"

"Your groans sounded sincere." He hesitated, and his tone grew heavy with meaning. "It was the shout at the end that I questioned."

The shout had been real, all right. She refused to look away. "I'm crushed you're second-guessing my enthusiasm."

His eyes held hers as the moments ticked by. When he spoke, there was suspicion and frustration in his tone. "I have no doubt your enthusiasm for your *job* is real."

Devastated by the insinuation, Carly could almost hear the creaking sound as his statement strained under the weighty load of meaning.

Outside of Thomas she'd never been involved with a man who'd hurt her when he'd walked away, as they all invariably did. Yet here she was, with a guy she wasn't even dating, wounded by his ability to take her in an explosion of hunger, calmly walk away, and with his next breath accuse her of dishonesty. Which meant he had a power over her no man had had ever before. Damn. The smile on her face grew tight, but she pushed back the need to pop the cork on her anger.

Don't go there. Don't let the emotion get the best of you.

But her aggravation was evident in her hardened tone. "I wonder if your doubt is a reflection of my past—" she moved closer, ignoring his wonderful scent and the hard physique encased in an elegant tuxedo "—or yours."

His gaze didn't waver, but a muscle in Hunter's cheek twitched. Four pounding heartbeats later he went on. "Before this conversation continues, I think a break is in order. I'll get us more champagne," he said as he took her empty glass, the heat smoldering in his eyes searing her to the bone, "but I'll be back."

She watched him head toward the bar and let out a breath, unaware she'd been holding it. But before she could relax another masculine voice spoke from behind.

"Hello, kitten."

At the sound of her childhood nickname her heart took an abrupt turn in her chest, speeding south. She briefly closed her eyes, preparing to face the man who doubted her more than most.

As Carly braced to face her father her stomach bunched into a knot. She was dreading his simmering judgment about her career, her life choices—and her *mistake*. She was used to the disapproving tone in his every comment. No matter how hard she tried, her efforts had never been good enough. But she was an adult now. She didn't need his praise. And she sure wouldn't beg him for approval.

Her moody, miserable, misunderstood teen years had been rough, and she'd constantly butted heads with her father. Unfortunately traces of that rebellious adolescent were reappearing more and more of late in his presence. She didn't like herself much when he was around. Which was the main reason she'd avoided him for the last six months.

Keep your cool, Carly. Keep it easy. And, whatever you do, don't let him see you cry.

Turning on her heel, she plastered a smile on her face. "Hello, Dad."

His hair now more gray than black, he was a striking figure of a man in his sixties. Tall. Fit. With his sharp features, he was imposing via the sheer volume of his eyebrows alone. And twenty-five years as head of a mega news corporation had honed his hard stare to a cutting edge.

"I assumed you wouldn't come," he said.

Good to see you too, Dad. I'm fine, thanks. How have you been?

She pushed aside the disappointment at his less than welcoming greeting. She knew better, and she really had to stop hoping for more. "Is that the only reason I was included on the guestlist?" she asked.

The muscles around his eyes tightened a touch. "If I didn't want you here I wouldn't have invited you."

Well," she said, trying to keep it light, "I suppose it would have looked bad if you'd invited everyone from the show except your own daughter."

His eyes grew wary and he frowned at her too-short dress, creating a flush of guilt-tinged resentment. Okay, so the hem length was a bit much. But she didn't need any more proof that he disapproved. Of course her father must have felt a sarcastic comment was in order.

"You've outdone even yourself tonight," he said. "Who's the poor guy this time?"

Her stomach balled tighter as she blinked back the pain. "I didn't bring a date." She tipped her head. "Disappointed?"

Her father's mouth went flat. "Can't say I'm eager to meet the latest good-for-nothing."

"Good-for-nothing?"

"Face it, Carly," he said, scanning the room before turning his gaze back to hers. "You should give your choice of men more thought before you hook up with them—or whatever you young folks call it these days."

Inhaling a calming breath, Carly straightened her shoulders, forcing an even tone. "Every guy I've *dated*," she said, mustering her patience, "has been a decent man."

"Every one of them has lacked ambition."

"I don't choose my dates based on the man's ambition for his job and his fat bank account." As a matter of fact, those attributes usually sent her screaming in the other direction. Hunter Philips was the single exception—for all the good it did her.

The displeasure in her father's eyes tunneled the hole deeper in her heart. "You set your standards too low, kitten."

"Maybe yours are set too high?" she countered.

The pause in the conversation was loaded as they regarded each other warily, and she wondered—*again*—why she'd bothered to come.

When her father went on, this time his tone was full of bewildered frustration. "The worst part is I don't think you care about your boyfriends that much. Instead you try on one fellow after another, and then wonder why they treat you so poorly in the end."

The words landed too close for comfort. "Is that what this party is really about?" Carly asked. "An excuse to get me here and harass me about my love-life?"

"It's a sad day when I have to throw a party just to see my own daughter." He let out the same long-suffering, resigned sigh he always did. The one that made her feel awful. "But as for your love-life," he went on, "you're an adult. Who you choose to run around with is your business."

"That's never stopped you from sharing your opinion."

"I'm more concerned about your professional choices."

Her heart withered a fraction as humiliation and shame came roaring back, and her patience slipped further from her grasp. "Come on, Dad. It's me. No need to sugar-coat your words." She stepped closer. "Why don't you just say you're worried I'll screw up again? Repeat past mistakes?" The frown on her father's face wasn't an answer, but it was all the response that Carly needed. "Well, there *is* good news. If I do muck it up a second time, at least it won't be on one of your newspapers. So you don't have to worry about that precious bottom line of yours."

Getting fired was her fault, not her dad's. But her sharp stab of doubt about his role in the debacle still cut deep.

She stared at her father, and for once the truth spilled out, free of sarcasm. "It's been three years, and I still can't decide if you were the one who ordered my dismissal or not."

Her dad's face flushed red, and he stepped closer. "Damn it, Carly," he said, the affectionate nickname long gone. "Your boss made that decision. Were you truly so naive as to think there wouldn't be repercussions?" He narrowed his eyes in disbelief, as if he still couldn't fathom how she could have been so stupid. "Just like you were naive enough to believe Thomas Weaver wasn't using you?"

"He *wasn't* using me. We didn't start dating until three months after my story ran." She lifted her chin, batting back the overwhelming emotion. "However I *was* naive enough to believe that the people who cared about me would stick around when things got ugly. But when the going got tough he turned his back on me to save himself. Just like you."

"What did you expect me to do, Carly?" he said. "Make excuses about my daughter's lack of judgment? Show a preference for my own flesh and blood? I run a tight ship, and business has to come first." His face shifted from anger and frustration—which she could handle—to the worst expression of all…disappointment. "I don't understand how you could have made such a rookie mistake."

She swallowed against a tight throat, her words thick. "I have a heart, Dad."

"Whether you choose to believe it or not, I do too."

"But I can't turn it on and off like you."

"As I've said…" His scowl grew deeper. "I couldn't step in on your behalf."

The pressure of budding tears burned her lids, and she tightened her grip on her purse. "Don't you get it, Daddy?" The name slipped out before she knew what she was saying. "I didn't *want* you to step in on my behalf," she said. She'd waited forever to hear her father say he believed in her. And here she was, three years later, still waiting in vain. "You have no faith in me at all, do you? I would *never* have asked you to show me that kind of favor." She fought to control the ferocious hurt. "But you didn't even trust me enough to give me the option of turning it down."

Though her dad's face broiled with anger, when Hunter appeared at her side with the champagne her father nodded in his direction and said, "Clearly *you're* too smart to fall prey to my daughter's charms."

Her heart convulsed, and Carly wasn't sure which was worse—the shame or the pain. She tried to respond, but her reply died when Hunter smoothly stepped closer to her side. A silent promise of protection.

His frigid, steel-like gaze focused on her father and he voiced an icy word of warning. "Careful."

But this was one encounter Hunter couldn't save her from. Wrestling with the need to cry, scream and lash out with her words, Carly blinked back the roiling anger. If she didn't leave now she'd make a fool of herself. After a last glance at her father's fuming face, she pivoted on her heel and headed out of the living room, leaving the murmur of happy chatter behind.

CHAPTER EIGHT

As WILLIAM WOLFE stomped off, Hunter watched Carly head down the hallway and wrestled with the intense urge to follow her, resisting the impulse. Despite the danger she posed, he'd shown up tonight because he couldn't seem to deny himself the pleasure of Carly Wolfe's company.

After they'd made love, his body completely spent, he'd realized the liberating release had been like none he'd experienced before. And he'd wanted her again. The moment the craving had hit he'd remembered exactly why she'd followed him into the shower room. Plagued by the disturbing thought she was using him, he'd had to bolt or risk losing himself in her a second time. And when he'd spied her sinfully sexy dress tonight, need had smashed him head-on. Angry at himself for being so susceptible, he'd provoked her. Insulted her...just like her father.

Regret churned in his gut. After the scene he'd just witnessed, he had a better understanding of the complex woman so full of softly rounded corners and sharp edges. Brashly forward, yet remarkably vulnerable. Driven at her job, yet oddly innocent at the same time. Hunter still wasn't entirely clear which side of the Carly equation *he* fell on—or, in the end, which side she would choose—but he was now convinced she was innocent of every accusation the press had thrown at her three years ago.

Fingers gripping the champagne flutes, he watched her turn into a room at the end of the hall feeling torn, grappling with the need not to be played for a fool again. But at least when he'd suffered his parents had supported him. Booker had stuck by him. But Carly...

When Carly had made her so-called mistake she'd been abandoned by the two people that had mattered most. The knowledge took a chink from his heart and burned in ways it shouldn't.

Jaw clenched, decision made, he left the party behind and strode down the long corridor, stopping in the open doorway at the end. Color high on her cheeks, mouth set, Carly paced the length of a masculine office done in forest-green, a bordering-on-indecent length of silky leg swishing back and forth beneath her red dress.

He hesitated, and debated changing his mind. Instead he said, "You want to tell me what just happened?"

She never broke her stride, and her tone matched the fury in her pace. "I want you to leave."

He was used to her charm-and-slash smile, the targeted sarcastic comments and the intentional flirting, but he'd never seen her so blatantly angry before. Not even when he'd insulted her.

Champagne in hand, he slowly entered the room. "I think you should talk about it."

"No," she bit out, looking close to either blowing her top or bursting into tears.

He set the glasses on a massive walnut desk. "You might feel better if you cried."

"No." Mid-stride, she heaved her purse onto the leather office chair. In a woman who normally brimmed with self-confidence the stark emotion, the seething vulnerability on her face, was hard to watch. "I promised myself I wouldn't cry about it again. Especially not *here*."

His heart twisted, but he ignored it. "Why not here?"

She reached the far wall and turned, heading back in his direction. "Right after the Weaver story blew up in my face and I got fired I came home, looking for support." Still pacing, she pointed in the direction of the desk, eyes burning with emotion. "And the moment I got back he sat me in this office and lectured me on a reporter's duty and the main goal of a paper...to make money. He went on and on about the importance of the financial bottom line." Her eyes looked suspiciously bright, but no tears welled. "He didn't give a *damn* how I felt."

It was the restraint that almost did him in.

She passed him, her scent trailing in her wake.

"Nothing I do is ever good enough. I've avoided him for six months." She fisted her hands. "Six *months*. And in less than two minutes he's making cracks about my love-life."

He watched her retrace her path across the room. "Has your relationship with your father always been difficult?"

"No," she said. "In some ways that would make it easier. Then I could just walk away. Instead I moved back to Miami." Her lips pressed in a thin line. "And like a moron I hang around, remembering how it used to be when I was younger..."

It was a dilemma he understood well. Lately he'd been spending a lot of time dealing with the past himself. He let out a long, slow breath. "It's hard to cut the good memories loose just to free yourself from the bad."

She stopped in the middle of the room and her gaze met his. "Exactly."

They studied one another for a moment. Several heartbeats passed and Hunter felt the pull, much as he had in the locker room. But this time it was so much more than sexual. Uncomfortable, he crossed his arms. "When did you two start having trouble?"

A shadow briefly flashed across her face, and she looked a little lost standing in the center of the room. "My mom died when I was a baby, so Dad's the only family I have. Things got rough when I hit my teens," she said, threading less than steady fingers through her hair. "Since then all he's done is berate me over every decision I make, all the way down to the clothes I choose to wear. Pretty soon, I just gave up." Her mouth twisted grimly, and she smoothed her hand down the silk covering her thighs. "I wore this dress tonight because I knew it would piss my father off." After a self-derisive scoff, she shook her head and turned to stare desolately out a night-blackened window. When she spoke it was almost as if to herself. "I don't know why I continue to antagonize him."

He knew. "Strike first before you get knocked out. It's a protective habit." He had a few of those himself.

She looked at him as if the idea was new to her. "Yeah," she said. "He's been known to throw a few fast punches. He once accused me of treating boyfriends like shoes from the sale rack." He lifted a brow in question, and she went on. "Tried on, adored for a few months, and then relegated to the back of the closet."

He leaned his shoulder against the wood-paneled wall. "Have there been a lot of men?"

"More than a few. Less than too many." She stared at him a moment before hiking her chin a touch. "Are you judging me?"

"No," he said truthfully. "It's not my place to judge. Why do these relationships end?"

"My fault, probably." With a self-conscious shrug, she sent him a small smile of defeat. "I get bored, and I suspect the guys can sense it."

Curious, he pushed off the wall and moved closer to Carly. "And what does the turnover rate provide you with?"

She let out a bark of laughter, as if the question was absurd. When he didn't return the humor she seemed to give the question some thought. "Mostly just a lot of embarrassing break-ups." She cocked her head. "Did you know there's a singing telegram service in town that specializes in break-up messages? I'm probably the only recipient in Miami whose address they know by heart." He bit back the smile as she went on dryly. "So the only thing the turnover rate provides me with is a lot of jokes in the office at my expense."

"And maybe another method of making your father angry?"

Her scowl was instantaneous. "No," she said, and then her expression softened to include a bit of uncertainty. "Maybe." She bit her lower lip, and then doubt replaced the frown completely. "I don't know," she said slowly, as if contemplating the possibility.

He stepped closer, looking down at her face. "Or maybe you don't want anyone around long enough to use you again. Like the senator did."

Denial surged, and her tone was adamant. "Thomas did *not* use me."

He studied her for a bit, wondering who she was trying to convince. Him…or herself.

"Are you sure?" He paused long enough to get her full attention. To hammer his point home. "That's hard to believe, seeing how when you finally became a hindrance instead of an asset he cut you loose."

"My story was already out. How was I an ass—?"

"With Wolfe Broadcasting in his pocket, winning elections would be a lot easier."

Carly closed her eyes, looking as if she'd been struck, and Hunter wanted to kick himself for being so blunt.

"Jeez." She paused, and then inhaled deeply as if to steady herself. "You're hell on a girl's ego, you know," she said softly. "I don't know what to believe anymore." She lifted her lids, and her gaze held an aching vulnerability that killed him. "All I know is…"

It seemed there was plenty she didn't *want* to know. "What?" he said quietly.

She scanned his gaze and her amber eyes lost a little of the gold as the brown intensified, growing darker. "All I know is that I want you again."

Heat and need socked him in the gut, setting off a sensual storm that promised to sweep away his resolve. This wasn't the reason he'd followed her here, but there was no flirtatious tone. No coy looks. No sassy challenge in her eyes. Just an open honesty that was clearly a cover for a painful defenselessness that made her scent, her soft skin and the desire in her eyes all the more difficult to resist.

His heart was pulling double duty, trying to keep the blood supporting his brain even as it drained to his groin. Outwardly he might appear calm, but Carly had to feel the earth quaking from the hammering in his chest. "Why?"

"Because you make me feel like nobody else ever has."

As he scrutinized her face, looking for the truth, he realized that making love to him in her father's house would be the perfect retribution for her.

Despite the need to pace, the restless urge to move, instead he said, "I should leave."

"Please stay."

His body now fully on board for anything she had planned, despite the fact his brain thought it a bad idea, he said, "It isn't fair, asking me while you're wearing that dress." His words were throatier than he would have liked. "I don't even think it's legal."

She tipped her head in that sexy way that slayed him. "Will you arrest me if it isn't?"

"I probably should," he muttered. He held her gaze, fiercely aroused and intensely troubled. Was he just another way for

Carly to get back at her father? Or an effective method for burying all those self-doubts?

For a brief moment he wondered if she wanted something more from him.

And what if she did?

Doubt battled desire, twisting his heart into impossible shapes, and he muttered his next thought out loud. "What other weapons do you have up your non-existent sleeves?"

She blinked several times and after a brief deliberation lifted her arms, placing her hands on her head in mock surrender. A position of submission. As if yielding all power to Hunter. "You can frisk me and look for more if you want," she said.

She steadily met his gaze...and he knew she was waiting for him to make his choice.

Gathering her courage, Carly waited, hating how much this man destroyed her usual confidence. He was hot, intriguing and dangerous, even when coming to her defense. And he never failed to step up on her behalf when it mattered most. She'd never fallen for a man before, and a part of her had always wondered why. With Hunter, she feared she was already more than halfway there...

Her heart skipped a beat and her stomach settled lower.

It's only lust, Carly.

She felt bare, exposed and defenseless as the seconds crawled by while he studied her, as if trying to decide what to do. Although the fire and focus in his eyes communicated he wanted her, it was obvious he questioned her motives.

But the unadorned truth was too hard to share: no matter how hard she worked, or how happy she tried to be, the sadness over her fractured relationship with her father made peace of mind impossible. Hunter's square-cut jaw, sensual lips and broad shoulders—and, more importantly, his protector mode she found so attractive—threatened to consume her as well. And she was desperate for the latter to win. Even if it was only for another sensually mind-boggling moment. It wasn't a difficult choice, really. Who wouldn't choose feel-good promise over dark disappointment?

Hope over despair?

Hands on her head, she stared at him, dying to know if he was as good as she remembered. Maybe she'd just been pathetically grateful for his on-air act of gallantry, sacrificing himself for her? Maybe it had been how hard he'd fought her in the locker room, and how utterly beautiful he'd been when he'd taken the fall? Or maybe she was simply tired of guys so laid-back they were just one step above dead?

"Frisk you?" he mused as he finally closed the last bit of distance between them, his rumbling voice shimmying down her spine. "I probably should." Meeting her gaze, he laid his hands on her wrists, skimming his way down her bare arms. The skin-on-skin feel left goosebumps in their wake. "Just to be safe." He smoothed his palms down her sides, his thumbs brushing the outer edges of her breasts in tantalizing promise before slowing to a crawl at her hips.

His gaze burned into hers, the warm hands scalding her through thin silk. "What are you wearing underneath?" he said.

"A thong."

His eyes turned darker as he slowly crouched. "Anything else?" he said, smoothing his sizzling hands down her legs.

Anticipation reached critical levels, and her palms grew hot against her head. "Nothing."

He looked up at her from his squatting position, hands on her shins. "That means there aren't many hiding places under this dress."

Her heart pounded at the memories of the last time he'd knelt in front of her. "It depends on how thorough you are."

The mysterious smile was instantaneous. He smoothed his hands up over her knees, higher along her thighs, and stroked the sensitive nub between her legs. Awash in pleasure, heart battering her chest, Carly maintained his gaze even as her thong grew wet.

"I'm motivated to be very thorough," he murmured.

He lingered a moment, eyes so dark it was hard to remember them ever being cold. Her body was so hot and damp it was hard to be much more than a mass of needy nerve endings.

"Because you're a G-man following procedure?" she said, her voice breathless.

"Why else?" He stood, his hands smoothing up her belly, between her breasts, out and around both, before finally cupping the curves. "Technically I should check your back too." His thumbs skimmed her now taut nipples and pleasure surged, her body melting more. She fought to focus as he said, "But it's occurred to me you don't need any armaments beyond this."

His mouth claimed hers and she kissed him back with all the pent-up, conflicting emotions in her chest. Desire for Hunter, and fear of giving him too much power over her. Hunter simply took what he wanted, demanding everything, and Carly could do little more than comply.

Heat infused her every cell as his hands slid under her dress to clasp her buttocks, pulling her firmly against his hard length. She arched against him in agreement, their mouths engaged in a primal duel even as his thumbs smoothed soothing circles low on her back.

"We need to lock the door," she murmured between rough kisses.

"We need a condom," he said against her mouth.

"The second one from the dispenser is in my purse."

At her words, he pulled his head back, eyes still fiery with

need, his brow creased in surprise. She had grabbed the condom on impulse, wanting a memento, and she wasn't sure if
he found her charmingly funny or entirely too bold. For the
first time in her life she didn't know where she stood with a
man, and it was driving her insane.

After a split second, he said, "I'll get the door. You get
the condom."

Fortunately neither endeavor took long. When they met
back in the center of the room Hunter removed her dress and
tossed it aside. "This time—" with a firm hand he gently
pushed her down to the plush carpet and a thrill rushed
through her "—I'm in charge." He kept pressing until she
was lying back, and then he slipped off her thong.

Throat tight, body aching for him, she watched Hunter
take off his tux, starting with the coat, bow tie, and then his
shirt. The sight of the finely honed torso—the one he'd placed
between her and her dad after her father's insult—left her
dying to take control. The acute need to worship lean muscle,
warm skin and the hard, protective planes of his chest was
strong. But when he shed his pants, was naked, his erection
visible in all its glory, her heart pumped so hard she feared it
would break free from her chest and flop to the floor.

Maybe it was a good thing he was taking the lead.

He knelt and lifted her leg, kissing her ankle. He nipped
his way higher, scraping his teeth across her skin, palms
soothing the fire his mouth left behind. When he reached
her inner thigh, with a quick dart of his tongue he licked the
nub between her legs, and a sensual jolt shocked every cell.

Before she could catch her breath he moved his attention
to the other leg, giving it equal time. As his teeth nipped up
her second thigh she closed her eyes, body humming, nerves
straining, and arched to meet him. His lips landed on her center again and lingered, sending hot pleasure rushing through

her. She gripped the thick carpet, a moan escaping her lips and sweat dotting her temples.

Time hovered, her mind expanding even as her muscles contracted, focusing on the point where Hunter's lips, teeth and tongue brought her to an ecstasy that washed everything away. There was no yesterday to regret. No tomorrow to worry about. Only the beautiful way Hunter made her feel.

Mouth between her legs, he worked his sensual magic, pushing her closer to the brink, so close to climax her whole body tensed.

He drew back and, crushed, she let out a cry. *"Wait."*

"You'll have to," he said, and calmly rolled on the condom. And then, eyes on hers, he shifted up her body. Instinctively she welcomed him. He arched between her thighs, going deep. Relief shuddered through her and she shifted to absorb more of him, meeting him thrust for thrust. There was no doubt. No uncertainty or distrust. Just a desire strong enough, sure enough, to push aside all the worries.

Heart pumping in her chest, hair damp at her neck, she closed her eyes as their hips strained against each other, her release just moments away.

This time when he pulled out her eyes flew open and Carly clutched his shoulders, speechless as he began to kiss his way down her neck to her collarbone. She found her voice, frustrated and flabbergasted. "What are you do—?"

His mouth landed on a nipple, eliciting a sharp hiss, cutting off her words. He nipped and kissed, as if relishing her flavor, and the sounds of her soft cries filled the room. Gradually she grew louder, spurring him on as his lips traced a path down her abdomen. He licked the tiny dip at her navel, drawing out a groan from Carly before he continued down. When his lips landed back on the sensitive center between her legs she called out his name. He lingered, apparently taking delight in pushing her higher, until she was close again, so close to completion she almost felt it.

Once more, before she could peak, he swooped up her body and drove deep between her legs. Arching his hips, he took all he could, and this time her body's response bordered on frantic. She let out a sob, the pleasure and need so great she dug her nails into his back, her legs aiding his thrusts as their hips bucked in unison. Tears of frustration burned her lids. The intensity of his gaze and the dark, determined look on his face shoved her closer to the edge. She began to whimper. And his movements, though controlled, grew carnal. Rough. Primal.

Mind spinning, muscles straining, she marveled at his strength. At the hard body that pushed her to the brink, exposing her even as he held her close. The hips that drove her closer to a dangerous ledge, his arms providing security.

Laying her open even as he protected.

Until she burst through the barrier, crying out from the force of her orgasm. And clung to Hunter as he joined her, the quake shaking her body with a ferocity that rocked the very foundation of her world.

"Looks like that cloud is bringing rain," Abby said.

From the lounge chair beside her, Carly shaded her eyes from the glare. "I think we'll be fine," she said, staring at the single gray ball of fluff blotting the horizon.

The noontime sun sparkled in the brilliant blue Miami sky—clear except for the single offending cloud—and the lingering cold weather added a slight nip to the breeze. The utilitarian concrete rooftop of Carly's apartment building was strictly for maintenance access. It wasn't as nice as her multimillion-dollar childhood home overlooking the Atlantic. But Carly had added a few potted ferns, along with some used patio furniture, and with the city sprawled out in front she considered it heaven. After about a week of wondering where she stood with Hunter Philips, right now she needed the tranquil haven.

"Pete Booker asked me to spend the weekend with him," Abby said.

Carly sent her a pleased grin. "And you said he wouldn't ask you out after the last date."

"Yeah, well…" Abby picked at her black leggings and smoothed her hand down the dark top with sleeves that flared at the wrists. "There's always a chance he'll change his mind."

Carly studied her friend, her tone soft. "Not every relationship ends in catastrophe, Abby."

"All mine have." She twisted to face Carly, her black hair in pigtails. "And unless you're holding out on me," she shot her a meaningful look, "so have yours." Carly resisted the urge to wince at the truth, and Abby went on. "Speaking of questionable relationships—have you heard from Hunter?"

Carly's heart took a tumble. "Not since my dad's party."

"You'd think by now he'd, like…you know…actually ask you out on a date."

Carly slunk down in her chair and pulled her sun visor lower, shading her eyes. Too bad she couldn't block her concerns as easily.

Confused, emotionally and physically exhausted from the evening, the moment she and Hunter had rejoined the party Carly had left. And she'd spent the last seven days wondering what Hunter would have done if she hadn't begged him to make love to her. No longer sidetracked by his disturbingly delicious presence, it was impossible not to scold herself for continuing to pursue a man who didn't trust her. Wasn't it enough to beat her head against the stubborn attitude of her father?

Must she continue to seek approval from those who doubted her the most?

After deliberating for hours, she'd decided it was time to cut her losses. Apparently self-control was impossible when it came to Hunter. She had no choice but to face him on the third show, but she could stay far, far away from him until then.

As plans went, it was all she had.

"And speaking of catastrophes," Abby said in a grim tone, as if she'd read her mind, "you put a lot of effort into getting approval to write a piece on Hunter Philips. Now that our boss has finally said yes what are you going to tell her?"

Carly stared at her friend, and tension flooded her faster than she could reason away her fears. The look on Abby's face reflected all the dark predictions she'd made from the beginning. For the first time Carly feared her friend wasn't so much a pessimist as a realist.

And then Hunter's voice came from behind. "Hello, Carly."

Carly's heart plunged to her stomach, and Abby shot from her chair, mumbling excuses about rain, getting wet, catching pneumonia, dying and burning in hell as she made a beeline for the exit. Gathering her courage, Carly twisted in her seat to watch Hunter approach, clad in a sleek leather jacket, pants and a dress shirt. He looked fresh and rested, but she hadn't slept well for a week, reliving every moment with Hunter in her father's house.

He sank into the lounge chair vacated by Abby. "Nice view," he said, nodding at the city.

She doubted he was here to take in the sights. "How did you find me?"

"I saw your car in the garage and asked your neighbor where you were."

They stared at each other, and silence fell. After her tumultuous family reunion, not to mention their sizzling interlude in the study, she was unable to play games or pretend to be polite—her nerves were too raw for her usual charm.

She needed peace—which meant she needed him to leave. "What do you want, Hunter?" she said bluntly.

His voice was low, sincere. His blue eyes warmer than normal, their usual frost…gone. "I have to attend a conference in Las Vegas this weekend." His gaze was steady. "I'd like you to come with me."

Stunned, Carly bit her lower lip, struggling to adjust to the development. A weekend together didn't exactly jive with her goal of avoiding the man. Unfortunately she loved how he made her feel, and it went well beyond what he did to her in bed—not that they'd technically made it to a bedroom yet. A part of her was tempted to risk a bigger piece of her heart just to spend more time with him. Another part was scared as hell.

She really should refuse.

Heart thumping with the force of a thousand bass drums, she tried to play it cool and keep it light. She hiked a teasing brow. "It won't make me go easy on you on the show."

"I'm not afraid," he said, his faint smile utterly seductive.

Her resolve slipped a bit. "I'm still going to challenge you to pull The Ditchinator."

"I can handle it."

Her heart thudded, and her attempt at keeping it light died. "My boss has accepted my request to do a story on you." If that didn't get him to bolt, nothing would. And, though his body didn't move, his whole demeanor tensed as her words hung in the air.

"And if I refuse?" he said.

"It doesn't matter. We've slept together. I can't write it now."

He cocked his head. "Have you told your boss?"

Ah, yes. There *was* that little hiccup to contend with. Carly briefly closed her eyes as panic threatened to overtake her, but she fought it back. After months of chasing Sue about potential story ideas, and having spent a considerable amount of time pointing out the advantages of a story on Hunter—including his current popularity with the local press—now she had to figure out a way to tell her boss no. Short of claiming the public's interest had waned, or sharing that she'd slept with the man, she was out of ideas. The first was an obvious lie. The second could get her fired. Again.

Swallowing past the boulder in her throat, she met his gaze. "I'll tell her soon."

She just had to figure out how. Sleeping with him hadn't been the smart thing to do. But the enigmatic Hunter Philips had captured her attention where every other man had barely registered a "huh." And now he was here offering her a whole weekend with him.

A gift that could eventually bite her in the backside.

Delay tactics were in order. "What kind of conference?" she said.

"The largest hacker convention in the US. Hackers, security experts, even law enforcement attend to keep up with the latest tricks. I've gone to Defcon every year since I was a teen."

"Did your dad take you?"

Hunter let out a laugh. Stunned, Carly watched amusement roll off the man. "No, my dad's not into technology—though he *is* retired FBI," he said. "His dad was a Fed too."

The news explained a lot. "It's in your blood?"

"Absolutely. But not in the same way. Dad is old school, and doesn't like reliance on computers, so we've had a few heated debates in our time," he said dryly, giving the impression he was understating the truth. And she knew a lot about heated family debates. "But..." His expression grew thoughtful as he looked out over the city. "Even when we disagreed about everything else," he said, and then turned to face her, "the law and justice were two subjects where we always saw eye to eye."

She tipped her head. "Fidelity. Bravery. Integrity..." she mused softly. Would that *her* family mantra was so noble. "You grew up living the FBI motto."

A dark look flitted across his face, and he shifted his gaze away. "Not exactly."

Surprised, Carly crossed her arms. "You mean you *haven't* always lived the life of a justice-seeking action hero?" Silence followed, and her teasing statement grew awkward as his expression remained serious, his eyes studying the skyline. Curiosity now at full throttle, Carly said, "Do tell."

Hunter didn't move, as if weighing his options, and it was a full minute before he finally spoke. "Booker and I grew up together," he said. "Being an eccentric genius works as an adult, but back then he was the target of every clique in school."

Given what she knew of Pete Booker, the news wasn't a surprise. She lifted her brows, waiting for him to go on. Instead she had to prompt him. "And...?"

"And until we became friends I never lifted a finger to stop them," he said bluntly, finally meeting her gaze, his eyes heavy with regret. "Our sophomore year, the wrestling team tossed him in a Dumpster while I stood by and did nothing." He let out a soft, self-derisive scoff. "That's just one of several instances Booker has never mentioned, though I'm sure he remembers." Hunter gazed out over the skyline, as if the memories were too distasteful to contemplate. "I know I do..."

Carly stared at his profile, remembering the teen years she'd spent clashing with her father. "Adolescents do stupid things," she said. "How did you two wind up friends?"

"When we were assigned a joint project in high school we discovered a mutual interest in computers. Booker invited me along to the Defcon conference with him and his dad." He smiled. "And I learned that, along with his bizarre and occasionally wicked sense of humor, he's a really good guy."

"I bet that changed things at school," she said softly.

He shot her a look with the remnants of a lethal intensity that had no doubt kept others in line. "After that I never stood by and did nothing again," he said. "No matter who was the target."

Carly's heart melted. Hunter was the most honorable man she'd ever met. With Carly he had put up the good fight, and probably still would. But when it came to push or shove the good guy inside of him always won out. Deep down, where it really counted, he *did* embody the FBI motto.

What would it be like to have a man like that in her life?

She blinked back the rushing rise of emotion, the last of her resolve slipping away. "So…" she said. "When do we leave for Vegas?"

Hunter's expression eased as he reached out and traced a line along her arm. The touch was simple. Warm. And clear in its intent. "Tomorrow night," he said, and he lifted his slate-blue gaze back to hers, sending a thrill skittering up her spine.

She wondered what the noise was, until she realized it was herself trying to breathe.

The light in his eyes made them breathtakingly beautiful as he said, "Right after I spend the day teaching you how to handle my gun."

CHAPTER NINE

JIM'S INDOOR FIRING RANGE was busy, but the shots fired by the patron in the adjacent booth were muted by the thick concrete walls and Hunter's headset. Fortunately the heavy earphones they were wearing had a built-in microphone system that allowed him to hear Carly's voice, including her sarcasm, albeit with a tinny sound.

"Is this how you dazzle the women you date?" she said.

His lips twitched as he reloaded the gun. "I wouldn't think you'd be so easily impressed."

"It's hard not to be. You handle that weapon like it's an extension of yourself." She nodded in the direction of the distant bullseye where Hunter's shots had been recorded electronically. "You hit dead center every time. I'm feeling inadequate already."

"You have other areas of expertise," he said, amused when she rolled her eyes.

Like holding a new firearm for the first time, it felt odd having her here—not necessarily wrong, just…different. And most likely that feeling would return when they boarded the plane for Las Vegas tonight. He'd never taken a woman to Defcon before—his days there were strictly his own. Mandy had wanted to come along once, but he'd talked her out of it, convinced she would have been bored. But this time he'd hated the idea of a weekend without seeing Carly. A disturbing trend it was best not to think too much about.

Concentrating on his current agenda was a better course of action.

Hunter attempted a serious tone as, with his nine-millimeter Glock 17 in hand, he stepped behind her. Both of them were facing the bullseye. "The safety is on, but remember to always treat a gun as if it's loaded and the safety is off." Mindful of her inexperience, he shifted closer, until he could feel the heat from her skin. Serious became harder to maintain. "Now, square your hips and shoulders with the target." He placed one hand on her hip, ignoring the delicious curve, and checked her alignment as he passed her the weapon.

Arms extended, she gripped the gun as he'd instructed earlier, and targeted the bullseye at the far end of the room. Her hip shifted beneath his hand, and her voice was almost... distracted. "Are you intentionally trying to mess me up?"

Biting back a smile, he said, "You're drifting down." He reached around her to lift her wrists—a pseudo-embrace from behind.

"Not. Helping."

"Just ignore me," he said, amused even as he tried to apply the advice to himself. Arms extended alongside hers, he leaned in to help her aim, his mouth at the level of her temple. The scent of citrus and the feel of her skin set his heart thumping dangerously. "Look down the barrel and square the sights with the target."

"I'm trying," she muttered. "And you'd think I'd get a few lessons *before* I learned to deal with distractions."

His lips quirked. "You're a quick study. I'm sure you'll have no problem. Now," he said, forcing the serious tone back to his voice. He lightly gripped her elbows. "Brace for the kickback. When you're ready, release the safety, check your alignment again, and slowly pull the trigger."

She did as told, and the gun fired with a loud bang. Carly didn't squeal, jump, or even flinch at the discharge. Instead she fired off two more shots in quick succession. When the echoing sound and the smell of gunpowder cleared, Carly finally spoke.

"Wow," she said with an awed tone. "The kickback is a shocker."

Maintaining her position, she turned her head to look at him curiously. Her lips close to his were heating his blood.

"Does the surprise ever go away?" she said.

"You get used to it," he said, doubting the same was true of touching Carly. He dropped his hands to her waist and shifted, his length now molded to hers from hip to thigh. Desire shot like bottle rockets, as forceful as any kickback from a gun. All parts of him tense and ready for action, he had to force his mind to focus. "You did a nice job."

"Purely a credit to your detailed instructions." She faced the bullseye. "You must spend a lot of time here."

"Every Friday morning before work."

After a pause, arms extended, gun aimed at the target, Carly fired off several mores shots before she turned her head again. Her bold gaze was mere inches from Hunter's. "You never did tell me why you still come."

He searched for an appropriate reply. In the end, a version of the truth seemed best. "I guess a part of me still misses my old job," he said, the understatement sitting uneasily in his gut.

After slipping the safety on the now empty Glock, Carly lowered her arms, twisting her shoulders to face him. "So why did you go into private business?"

The old resentment surged, and he stepped to the side and took his gun from her, careful to keep his tone even. "It was time to move on."

"It's a far cry from catching criminals."

"It's a living."

"So is writing columns about art gallery openings, night-clubs…" her lips quirked "…and trendy apps." A brief moment of amusement passed between them.

"Not your favorite kinds of assignments?" he said, holding her gaze.

"No." Her grin grew wistful. "I'm a nosy reporter that prefers people to facts."

"Who also has a tendency to get herself into trouble," he said dryly.

"I think that's why you've been following me around," she said. "I've decided I'm an outlet for your overdeveloped need to safeguard others. A need that hasn't been met since you left the FBI."

"That isn't the reason I joined the force."

Her eyes grew serious. "So what *did* you get out of it?"

He studied her for a moment, weighing his response carefully. But ultimately the unvarnished truth came out with more heat than he'd intended. "I got to catch the criminal bastards."

Either his tone or the words—or perhaps both—brought a smile of comprehension to Carly's lips. "You liked to outmaneuver them." Her grin grew bigger. "You liked the excitement of the chase."

The dull ache was back, and he clutched the handle of the Glock tight as she went on.

"Why don't you go back?" Her words were spoken innocently, as if it was that simple.

But innocence hadn't helped him much.

Gut churning, Hunter turned to the tables lining the wall, opening a gun case. There was a time when he'd been confident it would. When Truth, Honor and Justice—and all the other noble qualities he'd been raised to believe in—had meant something.

"That isn't my job anymore." He jettisoned the empty clip from the Glock, his back to Carly. "I have a business to run. Responsibilities. Commitments. And Booker hates the business end of things." Hunter reached for another magazine to load. "We should get on with the lesson."

He could sense her eyes on his back as she said, "You haven't told him how you feel?"

His jaw tensed, and he stared down at the second clip clutched tightly in his hand, struggling against the emotion that had been eating at him for months.

Instead, he said, "I owe him."

Her tone was skeptical. "Because of something that happened back when you were a kid?"

"No," he said firmly. "It's more than that." Because the friend who'd proved himself through thick and the worst of the thin deserved better. With a hard shove of his palm, he popped the clip into the Glock, loading the gun for another round. "When I told Booker I was leaving to start my own business I asked him if he wanted to quit his consulting work for the FBI and join me. He didn't hesitate."

"I'm sure he left because he wanted to."

"You're right. He isn't a martyr." Checking the safety, he set the gun on the table and turned to stare at her. "But he *is* a loyal friend who deserves better than getting dumped with an aspect of the job that he has no interest in."

"How do you know he's not interested?" she said.

"You've met him," he pointed out. "He isn't what you'd call a people person."

"Hiding behind his computer doesn't necessarily mean he doesn't want to branch out. Maybe he just needs a little encouragement. And if his interaction with Abby is anything to go by," she said, a wry grin forming, "he might not need much encouragement at all."

Unconvinced, he didn't respond, hoping if he said nothing they'd move on to the task at hand.

Instead, she said, "Look, Hunter. I know how loyal you are to Pete. And I know you feel some sort of obligation. But you need to be honest with him. You can't let a ridiculous sense of duty rule the rest of your life." She lowered her voice, but not its intensity. "Are you happy?"

He swore under his breath and turned to stare at Carly's electronic score. As was fitting for a first attempt, her aim was way off. In her assessment of him, unfortunately, she was unerringly accurate. "No," he said, blowing out a breath. "I'm not happy. I'm bored."

He'd never admitted to the feeling out loud—though he'd thought it, *felt* it acutely, every day.

"Talk to him," she said. "Tell him how you feel. Work something out. Establish a new set of rules for your band-of-brothers, bro-code mentality." She laid a hand on his arm. "A real friend will be able to handle the truth."

Torn, he nodded down at the gun on the table and lifted a brow. "Do you want to shoot another clip or not?"

She paused, pursing her lips and studying him for a moment. "Are you going to distract me again?"

His grin returned. "I'll do my best."

She smiled back. "Then count me in."

"In retrospect, the *Star Trek* convention tickets I sent you as a bribe weren't so wrong," Carly said with a teasing smile.

"This is where sci-fi meets reality." Hunter gazed around the crowded Las Vegas convention hall at the attendees of the Defcon conference—the annual pilgrimage destination for hackers. At a table in front of them participants with laptops were competing to see who could hack into the most servers in under an hour. So far Booker was in the lead, Abby cheering him on from behind.

Hunter nodded his head in the direction of his friend. "I never did tell you that Booker enjoyed the *Star Trek* convention in my place."

Carly shifted closer to Hunter's side, setting his body humming. "Which reminds me of something I wanted to discuss with you," she said. Her citrusy scent enveloped him, bringing back sensual memories of the past two days, and he hoped she was thinking what he was thinking. Carly said, "Have you talked to him yet?"

He sighed. Apparently her mind wasn't in sync with his. "I don't want to talk to my partner. He isn't nearly as pretty as you."

She narrowed her eyes in amused suspicion. "You're using delaying tactics."

"No." A grin hijacked his mouth, and he leaned closer. "I'm enjoying my weekend."

Which was true. He hadn't enjoyed himself this much since… He paused, trying to remember. Intellectually it should have been when he was with Mandy. But he was quite sure that he had never felt as alive in Mandy's presence as he did in Carly's. It wasn't just her smart, sassy ways, or that the sex was better—though that was a definite plus. Carly made the funny funnier and the interesting more interesting.

He would certainly never look at *Hamlet* the same way again.

"And, by the way, the next time you plan on sending a gift as a bribe," he went on, "I do have a list of preferences." He had several—and all of them involved a beautiful woman who had taken his life by storm. The timbre of his voice gave away the under-the-sheets direction of his thoughts. "Do you want me to share my favorites with you?"

Carly's quasi-serious expression melted into a welcoming one, and Hunter's body registered its approval. He loved her infectious enthusiasm. He loved how she'd embraced the playful side of the conference, cheering on the participants that succeeded at the annual "Spot the Fed" game.

As a teen, for him the conference had been about fun. As an FBI agent and then a security specialist Hunter had focused entirely on the business aspect. But Carly had convinced him to enter the "Crack the Code" competition. She'd even lured him away from a lecture for a lunchtime rendezvous in their room yesterday. And he hadn't been getting much sleep at night, either...

"You have a list of gifts that won't get sent back to me?" she said as she stepped closer, and he wondered if she could hear his heart thumping appreciatively in response. "This I'd like to hear," she went on. "Because I still have that secret decoder ring you returned."

"You kept it?"

"As a memento of our first show."

"I hope you still have the dress," he said in a low voice.

"I do," she said with a seductive smile. "And I brought it with me."

"Good. I can finally live out my fantasy of making love to you with it on."

"I don't think it will fit you," she said silkily.

Hunter laughed, and then leaned in to whisper in her ear, savoring her scent. "I'd give it a whirl in private, if that's what you wanted."

"Oh..." She pulled back until they were face to face, and her gaze turned decidedly warmer. "I definitely want."

The look seared him, frying the very marrow of his bones. But the heat in her eyes suggested her statement wasn't just about the dress, or even the ridiculous notion of him putting it on. It was almost as if she hoped for more, and it was shocking to realize they might have moved beyond desire and into something else.

It was easy to get lost in the sensual web she wove so

easily, because his body had begun to insist it was time for another noontime rendezvous. But still… "Do you want to know what I really want?" he said.

"Yeah." She lifted her chin, as if ready for anything—and she always was. "I do."

For a heart-pounding moment he tried to figure out the truth. What did he want? When the answer wouldn't come, he dropped his gaze to her legs, plenty exposed in the shorts she was wearing. "I want to know if they make shorts any shorter than that."

"Of course," she said breezily. "They're called bathing suits. But I don't think I'll be allowed in the convention hall wearing one."

"I don't think anyone would complain."

She looked at the crowd that consisted of people of all ages. Most were excited to meet like-minded people, engaged in conversations she probably couldn't understand. "I don't think anyone would *notice*."

His smile grew bigger. "Except me."

She smoothed a hand over his button-down shirt with a light in her eyes and the sassy self-assurance that set his soul on fire. "Your focus is one of the things I like about you."

Hunter gazed down at Carly, and beyond the intense desire that was growing by the second there was a sense of rightness, a light of possibility, that refused to go away. The feeling had been coming with greater regularity, and while he didn't necessarily trust it, the wholehearted, unwavering resistance that used to accompany the emotion was growing less acute. In truth…it was beginning to fade quite a bit.

Which in and of itself should have been concerning.

But right now he was simply going to enjoy himself. "And the other things you like about me?"

"I'm rather fond of your gun." Her grin grew bigger. "Your ability to remain cool under pressure. And I like how you wear that white hat." She glanced up at his hatless head and then returned his gaze. The teasing light in her eyes faded a trace as she grew more serious and dropped her hand from his chest. "Why haven't you talked to Pete yet?"

Hunter stifled a groan and turned to face the competitors at the table that included his partner, the guilt weighing him down. It would have been easier to ask for more time to pursue other interests—to break free of the stifling responsibility of keeping the business going—if it didn't feel like such a noose around his neck. But right now his life felt, if not perfect, as close to happy as he could remember. And he didn't want to ruin it with thoughts of his lingering dissatisfaction at work.

Hunter put an arm around Carly's waist and pulled her closer to him. "I'll discuss it with him when the time is right." His hand drifted lower, as if to hold her hip, but he kept right on going until his palm cupped the outside of her upper thigh. The feel of silky skin brought the desire back tenfold, not to mention some outstanding memories. "Currently I have other things on my mind. Like yesterday afternoon…" His thumb smoothed across her thigh, slipping under her shorts and tracing the edge of her panties at her hip. The crowd around them blocked most everyone's view of his hand.

Though she parted her lips, as if to catch her breath, her lids narrowed just enough to let him know she was trying to continue her discussion. The flush on her cheeks gave her difficulty in focusing away.

"I *could* go discuss business with my partner." He leaned in and spoke at her ear, pushing aside his frustration with the topic in favor of overwhelming desire. "Or we could go back to the hotel room and start working our way down my list…"

When she didn't move or speak, he straightened a touch to look down at her face, and the look of pure need in her eyes was his undoing. His fingers discreetly stroked her thigh, and the energy flowing between them could have lit the LED light display that covered the massive expanse of ceiling.

"Still susceptible to a pretty face, I see," a man said from behind.

The familiar voice from his FBI days plunged Hunter's heart headlong into blackness, snuffing out the light in his good mood, and his fingers gripped Carly's hip. In a blinding flash intense resentment flared. The sharp taste of bitterness. The bite of betrayal filling his heart.

Carly's wide-eyed look helped him regain his composure. Through sheer force of will Hunter transferred the pressure in his grasp on Carly's hip to the muscles in his jaw.

"Hello, Terry," Hunter said as he turned to face his old colleague.

Stunned, Carly took in the cold look that frosted Hunter's eyes—worse than any she'd seen to date—and a chill crept up her spine at the dark emotion exuding from his every cell. He dropped his hand from her hip and she instantly missed the heat.

Since they'd been in Las Vegas he'd been relaxed. Not coiled, tense, ready for trouble at a moment's notice. But now the reserve was back, and it was shocking how fast the old wall could so thoroughly, and so quickly, be thrown back up. She sensed the tension, the seething energy around the two men.

The redhead's buzz cut barely concealed his scalp, but it was the gleam of smug satisfaction in his eyes as he looked at Hunter that left her wary. Despite the chatter in the convention hall, the ominous silence between the two threatened to engulf them—until the newcomer decided to put an end to it.

The freckle-faced gentleman stuck out a hand at Carly. "Terry Smith," he said.

She mumbled her name and returned the shake out of courtesy, dropping his hand as soon as polite.

"Old FBI buddy of Hunter's, from his days with the Cyber Division," the man finished, though Carly doubted the word "buddy" was an accurate description. "Do you hack, or are you into security?"

"Neither," she said. "I'm a journalist."

The slight widening of Terry Smith's eyes registered just how much of a shock her profession was to him, vaulting her reporter's curiosity to lunar levels. But as he slid a sideways glance at Hunter, Terry's smirk grew bigger. Carly's heart flinched in preparation for what she sensed was about to become a worse situation.

"What is with your fascination for members of the press?" Terry's gaze touched back on Carly's. "Though who can blame you? She's hot too…"

Carly's heart tripped and fell, landing painfully on his use of the word "too." Hunter's face went glacier, rivaling the polar icecaps for frigid first place, and the menacing look that crossed his face robbed her of the ability to function. Hunter took a half-step forward and Terry's eyes briefly flickered with alarm. But whatever Hunter had intended was stopped by the sudden appearance of Pete at his side. His friend placed a restraining hand on his shoulder.

More mocking than holding real humor, Pete's boyish grin was aimed at Terry. "How ya handling that alcoholic habit of yours, Terry?"

The agent's face registered relief before he narrowed his eyes suspiciously at Pete. "Funny how it works every year at Defcon. My hotel room gets charged with another guest's consumption of alcohol." He paused and crossed his arms, the generic dark suit pulling tight across his narrow shoulders, his words thick with meaning. "Almost as if someone hacks the hotel computer and sends the bar bill from their room to mine."

Hunter's clenched jaw loosened a fraction, as if he was amused by the indirect accusation. "There are a lot of hackers at this conference with nothing better to do than stir up trouble."

Pete tipped his head in false sympathy. "Yeah, and you Fed boys will always be a target."

"It's a big bill too," Terry said, clearly finding little humor in the prank. "Hundreds of dollars."

"Pretty prohibitive with your salary," Hunter said.

"I guess whoever it is must be throwing a party," Pete added.

"Probably all in your honor," Hunter said. The FBI agent's lips tightened, and his grim look only got worse when Hunter went on, "Rumor has it every year the bill gets paid anonymously."

"Yeah," Terry said softly, his eyes glittering with accusation. "It doesn't undo the illegal act, though." He shifted his gaze between Hunter and Pete, as if looking for clues to the crime in their faces and trying to determine which one was doing the hacking and which one was paying the bill. "And if I ever catch the person doing it," Terry said, "I'm bringing him down."

"Lighten up, Terry," Pete said with a laugh and a playful slap of the agent's shoulder. "It's probably a couple of kids having fun at your expense." Pete's smile developed an edge. "Of course, with your poor skills, whoever it is should consider themselves safe from detection."

The insult hung in the air, and none of the three men made a move, as if each was waiting to see what his adversary would do next.

"A few of us are meeting up at the bar tonight." Terry's gaze swept back to Carly. "If any of you guys want to catch up, reminisce about old times…" his grin was positively derisive "…stop by." And, with that, he headed into the crowd.

Carly's mind twirled in the aftermath. It was too much information to be processed quickly, and as she watched the FBI agent walk away a million questions swirled in her head. Her curiosity was so sharp she couldn't decide where to start. With the reporter comment? With the history of the animosity between the three men? Or perhaps with who was hacking the hotel computer and stiffing Terry with the bar bill?

But when she turned to speak with Hunter…he was gone.

Hunter sat on a chair in the corner of his hotel room, thick curtains blocking all but a thin swath of the dying embers of the setting sun. After his aimless wander along the noisy chaos of the well-lit Vegas strip the dim light and silence of the hotel room was a relief. Out on the sidewalk he'd passed three Elvis impersonators, four superheroes, and a gold-painted human statue of Midas. Carly would have loved every one of them. He shouldn't have left her so abruptly, but he'd needed time to regain control of his anger.

Nursing the same bourbon he'd poured when he'd returned to the room an hour ago, Hunter stared across the posh penthouse suite. In his days as an FBI agent, a government employee on a limited budget, he'd been assigned one of the cheapest rooms on the bottom floor. Now he could afford the best of the best at the top. A massive room, lavish with plush furniture, thick carpeting, and a well-stocked bar that deserved someone who drank more than him. Since his drinking binge following Mandy's defection his taste for alcohol had waned.

Running into Terry had triggered an avalanche of troubled emotions Hunter had battled for eight years. At one time the salary slur he'd tossed at Terry would have left Hunter satisfied, knowing that he could buy and sell the man's life ten times over and never pull a financial muscle. But in reality it was an empty win. Hunter hadn't minded the cheap rooms, the basic government-issue cars, or the limiting lifestyle of a G-man on a G-man's salary. The work, the satisfaction of his job had supplied him with all that he'd needed: a sense of purpose. A calling he believed in. And—the real chocolate frosting on the plain vanilla cake—the thrill of outwitting the crooks and beating them at their own game.

Until his integrity had been called into question.

The acrid memories of those dark days burned—the shame, frustration and humiliation of going to work while the agency's Office of Professional Responsibility had scrutinized his life. Being investigated like the criminals he'd been tracking for two years.

He clutched the cold tumbler in his hand, bitterness twining around his every cell, tightening its grip. Choking him. And twisting the knife still buried in his back.

A rustling came from the hall and Hunter tensed, not yet fit for human interaction. But the sound of a card swiping the outer lock was followed by the door opening, and a soft click as it closed.

Carly.

CHAPTER TEN

RELIEVED she'd finally found him, Carly paused, caught between her incessant need to know what had just transpired between Hunter and his old colleague and her intense longing to ease the expression on his face. She'd seen the Hope Diamond once, and his eyes resembled it now. Blue. Hard. Frozen. Though hope was hardly an apt description. There was such an underlying sense of…emptiness about him.

After the last few days with Hunter it was hard to adjust back to the elusiveness he'd exuded in the beginning. But the wall had returned, taller and stronger than ever, and his expression was sealed off—tighter than any super computer responsible for national secrets.

"After you left the convention hall," she said from across the room, "I came back here looking for you."

"I went for a walk."

She paused, refusing to be deterred by his less than approachable tone. "Agent Terry Smith is an ass."

"Yes, he is." He didn't even look at her when he went on. "He always has been."

"You two never got along?"

There was a pause before he spoke. "He considered me a rival at work."

Her eyes dropped to the glass in his hand, as she decided

how to proceed. "Is that bourbon you're drinking going on your hotel bill...or obnoxious Agent Smith's?"

The hardness in his expression lightened a touch, and the frosty look in his eyes thawed half a degree. "It's going on mine."

Encouraged, she crossed the last of the distance between them. "I figured as much," she said, tossing her purse on the bed as she passed by on her way to Hunter. "Pete's the one who's been hacking the hotel computer every year and switching the bar bills, isn't he? And you've been anonymously paying the tab." The scenario fit with everything she knew about the two. The eccentric mathematical genius and—ever the white-hat-sporting defender—his brilliant and fiercely loyal friend smoothing the way.

His brow crinkled in the faintest of amusement. "A little continued rivalry would be understandable, given our history. But hacking the hotel computer would be illegal," he said.

She came to a stop beside his chair, and something in the way he'd said the words, in his expression, made her question her assumption. "Are *you* the culprit?"

He finally looked up at her with a hint of a secretive smile on his face. "Why would I admit to a criminal act?"

Her heart untwisted and eased. She adored the look on his face and was relieved to see the barrier drop a fraction. But her curiosity climbed to heretofore unseen levels—and for her that was saying something.

"You're not going to tell me, are you?" she said.

"No," he said. "I'm not."

She fingered the strap of her dress, hesitating, but she had to ask. Although she suspected she knew the answer it was several seconds before she worked up the nerve. "Was your ex a reporter?"

Nothing changed in his demeanor, but his fingertips

blanched against his drink, as if crushing the glass. "Yes," he said. "She was."

The implications of the news were enormous. It explained a lot about his initial attitude toward her, and it opened up a slew of potential about what had happened between the couple. Was it more than just a girlfriend who had decided to move on? More than just a woman who'd changed her mind about a man she supposedly loved? Carly's thoughts spun with the possibilities.

She knew he wouldn't answer, but she tried anyway. "Were you ever going to tell me?"

The pause was lengthy. "Probably not."

His answer was more painful than she'd expected. "What happened?"

"It's not important," he said, his voice grim, and then he tossed back the last of his drink.

She blinked back the hurt and the growing sense of panic. Inviting her to the conference had seemed like a major step forward. Now she wasn't so sure. But there *had* to be hope, and the pain she sensed he'd buried for years currently outweighed her own. Her own need to heal his hurts, to tear down those barriers once and for all.

Exactly why she felt it so keenly wasn't a matter up for consideration. The last thing she wanted to do was examine just how much she needed to get back to the connection they'd shared the last few days. It had felt like a real relationship, not the over-him-in-forty-eight-hours kind. More like an intense, never-will-recover, want-to-be-with-him-forever kind.

The thought of this man walking away came perilously close to being frightening.

He carefully set his glass on a nearby table and looked up at her with an expression that squeezed her chest—utter bleakness, infused with a burning desire. A compelling combination that made his tone gruff. "Did you put that outfit on for me?"

Heart now rapping hard, she glanced down at the leopard print slip dress she'd worn the night of their first TV show. She'd put it on earlier, with the thought of teasing him into a better mood when she found him, but now it seemed inappropriate. And very, very wrong. The light in his eyes was encouraging, but the fatigue, the sense of emptiness he kept buried beneath it all, was unmistakable.

"Hunter," she said, looking down at him. "It's been a difficult day, and you're tired."

"I'm fine."

"Have you eaten?"

Eyes on hers, he clasped her wrist, his grip firm. "I'm not hungry."

Pulse pounding harder, her resolve melted a touch. "You need to rest. You need to eat—"

"No." Gaze intense, fingers around her wrist, he reached up and cupped her neck, bringing her head closer as he murmured roughly, "I need *you*."

Her heart went wild in her chest as his mouth claimed hers from below. His lips and tongue held a desperation that was about more than just sexual need. It was intense, yes. Hot too. But the demand in his mouth was like that of a drowning man who seemed intent on taking her down with him.

She loved the way he made her feel. Special. Worthy of a sacrifice. But right now it was as if he needed her as much as she needed him...

Okay, Carly. This is obviously more than just lust.

The disturbing thoughts, the fear of wanting too much, were shoved aside when his hands raked up her thighs and over her hips. The despair and dogged determination in his touch set her skin on fire until she was sure her mostly naked body beneath the fabric would scorch her dress from the in-side out.

With his mouth on hers, his palms consuming her body, her own need grew urgent. She began to unbutton his shirt, fingers clumsy with emotion, embarrassed at just how much this meant to her. This wasn't about control or dominance. It was about surrender—not to each other, but yielding to the intense need they shared. She unfastened his bottom button and smoothed her hand across his chest, craving the feel of crisp hair, warm skin and hard muscle. Meeting his mouth, kiss for kiss, she tried to absorb every sensation. Afraid it would be over too soon.

Dying to draw out the moment of being so desperately needed by this man—as if he could never walk away—she pulled her head back and knelt beside him. Her fingers fumbled as she tried to unfasten his pants, and she let out a small, self-conscious laugh. "I hope I don't hurt you."

"I'm not afraid."

Carly's hands stilled as she stared up at him, her heart pumping in her chest. Because he scared the hell out of her. But the frank desire in his eyes gave her courage, so she pulled out his erection and lowered her mouth to take a taste. Hunter's low groan drove her on, and she loved the way his hand threaded through her hair, cupping her head. Not with a sense of power or control, but one of almost vulnerability. A moment where his wall was at its lowest point. No reserve. No guard. Just his need in her hands.

Her mouth and her touch grew bolder, more demanding. Her hands, lips and tongue smoothed their way along the soft skin covering the hard shaft. Satin covering steel. The protector, the coolly controlled man, poised and ready at a moment's notice.

The desperation in his tone was her undoing, his voice ragged. "Carly…"

Hearing his plea, she stood and reached for the hem of her dress.

"No," he said, his eyes burning into hers, his voice tight with desire. "Leave it on."

Slick with need, throbbing from the force of the desire coursing through her veins, she slid her thong down, kicked it aside and fetched a condom from her purse. Fear, hope, and a feeling that came too close to love twined tightly in her heart. She concentrated on Hunter's almost desperate grip on her thighs as she straddled his legs, sitting on his lap as she sheathed him in latex.

Pulse doing double time, her breathing too fast, she said, "You seemed more amused than affected the first time I wore this dress."

His words came out a throaty rumble. "I was affected." He bunched her dress to her hips and positioned her over him, leaving her holding her breath. "*Very* affected."

Helpless in his arms, she arched her back as he began to slide inside.

"God help me," he groaned, filling her inch by delicious inch as he went on. "I still am."

Try as he might, Hunter couldn't hold back the moan of pleasure as he entered Carly. Her body was more than ready. Beyond welcoming. Wrapping him in a warmth that was less about heat and more about alleviating the years of ache within. Overcome by the sensation, he paused for a moment. With him embedded deep inside her, she cupped his face for a kiss that was part healing balm, part all-consuming need, and a very big part an emotion he refused to name. She pulled her lips back a fraction, hands on his cheeks, her warm amber gaze locked with his, and he began to move.

Their hips rocked in unison, slow yet sure, as they savored every sensation. And Carly let out a sigh, her eyes growing darker.

Somewhere along the way the teasing tones and the playful challenge had been left far behind. All that remained was his need to lose himself in Carly. The selfless way she matched his rhythm, held his face and looked into his eyes, mended the cracks he'd sworn were too massive to be repaired. The doubts and misgivings he'd clung to in order to preserve his sanity were slipping. His heart was now too large to be contained in a cynical box. The woman was a seductive mix of sassy strength and endearing vulnerability, but it was the caring in her gaze that drew him in. Called him to wade further, venture deeper.

Death by drowning didn't seem a bad way to go, so long as it was Carly he was submerged in.

Giving himself over to the sensation, he wrapped one arm around her waist, the other hand low on her back, and closed his eyes, burying his nose at her neck, immersing himself as he succumbed to the spell she cast. Turning himself over to the sensation, he basked in her citrus scent, her soft skin and the emotion she shared so readily. So freely. And so honestly.

The unequivocal return of passion in her hips as they met his urged him on. Every savoring thrust increased his greed. Wanting to claim it all, to absorb the very essence of this woman, he fisted his hands in her hair, raking his teeth across the pulse pounding at her neck. His breath turned ragged against her damp skin and she clung to him, each of them lost in the other. Although he maintained the unhurried pace, the slow, strong strokes of his shaft grew rough, rugged. And needy.

Until Carly let out a soft cry.

The brutally frank need built higher. Both frightening in its intensity and healing in its authenticity. Weakening him and strengthening him at the same time. And as her cries of surrender turned into a call of completion the start of her orgasm gave him a final push. He took the leap with her, following her off the cliff and plunging headlong toward the ocean. And then the pleasure hit hard and closed over his head.

Well, it wasn't quite what she'd envisioned, but there was no denying it now.

She was in love.

Carly's chest hitched on a painful breath as she lay next to a sleeping Hunter, staring up at the ceiling of the hotel room. For years she'd wondered how the emotion would feel—perhaps like double rainbows with pots of gold, or frolicking unicorns, or any other number of mythical, magical things she'd heard of through the years. It was supposed to leave her believing she could leap tall buildings in a single bound, not longing to hide out in a basement.

She'd expected to feel energized and ready to take on the world, not left flattened in its wake.

Carly squeezed her eyes shut, blocking out the fear and forcing her breaths to come at a more doable rate—one that didn't make her feel quite so dizzy or panicky. She turned her head to look at Hunter—which didn't help her light-headed sense of anxiety either. The masculine edges of his face looked relaxed in sleep, as did the sensual lips that had minutes before consumed hers. This time had been different. He had made love to her as if all the barriers were gone. As if desperate to satisfy an emotional need via a physical one.

Or maybe that was her being naive again. Because sex was just sex, and with Hunter it had always been good, so what did it really mean?

Confused, she covered her eyes with her hand. Love hadn't brought the kind of harmony and feel-good vibes she'd always imagined. And how could she rely on a feeling of closeness in bed to mean anything? Perhaps, for Hunter, it really was all about the physical?

But she couldn't get beyond the feeling that facing his old colleague had brought all the old memories to the surface. That he had turned to her in a moment of pain—trusting her to see him through, having faith in the two of them.

And maybe pots of gold and frolicking unicorns were real and waiting for her right outside the hotel room.

With a subdued sigh, her doubts and fears too loud to be silenced, she rolled out of bed and quietly changed into jeans and a T-shirt. She combed her hair, slipped out of the room, and wandered down the hallway and into an elevator, pushing the button for the ground floor. As she descended Carly stared at her reflection in the mirrored wall, looking for the radiant glow that women in love were supposed to emit.

But where was the inner peace? The empowering sense of resolve? Or, for God's sake, at least her usual confidence? According to the generally accepted unwritten rules of romance she was now supposed to be an *über*-strong, formidable woman, endowed with the heroic ability to overcome all manner of obstacles simply with the power of the love in her heart.

All she felt was an overwhelming sense that she was no closer to breaching Hunter's mighty defenses than she had been *before* she knew she'd taken the emotional fall—but now failing to lure him out of his shell wasn't just about his happiness, but hers too.

Because, with those cool blue eyes, there was no way of being certain about anything.

The elevator doors opened and Carly made her way into the lobby, coming to a stop beside the marble fountain in the center. Feeling lost, she scanned the elegant scene. And then she spied obnoxious agent Terry Smith at the lobby bar.

A wave of discomfort settled deep in her belly. No surprise

that he lacked the imagination to seek out one of the many Las Vegas establishments that offered more than canned elevator music, hardwood floors, and an elegance so subdued it bordered on bland, generic posh.

She chewed on her lip, staring at the agent. He might lack imagination, but one thing he *did* have was knowledge about Hunter's past. All those tidbits Hunter hadn't shared…like the fact his former girlfriend had been a reporter.

Her heart and her brain crashed into one another again, leaving her struggling to adjust.

That little nugget of news about his ex had been relentlessly chugging around in circles in Carly's mind since she'd first learned the truth. Was there a link between Hunter's break with his girlfriend and his reasons for quitting the FBI? So far she had considered the events to be unrelated, but now she had a strong suspicion they weren't. With his ex being a reporter, it made the incidents a whole lot more likely to be connected.

And why hadn't he trusted her enough to tell her?

The ache returned, leaving her feeling vulnerable, and suddenly her need to know overwhelmed everything. She didn't require the nitty-gritty details, she didn't want a blow-by-blow account—though she would have gladly accepted both from Hunter if he'd suddenly decided to quit hiding behind unbreachable emotional barricades. She just wanted the answer to one question: had Hunter's girlfriend been involved with the leak that had led to him leaving the FBI?

And the only way to find out was to ask. She stared at the redhead, his scalp gleaming beneath the buzz cut.

Don't do it, Carly. Don't do it.

But, damn it, Hunter's past was about more than just *his* life now. It was about hers too. Love might not endow her with superpowers, but it did provide one indisputable truth— he held her future happiness in his hands.

Fear gripped her, more powerful than ever before. Retreating to what she did the best—seeking out answers, nosing out the truth—was the only way she knew how to take back a little of the massive control that had just been handed to Hunter. He now held her heart on a platter.

With a renewed sense of determination, she headed in the direction of the agent.

As the hotel elevator descended, Hunter cursed himself for conking out so fast. The late nights had caught up with him, and while Carly had slept in to make up for lost sleep Hunter had been up early, attending lectures at the conference. Still, the lost shut-eye had been a small price to pay for making love to Carly. Tonight, even after they were done, he'd pulled her close, wanting to stay awake and enjoy the sensation that had permeated every muscle in his body, making them slack. Loose. Unrestricted by the tension that had kept him bound tight for so long he couldn't remember the last time he'd felt so relaxed. The deep feeling of contentment, of *rightness*, came from holding Carly close. From making love to the woman who had wormed her way under his skin in a way that he'd never thought possible.

With her quirky love for the bizarre, her sense of humor, and her sexy, spirited love of fun, Carly had charged into his life and powered his way into his heart in a matter of weeks. Despite all his efforts he'd fallen so fast he was still struggling from the force of the impact. Life without her in it had become unthinkable. And the way she'd made love to him tonight suggested she felt the same way.

So why had he woken up alone?

Eager to be near her again, even if it was to inhale the fresh scent of her skin, to feel the warmth of her body sleeping next to his, he'd left the room with one purpose in mind: to tell Carly how he felt. That the stark emptiness that had threatened to swallow him whole was now filled with the smell of citrus…and the smile of a woman that filled gaps in places he hadn't known there were holes.

When the elevator doors parted on the ground floor Hunter exited and headed into the lobby. Pleasure hit when he spied Carly leaning against the counter at the bar. But the sense of well-being crashed when he spied who sat opposite her…

Special Agent Terry Smith.

The sucker punch to the gut almost dropped him to his knees. The emotional hit was so hard it knocked the air from his chest.

Heart pumping painfully, Hunter stood, frozen, staring at the two of them as the familiar, nauseating swell of betrayal set fire to his previous lighthearted thoughts, incinerating them in an instant. There was only one thing the two of them had in common. Him. And Hunter was one hundred percent certain he was the topic of conversation.

Instantly several memories flashed through his mind: Carly using her blog to rake him over the coals—subsequently making him the current subject of interest for the Miami press. Carly winning her boss's approval to do an in-depth piece on Hunter. And Carly making love to him—the first two times leaving him wondering what she had to gain.

Until tonight, when it had felt so different, so raw, it had lulled him into a sexually induced state of lethargy. Yet when he'd woken…she was gone.

Now she was talking to his former colleague. A man who knew every sordid detail about Hunter being duped by another woman. The duplicity, the slur on his good name, and the humiliatingly degrading days of being the subject of an inquiry by the department he'd sworn to serve.

Why was she talking to the FBI agent?

Hunter couldn't see beyond the most obvious answer. His story.

His vision tunneled and the edges grew gray, enveloping him in a black cloak that cut off every thought outside of confronting Carly Wolfe.

"Here you are," Hunter said from behind her, his voice encrusted with frost.

If she'd been a cat, his tone would have shaved several lives from Carly. She turned, and the look on Hunter's face left her frigid, chilling her to the core. Her heart thumped hard, forcing the blood through her frozen veins at an astronomical rate.

Terry Smith responded before her mouth could locate her tongue. "Hunter, come join our party. And just to prove there are no hard feelings—" the agent's smile was empty "—I'll buy you a drink."

Hunter's gaze remained fixed on Carly. "I'm not interested."

Carly's heart pumped harder and the strained atmosphere grew taut, the air dense from the tension. Was the anger on his face directed at his old coworker...or her? She had the horrible sinking feeling she was the cause.

The agent's grin lacked humor. "After you've paid my mixed-up hotel bar bill all these years, I owe you several hundred rounds at least."

"You don't owe me a thing," Hunter said.

His emphatic words about the yearly prank again left Carly with the impression that Hunter had done the hacking and Pete had done the paying.

"Not even one bourbon for old times' sake?" Terry said.

"I didn't want to drink with you back then," Hunter said, his tone lethally even, "and I don't want to drink with you now."

The agent refused to shut up. "Come on, Hunter. All Carly's been doing is asking questions about you."

Hunter's face went dark, and Carly's heart sank like an anchor. She opened her mouth to refute Terry's exaggerated claim, but the agent went on.

"So it wasn't like I got to enjoy a nice chat with your girlfriend," he said, and the up-and-down perusal the man gave Carly came dangerously close to a leer.

Up until now he'd been almost pleasant, and certainly not inappropriate. Carly had the impression Terry's offensive look was more about making Hunter angry than anything else.

The agent's words as he went on confirmed her theory. "Tell me—is she worth it?" Terry said. "Maybe if I found the right angle she'd offer to sleep with *me* for a story too."

Before Carly could fully register the insult, Hunter's fist connected with the agent's chin with a loud snap. One moment Terry Smith was sitting on a barstool, and the next he was sprawled on the floor. The gasps from the guests were loud, and a waitress dropped her tray, shattering glasses on the hardwood floor. Silence followed. The whole room was shocked into momentary stillness.

The two bartenders rounded the bar and Hunter took a step back, hands raised in a non-threatening gesture. His gaze pivoted from Terry—still lying on the floor, rubbing his chin—back to Carly. "No need to remove me, gentlemen," Hunter said to the staff, his slate-blue gaze on hers, so empty the negative pressure threatened to suck the very life from Carly's soul. "I'm done here." And, with an air of finality, he swiveled on his heel, heading toward the lobby.

The murmurs of the guests at the bar returned as a bartender helped Terry to his feet. The agent was sullen as he angrily waved the help away. It took Carly all of eight seconds to recover fully from the incident before she took off across the lobby, chasing after Hunter's retreating form.

"What are you doing?" she said.

He didn't stop walking. "I'm leaving."

"Where are you going?"

He didn't slow his pace. "Home."

Her patience was rapidly growing slimmer. "What is your problem?"

"Apparently my ability to choose who I sleep with. Did you find out anything good?"

Frustrated, and more than a little annoyed, Carly struggled to keep up, her legs stretching to match the longer length of his. "I didn't get a chance to ask him much of anything. You barged in and dropped him with a lethal right hook before I got a chance."

"Sorry to ruin your interview."

Anger flared. "Damn it, Hunter," she said, grabbing his arm. But he was bigger and stronger and powered by a fury that was almost frightening. The momentum of his emotion and his strength carried them both forward as she clutched his arm and went on. "It wasn't an interview."

"Then why were you talking to him?"

She bit her lip, her steps still carried forward by her grip on his arm as he made his way to the elevator. Dismayed, she struggled for a way to explain.

Curiosity hadn't killed the cat, because death would have been too easy.

In the end, the truth was all she had. "I wanted to ask him a question."

He stopped to face her and shook off her arm, stepping closer. "What question?" His eyes were iced over, his face hard, and he looked so distant it was difficult to remember anything other than this coldly reserved Hunter.

"I wanted to know why you left the FBI," she said. He stared at her, as if sensing there was more. "And I wanted to know if your girlfriend had anything to do with it."

"You could have asked me."

"I *did* ask you, but you said it wasn't important."

"Sorry I wasn't cooperative enough for you. I didn't mean to ruin your plans. Or maybe this *was* your plan all along?"

Her patience lost so much weight it disappeared. "What the hell are you talking about?"

"Your plan to lull me into sleep with a good round of sex and then slip away to find Terry. Get the story you've wanted all along."

Carly was proud she didn't stomp her foot, and even more amazed she didn't slug him with her fist. But his jaw was so set, his expression so stony, she would have broken her hand while he would have hardly registered the tap to his face. Instead, hope died. Her heart burst. And her soul curled up in the corner and immediately began to lick its mortal wounds.

He'd made her feel worth protecting. But that was a reflection of him. That was who he was and what he did. It was no reflection of his belief in her. He'd faced down two supposed thugs because he would shield anyone who was threatened. He'd slugged a man because of a vile insult, but not because he considered *her* honorable. The need to defend and protect was simply hardwired into his being. He didn't trust her. Had absolutely no faith in her. And he never would.

The tears stung, but she'd had years of practice fighting them back. "You're not even going to give me a chance to explain."

The old feeling of helplessness, of abandonment, came rushing back. First Thomas, then her father. And now Hunter.

His face was so rigid she feared it would crack. "I came to find you because I missed you."

The stinging tears grew sharp, and her every breath felt heavy, as if she were breathing against a thick mask. "I came here to find some answers," she said, her voice thick with emotion. "Because I love yo—"

"Don't." He bit out the word so sharply it startled a nearby

guest, and he stepped closer, towering over her, his voice low. "Don't say it," he ground out.

Heart pounding, she froze, trying to find her voice again. "Hunter, I didn't learn a thing. I told you. I wanted to know the truth, and since you wouldn't tell me—"

"You want to hear what happened? Okay," he said, crossing his arms, his face hardly the picture of acceptance. "On the record, so you can use it to your heart's content and impress your boss with your in-depth knowledge."

Carly's soul curled up tighter, bled a little harder.

Hunter either didn't notice or didn't care. "I was used by a woman until she got what she wanted and left. I don't know if Mandy hooked up with me with that intention or not. I suspect my job simply pricked her interest and she decided to see where it led. But ultimately the story was more important than our relationship."

Despite her own pain, she hated the blank look on his face. "I'm sorry."

Hunter went on, ignoring her attempt at offering sympathy. "She wrote an article that revealed protected information about a cybercrime ring affiliated with the mob in Chicago. Information only our department knew. I'd been working on the case for two years, and I suspect she used a friend of mine from work—an FBI consultant—as her source. All I know is that it wasn't me," he said. Defeat joined forces with the anger in his voice and his lips twisted wryly, his bitter humor black. "But you can't prove a negative. And while a lack of evidence protects you from charges, it doesn't protect you from your colleagues' opinions." Hunter raked a hand through his hair, leaving it spiked on the top. "So I could have stayed and kept my job with restricted access, but I'd lost my zest for the work. Making money in a consulting business seemed the better option."

Her heart ached for him—the honorable man being accused. "I am not going to use the story," she said.

He continued as if she hadn't spoken. "Or maybe you need a little more blood and guts to really impact the reader?" He hiked a brow loaded with bitterness. "Like how devastating it was to be used by a woman I loved. How humiliating it was to be accused of putting the case I'd bled for at risk. The FBI was more than just a job. It was my life." He turned and headed for the bank of elevators.

Carly followed him. "I told you, I'm not printing a word."

Clearly unmoved by her words, he glanced down at her as he kept walking. "You forget I know how badly you want to prove to your father you've earned your stripes back." Reaching the elevators, he stepped inside one, turning to hold the doors open with his hands—blocking her entry. "So try this on for size, Carly," he said, looming over her. "You are a remarkable woman, but you should be less concerned about your father's opinion of you and more about your own. You can't earn your dad's respect until you grow up, act like an adult and develop a little respect for yourself." His gaze was relentless. "And that includes refraining from hopping from one loser's bed to the next."

Her hand connected with his cheek with a loud slap, but the sting in her palm was nothing compared to the pain in her heart. The words had landed too close to home. The last sliver of hope shriveled and died, and her words rasped out, heavy with a furious sarcasm. "As opposed to someone like you," she said, holding his gaze. "Well, here's a newsflash for you, Mr. Philips. You don't hold a monopoly on fidelity, bravery or *integrity*." Livid, frustrated he was taking the wounds from his past out on her, she bit out, "One judgmental man in my life is enough, so you can take your paternalistic attitude and go to hell."

His expression didn't ease. "That's not a problem," he said. "Because I expect more from the woman I love."

Carly's heart soared even as the floor dropped out from beneath her stomach, the twin sensations leaving her sick. The sting in her eyes grew sharper, because the horrible part was she knew it was true. She'd felt the emotion when he'd clung to her in the hotel room. Hunter *did* love her. But she also realized why that news didn't bring the happiness she'd always dreamed it would.

Because there were all kinds of love. The unrequited kind, that often left one bitter. The kind that was reciprocated, sure and strong, which made a person feel invincible. And then there was the kind that was returned but wasn't mature enough to last, stunted by the shadows of the past.

And that was what she had with Hunter.

"I expected more from the man *I* love," she said. Hunter's expression remained walled up as she went on. "I need a man who'll stick by my side. Who has faith in me." She fisted her hands at her side. "I need someone who *believes* in me."

His voice was dangerously soft. "Unfortunately," he said as he straightened up to push the elevator button, "that man isn't me."

Stricken, Carly stared at Hunter's *over you* expression as the elevator door closed, cutting off the excruciating view.

CHAPTER ELEVEN

"LIFE sucks." Carly flopped back onto the plush comforter of the king size bed in the hotel room, staring up at the ceiling.

Abby shot her a sympathetic look. "I don't think Hunter meant the things that he said, Carly."

Carly dragged the back of her hand across her eyes, impatient with herself. She was tired of being madder than hell. And she was equally fatigued from feeling as if Hunter had whipped out a gun and blasted a shot at her chest at close range, leaving her bleeding in the wake of his retreat. Since he'd packed up and left, gallantly paying the bill for an extra day—as if she'd *want* to stay and gamble her money when she'd already lost her heart—she'd fought back the urge to hunt him down. To knock that dumb metaphorical white hat off of his head, stomping on it until it was good and flat.

The exhaustive flip-flopping of her emotions had left her wrung out and empty.

Abby sat on the bed beside Carly. "Look at it this way," Abby said. She placed a comforting hand on Carly's shoulder and crinkled her brow, the jet-black pigtails shifting in response. "He wouldn't have been so upset about finding you talking to his old colleague if he didn't really care about you."

Care? He'd *said* he loved her. For years she'd dreamed of hearing those words from someone she loved in return, but she'd never imagined that the moment could bring such agony.

"I don't know," Carly said. Which was true. She didn't know anything anymore.

"Well…" The doubt on her friend's face was hardly encouraging. "He decked that guy for the comment he made about you." Her overly bright smile looked forced, and it was painful to watch. "That has to mean something."

"It means he found an excuse to do what he's probably wanted to do for years, using *my* supposed honor as an excuse." Carly rolled onto her stomach and buried her face in her arms. Her voice was muffled, which made going on easier—because the next set of words were the hardest she'd ever formed. "Except he doesn't see me as honorable."

"You love him," Abby said softly.

Spoken out loud, the words doubled Carly's misery, and the weight of the monstrous entity was a burden that threatened to drown her.

Carly turned her head on her arms, looking up at Abby. "You said it yourself. These things rarely work out."

"Sometimes they do," Abby said. "You just have to believe that they will."

With monumental effort, Carly briefly pushed aside her pain and stared up at her friend. She wasn't sure which was harder: enduring the expected pessimism while lost in a mire of hopeless misery, or the bud of hope that was now emanating from her friend's face. "Since when have you been a love convert?"

Guilt flickered through Abby's eyes. "Since I got married."

The words lingered in the air and gradually seeped into Carly's consciousness, her eyelids slowly stretching wide as the news settled deeper. It took a moment for the rest of her body to respond. When it did, she shot up, kneeling on the bed. "Married?"

"Pete and I visited a chapel on the strip yesterday," she said with a smile. "Elvis officiated."

Blinking hard, Carly tried to reconcile the pessimistic, down-on-relationships woman she knew with the glowing, almost upbeat woman in front of her. Happiness for her deserving friend and sadness for herself combined to overwhelm her, and she leaned forward, gathering Abby in a fierce hug. "I'm so pleased for you," she said, her throat clogged with emotion. Carly closed her eyes, resisting the urge to burst into tears. This would hardly be the I'm-happy-for-you moment her friend must have envisioned.

Abby held her tight. "One day I'll return the sentiment."

Carly didn't have the heart to rain on her friend's newfound joy, so she said nothing. The words that wanted to form were all negative. She had no clue how to tell her boss the truth about Hunter without losing her job. She had no idea how to heal the rift with her father, especially now that she'd screwed up again. And, worse, she was sure she'd never recover from loving Hunter. Though the word "recover" was probably better suited to catastrophic events.

Well, as far as Carly was concerned, love ranked right up there with floods, hurricanes and other natural disasters.

Abby pulled back, holding Carly's arms. "What are you going to do now?"

Carly knew her colleague was referring to more than just Hunter, and she pressed her lips together, potential answers swirling in her brain. Run away? Leave everything behind and start all over again? It was tempting, but it hadn't helped her three years ago when she'd come limping back home. And it hardly seemed the best solution now.

Gathering her resolve, she met her newly married friend's gaze with as much confidence as she could muster. "I'm going back to fix what I can." She blew out a shaky breath. "Starting with my dad."

Carly turned into the long, oak-tree-lined driveway of her childhood home, half wishing it would extend forever and she could avoid what waited for her at the end. She could just drive on indefinitely, enjoying the sunshine and the song on the radio, pretending her life was okay. Moving toward the moment of truth, or one of them anyway, but without having to actually face her father.

Nice try, Carly.

She was exhausted from the trip home and missing Hunter like she'd never thought possible. No easy-breezy forty-eight hour recovery this time. Honestly, she wasn't sure forty-eight *years* would lessen the pain. But it was time to tell her father what had happened. She hadn't just screwed up again— would probably get fired *again*—this time she'd also lost the one man she'd ever loved in the process. So...not only had she managed to repeat past mistakes, she'd gone and topped her previous efforts.

What father wouldn't be proud of such an accomplishment?

Carly's lips twisted at the grim irony as she parked in the drive and stared up at the massive colonial house, hoping to find a little courage in the view. It hadn't always been associated with unpleasant memories. Her childhood had been as happy as it could be, given she'd been minus a mother and her tiny two-person family was all she'd ever known. They'd muddled through contentedly enough until she'd hit puberty. But she could no longer afford to be the resentful adolescent who'd felt inadequate and misunderstood, and it was time to let the hurt go. Time for her to stop stubbornly waiting for her father to apologize and take the first step toward reconciliation.

Because it was either forgive him for letting her down or give up on their relationship forever.

She briefly pressed her lids together, seeking a happier place, and then exited, closing the car door with a determined thunk—praying her resolve was strong enough to withstand the next few minutes. Losing her newfound sense of inner peace at the first test was hardly the new and improved, more mature Carly she was striving to be.

A few minutes later she found her father under the back brick portico, standing next to one of the giant pillars that faced the Atlantic. He looked as if he'd aged since last week. And, despite her obstinate refusal to move on, she wasn't getting any younger either.

"Dad," she said, and then hesitated, at a loss what to say next.

He turned, and she braced, waiting for one of the subtle sarcastic slurs he always tossed in her direction. Or maybe she was the one who fired first, in an effort to beat him to it. Perhaps they'd taken turns. She couldn't remember. Either way, it always ended with one of them, or both, too angry to continue the conversation.

Two stubborn people stuck in the same behavioral pattern for years. In retrospect, given all she'd lost, it seemed petty and pointless.

His face was closed off and hardly welcoming. "Hello, kitten."

The stupid tears that lived just a heartbeat away bubbled to the surface, but she blinked them back. If he noticed, he didn't say anything. He simply turned and leaned a shoulder against the column, staring out over the Atlantic, while Carly struggled to find the right words.

It was a full minute before he said, "I was just thinking about that time you disguised yourself as a waitress at a party I threw for the mayor." He turned to study her. "How old were you? Sixteen? Seventeen?"

It wasn't the conversation she'd planned on having, and she certainly didn't relish the thought of rehashing old arguments. Dealing with the current ones seemed ambitious enough.

"Fifteen," she said. "You were so angry you grounded me for a month."

He shot her a sharp look. "I didn't have much choice."

"A month is forever to a fifteen-year-old."

"The mayor complained that you were *stalking* him at the gala."

She chewed on her lower lip before responding. "That wasn't entirely accurate," she said, debating the wisdom of sharing the truth. Carly shifted on her feet. "I was actually trying to question his wife about his mistress."

Her father's heavy eyebrows shot up in surprise as he let out a faintly amused scoff. "You never told me that."

She gave a small shrug. "I thought it best you didn't know."

"No wonder the mayor was so livid," he mused.

A pause followed, and Carly wasn't sure if he was amused by her stunt, impressed with her teenage chutzpah or annoyed by the memories of raising a frustratingly independent adolescent. And the closer she'd grown to adulthood, the more her father had been unhappy with his daughter's choices. Now that she was grown up, it seemed nothing she ever did measured up in his eyes. It was a bitter pill that sat in her stomach, refusing to dissolve.

His brow dug deep furrows. "Why are you here, Carly?"

"I need—" Her throat clamped hard, blocking the rest of her words, but she forced her feet to carry her closer to her father. She scanned the turquoise waters of the Atlantic. The late afternoon sun was sparkling on the surface and the salty breeze was balmy. The cold weather that had arrived when she'd first met Hunter had finally passed and moved on. Much like Hunter himself. Pain pierced her. His absence was like an empty chair at a crowded table, a constant reminder he'd walked away. But he'd been right. It was past time to deal with her father as an adult.

"I don't want to fight with you anymore," she said. She drew in a breath. "I know raising me wasn't easy."

A small frown slipped up his face and he looked uncomfortable with the topic—or maybe he was simply suspicious of her intentions. It was several seconds before he responded. "I run a multi-billion dollar company with hundreds of people on the payroll," he said, his voice a mixture of exasperation and defeat. "But I never knew how to handle you."

"I'm not a staff member to be managed, Dad," she said. "I'm your daughter."

He sent her an aggravated look. "Employees are easier."

"Yes, because you can simply dictate what you want." Carly sighed and crossed her arms. "People in *real* relationships don't respond well to the method."

He stared at her for what felt like forever, and then shook his head, looking a hundred years older than he should. "I'm sure your mother would have done a better job," he said, his face haggard.

The sting of tears returned. "I'm sorry I was a difficult teen."

"It's just…" He blew out a breath and rubbed a hand across his forehead, leaving the wild eyebrows in even more disarray. He caught her gaze with an almost urgent intensity. "I won't be around forever," he said, his voice firm yet sincere. "And one of these days your choices are going to get you into *real* trouble."

A dull ache thumped, and Carly pressed her fingers to her temples, hoping to ease the sudden pounding. "Okay," she went on reluctantly. "You were right. Thomas was using me." She dropped her hands to her side. "But I didn't love him," she said. That fact had been made abundantly clear when she fell in love with Hunter.

The constant free-falling feeling returned and fear froze

her chest, making its work difficult. For a moment she could scarcely breathe.

Damn. Love didn't just hurt. It *paralyzed*.

"I know," he said.

Surprise drew her brows together in confusion, but her father went on with a small wave of his hand.

"Oh, I didn't believe that you'd slept with the senator for the story any more than I believed the rumor you'd fallen in love with him and let your emotions cloud your objectivity. I knew better. And in some ways…" he shook his head with a grim look "…I almost wished the latter was true."

Shocked, she stared at him, her mouth gaping as she tried to make sense of the words. "I don't understand."

He heaved out another heavy breath. "At least then you would have risked your career for something more than a fascination for a man just because he'd been labeled an individualist."

Carly held still, absorbing the words that were hard to hear even as her father went on, serving up more of the same.

"And since then you've been in and out of a number of relationships. Most of the men weren't worthy of your time, but I wouldn't have cared so much if you'd actually *loved* one of them."

She opened her mouth to speak, but there were no words of defense. And so far love had yet to provide her that warm, fuzzy feeling that got paired with the condition. Since the moment those elevator doors had closed in her face, with Hunter's words haunting her, she'd started to wonder if her relationships since Thomas had been about avoiding the big L. Because Hunter's accusations had left her raw, bleeding, for the second time in her life—abandoned again, without the chance to explain herself. Her father hadn't wanted to hear her side three years ago, and Hunter didn't want to hear hers now.

But maybe her father was finally ready to listen.

"Thomas and I didn't start seeing one another until after the story was done," she said.

"I know that now." He paused, his frank expression brutally painful. "I wasn't as convinced back then."

It hurt to hear the truth and it seemed horribly unfair. But life wasn't fair, and maybe it was never meant to be. Regardless, it was up to her to handle herself, despite feeling she'd been wronged. And maybe that was the ultimate lesson.

The only control she had was over her own behavior.

"Carly," her father said, "when are you going to grow up and stop flitting from one guy to the next?"

Her heart wrenched, the pain stealing her breath. The time to come clean was now. Would he be happy to hear she'd finally fallen in love when he learned that in all probability her emotional development came at the cost of her job? Her boss had hired her despite her past, giving her the second chance that she'd just destroyed.

But the agony of losing Hunter put the threat in perspective.

"I've been asking my boss for approval to write a story on Hunter Philips." The tone in her voice must have held the warning that bad news was ahead, because her father looked as if he was bracing for the impact, and a little part of her heart died again. "She finally gave me the go-ahead, but…" Her voice stalled. She was too afraid to go on, dreading the look of disappointment in his face. Apparently her expression said it all.

"You've slept with him," he said, his face resigned.

Her heart clenched even as her stomach rolled. He eyed her steadily, and she wished she could read more beneath the weary acceptance.

"You can't do the story now," he said.

"I realize that."

"You have to tell your boss why."

"I realize that too."

Neither one of them spoke of the obvious.

Her throat so tight it was painful, she said, "I'm in love with him."

The expression on her face must have conveyed the massive ache in her heart, because her father didn't look happy for her. He looked like he was sharing her pain but wasn't sure what to do about it.

He took a hesitant step closer. "Carly…"

Letting the emotion wash through her, Carly crossed the last few feet, and he folded her awkwardly in his arms.

The hug was brief, but full of the familiar smell of the peppermints he loved, before he set her back. "I'm sorry he hurt you," her father said gruffly.

Conscious of his discomfort—her father would never be the touchy-feely sort—she tried to smile. She couldn't have her father thinking it was all Hunter's fault. She cleared her throat, clogged with unshed tears. "He's a good guy," she said. "An honorable one."

Too bad he couldn't believe she had the ability to be honorable too.

Her father raised a bushy eyebrow. "What are you going to tell your boss?"

She lifted her chin. "The truth," she said. And it was a good thing Hunter had pushed her to quit being stubborn about her dad, because she would need his support in the coming weeks. "I'm going to write the best damn profile piece I can on someone else and offer it as a replacement," she said, steadily meeting her father's gaze. "And then I'm going to go on Brian O'Connor's show, meet Hunter face to face, and finish what I started."

"Were you given a hard time when you backed out of tonight's Brian O'Connor show?" Booker asked.

Jaw clenched, eyes on the three-foot-long punching bag hanging in the well-stocked gym of his home, Hunter swung with his right arm. His fist connected with a satisfying thwack. "Not really," he said. He did his best to ignore the digital clock on the wall.

11:44 p.m.

A sickening feeling rose, burning his chest and his gut, as Hunter went on. "There isn't anything left to debate." Except maybe his sanity, considering he'd had to learn the same lesson all over again.

He landed another solid punch, forcing back the urge to pummel the bag in frustration, knowing Booker was waiting for him to say more. But Hunter was washed out, too tired from his workout—and the current state of his life—to engage in much conversation.

The week since he'd arrived home from Las Vegas had been busy, consumed by a job that at one time had seemed perfect. Hunter had managed to carve out some time to explore the idea he'd formulated after Carly had questioned his career priorities. But after all that had happened, dealing with Carly on live TV again went beyond his abilities. Surviving this evening, knowing she'd be on the air without him, was proving to be tough.

It would take a miracle to get through the next quarter of an hour without losing his mind, or his resolve *not* to watch the show. Hunter glanced at the clock.

11:45.

Hunter began to pummel the bag, the repeated thumps filling the silence until his friend spoke again.

"It's on in fifteen minutes," Booker said, as if every cell in Hunter's body wasn't acutely aware of that fact. "Are you gonna watch?"

Hunter's abdomen clenched as if hit. His chest and arm muscles burned from his intense workout, but in a way the pain was an improvement. Since his argument with Carly he'd moved through his days in a trancelike state. Numb. Anesthetized. Trying hard to forget the maddening sight of Carly talking with Terry.

And the devastated look on her face as the elevator doors had closed...

With a hard jab, Hunter's fist met the bag, jarring his left arm. But the sensation did nothing to ease the conflicting images in his head.

"Because I think you should tune in to see what she says," Booker went on.

"No." Hunter punctuated the word with a mighty slug. "I'm not watching the show."

Public curiosity had swelled since he'd backed out forty-eight hours ago. True to form, Carly hadn't canceled her commitment to appear. Whether she'd stuck with it for the publicity, or for some other reason, he wasn't sure. But he'd seen the advertisement announcing the replacement topic: the debut of Carly Wolfe's new series. A column spotlighting a different Miami resident every week. She'd finally reached her goal.

The question was, who had she chosen as her first subject?

The clock on the wall read 11:47, and bile rose in the back of his throat. His stomach churned at the thought of watching her discuss everything he'd vomited out in a fit of anger. Muscles coiled tight, he felt the dark potential twine its way around his limbs. He refused to watch as the woman he loved traded in all they'd shared to achieve the career goal she'd chased for three years.

The familiar feeling of betrayal, the boil of resentment, left him battering the stuffed leather bag with a one-two punch that jarred him all the way to his soul.

"I find this situation very interesting," Booker said. "I'm usually the one who sees a conspiracy at every turn."

Hunter raised a wry eyebrow at Booker. "Are you saying I'm being paranoid, like you?"

His shaggy brown hair was in need of a trim, and Booker's smile was wide as he brushed his bangs back. "Your suspicions don't involve whole nations and large governmental agencies. So, compared to me, you're small-time." His voice changed to a more serious note. "But you *are* skeptical of everything that moves, Hunt." He paused before going on. "And I think you're wrong about Carly."

Pushing aside the crushing doubt made worse by Booker's chastising expression, Hunter shot his partner a doubtful look. "Of course you'd say that. You married her best friend," Hunter said. He was still trying to adjust to *that* particular turn of events.

"Abby and I decided it would be better for our relationship if we didn't discuss you two."

"Smart move. Still, you might be biased."

"Or I might be right."

Hunter's chest clamped hard, squeezing with a grip so tight it made breathing and circulating his blood a mammoth chore. His heart still managed to pump the lingering fear to the far reaches of his body. Fear that he'd learn he'd screwed up the one good thing to happen to him in so long that he hadn't recognized it for what it was...

Real. Genuine. And built to last.

With a silent curse, Hunter closed his eyes. The last time he'd made love to Carly his heart had claimed it was legit. That she was on the up and up. But he'd taken one look at her talking to Terry and his heart had taken a sharp U-turn. All the old suspicions, the duplicities of the past, had come screaming back. The avalanche of anger, humiliation, the need for self-preservation had plowed into him with a force that had swept him up in its wake.

If Carly hadn't run the story he'd accused her of going after, what then?

He opened his eyes and began punching the bag again, the lingering question feeding the massive knot growing in his chest.

Hunter was saved from dwelling on the unbearable thought when his friend spoke.

"Is it back to business as usual, then?" Booker said.

Hunter stopped punching and turned to face his friend and business partner. Regardless of the outcome tonight, the status quo had changed. He couldn't continue to pretend his life was enjoyable. Actually, it wasn't even tolerable. Making money hand over clenched fist wasn't good enough anymore. It was time to come clean about his plans.

"I had a long talk with the special agent in charge of the Miami division of the FBI," Hunter said. With a look of surprise, Booker crossed his arms and leaned against the wall, clearly settling in to hear more. "They're very interested in help with their caseload," Hunter said, steadily meeting Booker's gaze as he went on. "I signed on to become a part-time consultant."

A few moments passed, and then a smile slowly crept up Booker's face. "Catching the criminals was always your specialty."

Relieved Booker understood, Hunter delivered the rest of his news as matter-of-factly as he could. "Which means I'm going to need more help in the day-to-day running of the business."

Booker didn't hesitate. "Not a problem."

Narrowing his eyes, he wondered if his friend understood exactly what he was asking. "I thought you hated dealing with the clients."

The pause lasted long enough for his partner's face to take

on a guarded look. His words were cautious. "You set some pretty high standards, Hunt," Booker said.

Hunter stared at his friend, the implication of the statement washing over him as Booker swiped a hand through his shaggy hair again and went on.

"I hate feeling as if I'm not doing a good enough job."

Stunned, Hunter stared at his friend. "Did I give you that impression?"

"Not directly. But you're a hard act to follow," he said. "And you're fairly demanding when it comes to your expectations."

The possibility that Booker had been avoiding clients for a reason outside his social discomfort had never occurred to Hunter. Booker's voice dropped, and Hunter got a disturbing feeling the topic had widened to include more than just work.

"Sometimes you hold the people in your life to pretty impossible standards," Booker said.

Hunter's throat constricted so tight swallowing was impossible. He glanced at the clock on the wall.

11:55.

Booker picked up the remote control to the flatscreen TV mounted on the wall, holding it out to Hunter. "Do yourself a favor, Hunt," Booker said. "Watch the show."

Heart thudding loudly in his chest, Hunter removed his gloves and took the remote. Without another word, his friend headed for the exit.

Hunter stared at the black TV screen for a full four minutes, the digital numbers on the clock marking the passage of time, minute by agonizing minute. Either way, he had to know. He just wasn't sure which would be worse. Losing Carly as a result of her actions…or *his*.

Finally, unable to take the tension any longer, he pushed the "on" button and flipped to the right channel. His fifty-eight inch TV was filled with the image of Carly sitting on

Brian O'Connor's couch. Beautiful, of course, in a gauzy top and skirt. But the sight of her lovely legs, glossy brunette hair, and warm, amber-colored eyes was nothing compared to the shock he got when the camera panned to the right. Sitting next to her were two young adults in typical urban street clothes. Thad and Marcus. The two graffiti artists she'd been interviewing that day in the alley. The first Miami residents to be featured in her new series. Not him, after all, then.

Hell.

Nausea boiled, his chest burned, and Hunter gripped the leather punching bag to steady himself, his mind churning with memories. The vile words from his mouth. The stricken expression on Carly's face. She'd said she needed a man who trusted her. A man who had faith in her. Who *believed* in her. He'd screwed up royally at the very moment he'd confessed he loved her.

So how could he ever convince her now?

CHAPTER TWELVE

DESPITE the ebony-colored tablecloths with their center-pieces consisting of dried dead roses, the ambiance on the restaurant's outdoor patio was festive. Carly was amazed that Pete and Abby had managed to find the perfect balance of Gothic and elegance to celebrate their recent marriage. Lit by candlelight that reflected off the blanket of fog covering the terrace floor, the evening was cast in an otherworldly glow. Waiters circulated, their platters laden with appetizers. Guests ordered drinks at two beautiful mahogany bars, crafted to resemble coffins. Or maybe they were real. If so, Carly hoped the caskets were new.

In jeans, sneakers and a black T-shirt, Pete Booker cast his wife of two weeks an adoring look, and Carly's heart tripped over a mix of envy and happiness.

Standing beside her, her father muttered, "This is the strangest wedding reception I've ever been to." He dubiously eyed a discreetly placed fog machine before turning his gaze to the bride's outfit.

Abby's black long-sleeved gloves were paired with a matching corset dress that flared into a full-length lace skirt, trailing to the floor with a Victorian flare and a Gothic attitude.

Carly's lips twitched in amusement. "Thanks for coming with me, Dad." She clutched the strap of her silver beaded evening purse, running a hand down her halter-top dress of midnight satin. It wasn't her usual choice, but all the guests had been requested to wear black. At least the color suited her mood. "I hated the thought of showing up alone."

"Yeah…" Her dad let out an awkward harrumph and shifted on his feet. "Well…" he went on uneasily, and Carly's mouth twitched harder.

"Don't worry," she said. "I won't start crying again."

Her dad sent her a look loaded with fear. "Please don't."

Carly almost laughed. She had rallied and poured on the charm for the final show, but when it was done she'd fallen apart—and her father had barely survived the onslaught of tears. She'd finally come to realize her dad did not handle a crying woman well—something she hadn't fully understood until now. He would never be the perfect parent, ready with an understanding hug, a reassuring smile and gentle words of wisdom. Then again, she was hardly the perfect daughter, either. But he was here tonight, supporting her in his own way. And for that she was inordinately grateful.

Because eventually Hunter would make an appearance.

Anxiety settled deep. If she ever decided to date again—like maybe a million years from now—she was going to give her choice more serious thought. Both for her sake and the man's. Hunter might have been protecting himself by throwing up walls, but outside of Carly at least he hadn't hurt anyone in the process. She, on the other hand, had left a trail of unhappy boyfriends in her wake.

All of them had deserved better than her pathetic attempts to stick with men who had no hope of capturing her heart.

When she spied Hunter heading in her direction, said heart sputtered to a stop, and she reached out to grasp the back of a nearby chair. After a few earth-shaking seconds she pushed away the budding, soul-sucking vortex of gloom.

Her father glanced at Hunter and then shot her a worried look. "Do you want me to stay?" he asked, almost as if he hoped she'd say no. "Or do you want me to fetch you a drink?"

She was tempted to keep him around as a shield. But she'd made a pact with herself today that there would be no more wallowing.

She tried for a reassuring smile. "Drink, please," she said to her father. With a deep breath, she straightened her shoulders and met Hunter's gaze as he strode through the crowd in her direction. "I'm going to need it," she muttered.

Her dad headed for a casket lined with bottles, shooting Hunter a glare infused with a good bit of concern.

Hunter came to a stop a few feet from her. In an impeccably cut black suit, he looked as handsome and intimidating as ever—every muscle poised, prepared for battle. His cool slate-blue eyes were trained on her face. But this time his hair was spiked in front, as if he'd run an impatient hand through it multiple times. A brief flicker of uncertainty came and went, replaced with his usual determined gaze.

It took several moments and more than a few blinks of her eyelids to jumpstart her heart again. His presence had robbed her of her earlier confidence, so she'd just have to fake it until her mojo returned for real.

"I came to tell you I spoke with Booker and we're all square," he said carefully, his eyes probing, as if testing her response. "We've worked out a plan for me to put in some time doing consulting work for the FBI."

She refused to be swayed by the news. "Glad to hear it."

Neither mentioned their parting words at the elevator, but the ghost of their painful falling-out hung in the air, as if lurking in the fog-blanketed shadows. His eyes held hers, and the determined focus, the sense of purpose radiating from his face, made her heart work harder.

After a tension-filled pause, he said, "Congratulations on

your new series too. How did you get your boss to agree to your plans for your column?"

"I didn't sleep with her, if that's what you're suggesting."

A small smile appeared, more sad than amused. "It's not."

"I confessed everything, and then handed her a story on Thad and Marcus that blew her socks off."

His tone broadcast just how pleased he was. "Good for you."

"Yeah," she said. Just for good measure, she hiked her chin higher. "Go, me." Smart words, in retrospect. Because right about now leaving sounded like a wise plan. She'd missed him, had ached for him, but he also brought a host of sharp emotions along with the longing. Ultimately, it was the confusion and pain that drove her away. "Well…" She cleared her throat, the sound awkward. "I should find my dad." She turned on her heel.

He put his hand on her arm to stop her, his touch setting off all kinds of alarms. "I shouldn't haven't insulted you," he said, the regret in his eyes profound. "I'm sorry."

Ignoring the feel of his fingers on her skin, she took a deep breath, glad the initial icy tension was broken. His apology didn't make up for not believing in her, but it helped ease the ending. "I shouldn't have slapped you," she said with a tiny sheepish shrug. "It was an impulse reaction."

"I deserved it."

Oh, dear God, it was the agreeable Hunter from the first show. The one who was so hard to argue with. The one who knew how to work her to get just what he wanted, whether it be irritation, confessing her deepest doubts…or a sensual surrender.

The question was, what did he want now?

"Hunter," she said with a sigh, pulling her arm away. "I think we've said everything there is to say." Like he might love her, but didn't really know how. Not in the way she needed. The sharp ache resurfaced.

"I'm not finished," he said. "I wanted to tell you I spent the last week trying to perfect my new app."

She frowned, confused. "I don't care about—"

"Marry me," he said bluntly.

She sucked in a breath, feeling the hit, and her stomach clamped into a knot.

She shot him a look, trying to hide her weakening resolve. "You show up, after all this time, and just expect me to accept your proposal? It's been *seven days* since you left me high and dry on the TV show, and—"

"I had some work to do before I could face you."

She lifted an incredulous brow. "You confronted two men in a dangerous Miami alley, yet you couldn't deal with me face to face?"

"Not after the mistake that I'd made."

They'd both made several, and it was more than a few rapid heartbeats that passed before she was able to respond. When she did, the word came out soft. "Coward."

His lips twisted grimly. "In some things, yes."

Put an innocent in harm's way and he would bravely confront the most fearsome of opponents. But when faced with an emotional risk he cut and ran. It was a truth she needed to remember, despite the fact he was here now…looking wonderful…and her body was remembering the advantage of making love to a man with a fighter's muscles…her heart was remembering how the action-hero defender made her feel.

Protected. *Loved.*

Gathering her wits, she shifted her gaze away, blinking hard to maintain her composure. The guests were lining up at the unusual wedding cake: a six-tiered confection of white icing thick with a thorny trimming done in black. Carly tried to imagine taking the marital leap with Hunter, waiting for him to walk out…

"I can't marry you," she said. And with as much grace as she could muster, she headed for the bar and her father.

Halfway there her cellphone chirped, and she pulled it from her purse and opened the message. The soulful sounds of the song "Share My Life" crooned from her phone, and the screen filled with the words "Marry Me."

She gripped her cellular, her stomach settling on top of her toes. She hadn't recovered from the first proposal, and now he was sending a second. Another proposal that left her confused, doubting her resolve to be strong. Fingers shaky, she selected "No" and scrolled through the list of rejection songs to accompany her response. There were only ten. With feeling, she firmly jabbed the button next to "Love Stinks."

From behind her, the reedy sound of the song filled the air.

Carly whirled around to face Hunter, and his gaze held hers as he crossed closer, coming to a stop in front of her.

Now that she knew his plan, her whole body was filled with caution. "You *have* been busy."

"Designing the app is the easy part. Finding the right songs is hard." He eyed her levelly as he said, "I also discontinued The Ditchinator."

She gave him no leeway with her expression and she forced herself to maintain eye contact, desperately trying to calm her nerves. But she tipped her head, her voice reflecting her curiosity. "Why?"

His eyes held hers with conviction. "Because you wanted me to."

Feeling raw, Carly fought the urge to get misty-eyed. He'd done it to make her happy.

"I also decided you'd prefer something more positive," he said. "So I replaced The Ditchinator with The Hitchinator."

At the name, humor briefly overrode the angst, and her

mouth worked, biting back a smile. "Your new app needs a lot of work," she said, as lightly as she could, but all her doubts made it a tough sell. "The Hitchinator is a bit of a retreaded name, and the selection of music to accompany a refusal is pretty limited."

He tipped his head meaningfully. "But there are thirty ways to say yes."

"Do you think it will sell well?"

"I'm only worried about winning over one customer." His voice dropped a notch. "You."

Her heart pounded out its approval even as she struggled to remain strong.

"I didn't expect you to say yes...the first time," he said, taking a half-step closer.

She ignored the chaotic pumping in her chest, the surge of heat in her veins. The longing that went beyond the physical and traveled all the way to her soul. She forced herself to maintain his gaze, though her heart and her heated blood screamed *retreat*. To end the torture of continuing to tell him no.

"I should go find my father," she said, and turned and headed in the direction of her dad at the bar.

Ten feet from her intended destination, her safe haven, another chirp came from her cellphone. She stopped mid-step and glanced at her cellular with a powerful blend of dread... and hope. She pressed the button and the words "Marry Me" reappeared. The phone vibrated to the tune of Billy Idol's "White Wedding." Carly couldn't restrain the small bark of laughter. When the humor passed, again she pushed "No" and scrolled through the rejection choices, choosing one. But this time her fingers hovered hesitantly for several seconds. Biting her lip, she pushed "send."

Her selection of "Bad Romance" filled the air, coming from *directly* behind her, and Carly closed her eyes.

Don't let him charm you, Carly.

But her heart felt more vulnerable when she turned to face Hunter, standing just three feet from her. She gripped the strap of her purse. How could she survive this encounter when he was so close, looking and smelling wonderful and depriving her of her ability to breathe?

"Did you think Billy Idol's 'White Wedding' would endear me to your cause?" she said, knowing he knew it had.

"The first song was too obvious. And I know how much you love the unexpected," he said. "Besides…" He looked at a nearby table topped with an ornate haunted-house style candelabra, flickering in the night. "I've seen the video. 'White Wedding' seemed appropriate, given our current setting."

"Hunter—"

"I'm sorry I didn't believe you," he interrupted firmly, his eyes intense.

Her heart knocked faster, begging to be set free from its self-imposed cage, and panic squeezed Carly's chest. "Too little, too late," she said. "Before the last show I was hoping you'd turn up and say you'd changed your mind. That you trusted me and didn't need any proof beyond your belief in me." She stared at him, dwelling on those painful days. "An apology would have meant something *before* you had evidence I was telling the truth."

A host of emotions filtered across his face before landing on regret. "I know."

With a single finger he touched her hand, and her heart rattled the bars of its pen. But she fought the weakness and her growing doubts as he went on.

"I'm hoping you'll accept my apology anyway," he said. "And I'd be even more pleased if you'd agree to marry me."

Her throat ached as she fought back the tears and the overwhelming need to say *yes*. Good God, she was tired of crying. "Why should I?"

"Because I'd like a second chance." Her throat closed over completely, and when she didn't respond he continued. "I made a mistake," he said, his voice harsh with emotion. "But it doesn't mean I don't love you."

"I know you do," she said. "But Hunter—"

He opened his mouth to cut her off again, but Carly placed her fingers on his lips, stopping his words.

Shifting her gaze between two beautiful slate-blue eyes, she said in a low voice, "I can't live my life walking on eggshells, worrying that I might do or say something that shakes your trust in me again." She ignored the intense heat in his gaze and the feel of his lips, the unyielding softness that was oh, so uniquely Hunter. Her chest caught, and breathing became difficult. She dropped her arm, gathering the courage to continue. "All because you can't move on."

"I can," he fired off in a low voice. He shifted closer, towering over her, his tone softening. "Give me a second chance to prove it."

She still hadn't heard a good enough reason. "Why should I?" she repeated.

His words tumbled out. "Because I let my fear push you away," he said gruffly. Face frustrated, he raked a hand through his hair and looked across the crowded terrace. The pause felt like forever, but when he finally turned back, his expression was frank. Raw.

The last barrier was gone.

"I knew you loved me," he said, his words rough, heavy with the truth. "But I didn't trust the feeling and I was too scared to believe you. I don't deserve another chance. But I'm asking anyway," he said. "Because I'm tired of being unhappy and alone. All because I'm a gutless coward."

As if taking a moment to collect himself, he dropped his gaze to her bare shoulder and brushed her hair back, leaving a skitter of goosebumps. His hand settled between her shoulder blades, cupping her skin as if it planned to stay. He lifted his eyes to hers, and the brutal honesty stole what little composure she had left.

"And I think fear is driving your decisions now," he said.

Her mind balked at the idea and she hiked her chin, forcing the tears away with a watery sniff. "I am *not* scared."

The words sounded hollow even to her own ears.

Several seconds ticked by, and though his gaze was intense there was a touch of humor mixed with a hint of desperation. His voice, however, was pure daring conviction. "Then marrying me shouldn't be a problem."

As his warm palm cradled her back, Carly's heart thumped loudly in her chest, reinforcing the message that he could have called her a coward too, but hadn't. Or that he *could* have insisted he was right, which he was.

Despite everything, she sent him a suspicious look. "Are you *daring* me to marry you?"

"The woman I love never walks away from a challenge."

Her lips twisted into a self-directed frustrated frown. "Damn it," she said in a low tone. "I hate that you're right."

The happy sounds of chatter filled the air as his eyes continued to scan hers in a question, stripping her to the emotional bone. Until he said, "So, Carly Wolfe, which would you rather have?" Despite the words, in spite of the teasing light in his eyes, his tone was serious. "A life with me, learning how to do love right, or an endless succession of singing break-up telegrams?"

The question—and the skin-on-skin touch on her back—made breathing difficult. Which wasn't so good for formulating complicated responses. Fortunately the answer was simple. "You," she finally said. "I choose you."

Relief, joy and fire flashed in his eyes, and with a lightning-fast movement, Hunter hauled her against him. Her body collided with his and she sighed, her heart melting as she curled into his embrace.

His chest was hard. Protective.

The hand on her back was warm. And gentle.

Sandwiched between the perfect combination of unyielding strength and soothing comfort, she inhaled his familiar woodsy scent. The surge of happiness overwhelmed her and she buried her face against him, his soft jacket absorbing the embarrassing wet tracks on her cheek.

After a minute, Hunter said, "Just promise me something."

She slid her arms around his waist, blinked back the remaining tears and looked up at him. "Anything."

He glanced at the two coffin bars surrounded by guests dressed in black, their feet obscured by the mist from the fog machines. "No Elvis at the wedding," he said. "And no Goth-themed receptions."

Finally allowing herself to trust the joy, she let a smile creep up her face. "Can I ask the winner of the Pink Flamingo drag queen pageant to officiate?"

Hunter's eyes briefly flickered wider—but to his credit he said nothing.

She lifted an eyebrow. "Now who's afraid?"

"Good point," he said, his brow creased in humor, his fingers caressing her skin.

"So, tell me…" Her mojo firmly back in place, she flashed him her most charming smile and tipped her head curiously. "What kind of songs does The Hitchinator offer when I accept your proposal?"

A secretive smile spread across his face, and the light in his slate-blue eyes grew warmer. "I'll resend the message so you can hit 'Yes' and find out."

* * * * *

DOUBLE DARE

BY
TAWNY WEBER

Tawny Weber has always loved romance—all the way back to when she was checking out couple stories in the primary school library. Despite her family's warnings, all that romance stuff didn't warp her (too much). What's more rewarding than reading about the crazy twists and turns to happy ever after, and even better...steamy-hot love scenes? Nothing—those are the good things in life. Add to that a lifelong wish to write and a nudge from her husband to pursue her dreams. She took the leap. The result? Three Golden Heart nominations and a Harlequin Blaze contest win on the way to her coveted first sale to Blaze. And she's just getting started... Tawny's usually found dreaming up stories in her Northern California home, surrounded by dogs, cats and kids. Be sure to check out her website for upcoming books: www.TawnyWeber.com.

To my daughters, who gladly share me with
the Muse and don't think it odd that Mom works
in her jammies. Never give up on your dreams...
they really do come true.

To James, for being the most incredible hero a woman
could ask for. Thank you for the love, support
and unfailing belief in me.

To my Critique Partners for the laughter, patience
and gentle shoves when I was stuck.
You ladies rock!

And to my editor, Brenda Chin, for not only helping me
reach the point where she could buy my book...but for
feeding my husband so I could write more.

1

MAYBE SHE should have seen it coming, but a girl just didn't expect to get knifed in the back by her best friends.

"Wanna repeat that?" Audra Walker requested in a smooth, calm voice. She was rather proud of that tone. It didn't show the anger or the gut-wrenching hurt she was feeling. She was sure her face, carefully made up for this evening of revelry and celebration, was equally calm. After all, hiding her true feelings was old hat to her.

She spared a glance at her surroundings. The Wild Thing was typical of most of the clubs Audra's friends frequented. The beat of the music and voices reverberated in time with teal lights flashing overhead. Places like this were always bright and loud and hadn't ever bothered Audra before. Then again, her friends hadn't been idiots before, either.

"You're just not into it anymore, Audra. Face it, you no longer qualify as a Wicked Chick," Suzi Willits said, her breathy voice as serious as it ever got. The buxom blonde shrugged one toned shoulder, making her ample breasts bounce under her leopard print tank top. "We might not mean much to you these days, but we do have standards to uphold, you know."

"The Standard of the Double D. Of course I know," she said with a roll of her eyes. Maybe this was a joke? They'd rib her for a while, then spring a congratulations-on-your-promotion present on her or something. To stifle the simmering panic in her belly, Audra shifted in her seat and breathed deeply. The scent of her friends' perfume was as familiar to her as her own.

"I'm the one who came up with it. Dudes and drinks, the Wicked Chick's tools of the trade."

"Right, so you know better than anyone how important it is to keep those tools sharp and fresh, don't you?" Suzi challenged. It wasn't her tone that forced Audra to accept they were serious. It was the fact that Suzi waved away the hot guy who'd just signaled her to come dance with him.

Audra's gaze flicked from Suzi to Bea Tanner. Rather than meeting her eyes, the redhead kept her gaze averted, making a show of swirling a piece of mango through the froth of her margarita.

Audra thought about laughing in their faces. It'd be easy enough to toss back her drink, slide from the barstool and tell them both to kiss her ass before sashaying out of the nightclub. The only thing stopping her was the fact that Suzi and Bea were two of her closest friends. And while they might not be the poster children for loving support, the three of them had been hanging together since were Wicked Chicks in Training at fourteen, doing junior high detention together.

Ten years later, and still a hard-ass with a bad attitude, Audra didn't have many friends other than Bea, Suzi and Isabel. Most people, both back then and now, looked at her and saw imminent failure. She'd never cared, since those three were always there for her. With her dismal upbringing, she'd always considered these women her family, albeit a little dysfunctional at times. Without them, she was just a hard-ass with killer curves. They'd been the ones to show her how to *use* those curves.

She glanced over as the last member of their little party

rejoined them at the table. Slightly winded from her dance, the dark-haired woman gulped down her soda. Isabel Santos had been hanging out with Audra since they had both worn ruffled panties. Although not a member of the Wicked Chicks, Isabel had spent time with the other women off and on over the years. After school, though, Isabel had focused on her own career, while the Wicked Chicks had focused on enjoying life. At least, until Audra had the temerity to pursue an actual career.

"You're always hanging out with that Natasha chick now," Bea accused. She poked her silicone-filled bottom lip out in a practiced pout. Her newly colored titian hair framed a face that had graced a magazine cover, as Bea was always quick to point out. But the look on that face, half-sneer and half-dejection, assured Audra they were dead serious. They were kicking her out of the Wicked Chicks.

"That Natasha chick is a) my sister-in-law and b) my boss. And now she's about to launch a new lingerie line that is exclusively my designs." Which is what Audra had thought she was at the club to celebrate. Her promotion to head designer for Simply Sensual Lingerie. The achievement of her dreams.

"See, it's that kind of crap that's the problem," Suzi pointed out. "That's all we've heard this last year. You have to work. You have to study. You can't party with us because you have early classes. I thought it'd end when you graduated a few months ago, but now you're all about work instead."

"Oh, please," Audra scoffed, "like the two of you don't have jobs and responsibilities?"

Bea did tend to drift from job to job, but she always worked. Suzi cut hair in a high-end hair salon in San Francisco and Isabel's florist shop was flourishing.

"How come your jobs aren't the issue here?" Audra asked.

"*We* are able to maintain a balance between our jobs and our real lives," Suzi said in perfect imitation of an upper-class snob.

"And what am I doing?"

"You're building a career," Bea pointed out quietly. She said it as if Audra were building a weapon of mass destruction, her voice a combination of bemusement, aversion and fear.

"Why shouldn't Audra build a career? She's a great designer. This is her dream opportunity. Aren't you excited for her?" Isabel asked in a surprised tone. Her gray eyes flashed as indignation built. "Don't you guys think you're being a little unfair?"

"Fair, schmair," Suzi shot back. "Friends don't let friends blow their prime years chasing careers. That's the kind of crap you do later…after you've lost your sexual mojo."

Audra tuned out the inevitable debate between Isabel and Suzi over sexual status, aging, equal rights and staying true to friends. It was old news.

She bit back a scream. All she'd ever heard from her older brother was how her friends were trouble and would screw up her life. Isabel was always nagging her to set goals and prioritize her plans. And now she was hearing from her friends that she wasn't one of them anymore because she was trying to build a future. Not one damn person in her life was willing to simply accept her. All of her.

"I can have both a career and my friends," Audra insisted. Wasn't that the women's right of the new millennium? She could have it all? It wasn't as if Audra was looking to add a husband or anything stupid like that to the mix.

"Some career."

"I design lingerie," Audra pointed out, matching Suzi's sneer with one of her own. "That's hardly at odds with my Wicked Chick designation."

"You've always wanted to design sexy, wild lingerie," Suzi pointed out. And she'd know, since she and Bea spent years listening to Audra daydream about it, never once discouraging her.

"Instead," Suzi continued, "you settled for vanilla-sweet nighties for virginal brides."

"Everyone has to start somewhere," Isabel interjected in Audra's defense.

Before Suzi could retaliate, Bea pressed her hands to the table, bloodred nails spread like claws against the faux leather surface.

"Enough of this crap." The mellowest of them all, her distaste for the bickering and one-upmanship was clear on her face. "Audra, this is an intervention. You either prove you're still one of us, or you lose your Wicked Chick status."

Isabel gasped. "You've got to be kidding."

"Prove myself?" Oh jeez, it was junior high school all over again.

Suzi leaned forward with a challenging gleam shining in her midnight-blue eyes. "Prove yourself."

Audra rolled her eyes. "How? Outdrink you two? Dance topless on stage? Give up my job?"

Audra tossed the words out in an airy, unconcerned tone. But her insides twisted at the thought of either the first or the last. Given that she'd started her drinking in her early teens, she figured she'd done more than enough partying. That, and she'd watched what drinking had done to her mother, leaving her old and haggard-looking by forty. The booze wouldn't do Audra's skin, or her health, a bit of good. And she planned to keep both long into the future. Two drinks were her limit now, although she did a good job of hiding that from her friends.

And quit her job? Oh, God, no. She loved that job. Loved designing lingerie. She couldn't think of anything more satisfying than starting with a vision in her head, turning it into a reality and seeing a woman prance out of the boutique empowered by the result. They couldn't—wouldn't—be crazy enough to think she'd give that up.

"How about all thr—"

"No, much simpler," Bea interrupted with a dark look at the blonde. Suzi sat back with a huff and a roll of her eyes.

Audra waited. The music pounded a heavy beat around her, the cacophony of voices blending with the percussions.

"I dare you…" Bea began.

Oh, hell, she should have known.

"…to *do* the next guy to come through the door."

"This is silly," Isabel stated. Her gray eyes flashed with rare anger. She crossed her arms over her chest, her sweater pulling tight to curves she tended to hide, rather than display like the other three women. "Haven't you outgrown that silly game? I thought your club was all about empowerment, not pressure. Audra's your friend. She doesn't have to do anything to prove herself."

A voice in Audra's head agreed. She *didn't* have to. Like drinking, impersonal sex had long since lost its appeal. She could have just as good a time with her vibrator as with most guys. And at least her "D-celled" friend guaranteed she'd come. Swear to God, most guys didn't seem to know the difference between the G-spot and a parking spot.

But if she didn't, she'd be saying goodbye to something vital. Not just her friendships were on the line here, Audra realized with a start. So was her sense of self. The badass, wild part of her seemed to be fading away. And she didn't have a clue what, if anything, she'd find underneath.

"Hey, no problem. I never mind scratching that particular itch."

Ignoring Isabel's disappointed look, she gave the girls a wink, tossed back the last of her strawberry margarita and straightened her shoulders. Turning on the barstool, she leaned her elbows back on the table, faced the door and sent up a prayer that the next guy through knew how to park.

Holy cow. She eyed the sexy hunk standing in the doorway and exhaled a deep sigh of appreciation. Oh, yeah, he'd not only know how to park, but she'd bet he was hell on wheels. Audra took inventory, starting at what she estimated to be size twelve biker boots. Her gaze took a slow, appreciative tour up well-worn denim, lingering on a few particularly worn places.

Very nice.

She continued her tour over a well-defined chest and— m'm m'm good—perfect shoulders. The sleeves of the denim work shirt were rolled up to the elbows, and it was buttoned about halfway up to showcase that chest, wide and lightly dusted with a sprinkling of dark hair. How would that hair feel against her cheek? Soft and sensual? Wiry and erotic? Did it thicken as it meandered down his belly? Or did it taper to a very delicious point?

If he'd hurry up and walk through the door, she could find out. Anticipation made Audra antsy. She shifted in her seat and held her breath while her gaze rose to his face.

Oh, baby. Eyes half-mast, a wave of lust-induced appreciation crashed through her system. Now that was one hot man. Black hair tumbled around a face just this side of pretty. His full lower lip promised a sensual nature and, although she couldn't see his eyes in any detail, the man had cheekbones to die for. The only thing that saved him from being girly-pretty was a stubborn jaw and his nose, obviously broken a couple times.

"Good thing I wore my sexiest lingerie, hmm?"

Bea laughed and gave an appreciative hum. Even Isabel mouthed "wow," although the look in her eyes still screamed disapproval. Not surprising, since Isabel had never been comfortable with casual sex. At Suzi's silence, Audra glanced over. The blonde didn't look thrilled. If anything, she looked a little pouty. The rules of the dare were that neither of the others could come on to the dare guy. Which put hot, tall and sexy off limits for Suzi.

Audra couldn't resist taunting her. "One small step for him, one giant orgasm for me."

Suzi grinned and started to say something, then her eyes widened and she winced.

"Oops," Bea said under her breath.

Isabel cringed.

Stomach suddenly tight, Audra followed their gaze to the entrance where the hunk still stood in conversation with the bouncer just outside the arch that they deemed the official entrance for dares. Disappointment sunk like a chunk of lead in her stomach when she saw the source of her friends' horror. Shouldering the hunk aside was another guy. A nonhunky guy. A totally geeky, nonhunky guy. Audra's stomach turned, but did she see any way out of the dare? Not with her pride intact.

"Ya think he's got anything in that pocket protector you can get up?" Obviously trying to ease the tension, Suzi called the waitress over for a second round. "You'll need a drink before this one, Audra. My treat."

Was she supposed to be grateful?

"And as soon as you prove you've still got it in you to take a dare, maybe I'll go get myself a whole different kind of treat," Suzi mused. Audra followed her gaze to where hot, tall and sexy had taken a seat, two tables over from Audra's target. Rarely territorial over men, Audra was surprised to find that the thought of Suzi and the sexy hunk made her teeth clench.

She grimaced her thanks at the waitress and knocked back her margarita in one long gulp. Audra ran her index finger under her lower lip to make sure her lipstick wasn't smudged. Might as well get it over with. She slipped from the stool and sucked in a deep breath. A little shimmy of the shoulders to make sure everything was where it belonged, her fingertips brushed the hem of her leather mini and she let out her breath.

Isabel protested, "Audra, you don't have to go through with this. I'm sure Suzi and Bea are just riding you. You guys have been tight for years. You don't have to prove your friendship. Especially not by having random sex with some—" she grimaced at the geek "—creepy stranger."

She shot the other two women a dark look. Pink washed over Bea's cheeks and, with a half-hearted shrug, she averted her gaze.

Suzi, though, stuck out her chin.

"Hey, we never said jack about friendship. Audra knows we're all amigas. This is about being true to the Wicked Chicks code. Nobody's forcing her to re-up her membership. That's her call. *Hers.* Not yours."

With that statement, the underlying hurt and confusion in Suzi's tone, Audra realized her friends needed reassurance. This wasn't about where she stood with the Wicked Chicks. It was about where *they* stood with her.

Her friendship with Suzi and Bea was changing, sure. Did that matter?

Audra sucked in a breath. Yes, it mattered. These women were more than buddies to run around with. They were more than a part of her history. They'd accepted her, encouraged her. And, even if they were pains in the ass, they both gave her something nobody else, other than Isabel, ever had. Unconditional acceptance.

At least, they had until tonight.

The music pulsing around her, Audra knew she could shrug and—just like she'd grown out of acne, her spandex phase and the desperate anger that'd fueled her for so many years—let her ties with the other women go.

But being wicked wasn't just a designation. It defined her. She was a bad girl. From her prepubescent years under the bleachers to her wild cross-country rebellion when her father died, being bad was how she dealt with life.

Without it, what did she have left? Since she didn't know the answer, she obviously had no choice.

"I'm a lifetime member," she drawled. "Let's just hope the geek over there can handle me."

Isabel opened her mouth, probably to protest. Then, with a shrug and a sigh that summed up why she'd never quite fit in with the other women, she just rolled her eyes and sat back.

"Go get him, tiger," Bea said.

"Oh, yeah, have a great time," Suzi said with a wink.

Audra bit back a snarky response. Her gaze caught on the hunk again and she grinned. There was no rule against a nibble of an appetizer before hitting on the main course.

JESSE MARTINEZ looked around the nightclub and bit back a sigh. Purple walls were covered in teal neon lights. The dance floor was tri-level and the chrome bar wrapped around the room. The band was on break, but a deejay played Top Forty rock. Definitely not Jesse's kind of place. Crowded, loud and filled with psuedoperfect bodies, all on the make. How the hell had he ended up here?

Oh, he could blame it on work. Legitimately, he *was* on a job. But he could be back in his office with his computer. That was his job description, after all. A Cyber Crimes detective with the Sacramento PD, he wasn't required to follow dirtbags in person. He did it over the World Wide Web, instead. But, no, sucker that he was, he hadn't been able to back down from a coworker's dare that he get off his butt and get his hands dirty. Do real work. Show what he was made of. Damned if Jesse could back down from a dare, especially one couched in insults to his manhood.

He should probably work to reprogram that defective element of his personality. But since it was one of the few traits he actually appreciated having in common with his late father, he was loath to lose it.

Instead, he ended up in tacky nightclubs. Jesse sighed, but gave the waitress a smile and ordered a beer. He eyed the dorky dude a couple tables over. The guy was fidgety as hell, his fingers tapping on the table, his knee bouncing to a completely different rhythm. He looked like a virgin on a blind date with a porn queen. Or as if he were about to rob the place.

The guy's name was Dave Larson and he was a computer hacker with a taste for gambling. Jesse had it on good authority that Larson was butt deep in organized crime and determined to work his way up one of the dirtiest crime ladders in Northern California, the *Du Bing Li* Triad. Since there were any number of tasks a guy with Dave's computer skills could provide, Jesse wasn't sure just what the geek was up to. But one thing was sure, it was no good.

Which is why he'd followed him to the club.

The waitress returned with his beer. Jesse reached for his wallet when a slim hand pressed against his forearm.

"Let me get that for you."

Jesse's brain, at least the independent gentlemanly part, shut down. Apparently his vocal cords did too, because he couldn't say a word. All he could do was stare.

Temptation and pure sin, wrapped in black leather. The still functioning portion of Jesse's brain cataloged the woman's features. Huge doe eyes with a thick fringe of lashes dominated a narrow face. Shiny red lips looked as if she'd just eaten something juicy, tempting him to lean forward for a taste. Her short hair was jet-black, the spiky ends tipped with magenta.

Her body was a teenage boy's wet dream, all curves and sleek lines.

But it was her voice that had him in a trance. It was made for sex. The husky lisp brought to mind talking dirty in the dark. And he could tell in that one look, she definitely knew how to talk dirty.

The waitress snickered as she left and Jesse pulled himself together.

"Thanks for the offer, but I can handle paying for my own drink." He wished he didn't sound as if he had a stick up his ass, but that didn't appear to be happening.

A slow, wicked smile curved those sleek red lips and she leaned in close to whisper, "You look like a man who could handle just about anything."

She waited a beat, long enough for the image of just exactly how he'd like to handle her to fully form in his mind, then she leaned back and winked. "As for the drink, call it a welcome gesture. I haven't seen you in here before."

"You're here a lot, huh?" Jesse mentally groaned. Could he be any wittier? Of course she was here a lot; she obviously hadn't stumbled in on her way from a church social. For a computer geek like himself, she was the ultimate fantasy. Sexy as hell, and twice as aggressive. Not that Jesse didn't know how to please a woman in bed; he was damned good at it. But he was used to real women, flesh and blood. Not sexual goddesses such as the one standing in front of him. Close enough to touch, but totally out of reach.

"Actually I haven't been in here in, like, forever. But…" She looked left, then right, then whispered, "Shh, don't tell anyone or it'd ruin a great pickup line."

Jesse laughed with her, and just like that, she *was* within reach. He relaxed and lifted his beer to toast her.

"It'll be our little secret," he promised. "I'm Jesse."

"Audra," she said as she took his hand.

Damn. Jesse's body, all the vital parts, leaped to attention as sexual awareness surged through him at the touch of her hand in his. A hand that felt oddly delicate for a woman with such a powerful presence.

Which was closer to the real woman—the hot, sexy babe she appeared to be, or the soft, gentle woman both her fragile hand and her easy humor suggested? Unable to leave a puzzle unsolved, he knew his mind wouldn't rest until he'd figured her out. To say nothing of everything his *body* wanted to learn about her.

"The least I can do is buy you a drink in return," Jesse offered.

Her brown eyes lit up, then dimmed as her gaze slid away. "I'd love that, but I'm actually meeting someone else tonight. Blind date, of a sort, you know?"

Maybe it was ego, but he swore the regret in her voice was genuine.

"You don't sound excited."

"Hardly," she said with a laugh. She got a naughty look in her eye, shot a glance over her shoulder, then leaned close. "But you can help me."

"How?"

"A little fun, kind of like that spoonful of sugar that helps the medicine go down."

Before Jesse could laugh, she'd stepped close. So close only a bare inch separated her breasts from his forearm. Seated as he was on the stool, they were eye to eye. He automatically shifted so that his hand was on her hip, and she winked her approval.

Then she kissed him and blew his mind.

It started as a soft brush of her lips over his, just a whisper. Her breath mingled with his a moment as their eyes met, then something wild burned in hers before the thick fringe of lashes covered them. With a quick intake of breath, she slid her tongue along his lower lip. The act was so sensual in its simplicity, so seductive in its delicious temptation, Jesse almost whimpered.

Before he could respond, she stepped back and winked.

"Nice to meet you, Jesse. I'll see you later, maybe."

Fascinated, he murmured his goodbye and watched her walk away.

No maybe about it, he didn't plan to wait for later. Jesse started to slide off the barstool to follow her. Half out of his seat, he watched, baffled, as she stopped at Davey's table. She leaned across the narrow circular surface and said something that made the dork blush. Jesse watched the guy start stuttering and babbling.

With a frown, Jesse settled back on the barstool to watch. What did Audra have to do with a guy like Davey Larson? A simple blind date, like she'd said? A blind date, *of a sort?* What sort? Dave Larson was hip deep in crime, both organized and sloppy. Where did Audra come in?

Rumor had it Davey had caught the eye of the top echelon of a local crime ring. The head of that ring had a habit of using his women for deliveries. Was she the handoff? Delivery or receiving? Either way, it boded poorly for Jesse's shot at experiencing his ultimate fantasy.

A haze of jealousy blurred his vision when, instead of taking the seat opposite Davey, Audra slid around to sit next to him. Damn near in the dork's lap. When she tiptoed those delicate fingers of hers up the guy's butt-ugly tie, Jesse actually growled out loud.

Jesse watched Audra lean in close to Davey and whisper something. Whatever it was must have been a doozy, because Dave jumped as if she'd goosed him. A damp sheen coated his lanky face and his eyes bulged. Audra looped her finger through the knot on his tie and Davey skittered back. A group of partyers blocked Jesse's view. He craned his neck but could barely see the tops of their heads.

When the crowd shifted, Jesse saw Davey shaking his head like crazy. She said something, and Dave turned a little green around the gills, then jumped up from the table. Audra stared wide-eyed at him as he babbled. She was lucky not to get nailed in the face by the wild gestures the dork made. He finally ran out of steam. Mouth ajar, Audra looked stunned for a second, then said something. When Davey gave a frantic shake of his head, she held out her hand. Jesse couldn't see what she was holding, but Davey's eyes bulged in horror and he scampered away from the table, throwing one last comment over his skinny shoulder.

Jesse slid from his seat, prepared to follow Dave. He hesitated, glancing at Audra. Even with her mouth hanging open, she was the sexiest thing he'd ever seen. He debated between pursuing Dave or hooking up with Audra to find out what her connection was.

Before he could take a step toward her, though, she was surrounded by three women, their shocked expressions all matching Audra's. He eyed the blonde, redhead and brunette, but none popped up as criminals in his mental data bank. Then again, neither had Audra.

From the looks of them, the ladies would be around for a while. Davey, though, was scurrying off like a scared rat. Jesse hightailed it after the rat, but couldn't help shooting a final look of regret for the woman who'd briefly held the promise of fulfilling his every fantasy.

2

"WHAT THE HELL happened?" Suzi demanded, her voice filled with the same shock coursing through Audra's system. "I figured a geek like that would have lousy staying power, but you barely touched him."

"He didn't…" Bea gestured to her crotch area and scrunched up her face in disgust. "Just from you talking to him, did he?"

Audra squinted in question, then shuddered as Bea's meaning sank in. "Eww, no."

"Then why'd he run?"

Audra opened her mouth, then closed it with a baffled shake of her head. Her fingers clenched the strip of fabric in her hand. She had no clue. She'd made plenty of guys tremble over the years, but she'd never made one run before. When her friends had first started spouting off that she wasn't a Wicked Chick anymore, it had been easy to ignore them.

But now? Audra's breath hitched. Were they right? Was she losing it?

"I think he mistook me for someone else," Audra finally admitted. "He babbled a few things I didn't understand and when I suggested we get to know each other better, he ran like a sissy-lala."

Isabel took the tie from her, grimacing at the ugly green piece of patterned polyester.

Suzi flicked the flimsy fabric and wrinkled her nose. "Nice souvenir, Audra," she said. "What're you going to do with it?"

"I have no clue," she admitted. "I've rendered men dumb before, but none have ever hit the level of idiocy this guy did. I flirted, he babbled. I finally resorted to complimenting that ugly tie. He promptly ripped it off and tossed it at me just before he ran off like a scaredy-cat."

They all stared at the offense to fashion.

"Does this mean you failed the dare?" Suzi asked in a breathy tone of shock.

Audra's gaze shot to hers. Failed?

"She didn't fail," Bea snapped. "She isn't to blame if a guy can't keep it up. He obviously had issues and ran."

But Audra saw it in her friend's eyes. Even Isabel's held a faint glint of that dreaded emotion.

Pity.

Audra had failed. The first Wicked Chick to blow a dare.

"You're right, that wasn't failure," Suzi finally agreed. "Who knows, maybe he's not into chicks or something."

Bea gave a snort of laughter and shrugged. "So we, what? Chalk it up to a first? Wanna get another round of drinks and dance?"

Audra realized her friends would let it go then. They'd pushed the dare as a means to prove she hadn't moved on. That she was still one of the girls.

But now? Now she had something to prove to *herself.*

"Hey, I'm not done yet," she told them. "You dared me, I need to fulfill the dare."

"How?" Isabel wanted to know.

"New dare?" Bea suggested with a shrug.

"Like?" Audra asked.

"Simple," Suzi claimed. "You do the *next* guy to come through the door."

Audra sucked in a breath, ignored the voice in the back of her head claiming she was so over this dare crap, and nodded. Over it or not, she has something to prove. She eyed the tie as Isabel glanced at the ugly thing, then at Audra's tiny purse. With a grimace, her friend tucked it into her own hobo bag.

Audra glanced around for Jesse. Gone. At least he hadn't witnessed her failure. She didn't know why it mattered, but it did. Shoving the thought aside, she focused on the entryway and hoped to hell the next guy through the door wasn't a bigger geek than the one who'd just run away. It was probably asking too much for him to be as hot as the appetizer she'd enjoyed earlier.

JESSE SHOULDERED his way through the crowd waiting to enter the club and looked around for Davey. He didn't have to look far. The geek was huddled over his cell phone a few feet from the entrance, obviously waiting for a valet to bring his car around.

Jesse sidled closer, staying out of the guy's line of vision, until he could hear the one-sided conversation over the noise of the crowd.

"Look, I did my part. I passed the info to your bimbo. When do I get my money?"

Jesse leaned a shoulder against the building and let out a sigh. Not only could Audra undoubtedly talk dirty enough to have a man begging for release…she was dirty. As in, criminally dirty.

Damn.

He listened with half an ear as Davey negotiated fund transfers and time frames. He'd be able to track the payoff through Dave's computer, no problem.

Which meant he was that much closer to solving the case. At least, a part of the case. He'd come to realize in the last few days that Dave Larson was a small piece of a much larger puzzle.

And Jesse wanted the bigger picture. And the promotion that would come with it.

Hell, he was twenty-eight. His late father had already made lieutenant by this age. Of course, Jesse had spent four years earning his degree in computer science, but he should still be farther up the food chain.

This case, the undercover work and proving he could step outside his cozy computer world would seal that promotion for him.

And prove once and for all that he was just as good a cop as his father had been. He grimaced. Being the son of a legend was definitely a pain in the ass.

He watched Davey slide into his car. From the grin on the kid's face, he must've overtipped the valet. Jesse debated following him, but there wasn't much point. He could track the payoff money easily enough by computer.

Right now he needed to connect with the next level. Which meant Audra. He remembered the taste of those luscious red lips beneath his with pleasure. Some days he loved his job.

Anticipation spinning through his system, he reentered the club. His gaze sought out the table where she'd met the geek. She was still there, surrounded by friends.

When their eyes met, hers grew huge and she ran her tongue over her lower lip before flashing a delighted smile. She murmured something and three other sets of eyes glanced his way, varying degrees of naughty smiles on the women's faces.

With a look filled with sexual promise, combined with an unexplained gratitude that made his body go on full alert, Audra slid from the barstool in a slow, sexy move. Would she do everything with the same deliberate sensuality? Would he find out?

No. She was now a suspect. A criminal. His key to breaking this case.

But as she walked toward him, the last thing on his brain was the case. His gaze traced long, sleek legs encased in sheer black hose, and his fingers itched to glide up their silky length.

Jesse realized with a sinking heart that after years of wondering if he had any more in common with his late father than their coloring, he'd just found proof positive. Good ole dad had not only had a penchant for dares, he'd had a taste for women who spelled trouble. God knew, this was a rotten time for the grand discovery. Because this woman definitely spelled trouble, in glowing neon letters.

"Looks like it's later already," she said when she reached him. He smiled in response to the humor in her husky tone.

"What happened to your date?" he fished. "It didn't look like it went well."

"Oh." She glanced back at the table where her friends watched. She pressed her lips together, then shrugged. "You saw that, huh?"

"Bits and pieces. So that was your blind date?" He held his breath. If she admitted it was a business association, he could haul her in for questioning.

"Of a sort," she replied.

Damn it.

"A sort, huh?"

"Yeah, a sort." She hesitated, then gave a one-shouldered shrug. "You know, more like a dare. You ever get suckered into a dare? There is just no way out."

"Believe me, I know all about dares."

"Then you know how humiliating it is to back down from one, don't you?" As she spoke, Audra shifted so she stood between his legs. He wanted to pull her against him, to feel her body give way to the straining flesh pressing against his now too-tight jeans. She traced a finger over his mouth.

Jesse's lip tingled, and it was all he could do to keep from pulling that finger into his mouth and sucking on it. He was a passionate man—it was in his blood—but he'd never experienced this level of deep, dark excitement.

"Oh, yeah, a dare refused is a guarantee of humiliation," he agreed.

"Sometimes a dare accepted holds the same guarantee."

Was she talking about her deal with Davey? Larson could be involved in anything from credit card fraud to identity theft. What had he passed to Audra? Jesse was going to have to find out.

"It sounds like you're an expert on dares," he said.

Something dimmed the sparkle in her huge brown eyes. To Jesse, it looked like a combination of indecision and reluctance. Her gaze slid past him, a frown quirked her brow, and then she puffed out a little sigh.

"How about we blow this joint? Find a little privacy and get to know each other better?"

His mouth went so dry, Jesse couldn't reply. Instead, he nodded.

Desire ripping through him like a jagged knife, he followed Audra out of the nightclub, his gaze glued on the tantalizing sway of her leather-clad hips.

Jesse told himself he was just playing along for the case. He had to follow her to find out what she knew. That was all. He didn't intend to let it get out of hand.

But for the first time in his six-year career as a cop, he wondered if he could keep his pants on long enough to arrest a woman before having desperate, mind-blowing sex with her.

AUDRA WELCOMED the warm evening air after the stifling, sticky heat of the club. Her ears still ringing from the loud music, she took in a few deep breaths and wished for a breeze.

"Did you want to go somewhere? Get something to eat or some coffee?" Jesse offered. His hand warmed her hip as he shifted to protect her from being jostled by the partyers shoving past them to leave the club.

Did she want to go anywhere? Audra eyed the hunk at her side and puffed out a breath. He was hot, no question about it. But more, he had a layer of sweetness that had her alternating between wanting to hug him close and lick him all over. The latter boded well for her current predicament, the former was better avoided.

After all, thanks to that crazy man who'd freaked out over her offer to get friendly, Jesse had become her new dare. Not that she was proud to have the first failed dare chalked up under her name. But at least that failure came with a sweet reward. She eyed Jesse in delight. He'd make this dare a pleasure.

All she had to do was focus on the rush of sexual energy arcing between them like a rainbow, a bone-melting orgasm the promised reward. And ignore the spark of emotion, the weird desire to get to know him better. After a year of watching her brother and his bride grow closer, she'd probably just picked up on their couple vibe. Like a virus, that kind of thing could only be dangerous to her health, though. So she'd ignore it.

"How about we find someplace quiet," she suggested with a wink, "and see what comes up?"

From the widening of those delicious coffee-brown eyes, he got her message. The heat there told her he was all for it, but then his gaze shifted, became more reserved.

"There's a little coffee shop nearby," he countered. "We can order something to drink, maybe a piece of pie, and talk?"

He was kidding, right? Audra stopped and looked closer. There was a hint of color on his cheeks, but that could just be the neon lights. He was gorgeous, no question about that. And sexy as hell, but he didn't seem used to the club scene. Was he playing hard to get? Or was he one of those? A fabled good boy?

She squinted, taking in his shadowed jawline, his crooked nose, and the slight frown between his heavy brows. She couldn't tell for sure. After all, she'd never known a good boy.

"Wouldn't you rather go somewhere a little more private?" she asked.

He closed his eyes for a second, as if in prayer, then opened them and gave her a tight smile. "Let's talk a little first, huh?"

From the stiff set of his shoulders, he didn't mean dirty talk. Intrigued by the novelty, Audra smiled and nodded. "Okay, then. Your car or mine?"

"It's close. We can walk."

Audra laughed aloud. "Walk?" She lifted one foot to show off the four-inch heels of her spiked black pumps and pointed her toe. "These feet have been known to do many things," she paused suggestively, "but they don't walk any farther than necessary."

"Aren't you concerned about getting into a car with a strange man? A beautiful woman like yourself needs to be cautious."

From someone else, that might have sounded patronizing. Jesse, though, seemed genuinely concerned. His gaze locked on hers, warmth and sincerity clear in the brown depths. She noted the protective hand on her hip, not groping or sliding down her butt, but simply keeping her from being jostled.

Something warmed in Audra. Nobody had ever shown concern for her before. It felt…odd. A good kind of odd, though. Could he really be that sweet?

She gave him a warm smile and said, "I'm used to taking care of myself, promise. I'm a good judge of character and I fight nasty." The can of Mace in her purse didn't hurt, either. "Nobody tries anything with me I don't want without regretting it."

He gave a contemplative nod, but didn't try to pull any macho crap by arguing or trying to prove he was tough. Audra's respect rose a few notches. How wild. She was really liking this guy. She just might want to see if this dare could lead to something more.

Depending on his performance on her "O" scale, of course.

"Let's take my car," she suggested. "I prefer the driver's seat."

She slid her hand in his and shivered a little at the hard strength of his palm and long, narrow fingers.

"So," he said as they made their way to the parking lot, "that guy didn't look like your type."

Audra looked at the milling partiers in confusion. "Which guy?"

"The one in the club back there. You know, the dorky guy you had the 'sort of' date with."

"Oh, him. No, he's definitely not my type." Audra suppressed a shudder. What a geek.

"Do you have to deal with that a lot? I'd think a woman as gorgeous as you are wouldn't need blind dates."

"You know how that goes. You have to kiss a lot of toads before you nail a prince."

Thanks to the geek—or Dave, as he'd introduced himself—being a nervous wreck, she'd lucked out and wouldn't be locking lips with any toads tonight.

Would she be nailing this prince, though? Audra gave Jesse the once-over out of the corner of her eye. He sure looked like a prince. Hot, sexy and ready to be crowned.

They reached her car and she dropped Jesse's hand to fish through her purse for her keys.

"I'll bet you're going to have a few things to say to whatever *supposed* friend set you up, huh?"

"Why?"

"What kind of friend sets you up with a loser?"

"The kind who think they know best and are afraid I might break away from the gang."

"Gang?"

Audra frowned at the edge of cynicism in his tone. "Gang, club. You know, a group you hang with regularly? I take it you're not into clubs," she asked with a tilt of her head.

"I'm not into anything that pushes me to do things I'm uncomfortable doing."

She pursed her lips and gave him a long look. She'd bet she could push him to do quite a few things he hadn't been comfortable with before. And have him thanking her afterward. But she wasn't the kind to give away secrets, so she just smiled and gave a dismissive, one-shouldered shrug.

"Your date with that dork wasn't your idea, I take it?"

Audra grimaced. "Not hardly. More like I gave in to pressure and my need to keep my standing with my friends. And almost ended up with a very regrettable evening. Although—" she clicked the lock button on her key fob "—I have to say I came out the winner here. If not for them, I wouldn't be here with you, would I?"

Audra turned and in a smooth, easy move, pinned Jesse between her body and the car. She almost purred aloud. Even in heels, he still towered over her, the hard length of his body inviting her to lean into his warmth. Very nice. This dare was turning into pure pleasure, no longer a means to prove her Wicked Chick status to her friends. She wanted to get closer to Jesse. Just for herself.

With her slowest, most seductive smile, she watched him from under her fringe of lashes. His eyes had that slightly glazed look that assured her he liked the feel of her body against his. She shimmied a little, just to be sure she had his attention.

As she slid her free hand up his biceps, this time she did

purr aloud. "Yum. You're in fabulous shape. What do you do for a workout?"

"A little weights, some martial arts," he replied, his attention more on her caresses than her question. Both hands settled lightly on her hips, clenched, then gripped her curves fully. "So what made you pick this club tonight?"

"Hmm? Wild Thing? It's a fun place, one of the best in Sacramento. I'd planned a little celebration, although it didn't turn out quite the way I'd hoped. But I think you're the perfect celebratory present to myself."

Audra wrapped her arms around his neck and leaned further into his welcoming body. She brushed her lips over his, more a teasing temptation than a real kiss. Heated excitement swirled through her, making sensation spiral from her lips to the damp center between her legs. God, if he got her this turned on with barely a kiss, how would she feel when he put his hands on her? When he put his mouth on her body?

Desire was edged with impatience. She wanted to know. She had to know. She was sure Jesse would be a delicious lover. The kind that rated at least an eight on her "O" scale. She'd yet to find a perfect ten, but a solid eight could definitely be coached.

Backing off a little, she leaned her head back to see what he'd do. How he'd react.

"That's not much of a present," he commented.

Then he took her mouth. Took it in a way she'd only dreamt of before. His hands, gentle yet firm, cupped her head and held her where he wanted. Just for his pleasure. He nibbled at the corners of her mouth softly. Then, as she was smiling at the sweetness of it, he plunged his tongue between her lips in a swift, powerful move.

She was so used to being the aggressor that for the first couple of seconds she remained passive out of surprise. Then, pleasure shooting through her like an arrow, she met his tongue with hers in a dance of sexual delight.

Audra clenched her thighs to intensify the sensation. More. She definitely wanted more from this man.

"Wait," he breathed, breaking away from her mouth. "We should get to know each other better. You know, talk or something."

"I vote for 'or something.'"

"Did you say you got stuck on an almost sort-of date with that dork because your friend threatened you?" he asked, his words coming in a gasp as she pressed the beaded tips of her breasts against his chest. "Doesn't sound like much of a club to me."

"They're just worried about me."

Maybe they had reason to worry, too. Audra hadn't realized she wasn't much interested in meaningless sex and constant partying until tonight's fiasco. After all, at twenty-five, she was damned hot, exciting and interesting, even if she didn't get as wild as she used to. Maybe a part of her—deep inside— worried there wasn't any more to her than her bad girl persona. But as a rule, she tended to ignore that snarky worrying part. Even when snarky turned to screaming, as it had tonight.

"You know how it is when you get in tight with friends, people who've known you, like, most of your life? They want you to stay in their tidy box, keep with their perception of you. Sometimes you have to pacify them with proof you're still a part of the gang, you know?"

To distract them both, she pulled away a bit to run her hands up the delicious, hard expanse of his chest. "Why are we wasting time talking about this? Let's move on to more exciting subjects. Like, say, how you look naked?"

3

JESSE SWORE his heart stopped. All blood rushed from his head to his…well, other head. Damn, he'd never been as turned on or as unable to do anything about it as he was right this minute. Audra, with her promise of hot, sticky-sweet pleasure, was technically off-limits.

But her hands were doing incredible things to his body. Long, delicate fingers traced a path from his shoulders, over his nipples and down to his belt. Jesse wanted to say screw police procedure and guide those fingers lower. He breathed in the rich scent of her perfume and tried to remember she was still a suspect.

And after her comments, especially her confession of gang affiliation, Jesse knew she was Davey's crime ring connection. And it was his job to find out exactly how she fit into the organization and use it to break the case. He might prefer to do that job behind a computer, but there were definite benefits to this unfamiliar fieldwork. The temptation of Audra's body pressed against his was proving to be an almost irresistible benefit.

"So tonight was the first time you'd met that guy?" he asked. "He seemed a little overwhelmed when he saw you."

Not that Jesse was surprised there. Davey was a dork, sure. But Audra was the kind of woman that would overwhelm any guy, present company included.

"He was a bit freaked, I guess," Audra said distractedly. Her attention was focused on the soft, damp kisses she was scattering over his jaw and throat. Jesse's eyes fluttered shut as his body, already turned on by their kiss and the feel of her pressed against him, went into overdrive when she reached the open collar of his shirt and trailed her tongue across his collarbone.

"Why don't we take this inside," she suggested in that husky lisp.

"Back in the club?" Maybe that would be safer? She'd still be temptation in spiked heels, but at least he'd have a crowd to remind him why taking those heels off to nibble on her toes was a bad idea.

"In the car."

His eyes flew open. He looked at her. Huge doe eyes stared back at him. Her lips were damp, a sleek, succulent red and it was all he could do not to sink into their ripe promise. He tore his gaze from her mouth to glance at her compact silver car.

"That's a little cramped, don't you think?"

"Let's find out."

With that, she nudged him aside and tugged the passenger door of her toy-like convertible open.

"I think this probably isn't such a good idea."

Audra tilted her head to the side and arched one perfect brow. "No? I think it's a great idea. I think maybe you're just a little…reserved." She pressed against him again until he felt the edge of the door frame against his calves. "I think maybe you're not used to being seduced."

"Is that what you're doing? Seducing me?"

Had he ever been seduced? Jesse flipped through his mental database of his past encounters. He'd had his share of flings, a few deeper relationships and one lady he'd been serious enough about to bring home to meet the family. He wouldn't call any of the women repressed, by any means. But, he realized, he'd always been the aggressor. The go-to-it guy.

He couldn't remember ever being in the passive role of seducee. Most women he'd been with were happy to let him lead. Hell, he'd discovered getting a woman to even voice what turned her on was a major accomplishment. And Audra wanted to seduce him? Oh, yeah, baby.

"I'll bet I can seduce you with words alone," she suggested softly.

"Just words?"

"Just words. You, of course, are free to touch. I, though, won't use anything but my voice."

Jesse grinned. That sounded safe enough. Her touch, he was sure he couldn't resist. But words? Hell, words wouldn't be a problem for him.

"You're on," he said.

"Have a seat, then." She gestured to the open door.

Jesse sat, swinging his long legs into the small car. He was enveloped in her scent, seeped as it was into the smooth leather seats and gunmetal interior. Giving him an excellent view of her smooth cleavage under the neckline of her top, Audra leaned down. Her face almost in his crotch, she reached between his legs. Jesse's jeans grew tight and he caught his breath as anticipation hammered through him. "What happened to just voice?"

She turned her head, the parking lot lights making the magenta tips of her hair glow. She gave him a grin and he heard a click. Then the seat slid back. She rose with a wink and, leaning across him so her breasts were at eye level, she flicked off the interior light.

"Just making sure you're comfortable," she said. Then with a twist, a little shimmy in that tight black leather dress, she sat on his lap so that her back was to the driver's seat and her deliciously long legs were resting on the open door's armrest.

The nearest light was a half dozen or so cars away, and the parking lot deserted, so they had the illusion of privacy. But it wasn't private, and the door was wide open. Maybe if Jesse repeated that to himself a few dozen times, he could find the strength to care.

The temptation of those legs, encased in silky black stockings, was too much for him. Reveling in the feel of her toned limbs, he slid his hand down her thigh.

"Mmm, you have good hands. I'll bet you can work wonders with those fingers of yours." She laid her hand over his and guided it back up her thigh, just to the edge of the butter-soft leather hem. A hem that was inches, bare inches, from the promise of heaven between those glorious thighs. "I'd like to feel those hands on my body. You could start by unzipping my dress. All I'd have to do is stand up and it would slide to the ground, leaving me in silky little bits of nothing."

"Computers," he blurted.

"Beg your pardon?"

"I work with computers. That's how I keep my fingers limber." And how he'd dulled his social skills. Damn, could he sound any more stupid? Maybe he could sweet-talk her with some HTML code next? "Are you much into computers?"

Maybe that was her link with crime ring? Although with Davey on board, they probably didn't need any hacking help, as the dork was second only to Jesse himself in computer expertise. Nah, she had to be the handoff.

"Computers? I know about enough to turn one on."

"I'll bet you do," he murmured.

"I suppose that explains it," she mused.

He gave her a questioning look.

"Under that hunky exterior, you've got a brainy thing going on."

"Brainy?" Dammit, why brainy? Not that he sucked at attracting women, but there was always that layer of intellectual connection. His family was dead set on reducing him to a brain, albeit a handy brain when they needed heavy furniture moved. His coworkers and captain in Cyber Crimes valued his brains, counted on them to break the hardest cases. But the last thing he wanted to be noted for when he had the sexiest women he'd ever met in his lap was what was in his head. At least, not the one on his shoulders.

But, hunky? He knew it was immature, but his biceps clenched to support his hunk title. He could live with hunky.

"Yeah, you have a look in your eyes that tells me you think things through. Which is good. That means you'll think long and hard—" she paused for effect, then to punctuate her point, she wiggled her butt just a little "—about doing any job the best you can."

"Well, yeah. I do take pride in doing my best."

"I'll bet you do. Someone with that thoughtfulness, that attention to detail, you're sure to hit at least a seven, maybe even an eight, on the orgasm scale."

"Orgasm scale?" It was as if she'd posted a challenge sign. His testosterone demanded he grab that gauntlet and prove his manhood. "What's the scale? One to eight?"

Audra placed her fingers, just the tips, on the back of his hand and slid it under the edge of her skirt. Then she leaned close so he could feel her warm, sweet breath on his face. "Ten, baby. The top of the scale is a ten."

"What's the criteria for placement on this scale of yours?" He stifled a groan when he realized those luscious black hose covering her long legs stopped at the top of her thighs. He traced the rough, lacy band and told himself mewling pitifully would probably not rate high on her scale.

"Visual stimulation is the first step," she explained, her

husky lisp stimulating him more than most women could with a naked body and a can of whipped cream. "A look across the room, the sexual energy that sparks between two people when their eyes meet."

He slid his index finger under the band of her stockings, imagining how it'd feel to roll the silky fabric down her thighs, leaving her flesh bare for his lips.

"Do you know how it is when you meet someone's eyes, and your body responds sexually? For a man, you might get a little hard, might feel your muscles tighten. Me, I get damp. Damp is always a good sign in climbing the orgasm scale."

"I'll admit, I did get hard when our eyes met," he said.

She smiled her approval, obviously delighted he was willing to play along.

"Why don't you find out if I got damp?"

"We're a little past the meeting-of-the-eyes stage," he reminded her.

"Then why don't you see if I'm wet?"

Jesse couldn't resist. He slid his fingers higher on her thigh, brushing the tips over the lacy fabric of her panties. He groaned aloud. Wet. Deliciously wet.

"See, you're well on your way to an eight."

"I'm sure I can hit higher than an eight on that particular scale," he assured her fervently.

"Babe, nobody's gotten higher than an eight. That fabled ten on the orgasm scale is a myth."

"Then why not lower the scale?"

"Please," she insisted with a haughty look only a woman confident in her sexual worth could pull off. "Why would I lower my standards?"

Good point. Jesse grinned. It was a challenge he couldn't resist.

He leaned over and took her mouth with his.

And lost himself in the dark delight she offered. Pure sex, with that underlying sweet humor. She was his ultimate fantasy. When she sucked his tongue into her mouth, Jesse realized his fantasies were about to upgrade.

Audra's fingers brushed his skin like little electric shocks as she slipped the buttons of his shirt free. He nudged the elastic band of her panties aside to delight in her wet folds. When she scraped her fingernail over his nipple, an intense wave of desire washed over him and all thought fled.

With his fingers between her legs, his tongue working her mouth, Jesse gave himself over to a single goal. Bringing her that orgasm.

"Mmm," she moaned as he nibbled his way over the curves flowing out the top of her leather bodice. "I am so glad you came into the club tonight."

Club. Davey. The case. Dammit. Jesse lifted his head and blinked, shocked for some reason to realize they were still in the parking lot. A freaking parking lot, for God's sake. With a suspect of his case.

"I can't," Jesse said with a quick breath.

With not only his virtue, but his ethics on the line, he pulled back and shifted Audra so she was curled in his arms. And more importantly, so she was angled so he couldn't put his hand back up her skirt.

"Can't? Babe, you're hard enough to shoot for level nine if you tried. Believe me, I have faith you can."

Oh, God. Damned right he could. He was so hard, just the feel of her ass pressed against him was almost more pressure than he could stand. But he was pushing boundaries already. No way was he crossing that particular line.

"No condom," he claimed in desperation. "I don't have protection."

"Is that all?" Audra gave him a sultry smile that blurred

those ethical lines again. She reached behind her for the tiny purse she'd tossed on the driver's seat and did a quick finger rifle through it. Obviously not finding what she wanted, she upended the contents. Coming up empty, she frowned and gave a little shrug as she pulled open her wallet.

While she peered through the little pockets, Jesse eyed the disarray, looking for whatever Davey boy had given her. Lipstick, mints, a clear change purse holding a twenty and some coins. He spied her driver's license. Perfect.

"Wow, you look good," he said, slipping the small plastic card from the seat. He mentally patted himself on the back for such a sly move. "I thought crappy driver's license pictures were some kind of law."

"Laws aren't really rules, they're more like guidelines," Audra joked. Jesse cringed at her attitude but didn't figure he had room to take her to task, since he'd obviously broken a few ethical laws of his own. The underlying tightness in her voice distracted him from the pleasure of self-flagellation.

"And you aren't big on guidelines?" he asked with a frown. Frustrated with the lack of physical evidence of her connection to Davey, he told himself to get back in cop mode. Jesse memorized her full name, address and license number.

"Sure I am. It's a lot easier to break the rules if you know the guidelines first," she said with a wicked grin.

"Knowledge is the first step of preparation, huh?"

"Sure. And a Wicked Chick is always prepared." She leaned back toward the driver's seat and flipped open the glove box. She quickly shuffled through the messy pile of papers and frowned. "I have to have one in here."

She moved from shuffling papers to tossing them on the floor. "What the hell? How can I not have one? It's the Wicked Chicks number one rule. The only way to play safe is bring your own protection."

"I thought rules were more like guidelines." As soon as the words were out, Audra pinned him with a laser glare. Jesse winced. Maybe his sisters were right. Maybe he did always find the perfectly wrong thing to say.

Either way, he felt as if he'd been saved from a long fall off a very jagged cliff. He'd just ignore the part of him that was screaming in frustration at being denied that fall. Eight, his ass. He'd have shown her nine, easy. Ten, if he could use props and toys.

But that wasn't an option. At least, not right now. First he had to clear her or, if she was too involved with Dave Larson's current crimefest, bust her.

"To be honest, I'm not usually the kind of guy who gets that friendly on the first date."

Audra just continued to look at him, frustration and something deeper reflected in her eyes.

"I'd like to get together sometime, maybe a date?" Somewhere with a better setting for interrogation. First he'd do a little research, see if he could ferret out her connections. And practice the art of the cold shower.

"A date?"

"Yeah, you know, two people, out in public, getting to know each other."

"Sure. 'Cause guys are always interested in dating a woman they didn't get laid with, right?" she asked with a curl of her lip.

"Hey, what kind of guy do you think I am? I'm interested in you for more than sex."

"Sure," she repeated. With a wiggle that made him want to beg, she used her foot to push wide the partially open car door and slid off his lap to stand outside the car. As Jesse painfully unfolded himself from the vehicle, she reached into her purse and pulled out a piece of paper.

"Tell you what, here's my business card. You go ahead and give me a call, we'll do that date."

Jesse read it. Audra Walker, Simply Sensual Lingerie. Designer. "Lingerie, huh?"

"Oh, yeah, lingerie. And I'm damned good. Give me that call, I'll model some for you."

Maybe it wasn't too late to climb back in the car? He'd make do without intercourse. They could skip the whole condom issue.

She swung the car door shut and leaned against the fender. Smoothing her hands over her hips, she winked. "Don't forget the condom, huh?"

EVEN AS A BAD GIRL, lies didn't come easy to Audra. She hadn't been able to admit another failure, so when she'd sashayed back into the club, she'd smiled and let her friends assume she'd done the deed.

Five blood-pumping dances and an order of nachos hadn't blunted her sexual frustration. Finally tired of the unearned congratulations from Suzi and Bea, and the unspoken judgment of Isabel, she'd told the girls she was heading out. It would've been a clean break if not for the fact that she was Isabel's ride home.

Now, with her oldest friend in the passenger seat next to her, Audra flew down the freeway toward Auburn and the small neighborhood they'd grown up in.

Unlike Suzi and Bea, Isabel was into the whole focus-on-building-a-career thing. She'd taken over her parents' florist shop and was looking for ways to turn it from a small-town posey-pusher into one of the area's prominent florists.

Audra and Isabel had grown up next door to each other, both living over their parents' business. That Isabel had lived over the florist and Audra over a bar probably played into their personalities a bit. As a child, Isabel had been quiet, sweet and a little pudgy. Audra? She'd always been trouble.

Somehow, the two balanced each other out, though.

"Congratulations again on netting that deal with the mall," Audra said, remembering Isabel's earlier news. "You've been trying to snag that account for almost a year now. That's great that it finally came together."

They shared a smile. It was obviously a night to celebrate career achievements. Then Audra remembered the by-product of her latest achievement, her failure to live up to the code of the Wicked Chicks, and her mouth drooped.

"There's nothing wrong with being ambitious, Audra," Isabel said, obviously misreading her expression and figuring her frustration was career-focused. After all, for Isabel, most things were. "You worked your butt off going to school full-time and working in the boutique, too. You deserved to celebrate your success."

"Designing vanilla fluff."

"Oh, c'mon. Don't let that kind of defeatist thinking take hold. You have to start somewhere. How many people can claim the title of head designer right out of school? So you're not creating quite the kind of thing you want. Put in your time, pay your dues, and you'll be there soon enough."

Audra lifted her chin and pulled back her shoulders. Right. She'd get there. Damned if she wouldn't.

"Did you want to read that book I was telling you about yesterday?" Isabel asked, referring to the latest motivational tome she'd discovered. Audra had to hand it to her friend: Isabel was just as confident and determined to make her business a success as the Wicked Chicks were to live life to the fullest.

"Nah, I'll let you read it and give me the rundown, as always," Audra said with a wink.

Instead of her usual nod of agreement, Isabel frowned.

"You know," she said hesitantly, "you might want to read it yourself. Maybe it'd help you figure out why you agreed to debase yourself with meaningless sex, just for the sake of a girls' club you've outgrown."

"Debase?" Audra asked, ignoring the club reference, "What's so debasing about doing a hot, sexy guy?" Now, if she'd had to do that geek, well, that would've been beyond debasing. But Jesse? Her mouth still watered at the memory of his fingers, his lips. Oh, God. His tongue. She squirmed in her seat and shook her head at Isabel. "Look, I like sex. Just because you're trying out this chastity thing doesn't mean my choices are wrong."

"But this wasn't your choice, Audra. Why do you let them push you into those dares? I thought you said you were glad you'd grown out of that type of thing."

Audra's jaw worked. So what if she'd backslid a little? It wasn't just that Suzi and Bea were two of her closest friends. Her image, the sexy persona she'd developed in her teens, defined her. It made her special. Made her more than the pitiful little castoff of dismal parents who fought over her custody. Not over who got to keep her, but over who *had* to keep her.

It gave her control. Over herself, her life, the people around her. Isabel just didn't get that. She had two parents who adored her, who thought she'd hung the moon. Sure, she'd dealt with her share of crap growing up. But not like Audra.

Unlike the Wicked Chicks, Isabel preferred to stay in the background, to live the quiet life. In a lot of ways, it was amazing she and Audra had been able to maintain their friendship all these years.

Especially in the face of snotty-ass attitudes like she was currently copping.

"Look, Audra, I'm not judging you."

At Audra's sneer, she shrugged and admitted, "Okay, maybe a little. But that's just, you know…me. I don't get the whole sex-without-emotions thing."

"Emotions can't be trusted. Not when it comes to men," Audra stated adamantly as she pulled off the freeway. She'd learned that the hard way. The only guy she even considered semireliable was her brother. And that was more because she trusted his wife than out of any deep faith in him sticking around.

"Think of guys like dessert. Some you want to spend a lot of time on, savor. Get to know, maybe try a few more times to see if they're as good as you remember. Others are like M&M's. Quick, easy and clean. An easy between-meal treat that satisfies, but isn't really worth remembering afterward."

Isabel's laughter gurgled out, as Audra had intended. She glanced over and gave her friend a wink. Isabel rolled her eyes and shrugged. They'd been through over this same ground too many times before. They knew the drill.

Audra focused on negotiating streets she knew like the back of her hand. Finally, she pulled up in front of the small building that housed Isabel's flower shop and her apartment above. Audra's gaze landed on the neon lights flashing beer logos in the windows of the Good Times Sports Bar.

The difference in the two was as glaring-bright. Audra's brother, Drew, had taken over the bar after their father died. He'd put some effort into cleaning it up, but it was still a bar. Its edgy brick facade was in sharp contrast to the pale green florist shop with its apricot trim and flower-filled window boxes.

It was above that bar Audra had learned to set her goals, bust her ass and stand up for herself.

"So…what was this guy?" Isabel asked. "Tiramisu or M&M's?"

After barely a taste, she'd bet he was tiramisu all the way.

Since Wicked Chicks didn't admit failure, Audra gave her friend a wink and her naughtiest grin.

"Let's just say it would be my pleasure to try another taste of him," she drawled.

"It's probably just as well you won't," Isabel advised as she gathered her bag and opened the car door. "You need to focus on your career. This is no time to let some three-course dessert pull you off track."

"Hey, when have I ever let a guy matter enough to distract me from anything?"

As soon as the words were out of her mouth, Audra winced. While that would have worked with Suzi or Bea, Isabel knew Audra's history as well as her own. Once upon a time, Audra had thought love might exist. She'd believed a guy was more important than she was and had gladly handed him her dreams on a silver platter. Too bad he hadn't been interested enough to even lift the lid.

Luckily, her friend didn't press her advantage. She just patted Audra's hand where it rested on the gearshift knob and slid out of the car.

"Oh, hey, I almost forgot your souvenir." Isabel grinned and pulled a long strip of tacky green fabric from her bag. The tie. Audra took it with a wince. Ugly.

Isabel's grin faded as she shut the car door with a little wave. "You're there, Audra. Staring success in the face. Don't blow it."

Audra rolled her eyes and, without a word, slammed the car in gear and shot away from the curb.

Tension flamed its way over her shoulders and down her neck. And no wonder. She'd been fighting to prove herself all freaking night. Sure, she'd convinced her friends to chill out.

The cost? Instead of celebrating the first step of achieving her dreams, she was now wrestling with a pack of doubts. To say nothing of feeling overwhelmed by what could only be described as an identity crisis.

At this rate, she'd soon be one of those boring goody-goodys who worked all week for someone else's glory. Then spent Saturday night home alone. Maybe a pint of Chunky Monkey for company. Her friends would drop her a line now and then, a pity call for old times sake.

She was worried. Hell, she should be worried.

And yet all she could think about was whether or not she'd ever hear from Jesse again to finish what they'd started.

Maybe Isabel had a point?

4

AT HER DRAWING TABLE Monday morning, Audra stared at the design she was supposed to be finishing. Instead, she'd been sitting here, staring, for over an hour. Blocked. She'd never been blocked before. But now, she looked at the sketch of a white silk chemise and all she saw was blah, boring, vanilla.

Had she sold out? Had she put the idea of building a career, of making a name for herself in the lingerie design business, ahead of her individuality? Hell, did she even have individuality anymore? The things she'd counted on most of her life seemed to be slipping away. Her friends, her wicked persona. Her sexy attitude and ability to wow a guy speechless.

She eyed the tie she'd tossed on her table and rolled her eyes. Well, maybe she hadn't lost the speechless thing. That geek hadn't been able to weave three words together.

Audra looked at the wall over her table, sketches for the fall line in various stages of completion tacked across it. Some were, yes…vanilla. But only a couple. Most were hot. Empowering. An invitation for a woman to embrace her sensuality, to dress herself up in a way that would guarantee she felt strong and sexy.

Dammit, she was proud of those designs.

For a girl with few standout traits—at least, ones she wanted to market—the acclaim and attention she'd received designing lingerie were amazing. Audra had never stood out for anything but her looks and her badass attitude. So to take the sexy little designs she dreamed up from sketch to finished product gave her a sense of accomplishment she'd never imagined growing up as a number on a social worker's case file.

To have others actually pay money for that lingerie? It rocked, plain and simple.

So maybe she was focusing on the vanilla aspect, for now. It was a place to start. Soon, she'd layer in some rich, bittersweet chocolate syrup, maybe a little whipped cream. If she followed Isabel's advice and all that career planning stuff her friend spouted, Audra figured she'd have her cherry-topped dreams before she was thirty.

Nothing to worry about. She wasn't losing herself in the dream. Just working toward making her starring role a little better.

Semireassured, she forced herself to shake off the irritating introspection and took a swig of her energy drink.

She fingered her memento from Saturday night, the geek's hideous tie. It was a poorly-sewn-together monstrosity of blue geometric shapes strewn over an eye-watering green polyester background. She ought to toss it in the trash, but for some reason she couldn't. Probably because it reminded her of the delight she'd almost had, and how she'd let it get away.

"What's that? A new design?" Natasha, Audra's sister-in-law and boss, asked as she entered the small office-slash-design room. She reached out to touch the tie and grimaced. "No offense, Audra, but that's butt-ugly. Is that the kind of thing you're going to do now that you've graduated textile design school with all those honors?"

Audra fought back a blush. Honors. Who'd have thunk it? She was so *not* an honors kind of chick. For a woman who'd gotten her high school diploma through the G.E.D. program, school was not the gig of choice. But the Textile and Fashion

Design Academy? She'd found heaven. People who admired her for more than her bust, who were more interested in the designs she envisioned and brought to life than how much she could drink.

"No," she said in answer to the question, "this isn't a design for Simply Sensual. It's more like a reminder."

"Of what not to wear, I hope."

More like of the hottest guy she'd ever almost had, to say nothing of her fall from Wicked Chick status. Two dares failed in one night. How humiliating. A wave of despair washed over her. Were her friends right? Was she changing? Losing her edge in her drive to build a career? The missing condom definitely supported that theory.

She looked around the work space, its soft blues and deep burgundies edged with gilt and curlicues. Pure femininity. The colors and lines definitely weren't what she'd call her style, yet she was perfectly comfortable here. Productive, even more so than in the vivid purple and red decor of her apartment.

It was a Monday morning, and she'd shown up at work before Natasha to open the shop. Again, a sign of responsibility at odds with her bad girl reputation of swinging in whenever the whim took her.

It was enough to make a girl panic. But Audra ignored the sick tension in her stomach and the freaked-out thoughts swirling through her brain. She was made of sterner stuff than that. Dammit, she could have it all. She'd prove her badness, *and* make her mark on the lingerie world.

Since that wasn't the kind of thing she could share, though, she just smiled. In looks, Natasha was her complete opposite. Blond, ladylike and subdued. It was only after Audra had gotten to know her that she'd recognized the wild woman under Natasha's tidy exterior.

"I like to think of it as a design with an identity crisis," Audra said of the tie. Like a game show hostess, she held it high in one hand and trailed the back of her fingers over it with the other. It was so poorly constructed, it felt as if they'd left a needle or something between the layers.

"Identity crisis?" Natasha repeated with a laugh. "That tie is just ugly."

Damned good thing she hadn't ended up with its owner. Who knew what else of his was poorly constructed? Audra suppressed a shudder and shrugged. "Some ideas might come of it."

Hopefully ideas on how to find balance between her ambitions and her friends instead of the sexual fantasies she'd entertained about Jesse and all the alternate endings to their encounter. Alternate endings she had no way to engineer since she'd not only become wuss girl without the condom, but hadn't even got the man's phone number.

God, what was happening to her?

"If anyone can find inspiration from it to use in a lingerie design, you can," said Natasha. "After all, your latest nightie is selling like gangbusters. Didn't you say it was inspired by one of those plastic six-pack carriers?"

Audra grinned. She loved the nightie Natasha mentioned. Its random circles of opaque fabric stamped over sheer organza offered tantalizing peeks of bare flesh, all in a baby doll style that screamed sassy fun.

"This just goes to prove the brilliance of my decision to make you head designer," Natasha claimed with a satisfied smile.

To hide her infinitesimal wince, Audra shrugged. Head designer. It sounded so…uptight, official. So not her. She wasn't sure if it was the designation or the implied responsibility that gave her the willies. Then again…if it kept her on the road to that cherry-topped dream, she'd deal with it. Willies and all.

She pinned the tie to the wall next to her sketches. She was just about to pitch the changes she'd been dying to make for the new fall line when Natasha jumped up and clapped her hands.

"Oh, that reminds me." Excitement rang clear in her sister-in-law's voice. "I had a call. A very special call, as a matter of fact. From Hantai Lingerie. They definitely want to talk business."

Audra's mouth went dry. Business? International business? Visions of her latest design ideas flashed through her mind. Now that she was head designer, she'd be able to get a little wild, instead of the more demure, subtle designs Natasha favored. Where better to launch them than in a new country? Excitement whipped through her.

This was why she was teetering on the edge of losing her Wicked Chick status and even the respect of her friends. For a shot at making these visions a reality. To make her mark on the design world with lingerie and finally prove she was a success. Go beyond bridal fluff and get into truly sexy creativity.

"This is it, Audra. We're heading for the big time. That makes the third China-based lingerie distributor wanting to carry our fall line."

Natasha grinned and grabbed Audra, pulling her out of her chair for a hug. Still unused to the ready affection, Audra was stiff at first, but Natasha didn't let up. A few seconds was all it took Audra to loosen up and join her sister-in-law in the celebration. They did a wild butt-swinging boogie and slapped hands before dropping to their chairs.

"Rock on. I've been thinking of some designs to spice up the line. You know, add a few options to grab the more adventurous customers." It was all Audra could do to keep her cool and not bounce in her seat like a little schoolgirl.

Natasha's smile dimmed and her face got that let's-let-her-down-gently look.

Audra didn't even need to hear the words to know she was being denied.

"I'd love to see your ideas. I'm sure there's a solid market for more adventurous designs. I'll bet you have some exciting things in mind."

Nice words, but a shutdown, none the less.

"But…"

Here it was.

"Simply Sensual has built its reputation in a more demure and subtle direction. I think, at least for the fall line, we should keep our focus there. That's what these distributors have recognized us for, what they are interested in. After all, we can't afford to experiment at this point. We just don't have the time or the financial resources."

In other words, more fluffy sweet designs. Audra bit back a sigh. Not that she didn't enjoy the challenge of making something demure scream "Do me." But she'd thought she'd be able to spread her wings a little now. Wasn't that what head designer meant? That she was in charge of the designs?

Before she could find an unchallenging way to ask, Natasha leaned forward to tap the papers spread over the drafting table.

"Let's focus on signing these Chinese distributors. We'll keep the fall line in sync with our current image. But draw me up these designs you have in mind, and we'll see what we can do about incorporating some aspect of them into the spring additions, okay?"

After a brief struggle with impatience, Audra grimaced and shrugged. Heck, she was getting her way, right? Maybe not as fast as she'd prefer, but Natasha's explanation made sense.

"I've been thinking about it," Natasha said, her fair face

flushed from dancing. "I know I said I didn't want to borrow any money from a bank because I need all the capital and collateral available for this next big order. But I talked to my aunt last week. She's willing to loan me enough money to guarantee we nail this deal."

Natasha's aunt was rolling in snooty, upscale money.

"I think it'd be smart if one of us went over to Beijing and met with these companies," Natasha continued. "You know, talk us up and personally present the designs. Be there to get them to sign the contracts."

From the serious look on the blonde's aristocratic face, she'd put a lot of thought into this. The lure of China stifled Audra's still simmering impatience to branch out with her designs.

"Okay. That's smart," Audra agreed with a nod. She didn't even ask which one of them would go. She might be the newly appointed head designer, but the businesswoman thing was obviously not her specialty. "It'll cost a bit of capital, but if the loan will cover it, it's worth it. I think the connection we'll make by face-to-face meetings will pay off in the long run."

But didn't this mean there was more money available? Like, money that could go toward some hot, sexy designs? Audra pressed her lips together, but didn't say anything. Bottom line, it was Natasha's business. As much as Audra might want to push for her rights as head designer, she'd wait. She'd watch for the opportune moment. Any bad girl worth her garter belt knew how to turn a no into a yes. It was all in the timing.

Simply Sensual would be a success. Thanks, in part, to her. This would be the first major step they'd taken since Natasha had bought the company from her aunt almost two years before, one they couldn't have made without Audra's talent.

She sucked in a breath and held it, her cheeks puffed out.

Focus on the trip. China, so much to see and do. She'd never traveled outside the country. Not that she'd be going this time, but wouldn't it be cool if she could? Make big deals, wow the distributors with her charm and moxie.

"Which one of us is going to go?" she asked, just in case a miracle happened and Natasha thought knowledge of the designs would be a bigger asset on this trip than knowing the business.

"I'm not sure," Natasha admitted with a grimace. "You did the designs. But I know the business end. You know, what we need to make this deal work."

Not sure, her ass. When it was put that way, Audra could hardly argue. She really wasn't disappointed. And maybe if she repeated it enough, she'd believe it.

Besides, she had enough at stake already, trying to wade through her personal identity crisis. The exhilaration fading, Audra wanted to sink into her chair and bury her head in her hands, but couldn't. Not while Natasha was here. To admit such a problem—hell, to admit any weakness—wasn't her way.

"You'd make a stronger impression on the suits" was all Audra could come up with. And it was true. While Audra might wow them, the impression Natasha would make would likely net more business.

"Are you sure?"

"I'm sure. You go. Hell, you should take Drew," Audra suggested, certain her brother would love the idea of a second honeymoon. He'd been so focused on saving their deceased father's bar, then on building enough business to keep Aaron Walker's legacy in the black, that he hardly ever took time off. Besides, not only had he been the one to nag Audra into going to design school, he'd even paid her way.

The least she could do was make sure big brother got a little international nooky with his wife. "He'd get a charge out

of it. I'll bet it'd make a better impression on those business-
men, too, you being solidly married and all that."

"Oh, good point." Natasha scooted around the desk and
grabbed a pad and pen. Audra grinned when she started
scratching out a list of things to do. Then Natasha paused and
tucked a long strand of hair behind her ear and peered at Audra.

"Um, you'd have to handle the boutique on your own. I
think I could get Aunt Sharon to help behind the counter once
in a while, but mostly it'd fall on you. I'd have to be gone
about two weeks, I think."

Unspoken was the fact that the longest Audra had been responsible for Simply Sensual was a three-day weekend. That
was the weekend she'd ended up hosting an impromptu bridal
shower in the boutique, complete with male strippers. It
probably wouldn't have been too big a deal if Natasha's aunt
hadn't chosen to stop in just as the bride-to-be and the stripper
had been acting out an explicit sexual act on the checkout
counter. They'd sold a hell of a lot of lingerie that evening,
she remembered, suppressing a naughty grin.

Natasha's doubts, so politely unsaid, were clear on her
face. Audra knew her sister-in-law would be enlisting her
aunt as a babysitter, as well as temporary clerk. Audra's
amusement fell away. No matter how she sugarcoated it, her
sister-in-law expected her to drop the ball.

Jeez, how hard could it be to take charge of the boutique
for a couple weeks? Audra ran through a checklist of what
she knew about running the business. It was a dismally short
list.

Damn.

Maybe Natasha was right to worry about the wisdom of
leaving it all in her hands. But if there was one thing Audra
refused to do, it was to appear needy. Nope, she'd suck up the
insecurity and do a kick-ass job.

"When do you think you'll go?"

Natasha tapped the pencil on the pad of paper, the dull thump keeping rhythm with Aerosmith belting out "Just Push Play" on the radio.

"I can call Aunt Sharon and get the money transferred today. The sooner we get the contracts and an idea of what kind of numbers we'll be producing, the faster we can deliver product. What do you think about me leaving tomorrow? It's like an all-day flight, but I can set up meetings starting on Wednesday."

"Sounds like a plan. Let's get this party rockin'."

Natasha settled behind her desk with a cup of peppermint tea while Audra knocked back a Red Bull. For the next half hour they sketched out a plan of action, then went over the boutique responsibilities for the next week or so.

"I think that's everything," Natasha said as she tidied her notes into a stack. "And just in time to open the doors."

She came around her desk and gave Audra an excited hug.

"We're making it, Audra. Big-time. Drew is so proud of you." She pulled back, obviously realizing all this sentimental stuff made Audra uncomfortable. "So we're set. Are you sure you can handle everything alone?"

Audra considered her performance over the last week since graduating the textile and design academy.

She'd lost an order, told a customer the fishnets made her cellulite look like a bag full of marbles and almost got the delivery guy fired for flirting on company time.

Hardly management material.

But if she wanted to be trusted with something as major as bringing her vision to the spring line, she'd have to prove she could handle running the boutique.

Rarely felt nerves made their way through her stomach with a nasty flutter.

"I can handle it," she vowed. She'd make sure of it. "As long as I don't have to remember to bring a condom," she muttered under her breath.

"Um, no, I doubt you'll need to worry about that. At least, not for the boutique—unless you're planning another party," Natasha said with a wink and laugh.

Maybe she'd overreacted and Natasha wasn't worried about leaving her in charge. Audra frowned.

Dammit, she should worry. Two years ago, heck, two months ago, she'd have worried. Now, though, Audra was, what? Such a goody-goody she could be trusted to be well-behaved? She sank into her chair with a morose sigh. All these yo-yoing emotions were exhausting. Just because she wasn't a loser didn't mean she was a goody-goody. There was an in-between there. Somewhere.

"But, you know it's better to be safe than sorry. I'd strongly suggest keeping a few condoms on hand, since you never know what will come up." Laughing at her own joke, Natasha headed out to the showroom to open the boutique for the day.

Audra made a face at her sister-in-law's retreating back and mocked, "Ha ha."

But inside, she groaned. How freaking pitiful was she? Even Natasha knew to be prepared.

After Natasha left, Audra contemplated the ugly tie pinned to the wall. The green was an insult to the eyes, and the crappy construction mocked her devotion to design details.

She should throw it away. It was stupid to hold on to some geek's tie. A geek who'd run out on her, making her a loser in her friends' eyes. Sure, they'd tossed her a second dare. But look how that had turned out.

But no, here she was, a sappy sentimental wuss who should have her Wicked Chick membership revoked. Courting silly thoughts about what a guy was like out of bed and wonder-

ing if he'd really call her for a date. Holding on to some butt-
ugly memento as a reminder of the night she'd met the hottest
guy to ever keep her awake without even being there.

Talk about an identity crisis.

A JUMBO COFFEE at his elbow, heavily laced with cream to
disguise the bitter taste, Jesse's fingers cruised with loving
familiarity over the computer keyboard. He ignored the usual
Tuesday morning noise in the cop shop as he patiently hacked
through Dave Larson's personal life.

Two steps forward, five steps back.

A dance Jesse loved. Larson was dirtier than a meth fiend
on a street corner. The last two years he'd been up to his ass
in debt, conning Peter to rob Paul. Now, suddenly, he was
rolling in the green. Enough cash flying through his secon-
dary account to rent a BMW, pay for a Nordstrom shopping
spree and buy one hell of a lot of porn on the Internet. Davey
Larson was definitely being paid well.

Jesse hit Print to add the financials to his file and continued digging. An hour later, the phone on the corner of his desk
jangled. He ignored it until someone yelled his name.

"Hey, Martinez. Phone. Dude wants to talk to you."

Jesse waved his thanks and grabbed the phone, still
working the keyboard with one hand.

"Martinez here."

Five minutes later, he stared at his scribbled notes. It wasn't
the chicken-scratch mess that had the coffee churning in his
stomach. His informant had confirmed the rumors. Dave
Larson wasn't just dabbling in organized crime. He was
playing with the big boys. Chinatown-based mafia *Du Bing
Li* big. It seemed Dave had finally scored the underworld
connections he'd sought through the most unlikely source.
His porn addiction.

And the woman who'd lured him in was said to be one hot babe who favored The Wild Thing as her club of choice.

Audra's image flashed through his brain. Jesse tried to wash out the dirty taste in his mouth with a swig of tepid coffee. Pulling a face, he shoved the cup away. He couldn't stand the flavor of the stuff, but it was the best caffeine bang for the buck, and his energy level was nil in the morning.

Dammit. Jesse slapped the notepad aside. He hated that she was dirty. Sure, she came across as a man-eater who knew the score, but there was an underlying sweetness that had tugged at his heart.

"What's up?"

Jesse glanced over at Rob Dutton, the cop whose desk faced his. A tall, lanky redhead with a penchant for practical jokes, he was the reason Jesse found himself in this moral mess. After all, it'd been Rob who'd dared him to get out of his comfort zone and try a little undercover for a change.

The bastard.

"The evidence against Larson is building," Jesse told him.

"Good thing you tailed him, huh? Did you get the goods Saturday night?"

Not for lack of willingness on his body's part. With a shiver, Jesse remembered the cold shower he'd taken Saturday night after leaving Audra.

"I trailed him, identified his connection and made contact." The memory of that contact sent a wave of heat over Jesse, making him shift in his chair.

"Dude, you crack this case, you might snag a promotion. Your work here in Cyber Crimes is noteworthy, sure. But the extra steps you're taking, going undercover? The brass will love that. Hero stuff must run in the family," Rob teased.

Jesse responded with a shrug as Rob took a phone call, but his mind raced.

The brass. Always close to the surface, the memory of his late father rose in Jesse's head. Even though he'd been gone five years now, Jesse still imagined his father was watching over his shoulder—always judging his job performance, his life choices—and shaking his head with a frown of disapproval.

A man's man, Diego Martinez had been one hell of a cop. The brass said he'd died a hero's death. Jesse knew the reality was Diego had trusted the wrong woman. While Jesse might feel compelled to constantly prove he was as good a cop as his father, he wasn't about to repeat the man's mistakes.

So he would run an in-depth check on Audra Walker. As soon as he'd built enough evidence against her, he'd lose this fascination. Maybe then he could lay off the cold showers. His body would thank him. Hell, just the thought of Audra got him horny as hell. For another chance to see her, touch her, his body would weep in gratitude.

Ten minutes later, Jesse was wishing he'd started his day with something stronger than coffee.

"Damn," he breathed. He hadn't even had to dig. It was all right there. Cocky and in-your-face, just like Audra herself. It hadn't taken Jesse more than a couple of keystrokes to find the proof he needed.

He stared at the monitor with a sinking feeling in his gut. A part of him had secretly hoped he'd discover her innocence. The evidence pointed to the contrary.

"Martinez? Report."

This day was going downhill fast. Jesse grimaced. Then, clearing his face, he spun in his chair to face his captain.

"There's a break in the Larson case. I've solidly tied him to the *Du Bing Li* triad."

Captain Shale's bushy blond brows rose, and he tugged at his chin, signaling he was cautiously impressed.

"We've been trying to infiltrate *Du Bing Li* for months now. We've got a guy from San Francisco PD working Chinatown, but nobody's been able to tie them to the Cantonese *Wo Shing Wo* triad. Do you have anything solid?"

"I know he's passing information, sir. It could be fraud, ID theft or, given Larson's history, credit card theft. I haven't narrowed down the specifics yet. But I'm close. Give me a few more days." Jesse pulled out a file on the triad and handed it, along with the Larson file, to the captain.

Shale flipped through the report, humming a couple times, but otherwise silent. When he got to the most recent pages Jesse had added, the captain's brows rose again and his hum turned into an *aha*. He'd obviously reached the part pertaining to Audra Walker.

Jesse felt like hurling those large quantities of coffee he'd used to pry his eyes open that morning.

"Walker? You run her sheet?"

"Yes, sir. Her adult record is clean, but she's got a sealed juvie."

"You verified this deposit?"

"Yeah, the money was deposited in the account last night. It's not her account, but the business she works for." As if that minute detail mattered. "I haven't been able to track the source yet." The sick feeling spread from his stomach to his head. It just felt wrong planning to arrest a woman after he'd had his hands in her panties. Unlike his father, he didn't prescribe to the any-method-to-crack-the-case code. Jesse stretched his neck from side to side with a loud crack of tension.

"Two plane tickets to Beijing?"

"Yes, sir. They're booked in her boss's name, though."

As if that were any big defense. It only meant both women were involved. Jesse hadn't had time yet to check further into

Natasha Walker, other than to discover she was related to Audra by marriage. A family that plays together stays together.

"Your cover is solid? You've made contact with her?"

With all parts of her. Jesse's fingers tingled at the memory of the sweet heat of her juices.

"Yeah, it's solid" was all he said. He knew there were officers who had no problem going into deep cover, could justify any action in the name of getting the job done. His father had been one of them.

Jesse, though, didn't. Couldn't.

"I don't have a case against her, yet," he reminded his boss. "So far, what I have is all circumstantial. It's possible it's all a coincidence."

"I don't believe in simple coincidence, Martinez, you know that. Keep digging on Larson, see if you can follow him, strike up a friendship. Maybe use your computer connection or check into infiltrating one of his online porn chats. But focus on Audra Walker. She's tied in somehow. I want you to find out how. Stay undercover, use whatever means necessary to get close to the woman. Break this case," he ordered.

His head pounding like a sledgehammer, Jesse thought of the condom he'd taken to carrying in his pocket. That probably wasn't the kind of means the captain had in mind. Then again, given the potential of this case, maybe it was. Knowing he had his captain's blessings didn't help Jesse's resolve to keep his dick in his pants and his hands off the luscious suspect.

"I JUST DON'T THINK naughty undies are in good taste," tittered a thirtysomething woman who looked as if she could use a good dose of naughty. Her mousy hair was pulled back so tight it made Audra's own face hurt, and her high-necked blouse did a damned good job of disguising her femininity.

"That's the great thing about lingerie. It can suit any mood from naughty to sweet," Audra assured her. "First and foremost, lingerie is about feeling good with yourself. It's like an affirmation of a woman's sexuality, her sensual self-worth."

"I just don't think I could wear some of this stuff," the woman murmured as she fingered a pink satin merry widow with rosebud detailing. She wrinkled her nose at the cord that comprised the G-string. "Wouldn't this chafe?"

"It's an acquired preference." Audra managed to keep a straight face and resisted adjusting the strap of the red leather bustier she wore with jeans and her cropped denim jacket. If the lady thought satin chafed, she'd definitely not be into leather. "If you're just beginning to explore lingerie, you might start by examining your own sexual fantasies. The merry widow is a popular choice. Sometimes you want to work up to that, though."

"Maybe I should start with something less intimidating?"

"Great idea." Audra gestured to a different display, this reminiscent of vintage Victorian. She held up a semisheer cotton sheath, and the woman's eyes lit up. "Something like this looks innocent and offers body coverage. Feel the fabric."

Hesitantly at first, the woman rubbed the cotton between her fingers.

"Oooh, so soft."

Audra quelled her triumphant grin at the look of delight on the woman's face.

"If you like that, wait until you see this corset set. It's the most comfortable thing you'll ever wear." Audra let her voice drop to a whisper as she leaned closer. "And the things it does for the cleavage. Very impressive."

The woman grinned and nodded enthusiastically.

Oh, yeah, baby, haul out the plastic.

Audra kept her smile in place as she rang up the sale, but

as soon as the door closed behind yet another lingerie convert, she let it fall away. God, what a week. Natasha had only been gone three days and Audra was ready to scream.

Only a half hour until closing. Then she'd be able to relax a little, shake off this stressed-out feeling. Maybe she should call the girls, see if they wanted to get together? She could loosen up and relax. And best of all, there was a good chance she'd meet a guy, get lucky and take the edge off.

Didn't it freaking suck that the only guy she wanted was Jesse? At least half her distraction this week could be firmly placed at his feet. After all, sexual frustration was not something Audra was used to feeling. Until now.

The soft chime of bells indicated a new customer. She wiped the pissy expression off her face and looked at the entrance.

Like a dream conjured from her naughtiest wishes, Jesse walked through the door. She gave an unconscious sigh of appreciation. He really was as hot as she remembered. Well-worn jeans cupped a promising package, while a plain black workshirt covered his drool-inspiring chest. Lust rushed through her at the delicious sight.

"Hey, gorgeous," she said leaning forward on the counter in a way she knew gave a generous view of her cleavage. "What a *very* nice surprise."

With a sexy grin, he held up a condom. The sunlight coming through the large plate glass windows glinted off the foil wrapper. "Didn't you say something about modeling lingerie for me?"

5

DAVE LARSON stood in the entrance to The Wild Thing and swiped the back of his hand over his forehead to keep the sweat from trickling into his eyes. He'd gone through two sticks of antiperspirant in the last week. Ever since he'd found out he'd handed off the computer chip to the wrong woman, he'd been sweating like a pig. For a fastidious man, it was pure hell.

That triad pinhead had woken him Sunday morning from a dead sleep, beating down his door and spouting a whole litany of threats. It had taken Dave a few minutes to figure out what the problem was. After all, not that he'd admit it to the pinhead, but it wasn't like women came on to him all that often. How the hell was he to know the hot chickie wasn't their connection? Hell, she'd fit the look, she'd complimented his tie, not quite the code word, but close enough. What more was he supposed to have waited for? Her friggin' ID?

That'd been when the pinhead had got pissed. The guy had started talking conspiracy, rival gangs and infiltration. Dave had just rolled his eyes. It was all too much paranoid drama for his blood.

It hadn't been until the pinhead had sicced his goon on one of Dave's computers, beating it into a pile of plastic and metal, that Dave had gotten scared.

It seemed that even though Dave had been a loyal employee for the past six months, although he'd followed their instructions, he'd worked his fingers sore hacking enough numbers to meet their dirty needs, the mix-up was all *his* fault. And while Dave was willing to take the blame—especially since the goon had still been hefting the baseball bat he'd whacked the computer with—the pinhead wasn't willing to let him off the hook.

Probably because Dave had gambled away a good portion of the first installment *Du Bing Li* had fronted. Not that he'd told them that, or apparently that it would have mattered. They wanted the chip. The original, not a copy, not a new batch of names. It had to be that one.

As proof of Dave's desire to live.

Here he was, Mr. Nice Guy, doing them a favor by offering up the goods. Dave knew the value of the info he'd hacked. Full identities. Names, addresses, social security numbers, mothers' maiden names. The works. All those tidy little tidbits of information a savvy group such as *Du Bing Li* could use.

Dave was a smart man. He knew *Du Bing Li* was tied to *Wo Shing Wo,* and the word on the street was they were looking to start transporting their human cargo into the good ole U.S. of A. For that, a computer chip of cleanly hacked IDs was a goldmine.

Now he had to get it back from some club tramp, or lose his ass.

"Move, dude."

Dave waited until the refrigerator-sized bouncer was past him before he sneered and gave him the finger.

He swiped his forehead again and stepped into the club. Damned flashing lights made it hard to see, so he squinted, looking for the woman.

He could barely remember what she looked like. Hot, sure. But the details? Jeez, all women looked alike from the neck up; he never paid much attention.

Finally, he spotted a blonde who seemed familiar. She had

been here that night. He was sure, because he remembered thinking that in the animal-print thing she'd been wearing, she'd looked exactly like one of the porn queens he idolized. She wasn't the woman he was looking for, but maybe she could help him find her.

He timed it right, waiting until she and the woman she was with waved to the waitress for drink refills. Then he sauntered over, hand on his wallet ready to make an impression.

"Ladies, how ya doin'?"

"We're out of your league, dude. Get lost," the blonde said, with barely a glance his way.

The other one, a redhead with a nice rack, gave him a sympathetic look and little shrug. It was that shrug, the dainty apology of it, that made Dave look again.

She was gorgeous. It wasn't just the sweet curve of her breasts pressing against her dress or the way her hair curled down her back, inspiring one of his favorite fantasies. It was the polished, moneyed look of her. Dave was an expert at recognizing money and what it could do for a person. Which was why he'd dedicated his life to amassing as much of it as he could.

A man such as himself could definitely appreciate the silky richness of a woman like this one.

"Don't underestimate me," he told the blonde. "There's a lot more to me than meets the eye."

The blonde snorted.

Normally, that kind of crap would send him back to the safety of his computer and his agreeable online ladies. But damned if he'd be brushed off when he'd found his dream woman. Especially when his ass was on the line, too.

"You might be overestimating yourself if you think you could handle either of us, dude." This time, the blonde actually turned to face him. Davey recognized the look in her eyes, the combination of pity and disinterest.

Davey fought off his natural instinct to run away. He needed the chip. To get the chip, he needed to find out who that woman was, and once he did, find a way to get to her. He was sure she'd been with these women that night. Which meant they might know her name and address. And hopefully, they meant enough to her to be bait if necessary.

"Let me buy you ladies drinks and I'll show you how wrong you are." Dave pulled out his wallet and, hiding a grimace, handed the waitress enough to cover the drinks she'd just delivered. "I'll bet women as hot as the two of you are used to all the studs hitting on you. Bunch of egocentric, selfish guys, all out for whatever they can get off you."

"Obviously any guy can hit. Who we let connect is what counts."

"Sure, sure. You're hot, you're in the driver's seat. But what I'm saying is, you ladies, hot as you are, have to get sick of the users around here. Me, I'm all about what I can do for you."

"Nice try, and points for creativity." The blonde rolled her eyes at him in obvious dismissal. "But, no thanks."

Davey ignored the blonde's disinterest. It was the redhead's reaction that sent the surge of triumph through him. Her slight nod and the droop of her mouth screamed "Score."

The gorgeous rich girl was the key. Anticipation swirled through him at the idea of working on her to get the information he needed.

Like a hawk focused on its prey, he shifted his weight just a bit. Enough to face her, but not enough to scare her off.

Her soft blue gaze met his, sending Cupid's arrow straight through his heart. He skimmed his gaze over her, taking in the designer clothes, flash of sparkles at her ears and pricey cosmetics. The only thing that turned him on more than a gorgeous woman with a C cup was one who came wrapped in wealth.

Unfortunately, as he did whenever he was faced with a fantasy woman, his tongue tied itself in knots and he lost the ability to think coherently.

Dave quelled the panicky feeling in his belly and tried to get his brain to work. He needed that chip. To get it, he needed the name of their friend. That wasn't gonna happen unless one of them trusted him. Since his body screamed out for the hot redhead, he'd focus on her. After all, the blonde scared him.

Dave put on his most trustworthy face and hid his fists in his pockets. Sucking in a deep breath, he almost choked on the mix of perfumes, BO and booze in the air. He ignored it and pasted a big smile on his face.

"Your friend's loss is your gain," he said to the redhead. Davey looked at her glass, almost empty, and hid a wince. She sure drank fast. Dammit, he might have to fork out more dough than he'd wanted. "Let me buy you a couple more drinks and tell you how well I'd treat you if you were my lady."

Three drinks, two painful dances and countless barbs from the blonde later, Davey was pretty happy with his progress. He had his hand on the redhead's—Bea's—ass. He'd got a buzz going and lost some of the edgy nerves that had dogged him since the pinhead had slammed down his door. Now to get that name.

"You ladies look familiar. Have you been in any commercials or print work I'd recognize?" he asked.

Bea's eyes lit up and she did a sweet little wiggle that sent her chest swaying. Before she could reply, though, the blonde gave a mean little laugh.

"Oh, please," sneered Suzi. "You're already feeling her up. Can't you do any better than that cheesy pickup line?"

"No, no. I've been on the cover of *California Girl*," Bea said with a glare at her friend. "He probably recognized me."

Davey didn't even recognize the magazine. But he grinned anyway and nodded.

"Of course, of course. I knew it. I've seen you recently, though. Maybe in person? Do you come in here a lot?"

"Actually," Bea said, giving him a long, slightly wasted look, "you look familiar, too."

"Gag me," Suzi murmured.

Davey had to force himself not to take her up on the offer. Instead, he offered her a sneer and his shoulder. She just laughed.

"I was in last Saturday scoping out talent. I'm a photographer," he told Bea, who's eyes sparked with excitement. "Maybe you were here then?"

"Saturday?" the blonde said with a shrug. "Maybe. We hit a lot of clubs."

Bea narrowed her eyes, then nodded. "We *were* here Saturday. That was Audra's party. Remember, Suzi?"

"Oh, yeah, I remember." Suzi giggled, the softest sound he'd heard from her. A self-professed expert at reading people, Dave wondered at the affection and regret in the blonde's eyes. "She hit on that geeky loser and he ran like a scared little girl, remember Bea?"

Bingo. Davey cracked his neck, pasted on a fake smile and hoped they didn't recognize him as the scared little girl. The Audra chick must have his computer chip. Dave wasn't too concerned, though. It wasn't as if she was the competition, out to sell it to the highest bidder. Nah, this was all gonna be fine. Just fine.

Davey leaned his elbows on the high table and turned on the charm. He'd find out if he had anything to worry about, get a name to retrieve his chip from and romance his dream woman in the bargain. Nobody was better at getting his way than Dave Larson.

AUDRA'S SMILE drew Jesse's attention away from the mouth-watering view of smooth flesh showcased in red leather. He knew the flesh was smooth because his fingers had memorized the feel of her.

"You'll have to tell me a little bit about your preferences," Audra told him. Straightening slowly, the view shifted and he saw her top only reached her midriff, leaving her stomach bare above low-slung jeans.

A bare stomach adorned with not only an ultrafine gold chain, but also a belly-button piercing—a glittery red jewel with dangling stars.

Jesse did his damnedest not to swallow his tongue.

"Preferences?" he asked. The possibilities ran through his mind at the speed of light, each one featuring a deliciously naked Audra.

"Yeah. You know, what look you like. What gets you excited?"

"You."

And she did. Instead of the magenta-tipped spikes he'd seen before, today her hair was fluffed around her head. Still edgy black, it was just a little softer. Her face seemed softer, too. Maybe it was the girly atmosphere of the boutique instead of the harsh lights of the club or the parking overheads. This easy, approachable look made it damned hard to think of her as a criminal.

Especially in this confection-style shop, with its gilded edges, swirly decorations and mass of frilly sex-inspired nighties.

She laughed a little and shook her head. "I mean what lingerie looks are you into? Any fashion preferences?"

"I like the look you have going on," he reiterated. "What style is that?"

Audra looked down at herself, then shrugged and grinned. "You won't find this in here. For the most part, Simply

Sensual's stock is more subtle. You know, satin and lace. Someday, I hope to bring in a little leather, maybe some metal detailing. But for now, the stock here is pretty sweet. I call this my last rebellion style."

"Do tell."

"When I started working here, I was the ultimate rebel. It was all about the design, not the boutique. Shop, retail, that was boring. I'd show up for work whenever I felt like it, take off when I wanted."

"Didn't your employer object?"

"Believe me, I didn't come with references," Audra said with a rueful laugh. "I remember my first job. I worked at this trendy little boutique. One day I saw a list of 'employee rules' posted in the office and realized I'd broken them all."

"Don't you worry about breaking rules?"

"Nah. I'm not big on rules. Usually the worst I get is a lecture and I'm used to that. I had a social worker once who was the queen of lectures."

"Social worker, huh?"

"No biggie," she said with a shrug, "I had a high school counselor who doubled as Dottie Do-Gooder. She was so sure I was gonna end up in jail or on the streets, ole Dottie called in Child Protective Services. They'd already tagged me as a lost cause, but this social worker figured she'd hang out and make me her project child."

Even though her tone was light, it was clearly a closed door. Jesse noted the tight, pained look around her eyes as she talked about the past. From the info he'd dug up, she'd never actually been in the foster system. It didn't sound as if she'd gotten off unscathed, though.

"So you're not big on rules, huh? What about losing your job?"

Her wide smile was obviously in thanks for changing the

subject. Jesse ignored what it did to his body and told himself to focus on the case. His body, of course, ignored him.

"Natasha knew what she was getting into when she signed me on. Actually, I started in the back doing design work while I went to school. Simpl Sensual has two functions. The boutique and the lingerie company. My focus is design, first and foremost. But somehow I got conned into creating displays, eventually got suckered into working the cash register."

"Sounds like your—" Jesse stopped himself before he let slip *sister-in-law* "—boss is pretty wily. She obviously knew what it would take to entice you into becoming the model employee." He eyed her bare belly and winked. "Especially if you get many men in here shopping."

"We get a few. And yeah, Natasha's okay. She just promoted me last week. Now I run the design department of the lingerie side of the business."

"And you still rebel?"

Audra laughed, a husky sound of delight.

"I'll always be a rebel. I'm just a little…less, now." Her tone drooped, kind of like the wispy bit of silk that dangled, one strap hanging forlornly, from the padded hanger. She reached over to adjust it, securing the loose strap over the fabric-covered button.

"Over the last few months, I suppose I have become the model employee. Hell, I even put the money in the cash register now so it all faces the same way." She gave a rueful laugh and walked toward him. The effortless swing of her hips tempted him to forget his resolve to stay on track. Jesse caught her distinctive scent and felt his body reacting with remembered yearning. "But a girl loses her edge if she doesn't keep that naughty side alive and kicking. So now I find other areas to be…bad."

His mouth watered as he envisioned her being bad on him. Over him. Under him. *Oh, hell. Focus, Martinez.* He needed to get a grip. She'd given him the perfect opening, he needed to think with his cop head.

"So what kind of bad are you into now?" he asked.

"Just about anything you have in mind, I'll bet I'd be into," she said, taking a few steps closer. So close, he could feel the heat radiating from her lush body. So close, his fingers tingled with the need to touch her. She was like a drug. She'd wormed her way into his system and he couldn't get enough of her. Then he frowned. Anything?

"Like what? I mean, how far do you go to be bad? Drugs?"

When her eyes popped wide, Jesse winced. Dammit, he belonged behind a computer keyboard, not here trying to sneak information out of a woman whose scent fogged his brain.

She gave him a long look, the most serious he'd ever seen from her. Then she offered a one-shouldered shrug. "I guess, given what some people call bad, I don't mind clarifying for you. I'm anti-drugs, and to be honest, I'm a very light drinker. I'm not big on artificial stimulation."

She paused, inspecting his face. She must have been satisfied with whatever she saw there, because she ran her tongue over her lower lip and moved close to him again.

"I am, however, very into physical stimulation. If memory serves, you're pretty good in that area."

"I can work magic with my hands," Jesse assured her. Sure, it was usually on a keyboard, but all that finger work limbered him up for much more intricate maneuvers.

"Really? Does that mean your wand is magic, too?" Her comment, combined with her wide-eyed innocent look, made him laugh with pleasure.

"You're so damned cute, you know that?" He was surprised at how much fun she was. How at odds her playful side was to the hot packaging.

"Cute? I don't think I've ever been called cute," she said with a snicker.

He winced. That probably wasn't the kind of thing a woman over twelve took as a compliment. But she didn't seem offended, just amused.

"Is that a bad thing? I know my sisters have this need to be taken seriously, and cute isn't synonymous with serious. Other women I've known seem to need compliments and—" he almost said "to be fawned over," but stopped himself in time "—you know, to be treated so carefully. You're probably the most comfortable person I've ever met."

"Comfortable? You're kidding, right?" She furrowed her brow and gave a little curl of her lip. But, again, she didn't seem offended.

"Comfortable with yourself, I mean. Not comfortable to be around. After all, I get a hard-on the minute I see you. That's not exactly what I'd call relaxing."

Her face cleared, and a wide smile flashed. With an impish look, she raised a brow and dropped her gaze to the zipper of his jeans. Already semierect, his dick reacted as if she'd run her hands, instead of just her eyes, over it.

"You know how to play, if that makes sense. To laugh and not take every little thing seriously."

"Why bother? Life is too short to be all uptight. I'd much rather play, as you put it. Have a good time, enjoy myself. As long as I don't hurt anyone else, why shouldn't I do whatever makes me happy?"

Damned if he didn't want to see what he could do to make her happy. Desire, never far from the surface when he was with her, engulfed Jesse. He reached out to grip her hips, his hands smoothing over the silky skin along the edge of the waistband of her jeans.

Intrigued by her body decorations, he traced his index

finger over the gold chain settled in the curve of her waist. He glanced up to meet her eyes. They had a soft, bidding look in them that invited him to enjoy himself.

And she was involved with one of the nastiest crime rings in the state?

It didn't compute. This woman, with her freewheeling-but-hurt-nobody-else philosophy, just didn't seem like a criminal. For all her bad girl image, Audra really wasn't hard enough. Which meant she was just entering the criminal life.

He bit back a sigh and ignored the bad taste in his mouth. If he could get her to turn evidence on Davey and the triad, he could get her out of the picture fast, solve the case. Then maybe ask her out for real.

With that promise to himself, he forced himself to stop playing with her belly chain and let go of her hip.

"So, you know, in the name of physical stimulation, are you into porn?" he blurted out.

Audra's mouth dropped, her eyes growing huge. Like he'd asked her to have a threesome with a goat.

Lucky for him, she recovered with a shake of her head, and rolled her eyes. "I know some people really get into it, but it's not my thing. Who needs to watch someone else get off? I'm selfish. If there's any moaning going on, I want it to either be me, or because of me."

Jesse frowned. His informant was sure Larson had been lured in by the triad through his porn obsession. The guy had even hinted that the hot babe Larson made the handoff to dabbled a bit in movies herself. That had purportedly been the clincher—the opportunity to be face-to-face with one of the women he fantasized about.

"Then you probably haven't done any films like that, huh?" he asked. As soon as the words were out, Jesse wanted to slap himself in the forehead. So much for subtle investigation.

"Films? You mean porn? As in starred in a skin flick? Me?"

"Yeah. I mean, I hear that's a hot turn-on for some people, doing it on film."

"I know a few who are into taping their personal encounters for their own viewing pleasure, if you know what I mean. But even that's a little much for me. I'm not shy, I've just never felt the need for a souvenir."

She squinted at him, a bemused smile on her face.

"What?"

"Nothing, really. I just wouldn't have taken you for one of those guys."

"What guys?" Jesse asked blankly.

"A guy with a porn fetish. You seem more into making your own moves than watching someone else's."

"You think I meant I…? No, I mean, sure I have, but I don't. I have, of course. That is, you know, bachelor parties and stuff. But not like date replacement or anything. I don't, um, you know, watch it for sexual aids or whatever."

Jesse wondered if he babbled long enough, whether he could distract her with bullshit so that she wouldn't notice the color heating his cheeks. He hadn't blushed this much since puberty. And that had probably been because of porn, too.

Audra gave a husky laugh. She curved the back of her hand over one of his still warm cheeks, then stepped closer. She leaned into his body, just the barest brush of her breasts against his chest. Before Jesse could moan, she'd pressed a soft, friendly kiss to his other cheek and stepped back.

"And you said *I* was cute?"

She turned away to lean over the counter, giving him a sweet view of her denim-clad butt. Turning back around, a set of keys dangling from her fingers, she winked.

"I have to lock up. Then I'll be happy to give you that show you asked for."

Shit. Now what was he supposed to do? The plan had been to get her to tell him what porn link she'd used to hook up with Davey. He'd figured he could use that to make his own connection with the guy, then lure him in. But it seemed she was somehow unconnected. Or one hell of an actress. But why would she bother to hide something like that? It would be pointless.

Since the porn thread had gone nowhere, he should tug on the gang affiliation. He needed a few names, maybe an idea of what other pies the triad had their sticky criminal fingers in.

He could hardly ask her if she was in a gang. Not after his rookie porn questions. So he'd go along with the fashion show and wait for the opportune moment.

And maybe if he told himself often enough that she was a suspect, seeing Audra in a few dozen slinky, sexy outfits wouldn't make him explode with desire.

6

AUDRA USED the time it took her to lock the boutique door and shut the blinds to catch her breath. She'd met a lot of different guys in her Wicked Chick days. Maybe, sometimes late at night, she might admit to herself that some of those men she regretted. But with all her experience, she'd never before met a guy like Jesse.

There was something special about him. She wasn't sure what it was, exactly, but she'd have to watch out for it. After all, he'd actually had her opening up about her past. And that was something Audra never did. Especially not crap about CPS and the endless stress dodging them had brought to her teen years. Other than her endless truancy reports, her only real run-in with the law trying to spring a dog from death row. Of course, the cops had always harassed her anyway, just because they thought she looked like the type to be trouble.

It was all a part of her life she was more than happy to lock the door on. The only information she shared with guys was the turn-them-on, keep-them-guessing kind.

Then again, Jesse wasn't her average kind of guy.

He was an intriguing mixture of sweet and sexy, shy and sensual. The way he flirted was a major turn-on for her. In her considered opinion, he could definitely deliver on the promise of that flirtation. After all, she hadn't been able to get the memory of his talented fingers and delicious mouth out of her head all week.

How many guys talked porn in such a cute, unobnoxious way? Audra had a strict personal policy to only do what brought her pleasure, what felt good to her. If a guy was into a form of kink she didn't like, she'd say so, straight up. Like she'd told him, she wasn't into watching sex. She was more a kinesthetic, hands-on kind of girl.

Having closed the boutique for the night, she turned to face Jesse. He stood there, all sexy male confusion, fingering a purple silk chemise.

Yum.

"So you never answered my question. What's your pleasure?" she asked him.

His gaze shot to hers and he grinned, a boyish flash of white teeth.

"Such a leading question," he returned.

"Isn't it, though? The real question is, do you want to do the leading or be led?"

"I think I'd like both, depending."

Audra sauntered over to where he stood, the purple silk between his fingers. His obvious sensual appreciation for the tactile fabric was a good sign. One she wanted to explore. Enough of this chitchat prelim crap; it was time to rock and roll.

"Why don't we take turns? I'll start." With that, she looped her arms around his neck and gently pulled his head down to meet her hungry mouth.

Mmm. Delicious.

She traced his lips with her tongue, reveling in their soft texture and the hint of something hot and dangerous just beneath the surface. Impatience, with its rough, edgy bite, ripped through her. She wanted more. Wanted to taste him, see how fast and far he could take her.

So she did. With teeth, tongue and lips, she gave herself over to desire. At her assault, Jesse groaned. He gripped her hips in his hands and pulled her tight against him. Pleased to feel evidence that he was as into the kiss as she was, Audra rubbed herself against the hardening flesh behind his zipper. Need, already coiled tight, sprang loose to spiral through her. From her avid mouth to the wetness between her legs, she was ready for him.

"Now," she gasped. She pulled back from his mouth just long enough to make the demand before trailing kisses over his rugged jaw and down the smooth flesh of his throat.

"Lingerie," he mumbled, one hand roaming her back while the other gripped her hip as if it were a lifeline.

"Huh?"

"Show. You said you'd show me your designs."

Audra pulled back to look into Jesse's eyes. He wanted a show? Now? Instead of sex? A woman with less faith in her sexuality might worry that he wasn't interested. Given her track record this week, Audra's own faith in her sexuality was teetering on a fine line. But she knew the signs. Not just the woody pressing into her belly, but his dilated pupils, slightly labored breathing and the way his fingers smoothed over the small of her back as if it were a precious jewel.

She narrowed her eyes. Was he playing a game? He stared back. There was nothing in his eyes except desire. So why was her bullshit meter sending her caution signals?

Audra's breath caught as she tried tamp down the panic at the idea that she wasn't the sexy, hot chick she defined herself as. If she'd lost her identity—her sexual mojo, to quote Suzi— to ambition, what the hell did that leave? Her self-image was so wrapped up in her sexuality that without it, she was lost.

"You'd rather see my designs than get hot 'n' heavy with me?" she asked.

"Hell, no," he exclaimed. "But I want to see those designs. You intrigue me. I want to get to know you better. You know, things besides what will make you scream in ecstasy."

Letting herself be soothed out of the panic-inducing identity crisis, Audra considered him. When had she become so cynical and jaded that a guy looking for an actual relationship would have her so suspicious? Was she stupid enough to walk away from someone who might want more than just sex from her? Because he wanted to get to know her?

To quote Jesse, *Hell, no.*

"As long as I don't lose out on those screams of ecstasy, I'd be happy to show you my stuff."

Audra looked around the boutique, hoping something would spark inspiration. The guy wanted to get to know her? Maybe she could get to know him, too. She'd never spent as much time wondering about a man as she had Jesse. Why not get a few of the answers to her musings? As the idea took hold, the odd feeling of rejection she'd barely admitted fell away and she started to get excited.

If nothing else, finding out what lingerie he preferred would be an interesting peek into his sexual fantasies. What would prime his pump? Stir his juices? It'd be fun to find out.

"As the guest of honor at this evening's private showing of Simply Sensual Lingerie, I'd like to invite you to peruse our wares. Choose as many outfits as appeal to you."

"Anything?"

"Sure. It's all pretty tame, to be honest. Simply Sensual caters to the upscale, ladylike sexual fantasies. I'm hoping to change that soon, though."

"Really?" Jesse's intrigued glance, and the clear interest in his voice, encouraged her to open up.

"I'd like to bring in some naughtier stuff," Audra said with a laugh. "Something more adventurous. You know, the exotic and erotic, the leather, the merry widow, the role-playing-styled lingerie. Fun stuff aimed at sexual fantasies of the wilder kind. I've got a few things in the works that I figure will make all my dreams come true."

He shot her a weird look, a deep frown creasing his forehead, but all he said was, "Sounds like that promotion is going to bring some interesting changes here, huh?"

She sure hoped so.

Audra watched Jesse take his time, carefully inspect each outfit on each rack. Every time he seemed interested, he stopped to rub the fabric between his fingers, then looked at her as if gauging how it would feel with her in it. Since her shopping MO was based on the thrill of impulse buys, this was killing her. Or maybe it was the ever-tightening thread of desire that curled through her. After all, she was going to be getting next-to-naked with this guy soon. If he'd just hurry up.

Finally, he'd chosen a half-dozen outfits. Audra cast a quick eye over them and grabbed a few accessories as well as boots from the shelves, tossed them in a wicker shopping basket then winked.

"It's showtime." She gestured to the hall. "Shall we?"

Jesse shot a confused look at the flowing letters over another hall marked Dressing Room. "Where are we going?'

"A few months after I started working here, I realized we were missing out by having those tiny dressing rooms up front. They're fine for women shopping alone, but it can be a major turn-on lingerie shopping with your man along. You know, letting him be a part of the fun."

He followed her down the short hallway. There were two doors, the second being her and Natasha's office. They stopped at the first one. The interior had been fitted as a comfortable waiting area.

A manly leather couch offset the overt femininity of the rest of the boutique. A low table in front of it to hold a drink or for a guy to put his feet up while he waited, with an array of magazines, including *Car Craft* and *GQ,* spread over the smooth wood surface. The corner had been fitted as a dressing area, with deep burgundy curtains for privacy. And in front of the small, mirrored wall was a pedestal, perfect for modeling purposes.

"It's not just about couples. We get brides in here wanting to try on their trousseau for their entourage. Sometimes girlfriends have fun putting on a group show. But the couples seem to appreciate it the most."

"Nice," Jesse said, taking it all in. He gestured to the couch. "That'd probably put a guy at ease, huh?"

"It does, yes. And guys at ease tend to hang out longer, buy more."

"Smart business." He sauntered over as if he was going to sit down, then hesitated. "Maybe this is a tacky question, but don't you worry the privacy, combined with the sensual atmosphere, might…you know?"

Faint color washed his cheeks. Damn, he was cute. Audra couldn't help but tease him.

"You know? What? Try on more lingerie?"

"No. You know, this place, the clothes, you. It's all so sexy. A guy comes in here, he's gonna be thinking sex. He gets back in this room, he's gonna be tempted to have sex. Some guys even get off on the semipublic aspect of it. Just knowing customers are a few feet away, it adds to the excitement."

"Do you?"

"Huh?"

"Do you get off on the semipublic aspect of it? You were asking about porn earlier. Is this another form of voyeurism?"

Jesse swallowed audibly.

"Yeah. In a way, I guess it is. I mean, I'm not into porn. Like you, watching isn't my thing. But I can see where there might be an added edge, an extra element of spice, to doing it in a semipublic place. Kinda like the other night in your car? Public parking lot, dark night. It was… Well, it was sexy as hell."

His voice gruff with emotion, combined with the look in his eyes, made Audra catch her breath. The memory of that night, of his fingers on her—in her—made her shiver with desire.

Had she ever wanted a man like this? What was it about him that had her at war with herself, wanting equally to get to know him better and to rip his clothes off and get him naked?

"It *was* sexy, wasn't it?"

Spying the brass rack, Jesse hung the lingerie on the bar and turned toward her. He took the basket from her hands, set it on the low table and faced her again. Excited by the anticipation, the wonder, she tensed. Her entire focus centered on him. On what he'd do next.

He stepped close, so close she could feel the heat off his body, smell the subtle spice of his shaving cream. Without actually touching her, he flicked the tiny stars dangling from her belly button, watching their movement with heated eyes.

"That night was about the sexiest experience I've ever had without an actual orgasm," he told her. "Everything with you seems to have that extra edge. A special something that takes it past anything I've ever felt before."

Audra didn't know what to say. She felt the same. Her feelings about Jesse, her reactions to him, were all new to her.

But she'd learned when she was young to guard her emotions, to keep those vulnerabilities to herself. After all, she'd tried that relationship thing once. But then she'd realized that she just didn't have it in her to change enough to make another person happy. Even though Jesse's honesty inspired her to share the same, she couldn't. Maybe that made her defective, or just overly cautious. But she couldn't open her heart. Couldn't let him peek into her soul.

Not out of any sense of privacy. No, Audra could admit to herself it was fear, pure and simple. Fear that if anyone ever saw into her heart, into her soul, they'd find out there was nothing really there.

Instead, she fell back on the tried and true, gave him her sexiest smile and leaned in close. With the softest brush of her lips against his, she whispered, "If you thought that was good, you ain't seen nothing yet."

Jesse laughed, and the air cleared of all that heavy emotional expectation. Relieved, Audra winked and gestured to the couch. With a flip of a couple switches, she dimmed the lights and cued the music. A low, bluesy tune wailed softly through the tiny speakers in the corners of the room.

"Get comfy," she suggested again. She waited until he settled on the couch before she made her way to the dressing area. "Do me a favor. Think of those outfits you picked out. Try and imagine me in each one. Picture what it will cover, what it will show. How the light will shimmer as it touches my skin. Imagine how the lingerie will look on my body. How it'll feel as you run your hands over it. Over me."

She watched his eyes dilate, grinned and slipped behind the curtain.

"Be right back."

JESSE SHIFTED on the couch, guilt making him wince. Damn, could he get any lower? A snake would look down on him in contempt, with good reason.

This kind of thing—a sexy suspect, questionable circumstances—had been tools of the trade for his father. Diego Martinez'd had a reputation for breaking his cases by using any method at his disposal, especially romancing the ladies.

Because of that, Jesse'd long ago promised himself never be in the position to borrow any pages from his father's book.

So much for promises.

Granted, he wasn't overly experienced with fieldwork or working face-to-face with suspects. But Audra simply didn't seem crooked. She was hot, sexy, sweet as hell. She might be aggressive and a little wild, but those things didn't make her a criminal.

Jesse shoved a hand through his hair and sighed. Since he'd already landed in a typical Diego Martinez situation, his father's philosophy was screaming in his head. *The more innocent they looked, the guiltier they were.*

Disgust with himself churned through Jesse's stomach. He didn't want to break the case this way. Audra wasn't a means to an end. Even knowing she was guilty, he was dangerously close to falling into serious lust with the woman. Bad business.

On top of that, she knew nothing about the porn connection. He'd do better to focus his investigation on Dave Larson. If he left now, he could get home in plenty of time to cruise the online porn sites Larson frequented, try and connect with the guy. He had a few other lines he could tug, too. Such as hacking into Larson's computer and finding a trail to his backup system. Jesse knew there had to be a backup system. The trick was to find it.

Either way, there was plenty Jesse could be doing. None of which included the torture of sitting here while Audra got naked behind that curtain. He couldn't even see her bare feet, but just knowing she was on the other side of that flimsy barrier— slipping those jeans down her long, sleek legs, unsnapping that leather bodice to free her lush breasts—was killing him.

He should skip out now, before she came out and gave life to one of the many fantasies he'd envisioned as he picked out lingerie. He could claim to be sick, to get a call, a forgotten emergency. Anything.

He'd tell her he'd call in a couple weeks. Go solve this case, arrest Larson, break up the *Du Bing Li* triad. Maybe by doing so, he could find a way to help Audra out of the criminal organization.

Jesse stood up. Just as he started to yell to let her know he'd had an emergency and had to run, she flipped aside the curtain.

His breath caught in his throat and his body went from semierect to rock-hard in three seconds flat. God help him. He couldn't walk away. Hell, he'd be lucky if he could *even* walk, as hard as he was. Standing before him, Audra made him want to weep. Hands down, she was his ultimate fantasy.

From her red velvet choker to the black satin corset with red lacing up the front, her look screamed wild sex. Golden flesh peeked through the crisscrossed laces, and the red satin ends hung loose, untied. A promise of easy access to the heaven beyond.

The skirt, some sheer material that gave him tempting glimpses of the outline of her legs, flowed to her calves. And beneath it? The one thing guaranteed to send Jesse into a drooling mess of testosterone. Boots. Knee-high, black suede, lace-up-the-front boots.

She'd fluffed her hair, done something to make her skin sparkle in the soft lighting. His gaze followed the glittering trail down her throat, over her collarbone and watched where it sank between her cleavage. He wanted to take that same path with his tongue.

Jesse groaned.

Audra gave him a saucy grin. Pure female confidence, she

stepped up onto the platform and pressed a button on the wall. The music changed from soft blues to the quicker, heavy beat of rock and roll.

Her gaze locked on his, Audra danced the length of the platform.

"You like?"

"I like very much."

Audra nodded as if she'd expected nothing less. She danced, totally unself-conscious, her moves both sexy and graceful.

"You have good taste. This is one of my favorite outfits. I call it Dominate Me. It's about the edgiest design we carry. It's turned out to be one of our best sellers."

"I can see why," he said, his vision glazed with desire. "You look good enough to make me hand over a whip and ask you to punish me, mistress."

Audra's brows winged up, a wicked grin curving her full lips.

"I like the way you think. Very sexy. I've never met such a sexy computer geek before." She sauntered off the platform, her hips swaying in hypnotic time to the rock beat. "Maybe you can take a look at my PC sometime? It's been acting funky lately."

"Sure," Jesse said with quick enthusiasm. It was all he could do to not jump up, grab her by the hand and run from the room. "We could do that now. Let's go."

Audra stopped, inches in front of him, and gave him a puzzled look.

"Now? You're kidding, right?"

Jesse's gaze swept the delicious feast of flesh encased in smooth black satin and tried not to groan. Hell, no, he wasn't kidding. He didn't know how he could stay here and resist touching her. Tasting her. He needed to get out of here, fast.

"Why not? Your computer is here?" Since the tickets to China had been purchased through Simply Sensual it was feasible any connections she had with Davey or *Du Bing Li* would be on the company computer. Give him a half hour with that PC and he'd have all the evidence he needed to nail her. He just hoped it was enough to push her into turning evidence on Davey and the gang.

"Nah, I don't have a personal computer here. Natasha handles all the books and business stuff on one. But I rarely use it. It's better that way. If I started thinking of computers as workhorses, I'd never play with one again."

She took a step closer, and Jesse almost swallowed his tongue. Just centimeters away, he could feel the heat from her body. He could see the outline of her nipples beneath the midnight satin. Her perfume, something musky and evocative, enveloped him. His mind fogged, and thought dribbled away like water between his fingers.

"My computer is at my place. Maybe we can go look at it later."

"Later?"

"Mmm-hmm. Later. We're busy right now. After all, you don't want to miss any of the show, now do you?"

AUDRA HELD her breath, waiting for Jesse's response. Her sex appeal on the line, she wasn't sure what she'd do if he said he'd rather check out her computer than her body.

Any other guy, she'd have flicked him off, sent him on his way at the slightest hint he wasn't totally into her. But Jesse? She couldn't help it, but she was mortally afraid she'd do whatever it took to get him—keep him—interested.

Lucky for her, those gorgeous brown eyes of his glowed with heated interest, and he gave her a slow, sweet smile.

"Show, huh? I did like that dance. You have a way of moving that makes a man want to give thanks."

"I have a few other moves you might like to see."

Jesse's eyes darkened to a deep, rich chocolate and muttered what sounded like a prayer before he reached out to pull her toward him. One hand flat against the small of her back, he combed the other through her hair to tug gently, holding her head.

"I've got a few of my own. Why don't we share?"

"Why don't we," she murmured just before his mouth took hers.

It was like a wildfire. The heat had been there already, swirling between them. But the touch of their lips set off the spark, sending those smoldering embers of desire into flames. Engulfing, life-changing flames that Audra welcomed like nothing she'd ever felt before.

She gave herself over to the kiss. Every slide of their tongues, nip of their teeth, fanned the flames hotter. She ran her hands down his arms and gave a shiver of delight at the clenched muscles beneath his shirtsleeves. Nothing turned her on more than a dude with a hot bod. She wanted to see just how hot Jesse's was.

She slipped her hands between their bodies and worked the buttons of his shirt loose. He released his hold on her head and, oh baby, cupped her breast instead. Audra paused on the buttons to fully give herself over to the pleasure of his fingers working her nipple beneath the slippery satin.

He pulled his mouth away and with two quick steps, swung her around so that she lay beneath him on the couch. She shifted so one leg wrapped around his and cupped him between her thighs. The feel of his hard flesh pressed against her swollen, aching center made her moan. Audra moved against his leg in a subtle, easy rhythm to enjoy the slow climb to ecstasy.

Jesse buried his mouth in the curve of her neck and slid his fingers up her thigh. She could feel the heat of his hand through the silky smooth stockings and waited, a half smile on her face. She let her head fall back, eyes closed to heighten the sensations, as he discovered her thighs were bare above the elastic thigh-high stockings. Her thighs and everything else.

He slid his body down just a bit, and she moaned as the movement put more pressure on her wet, throbbing nub.

"More," she demanded breathlessly.

Jesse used that oh-so-talented mouth to tug at the laces between her breasts. Loosened, the bodice fell open and she heard his hiss of pleasure at the sight. With her free hand, she reached up to cup one of her own breasts, offering it up for his pleasure. Then she felt his mouth on her flesh. He used his tongue to lightly circle her nipple, teasing, taunting. Audra wanted to scream. She needed more. Needed pressure.

He must have read her desperation. In a deliciously quick move, Jesse took her nipple in his mouth. He suckled it deep as he ran the tip of his finger over the wet, straining folds of flesh between her thighs.

Audra felt the climax building, a tight coil of sensation. She tried to pull back. It was too fast, and while she was all for selfish pleasure, she wanted more with Jesse.

But he wouldn't let her. With a gentle scrape of his teeth over her nipple, he worked her clitoris and sent her flying over the edge.

Audra gave a keening moan of pleasure and shuddered as the orgasm took her breath away. Lights flashed behind her closed eyes and she felt as if she were surfing on a wave of delight. Her body clenched, shuddering as the climax rippled through her.

While she floated somewhere in a cloud of bliss, Jesse gathered her close and shifted so that they lay side by side on the couch.

Her hand still clenched on his bicep, Audra slowly opened her eyes to see him staring down at her.

He winked and raised both brows. "I know it was just an opener, but I'd say that had to rate at least a six on your scale."

She stared blankly for a second, then burst out laughing. "At least a six. Probably even a six and a half. I can't wait to see what you do when we're naked."

Before she could make a move to find out, a tinny chime rang out. Jesse started, then looked around in confusion. A few notes into the tune, and Audra grimaced.

"Isn't that the song from *Pinocchio?* What's it called?"

"'When You Wish Upon a Star,'" she muttered, not meeting his eyes.

Five solid seconds of stunned silence was more than she could handle, though. She glanced up from his chest to see the look of bafflement in his eyes.

"Disney? Your cell phone rings Disney?"

"Well, not really."

He squinted at her.

"I have ring tones programmed in for some of my friends. That would be Isabel, and it's a joke. Sort of."

"Sort of?"

Audra sighed. Why did she have the feeling she wasn't going to get his clothes off without an explanation?

"When we were kids, Isabel had a habit of acting like that annoying little cricket."

His frown faded, and he laughed. "Your conscience?"

Give the man points for being quick. At least on the uptake. She'd bet he took his slow, sweet time with other things. Impatience rippled through her, since she wanted to get back to finding out.

"Right. And since she has a freakish record for interrupting me when I least want her to, I haven't changed it." Audra shifted and her still-sensitive nipples brushed against the hard planes of his chest. She sucked in a breath, then let it out as she pressed herself closer.

"She's gone now, so let's get back to more important matters. Like if you can top six and a half."

Impatient to find out, she shifted so she could undo the remainder of his shirt buttons.

Jesse's hands folded over hers. Audra looked up with a frown and tilted her head in question.

"We need to stop," he murmured. Regret shone in his brown eyes, still hot with desire.

"What? You're kidding, right? You just gave me one sweet little orgasm, but that's just an appetizer. I won't be satisfied unless I get the whole meal." Brows furrowed, she brushed a soft kiss over his mouth. "I want you to get the whole meal."

He gave a strained laugh and rested his forehead against hers. Sweet pleasure, something on another level than the physical release she'd just experienced, rushed through Audra.

"I'm sure it'd be one hell of a meal, at that. And I want to. You have no idea how bad I want to. But…I can't. I just can't."

"Why? What is it? You have a condom. I saw it. I even have a box of them here. Is there another reason? The phone call? Did you lose the mood?"

She shifted against his still straining hard-on and grinned. "You definitely didn't lose it where it counts."

"No, it's not that."

"What, then? Something physical?" A million thoughts ran through her brain, all of them a little gross.

He looked blank at first, then screwed up his face in denial. Relief surged through Audra.

"No! I mean, it's nothing physical. It's just…well, as insane as this sounds, I'm not that kind of guy."

All she could do was stare, her mind blank with shock.

"Oh. My. God," she breathed. She reached up to pull her bodice over her bare breasts. "I knew it. The signs were all there, but I kept sidestepping them. That voice in the back of my head kept pointing out the obvious, but I kept telling myself I was wrong."

He winced.

"You are a *good* boy, aren't you?"

"A good boy?" He squinted at her in silence for a few seconds. Then he frowned and nodded slowly. "Yeah, that's one way to put it. I'm a good boy. And, well, I can't do this yet. I want to. I want *you* insanely. Past the edge of reason. But…I can't."

"What? Is there some good boy code or something?"

"You could say that."

She waited.

He shrugged and gave her a sheepish smile.

"I'd really like to get to know you better before we make love."

Audra just stared. It sounded like a brush-off to her. She wasn't really sure, having never been brushed off before. But she'd brushed plenty herself, and it was definitely following the same pattern. She bit her lip and told herself she wasn't hurt.

The pain in her chest said differently. She was a big girl, though. She could ignore it.

Something must have shown on her face, because Jesse's expression clouded with concern. He slipped both hands, so warm and strong, over her jaw to cup her cheeks.

"What? You don't believe me?"

"It's not that, really. I mean, I don't think you're lying to me or anything." Maybe lying to himself? He seemed too sweet to try and deliberately deceive her. She'd known plenty of guys who were pros at the scam. Jesse radiated pure honesty. Such a good boy trait.

"I swear, I want to spend time with you. I can't think of anything I want more than to make love with you. To drive us both crazy, to see how many ways we can bring each other pleasure. You know, strive for that ultimate ten."

Audra, still damp, felt herself heat up again at his words. If she closed her eyes, she knew she'd be able to visualize them together. To imagine all the things they'd do with each other. To each other.

"I just… Well, I want to get to know you better first. So when we do get together, it means something."

Her eyes grew huge. He wasn't thinking all that mushy emotional stuff, was he? Obviously reading her, he grinned and shook his head.

"Not like that. As much as I want to see where this goes between us, it's not like I'm not looking for something permanent or, you know, all serious. I just, well, I believe that when two people get together, it should be more than the moment."

His wince was infinitesimal, but Audra saw it anyway. Maybe he figured she was such a hard-ass, she'd blast him for being a sentimental goofball. Once, she might have. But now?

Now the sentiment was appealing to her, for some reason. Maybe it was the source?

"So, dating, huh?"

"You game? Call it prolonged foreplay."

When Audra laughed, Jesse hugged her close. She closed her eyes and let herself absorb the warm comfort of his arms.

"It'll be cool. You'll see. Besides, I'm just not the kind of guy who goes all the way on the first date."

She laughed again and pulled away from him. Both arms outspread, she jutted one hip and tilted her head.

"You sure you want to wait?"

Jesse closed his eyes and groaned. But he still nodded.

"It'll be cool," he repeated. "We'll talk, get to know each other. Just the two of us, hit some hot spots, do things."

"What kind of things do you want to do?" Audra strained to think of nonsexual things to do with a man, but she came up blank. She tried to tell herself it was the remnants of heat, the faint tremors of that orgasm still coursing through her.

"What about a trip to Napa? Check out the wine country. Or we can go to San Francisco and hang out on Fisherman's Wharf. See a movie, catch a concert. Dinner and dancing? You know, dating things."

Audra frowned. They all sounded great. They'd all be better capped off with a night of sex, but who was she to quibble. Had she ever dated? For a woman whose longest relationship could be counted in weeks, it was a foreign concept.

To date and not have sex? It was more than foreign, it was totally alien.

But…for Jesse? She was drawn to him, and as much as she wanted to screw his brains out, she was intrigued by the man as much as by the body.

Just one more out-of-character thing to worry about.

Dating? It was worth a shot.

"For a while," she agreed. "But you have to promise, after the third date we get to have sex."

7

CLOSING TIME had never been so welcome, Audra thought. Or, she glanced at Bea, so distracting.

"C'mon, you have to help me out," Bea wheedled. She leaned against the boutique's sales counter and batted her lashes. "You're always there for me, right? Best buds?"

As if Audra was going to be influenced by a pair of big baby blues and carefully displayed cleavage? She knew it wasn't deliberate, though. That was just what Bea did. They'd met when Bea had rebelled against her rich daddy by talking her stepmom du jour into enrolling her in public school. The helpless sex-kitten persona was as much a part of Bea as her porcelain complexion and the way she cried at Hallmark commercials.

"Look, normally I would, you know that." That was the great thing about the Wicked Chicks, they *were* always there for each other. "But I don't have time right now. I've got too much to do here in the boutique. Between that and my deadline for the fall designs, I'm buried."

She'd be a lot further along with the designs if she hadn't spent so much time daydreaming about her time with Jesse on the couch the night before. And reliving the sweet rush of pleasure he'd given her.

"I'd pay extra," Bea offered. As soon as the words were out of her mouth, she winced and held up one hand in protest. "Don't say it. I'm sorry. Reflex brought on by retail mania."

Audra quirked a brow, but didn't respond. After all, Bea's generosity was as big as her heart. Unfortunately, the woman was getting used to daddy's money buying anything she wanted—again. It was a habit the Wicked Chicks had broken her of in their teen years. The girls had come from drastically different places—Bea, the poor little rich girl, Audra, a social worker's obligation, and Suzi, an orphan with a chip on her shoulder. But they'd all had the same badass attitude and faith in each other. Audra firmly believed it'd been that faith that had kept the three of them from becoming sad statistics.

Lately, though, Bea had given in to her father's nagging and emotional blackmail, and after his last divorce, had agreed to act as his hostess and social assistant.

The man was obviously a bad influence on her.

"It doesn't have to be a special design, then," Bea continued in her relentless way. "I mean, I love your stuff, you know that. I'd rather wear it than anything else. I just need some hot lingerie for this shoot."

Audra glanced over to see the redhead's lower lip hanging, her eyes puppy-dog sad.

Oh, jeez. As if she cared about a guilt trip? Audra ignored the subtle pressure of both Bea's pout and her own conscience. She continued counting Saturday's till. The boutique had just closed. All she needed to do was finish the deposit and grab her sketches, and she could hightail it home to a pair of cozy slippers, a cup of hot chocolate with extra whipped cream and her waiting pile of work.

That thought, the mundane boring reality of it, scared the hell out of her. Her fingers clenched the bills she was counting. It was Saturday night. She should be planning to go clubbing. Considering what hot outfit to wear, which of her three new pairs of heels would be best for dancing.

Contemplating what flavor of sex she was in the mood for.

Panic whispered in her ear, assuring her she really was washed up. She'd lost it.

Audra sucked in a swift breath to quell the freaked-out thoughts and tilted her chin at Bea.

"Tell me the deal again. Why has this photo shoot got you so excited?"

"I met this up-and-coming photographer and he's going to shoot a few rolls of film for my portfolio," Bea explained in a giddy tone. Bea dropped a name but, since she was unfamiliar with the fashion scene outside lingerie, Audra just shrugged. "This is it, Audra. With his edgy, high-fashion shots, I can have it all. Modeling, magazines, maybe even TV commercials."

"This guy told you all that?" Audra had to work to keep the sneer out of her voice. When would Bea learn that guys lied like rugs?

"Yeah. Suzi said he was full of shit and was just trying to get laid."

Suzi was smart that way.

"But he gave me his business card this morning, told me to check him out if I had any worries."

This morning. As in Bea had already done the guy. Audra sighed and wondered when she'd turned into Isabel. Who knew meaningless sex could bother her so much?

"Did you check him out?" she asked.

"Well, no. I mean, I don't know how to check a guy out, other than the obvious package assessment." From the look on her face, the guy's package hadn't been too impressive. "He did say he's not really computer savvy, so he just recently hired someone to set up a Web site for his company. He even mentioned using my picture for the launch page of his site after this photo shoot."

Maybe she was just jaded, but it still sounded like a line

of bullshit to her. Then again, he'd already got into Bea's panties, so why would he lie after the fact?

"Take a look around. You're welcome to anything here."

Obviously not thrilled to be shopping off the rack, Bea wrinkled her nose. But she started flipping through the lingerie racks anyway.

Five minutes later, Audra's jaw hurt from clenching it. Not that Bea had been bitchy or rude about the designs, but her expression was crystal clear. She was very unimpressed.

"What's the problem?" Audra finally challenged.

"Nothing. Really, these are sweet." Bea hesitated, obviously not wanting to be ungrateful. Then she shrugged, her hands lifting in defeat. "It's just… Well, they *are* sweet."

"Sweet?"

"Yeah. You know, the kind of thing you'd get your little sister for her wedding night or something. They hint at naughty, but don't scream *hot sex*."

Audra opened her mouth to protest. Then with a snap, she shut it again. After all, Bea was right.

"I just wanted something more, you know, spicy. Hot. Dirty, ya know?"

She knew. Stuff like she'd been seeing in her head. Leather, zippers, chrome. Designs that got a woman excited about herself. Dared her to push her own envelope a little. The kind that promised a guy he'd have to work damned hard to keep up.

The kind of design she'd been itching to create.

But couldn't, because she was already behind the eight ball with her current commitments. Maybe after Natasha returned from China?

Then again, she mused, this *would* be a great opportunity to sketch out a few of her visions, use Bea's request as an excuse to pitch them to Natasha.

"Tell you what," she proposed, "I don't have time to work

up anything new right now. But I can modify a couple to suit you. When did you say the shoot is?"

"Hopefully next week. He's going to book the studio and let me know the date."

"Okay, I'll work on it tonight." She shouldn't have too much trouble fitting a little altering and modification in between designs.

"You won't regret it," Bea promised. She giggled and gave Audra a tight hug. "I'll be a huge star and everyone will be clamoring for your lingerie."

A warm feeling, friendship mingled with comfort, settled over Audra. She might not be as bad as she once was, but at least she still had her friends.

That, combined with a chance to run with these design ideas, and her upcoming date with the sexiest man she'd ever come for... Well, her life was rockin' along nicely.

WITH A HUGE YAWN, Audra stretched her arms overhead and tried to work the kinks out of her shoulders. She glanced over at the stack of designs, in various stages of completion, scattered over her home drafting table. She'd spent the previous evening working on three outfits for Bea. She'd tailored each to showcase the redhead's curvy figure and rich coloring.

Sexual images, always at the forefront of her mind because of her nature and the nature of her work, had bombarded her all night. All she'd been able to think of was her not-even-close-to-enough sexual encounter with Jesse. She'd spent hours staring off in space, reliving the whole evening. Here she was, all hot and bothered, and the guy wanted to date.

Dating. Who'd figure she'd be excited about the idea? Maybe it was the novelty. Possibly the distraction from all the responsibility of Simply Sensual, or the worries over the unclear direction her life was going—or, rather, not going. Whatever the reason, she was fascinated with the concept.

Too bad their first date wasn't until Thursday night. She wouldn't mind a repeat of that level-six orgasm. If he could do that fully clothed, she just might have found a level-eight guy. With extensive coaching, possibly the fabled nine and a half.

She glanced at the clock on the wall, a Betty Boop figurine complete with finger on chin and her butt hitched in a seductive stance. Audra needed to get these designs done.

One of the keys to Simply Sensual's sales pitch was, in addition to key pieces from their current line of lingerie, a first look at their fall line and three exclusive designs to any distributor committing to a certain quantity.

While the current line was already available to show, the fall line wasn't complete yet. Which was what Audra was supposed to finish this weekend.

She'd lost a lot of time already, and Natasha was going to want the sketches faxed to her on Monday. Since that was tomorrow, Audra didn't have the luxury of daydreaming. Not if she wanted make good on Natasha's faith in her. And given that Natasha had given her a job, a career and a chance to prove herself, Audra was set on proving that faith justified.

She looked around her apartment, its funky style making her smile. Rich, jewel-toned paisley fabric covered the walls in lieu of paint. Peacock feathers, Mardi Gras masks and a black boa provided wall art, and the furniture was overstuffed and sensual. Tall pillar candles filled the air with musk, their flickering flame dancing with warmth. All in all, an invitation to play. Just the way she liked it.

She'd been on her own forever, it seemed. But this apartment, even months after she'd moved in, still made her proud. It was the most expensive place she'd lived. Very different from growing up with her father over the bar, or her mother in whatever dive she happened to be flopping at the time.

When she'd reunited with her brother, she hadn't had much faith in him. Or, to be honest, in herself. But he'd come through for her. He'd been determined to do whatever it took to fulfill their father's last request that they reconnect and that Drew help her get a job, get her life on track.

At first, Audra had screwed with Drew's head a lot. She'd told him she wanted work in a circus, a lemonade stand and her own phone sex business. Despite her crappy attitude, he hadn't given up. He'd pushed until she finally admitted her interest in design and lingerie.

Lucky for her, Drew's wife had just bought out her aunt's share of Simply Sensual and she'd taken Audra under her wing. Natasha had mentored her, given her a job both in the boutique and designing lingerie. While Drew had footed the bill, Natasha had helped Audra get into school to get her degree in fashion and design. The more Audra learned, the more Natasha had let her do, until Audra was doing all of the designs in-house.

Natasha has promised if Audra stuck with it and graduated, she'd make it worth her while. There weren't many people Audra trusted to keep their word. After all, other than Isabel, Bea and Suzi, nobody else in her life ever had. But Natasha and Drew had come through for her.

It still amazed her.

Finally, about six months ago, Audra had been comfortable enough to trust the income would last and had settled into her dream apartment. Two bedrooms, a sunken tub and, her secret passion, a gourmet kitchen. Not that she could cook more than microwave dinners. But there was something so sensual about food, and places where food was prepared. Like sex, she figured when she learned to cook, she'd be damned good at it.

She forced herself to concentrate on her current design. An oriental-inspired teddy, it was a combination of silk, embroidery and a modified mandarin collar. But she couldn't focus. Her mind was fogged with exhaustion and she could barely keep her eyes open. With a shrug, she decided she had the rest of the day. She could get it done later.

Audra gave into the decadent lure of her bedroom and cuddled under the downy warmth of her purple velour comforter. After a little nap, she'd be recharged to work on the designs.

THE JANGLING PHONE shrilled in Audra's ear. She moaned and pulled her pillow over her head, trying to ignore the summons.

Her answering machine, idiotically placed on the bedside table, whirred as it delivered the outgoing message.

"Audra? You have to be around. Where are you?" Natasha's voice crackled over the line. Not even the thousands of miles between them were enough to dull the sharp, frantic tone of her voice. "I have to talk to you right away. Can you—"

Audra grabbed the phone. "Yeah," she said.

She leaned on one elbow and squinted through the dusk-darkened room at the luminescent numbers of her clock radio. She'd slept two hours. At least she'd had a nice, hot erotic dream to show for it. Images of Jesse, leather wrist straps and decadent delights still flashed through her head as Audra stretched, one hand holding the phone and the other trailing down her body, over her still peaked nipples. Even awake, she could feel the heat, the wet pleasure between her legs.

"I'm here. What's up, Tash? You sound a little freaked."

"Freaked? Oh, man, that's putting it lightly. These people are crazy. They want the designs immediately."

Audra winced and sent a squint-eyed look past her

bedroom door to the drafting table backlit by the kitchen lights. Okay, no problem. She'd work all night, get the fall designs done and faxed first thing in the morning.

"The fall designs? Um, okay. I'll get them to you this week. I have the hotel's fax number, right?"

"Wrong. Hotel address."

"What? You need them expressed or something?"

"No." Panic came through the phone line loud and clear. "They aren't satisfied with the *promise* of three exclusive designs in addition to the fall line. They want to see what the designs will be."

"What?" Audra yelped, sitting up so fast her head spun.

"They want to see actual design boards on the custom designs. The real deal. No rough sketches, no samples of past designs to prove our quality. They want, in their demanding little fingers, the actual prototype designs. Fabric swatches, bead samples. The works."

"Shit." This sucked. Audra threw off the comforter and bounded out of bed. Maybe they could substitute a few from the fall line she'd been working on? She hurried into the living room and started flipping through her completed designs. Five. Dammit.

She had to do it, though. Natasha had gone all the way to China to court these distributors in person. To take Simply Sensual out of the domestic market and go international. This was their big break.

"How soon do you actually have to have them?"

"The sooner the better. I can send you their preferences, the looks they're hoping for. You have my appointment schedule. If you can get me the individualized design boards at least a day before each meeting, that'd still work."

"I doubt I can get them ready that fast, Natasha. I thought we had time. I thought you were just presenting ideas, remember. I was waiting to hear what they wanted for their custom look before I even tried to come up with designs."

Audra frowned and set aside the almost-complete design for a lace bridal teddy. Before she could think of another alternative, her sister-in-law was wailing again.

"This was crazy. We jumped before we were ready. I'm going to come home, we'll regroup, think this through. We might lose these distributors, sure, but we can pick up others."

"No!" Audra exclaimed. "No damned way. We spent a lot of time researching *these* distributors. We busted our asses finding companies that met all our requirements, including your demanding work ethic. That wasn't easy, Natasha. This is our shot. You're already there, you've had the initial meetings with them. If you leave, we've blown it."

"I don't want to leave, either, but I just don't see how we can do this. There is so much work involved. Work you are going to be stuck doing."

"We'll make it happen," she vowed. Somehow.

"Are you sure? Because if you can do it, I'm sure we'll snag at least two of these accounts. And on top of that, I was approached by a different distributor yesterday who's interested. We're meeting this week, as well. I need to research them, but it could mean an even bigger order. More success." Natasha sounded giddy and terrified, all at the same time.

Audra pressed a hand to her stomach. She knew how her sister-in-law felt.

"The thing is," Natasha continued, "this puts it all on your shoulders, Audra. That's four accounts to design for now. Can you handle it?"

Her anxiety came through loud and clear. It had been one thing to leave the boutique in Audra's hands while she was away for a short trip. But now? Now Audra was responsible for the boutique *and* the success of Simply Sensual.

The only thing Audra couldn't tell was whether Natasha felt bad about Audra carrying the extra load or if she simply didn't have the faith that Audra could pull it off.

Did it matter? Either way, it would take a miracle. But she wasn't going to tell Natasha that. The last thing she needed to do was confirm she couldn't handle the responsibility of the shop. Instead, she offered bogus assurances, hurried her sister-in-law through goodbyes and hung up.

"Shit," she said to the empty room. "Now what?"

Now she proved she was a responsible designer worthy of her new title, and not a pity case. Or she confirmed to the world at large, or at least her family, that she would never amount to more than an unreliable bad girl with a flair for design.

JESSE RUBBED his eyes and glared at the computer screen. He was finally getting a solid hook on Dave Larson. The guy had more screen names than Microsoft had patents. So far, though, he'd connected him with the enforcer of *Du Bing Li* triad, at least through e-mails, as well as three of the lower-ranking gang lieutenants. A couple were stupidly chatty in their online exchanges, probably thinking Dave's computer skills would shield them from detection.

Who knew the computer was the communication of choice for up-and-coming gangs?

"Martinez?"

Jesse turned to face his captain.

"Sir?"

"Any breaks on the triad case? Word on the street is they're moving on something big, but nobody can pinpoint what it is. Vice wants in, so give me something to keep this in our department."

Jesse bristled. "This isn't their arena, it's ours. From what

I've tracked so far, we'll be able to link them to high-level identity theft. Possibly credit card fraud and some money laundering, as well."

Shale grunted and took the file Jesse held out. The furrow between his brow deepened as he read through the case notes.

"If you're right, they'll be moving on this fast."

"I'd estimate they'll want to move before the month's out. I'm surprised they haven't already. All I can think of is maybe they had some trouble with the information? From what I can tell, Larson is scrambling. It looks like he screwed up somewhere."

"His loss, our gain."

"His loss might be more than he bargained for. He's always been small potatoes. This screwup, whatever it is, might cost him more than he'd imagined."

"Has a hit been ordered?"

"Not yet, but my narc seems to think it's in the works."

"Can you use that?"

Jesse considered. "Maybe. I've made contact with Larson online in a few different venues using different personas. He must have something else going on, though, since his online activity level is a lot lower than his M.O."

"Like you said, he's scrambling. Maybe he's busy trying to rebuild his info?"

"Or trying to recover it," Jesse mused. He had to nail down what had been handed off to Audra. Once he did, he'd have the evidence he needed to pull the guy in. Audra too, unfortunately. As far as he could tell, though, she hadn't had any further contact with Larson.

At Shale's look, Jesse shook his head and indicated the file. "Either way, he's on shaky ground."

"The shakier the better. See if you can set something up with him. Get his trust, see if he'll turn."

"Turning on anyone connected with *Du Bing Li* is dicey. I'd have to have some damned good incentive."

"If he did screw up, his ass is on the fast track to dead. That might be all the incentive you need."

Jesse nodded. It might. He'd see if he could come up with a little more, though.

"You nail the Walker chick yet?"

Didn't he wish? Jesse mentally groaned at the memory of Audra's body beneath his on the couch. The slide of her flesh against the slick leather. The feel of her exploding around his fingers. Damn.

"Not yet, but the evidence is building. Her business partner is over in China. So far, she's met with a few different lingerie distributors, which is in keeping with the lady's business. Nothing hokey until yesterday, when she had a meeting with a new company. A little digging and I found out they're a money laundering front for the *Wo Shing Wo* triad."

Shale nodded, obviously unsurprised. Unlike Jesse, who had been a little shocked to have the evidence drop into his lap that easily. He wanted to think it was too easy, but he was pretty sure that was the lusting side of his brain talking, not the cop side.

"Did you track the money?" Shale asked, tapping the printout of Simply Sensual's bank account and the large sum deposited the previous week.

"Not yet, except that it came from an offshore account."

"Both women have clean records, though. They're probably new," Shale mused.

While his boss focused on the file, Jesse didn't inform the captain that he'd broken into Audra's sealed juvie record. His superior would have no interest in the fact that Audra had been arrested for breaking into a dog pound.

Jesse, though, was fascinated. The woman was a mass of

contradictions. Sweet as hell, and equally hard. Funny and sexy, and now this humanitarian side? All he could think about was their date on Thursday night. If only he could break the case before then. Because it was going to be pure hell resisting her otherwise.

Jesse had never found a woman who appealed to him on so many levels. It was as if she was the answer to all of his most tempting dreams.

It was going to suck when he had to arrest her.

8

"HEY, AUDRA. You look whipped."

Audra glanced up from the counter, where she'd spread her designs, trim and the ugly tie the geek had tossed at her that night in the club, to see Isabel let the boutique door swing shut behind her.

"Hang on," she muttered. "I've almost got this design just right."

Sure, Natasha wanted to stick with the tried and true. But if Audra had to make up design boards to present the exclusive designs these distributors wanted to see, why not offer an interesting option?

She'd woke that morning from a hot dream where Jesse had tied her to the bedposts. All morning, she'd been trying to get the wild dominatrix idea out of her head. She hadn't been able to pull it from dream to reality until she'd spied the butt-ugly tie draped behind her desk. As soon as she'd seen the strip of tacky material, something had clicked. It was the color, the vivid garish rainbow, that she'd used for the wrist straps. The way the straps contrasted with the sexy black leather really made the design pop. It looked even better on paper than it had in her imagination.

She smothered a naughty grin. It wasn't that she was trying to get her own way by ignoring Natasha's wish to stick with the sweeter stuff. It was just that she felt sure she knew what was best for *her* designs. Wasn't that what a head designer was for?

"Party hard this weekend?" her friend asked. "You look like you haven't slept in days.

Dropping her pencil on the counter, Audra rubbed her burning eyes and glanced at the clock. It was only Monday morning and she was ready for the weekend. She'd been in this seat since six and her brain felt as if it were going to explode. She flexed her stiff shoulders and wished for just a thirty-minute nap. She swiveled to face Isabel and pasted a cheeky smile on her face. It was all she could do to keep it there when she got a good look at her friend's face.

"What's wrong?"

Isabel's lip jutted a little, and she tucked a black curl behind her ear as she shrugged. She flicked a finger down the peach lace of a chemise, then met Audra's eyes.

"I lost the account."

Her mind went blank for a moment. Audra started to ask what account, and then it hit her.

"The mall?" At Isabel's morose nod, she forced her stiff body off the stool and came around the counter. "What happened? You were meeting with the manager, right?"

"Right. This morning." Shoulders slumped, Isabel made her way toward Audra.

Her eyes still on her friend's face, Audra moved to grab a Red Bull from the minifridge behind the counter and handed it to her.

"Here, a shot of energy should help you shake it off. Then you can tell me the details."

Still droopy, Isabel popped open the can as she glanced over the sketches spread across the counter.

"See," she said with a sniff. "These designs are like us. The sweet florals are me. The leather and studs are you. Even if it does have those freaky-looking wrist bands."

Her brow wrinkled. What the hell was Isabel babbling about?

Audra looked at her little bit of rebellion. The leather teddy, complete with ugly-tie-inspired wrist restraints. Who knew such a blight against design as that piece of neckwear could inspire such a hot idea?

"Which one of these two can handle heavy flirting?" Isabel continued. "Which one screams, 'Do me with a dollop of whipped cream'? Which one would a guy go for?"

She took a swig of her drink. Then she faced Audra, her sweet face hard with determination.

"For the first time in my life, I want to be leather and studs," she declared.

Audra's eyes widened. *Come on over to the dark side,* she wanted to say. Afraid to jinx this breakthrough, though, she swallowed the invitation.

"What actually happened?" she asked instead.

Isabel took another look at the designs, then rolled her eyes. "Did you ever meet a guy who made you want to give him a bath with your tongue?"

Jesse's face flashed through her mind. She hadn't considered a tongue bath before. But now that she did, it had definite possibilities.

"I showed up this morning for my appointment. I was supposed to finalize everything and sign the contracts, right?" Before Audra could comment, Isabel continued, "I'm waiting in this guy's office and he's like twenty minutes late. I'd rather walk out, you know? Because the last thing I want to deal with is a rude client. If he's late for meetings, who knows what other bad business habits he has?"

Audra had barely finished nodding when Isabel barreled on. Now, though, she was pacing. Her wide-flying gestures didn't bother Audra so much as the open can in her hand.

"Finally, just as I decided no account, no matter how pretty a feather in my cap, was worth that rudeness, in walks this guy."

"The manager?"

"I wish. I've met the manager. He's balding, short and has an overbite. This guy is tall, hot and sexy. I guess he's the general manager or something."

"General manager? That's good, though, right? I mean, he's got the power to hire you for a lot of malls, not just one."

Isabel winced.

"Did he turn you down? He reneged on the verbal agreement?" Audra growled deep in her throat. Anger, rarely expressed, surged through her. With swift strides, she started pacing the length of the boutique, too. "I'll go to that mall myself and kick his sorry ass. Where does this guy get off?"

"He didn't renege, Audra. I ran."

Stopping so fast that her spiked heels should have been smoking, Audra squinted at her friend. "Huh?"

"I ran. He came in, all hot and sexy and I got tongue-tied. All I could think of was stripping his suit from his body and having him for breakfast. Then he..."

"He what?" Images flashed through her mind, none of them pretty. Her stomach cramped again.

Her voice so low that Audra had to strain to hear her, Isabel said, "He flirted with me."

Huh?

"Did he take his clothes off while he flirted?" Audra asked, perplexed.

"Of course not."

"Did he make kinky suggestions? Make you feel pressured to put out? Invite you to a threesome with the balding missing manager?"

"Don't be ridiculous. He didn't do any of that. He was just...you know, flirty. Like he was interested."

"So you ran away? Not only from a hot dude who'd likely give you a nice lube job, but from a huge business deal?"

And Isabel had worried Audra would blow *her* career?

"It sounds stupid when you say it. But I was overwhelmed. I'm not like you. I'm not used to such intense interest from a guy. I guess I ran from it. From him."

Isabel tossed her empty can into the trash and threw up her hands. "It's not like it really matters, right? I mean, I don't have to move on to the next stage of my business plan yet. I've improved the flower shop a lot already, right? Money is okay. So I've hit a career plateau."

Audra thought of her own struggles lately. That plateau seemed to be going around. Sure, she'd got a fancy promotion to head designer, but she was starting to feel that it was an empty promotion. Pretty words, no substance. Since she'd been fighting that particular perception most of her life, she should recognize it when it stared her in the face.

"No law says I have to move up *now,*" Isabel continued. "I'm fine waiting a few months. Maybe years."

"Years? Oh, my God, no way." The glaring comparison to her own situation was too obvious to ignore. Audra smothered the thought with a determined jut of her chin. She wasn't waiting years to have her cake. And neither was Isabel.

"Years, my ass. You get your butt back to that mall, sex that guy up and get that account."

"Sex him up? You're insane."

"You don't really have to sleep with him. Just flirt. Give him back the same as he's giving you. You know, go for the gusto."

"Isn't that a beer slogan?"

Audra rolled her eyes. "You know what I mean. You want to be leather and studs, go for it. Who's to say you have to take it slow? Don't you owe it to yourself to give every shot one hundred percent? Even if it might not be the perfect time?"

"I can't mix business with pleasure like that," Isabel objected. "It'd be like using my body to get the account."

"Jeez, Isabel. You were already promised the account. So go get it. If you use your body at this point, it's to celebrate the success. Quit making it a crime to have sex."

"Meaningless sex."

"There's no such thing," Audra reminder her. "Even M&M's satisfy."

Considering her words, Isabel flicked a finger over the leather design board. "I haven't seen any designs like this in the boutique. Are you branching out? To be honest, this is the kind of thing I'd always imagined you designing. You know, something that screamed naughty sex."

Audra contemplated the leather-studded design she'd been doodling. Isabel was right, this *was* one of the things that had attracted her to lingerie in the first place. And exactly what she intended to market. Some day.

"We don't carry this kind of thing yet, it's just something I'm working on. You know, kind of like cleansing my palate. I'm on overload right now and was hitting the point that if I had to draw one more pink rosebud, I'd scream."

"Well, this definitely isn't pink." Isabel wrinkled her nose and looked around the boutique. "Of course, I'm sure carrying something like this here is way down the road. After all, this store caters to the sweet, wedding trousseau styles. I doubt this will fit your target market or Natasha's marketing plan."

Audra sniffed, but didn't answer. Instead, she tidied up the counter and focused on building Isabel's confidence back up so she could take that manager by storm.

Five minutes, a few pats on the back and a satin chemise later, she waved Isabel out the door. Audra eyed the stack of custom designs she was sending to Natasha. The courier was due any second. Lips pursed, she eyed Leather Submission, as she'd titled the teddy she'd just finished, and the tie that had been its inspiration.

It wasn't a big deal to include it. She was just showing Natasha a few options. With a sly grin, she cut a chunk off the tie and stapled it to the design board. Natasha would recognize it from their conversation and realize the butt-ugly tie had inspired a design, just like she'd predicted. Audra slid the tie-decorated board and the other designs into the mail pouch going to China and sealed it all with a kiss.

Sure, she got the whole careful planning thing. She did appreciate the progress. Slow and steady. But dammit, she wanted the whole dream. Designing things that inspired her. For women like her.

She wanted the gusto for herself.

And she was gonna get it.

DAVE LARSON was living on easy street. Life didn't get much better than this. He lay back on the foofy pillows of Bea's overstuffed couch and toed off his shoes. He had it all. A hot chick and a growing reputation with the right people looking for his particular skills.

And thanks to his handy-dandy off-site backup system the triad had no idea about, it'd taken him a couple of keystrokes and he'd made a spanking brand-new copy of the chip they wanted. No point in wasting time chasing his tie and the other chip when it wasn't any kind of real threat. He'd asked Bea enough questions to know her friend wasn't a problem. If there was one thing Dave prided himself in, it was his judgment of people.

"Hey, snookums, did you want a beer?" Bea asked as she curled up on the couch next to him. "I'll get you one and you can tell me what you've heard about my photo shoots. I'm ready, you know. I've got the perfect lingerie coming and everything."

Dave grimaced. He might actually have to find a way to make that happen for her. But at this point, he didn't have a clue. Time to change the subject.

Even though he'd intended to wait until after sex, Dave pulled a box out of his jacket and handed it to Bea. Before, after, either way, he'd be getting sex. This little gift would just ensure it'd keep coming.

"A present?" Bea said in that cute little girly voice that got him all excited. "For me? How sweet of you."

She leaned over, her lush breasts pressed against his shoulder giving him shivers, and brushed a lip-gloss-infused kiss against his cheek. Even knowing he'd have a breakout as a result, Dave couldn't bring himself to wipe the stain away.

He forced himself to sit still as nerves scratched their way down his spine. This was the first present he'd given a woman, if you didn't count his mother. And he didn't. Had anything ever mattered as much as this moment? He felt he was putting everything on the line.

In the blink of an eye, Bea ripped through the wrapping he'd made the clerk redo three times until he'd been satisfied. When she lifted the lid of the velvet jeweler's case, her grin sparkled as bright as the diamonds nestled on the white satin.

"Oh, Davey," she squealed, leaping across the couch to wrap those long, tan arms around his neck. Dave groaned as he slid his hands over her curves. She was a dream come true. Sweet, a little dumb, with a body better than any of his favorite porn queens. He couldn't get enough of her.

She rained kisses over his face and neck, all the while hooking the five-carat diamond bracelet around her wrist. Dave sighed in pleasure.

"You like?" he asked as she held her arm out to admire the dangling ice. This was definitely worth tapping into his untraceable overseas account for the funds. "That's just the beginning. You stick with me, you'll be wearing jewels from head to toe."

Bea leaned back on her heels, her short dress hiked up to the thighs that he'd beg to taste again. The look she gave him was at odds with the airy persona he'd come to count on. "I appreciate the gift, Dave. But I'm not with you for presents. Or even for that magazine shoot you've promised me. I'm with you because I like you. I really admire what you've made of your life."

Dave ducked his head to hide his wince. Sure, she liked the picture he'd painted. Who wouldn't? He was custom-made for her, thanks to his ingenuity and brilliance. Not that he believed for a second that she'd stick around without jewels and incentives. But that was fine with Dave. It wasn't as if he'd stick around if she didn't have such well-stacked incentives herself.

"I mean, how many guys orphaned so young make a huge success like you did? You're a photographer to the stars. You're a self-made man. I admire all of that, especially what you told me about investing in the arts." Bea gave him a sexy look through her lashes. "I'd really love to learn more about art. It's so sexy."

Dave chewed the inside of his cheek while he tried to remember what he'd told her. He really needed to start writing these things down.

Before he had to come up with anything, though, his cell chimed.

"Hang on," he told her as he pulled it from the leather case on his belt. The tension in his body went into overdrive when he saw the three X's on the readout.

"Can I take this in your room? It's business and, you know, private."

She didn't even take her eyes from the sparkles as she waved him on his way. Dave hurried to the lush delights of Bea's bedroom, and, with a wince, answered.

"Larson here."

"Larson, my man. You've done us proud." The voice was as smooth as glass, but Dave knew it could cut deep enough to slice his jugular. A man didn't make top lieutenant in a group as powerful as the triad without a deadly reputation. "I wanted to personally thank you for the information on that chip. It's exactly what we were hoping for."

Dave wiped the bead of sweat from his upper lip. "You, uh, you got it all to open, right? No questions on anything?"

"You're information was both concise and user-friendly. Well done."

Dave tried to swallow, but he didn't have any spit in his mouth. If it was fine, why was the enforcer calling him?

As if he'd plucked the question straight from Dave's brain, the man continued in his whiskey-smooth tone, "I like to make it a point to let my people know when I'm pleased with them."

Dave's heart skipped a beat. *His* people. *Yes!* He'd made it. Time for the cushy jobs, the prime benefits.

"Of course, I was a little disturbed when I'd heard of your earlier…mistake." His pause was just long enough to let Dave become very aware of the sweat raining down his spine to soak the waistband of his slacks. "But you retrieved the temporarily misplaced information in a timely manner and didn't cause undue hardship for my people. I hate it when they have to take time away from their day-to-day jobs to…deal with issues."

Retrieved. Dave's vision blurred just a bit around the edges. Remade, retrieved. They were so close to the same thing. It didn't matter. Bea's friend was harmless. Just some bubbleheaded bimbo, hardly anyone to worry about. Hell, she'd likely tossed the tie by now.

"Hey, no problem," Dave finally said. "I mean, it was a simple mistake. Easy enough to rectify, ya know?"

"But it was rectified, which is what matters. I'm sure I don't have to tell you how damaging it would be to our operation should any of that information ever be used by any party other than us. An identity is a precious thing, and, of course, an exclusive thing. Should anyone else have the same identity, the same information, well…the picture isn't pretty, is it?"

Since the picture flashing through Dave's mind was of his body, dead in any horrifying variety of ways, he had to agree the image was ugly.

What if the chip slipped into the wrong hands? What if Bea's bubblehead friend somehow found it, even though it was expertly hidden in Dave's favorite tie? What would she do? Dave swiped the sweat off his chin with a shaky hand. Maybe he should check things out, try to get it back.

"As you know, I appreciate thoroughness in my people. After all, finding new ones is such a trial."

Since the triad had a reputation for never letting anyone leave employment alive after they'd "found" them, the threat was clear. The line went dead. Bile rose in his throat. Needing to wipe away the sweat dripping down his forehead and soaking his shirt, Dave headed for the bathroom to wash up.

He had to get that chip back. Not that the lieutenant had any idea the chip the triad had was anything other than the original. But just to be on the safe side, Davey'd better hook up with Bea's friend, Audra. He'd get his tie back, secure his deal. After all, he'd finally achieved his dreams. No way some loose thread was gonna screw that up for him.

BY WEDNESDAY, Audra was worn out and ready to scream. She'd just finished the final modifications to one of Simply Sensual's hottest designs for Bea. Now, the lilac lace screamed down-and-dirty sex instead of sweet, demure seduction.

It wasn't leather, but it'd suit Bea to a tee. She just hoped Bea wasn't disappointed. Her friend seemed to be putting a lot of hope into this guy's promises. Promises that sounded too good to be true.

Not that she hadn't cared about her friend's welfare and happiness in the past. She just didn't know how to interfere without sounding like an uptight idiot. As a rule, the three Wicked Chicks tended to live by a sink-or-swim policy, never interfering with or advising the others.

She thought of the final adjustments needed for Bea's last outfits.

Discontent weighed at her shoulders.

She didn't want to work.

No, what she wanted was Jesse. It'd been a long time since Friday night. Much too long since that delicious orgasm on the back couch. Even the barrage of erotic dreams she'd been enjoying all week weren't enough to satisfy her anymore.

She wanted Jesse.

She pulled a slip of paper out of the back pocket of her denim skirt. The creases were worn fuzzy, and looked about ready to rip apart from her unfolding and folding it. She stared down at the angular scrawl. *Jesse Martinez—cell.* Seven digits to delight.

She never called guys. Not out of any ladylike reserve, but because she never had to. But now? If she couldn't have Jesse's body, she'd settle for his voice.

Battling down nerves, she grabbed the boutique phone. Then, doubts racing through her head, she put it down and hurried back to the office for her phone. If she got lucky and it was a long call, she didn't want to have to hang up if she had to leave the boutique for any reason.

Cell phone in hand, she looked at the numbers again.

Two rings later and his deep voice was on the line. Anticipation made a heated journey through her erogenous zones. Audra settled in the plush chair toward the back of the shop and relaxed for the first time in days.

"Have you ever played Truth or Dare by telephone?" she asked in her sexiest voice.

Silence.

Then, "Audra?"

"How many other women are you playing phone sex games with?" she teased.

He laughed and she could almost hear his shrug. "I guess only you. Although, I have to admit, I've never seen Truth or Dare as a sex game."

"Then let me teach you the right way to play." Audra scanned the empty shop. She wanted to go back to the dressing room, take off her clothes and lay down on the leather couch. She could almost feel the cool grip of the leather against her hot, naked skin.

But it was still a half hour till closing. Damn this streak of responsibility.

"Is it a lot different than regular Truth or Dare?" Jesse asked.

"Just a smidge. Are you alone? Somewhere you can get comfortable?"

"Yeah," he said slowly. "I'm home alone. How comfortable?"

"Comfortable enough to touch yourself," she said in a husky voice.

His groan was as clear as if he'd been standing next to her. Audra grinned, biting back a giggle.

"How about I stick with truths?" he suggested. But Audra

was skilled at reading people, and she could tell from his voice that the truths held just as much worry as the dares.

Interesting.

She glanced around and spied a package of Naughty Games dice. With a grin, she grabbed it and ripped it open.

"We'll roll," Audra explained, making up her game as she looked at the hot pink dice. "Even number is truth, odd is dare."

"You carry dice with you?"

"You never know when you'll have the urge to do a little gambling," Audra teased. "After all, what's life without a risk?"

"Risk? Right."

Audra frowned at his tone. Was he too much a good boy to play with her? Maybe she was crazy to be drawn to someone so much her opposite.

"Okay, roll," he instructed.

"You're comfy?"

"Hell, no. But I'm ready to play with you."

With a grin of appreciation, she tossed the dice on the low display table.

"Odd."

"So you have to take a dare?"

She'd thought she was rolling for him. With a mental shrug, Audra stretched one arm overhead to release the tension in her lower spine. She wished she had one of those headsets in case this got to be a two-handed game.

"I have to take the dare," she agreed. "What's your pleasure?"

"My pleasure? I'm thinking more along the lines of what's your pleasure."

"Now that'd be a truth."

"Good point. Are you in a private place?"

Audra glanced toward the boutique door and raised blinds

on the bank of windows. She was partially obscured by a couple of clothes racks, but she'd hardly call it hidden.

"Private enough. Go for it."

His pause was filled with sparks of sexual awareness. Audra imagined him sitting somewhere, maybe a semidark room, fantasizing about her. Or more specifically, what he wanted her to do to herself.

She shifted a bit, adjusting her denim miniskirt in anticipation.

"Close your eyes," he instructed.

With a smile, anticipation coursing through her, she did.

"Now with your free hand, I want you to touch yourself."

She lightly scraped her nails up her thigh, heading toward the hem of her skirt.

"Start at your forehead," he instructed.

Audra's eyes flew open. Huh? What happened to phone sex? Was this some dumb idea of romance? What a waste of orgasm potential.

Before she could redirect his dare, he continued.

"C'mon, it's a dare. You have to do what I say, right?"

She pulled the phone away from her ear with a frown. How'd he know she wasn't? After rolling her eyes, she closed them and put the phone back to her ear. Then she followed the dare instructions and reached up to smooth her forehead.

"Imagine it's me, lightly tracing your face. Imagine that I'm sitting with you, staring at your beautiful features. Those sharp cheekbones, the little point of your chin. Imagine I'm rubbing my thumb across the full softness of your lower lip."

Audra's breath shuddered. Had any man ever looked at her like this? Ever memorized her features or taken such pleasure in imagining *himself* touching them?

"Slide your tongue out and wet your bottom lip," he said,

his voice a lyrical seduction. "Then suck your finger into your mouth. Imagine it's me."

She gasped, then squirmed in the chair. She wanted to touch herself, to ease the building pressure. But she couldn't. Not with one hand on the phone and the other in her mouth. Did he know that?

"Your turn," he said after a few seconds. From his indrawn breath and labored tone, she could tell he was imagining himself in her mouth, too.

Audra hesitated, not sure what to say. Usually phone sex was down-and-dirty instructions. Touch this, do that. Imagine me this way.

But with Jesse? She felt she had to dig deeper. To reach inside and really ask herself how to make this a special experience. To make it about more than simple physical release.

And damn if that didn't scare her.

"Audra?"

"Yeah. Um, hang on, I'm rolling the dice." She sucked in a breath and told herself to get a grip. Sex was sex. And she'd never run from sex.

"Even," she told him, looking at the snake eyes. "So you have to tell me the truth."

"Okay," he drew out. He sounded a little unsure.

Ha, served him right. He'd pushed her emotional buttons, she was gonna push his.

"Tell me, truthfully…what's your ultimate sexual fantasy?"

His laugh was low and slightly wicked. More wicked than she'd have thought a good boy would sound.

"Ooh, this sounds like a good one."

"I don't know if I can say it over the phone," Jesse admitted.

"Sure you can. Just pretend you're with me. We're lying together in a dark room, and you're whispering in my ear."

Would he share? How truthful would he be? He'd agreed, and Audra had the impression that Jesse's word was gold. So if he bared his soul and shared his real fantasy, how sexy was this gonna get? She was willing to bet it was either one of two fantasies. The tie-'em-up-in-the-bedroom naughtiness, or the two-women-pleasuring-him scenario.

Audra glanced at the clock. Twelve minutes until closing. Screw it.

"Hang on," she ordered.

She flew from the chair to the front of the store. A quick glance outside assured her nobody was heading toward the boutique. With a flick of her wrist, the door was locked. A quick tug had the blinds drawn.

"Okay, start talking," she demanded as she headed down the hall toward the dressing room.

"Well," he started, sounding uncomfortable, "I guess it starts with dinner."

"Dinner?" Audra pulled the phone away from her ear to give it a baffled look, then shrugged. Without bothering to turn on the lights, she dropped to the couch and lay her head on the arm, with one leg thrown over the back. "Like, what? A family dinner? Dinner out at a restaurant? What?"

"No, dinner in. Candlelight, roses, wine. Just me and, well, in this case, you."

She grinned. "Me, huh? So you've had this fantasy recently?"

"Oh, yeah. It's been getting a lot of mileage this last week. Although the memory of you on that couch in your dressing room has been replayed a number of times, too."

"I'm on that couch now," Audra said in a husky tone.

Jesse groaned.

"Nope, no sidetracking," she demanded. "So we're having a candlelit dinner?"

"No. I'm sitting at the table. The room is dark except the

candle flames. Soft rock, something with a solid beat but not a lot of lyrics, plays in the background."

Audra heard a creak, as if he was settling back in his chair or something. He sounded more relaxed, like he was getting into the story.

"Sounds pretty," she said softly. It did. Very romantic and nice. Not really a turn-on, though. Oh, well, so the guy didn't have a wild imagination. He was definitely talented with his hands and had one wild mouth. Phone sex might have added more to her fascination with him, so this was probably just as well.

"You walk in," he continued, "completely nude. Except for thigh-high leather boots, of course."

"Of course," she agreed, swallowing a surprised chuckle. So maybe he wasn't so tame, if he wanted her, naked, for dinner. "Am I carrying food or something? Maybe serving you dinner?"

"Nope, there's a sideboard filled with everything I need."

"Need? Like…?"

"You come to me and lean over for a kiss. It's hot, a lot of tongue. Like we're battling it out for who gets to be boss. The winner will eat dessert off the other's body."

Oh. Audra hummed her appreciation of the image, her eyes dropping to slits as she imagined eating off Jesse's hard body. Yeah, that was working for her.

"I win, of course."

"Why?"

"Because it's my fantasy," he said with a laugh.

Audra frowned. Wouldn't a guy's fantasy lean toward being pleasured?

"I grab you, kind of quick and rough, and you give this breathy little moan and curl up on my lap. You run your hands over my body, using your nails a little to scrape at my skin. Nothing hard or painful, just a little wild."

Her breath short, she ran her tongue over her bottom lip to wet it.

"I grab a jar of chocolate-butterscotch fudge off the table," he told her.

Audra sighed in pleasure. Her favorite flavor. How perfect.

"I scoop it up with my fingers. I rub some on your lips, and you lick it off. Then you lie back in my arm so I have full access to your breasts and stomach."

Audra curved her hand over one of her already aching breasts and squeezed.

"My hands sticky with the chocolate, I hold your breasts, squeezing at the same time I flick your nipples. I lick the chocolate off your mouth, careful to get that little drip from your chin. You taste delicious." His voice trailed off and she heard the snick of a zipper through the phone. Eyes closed, Audra smiled her pleasure and with one last tweak of her nipple, slid her hand down to the hem of her skirt.

She pulled it up, then pressed her fingers to her damp panties.

"You pull away from me," he said, his voice rougher now. "You slide up onto the table and take the chocolate from me. Then you scoop some out and swirl it over your nipples. As soon as I lick it off, you wipe more on yourself, this time a little lower. I keep licking, you keep going lower."

Audra's panties were off now. She carefully traced her swollen lips, letting the pleasure build as she let his words, his obvious delight in this fantasy, take her higher.

"With just my tongue and fingers, I get you moaning. You beg me for more, beg me to drive you crazy. I make you come. You scream out my name over and over."

"Mmm," she moaned. The pleasure was building, tightening. She'd be screaming his name, all right. Any minute now.

"Your screams die down, and you slide from the table. You take that syrup and do the same thing to me, nibbling your way down my body. Eating the sweet dessert off my flesh. I get harder, bigger. I feel like I'm about to explode as your mouth gets closer and closer to my dick."

Imagining it, Audra used one, then two fingers to take her pleasure to the next level. Desire tightened deep in her belly, and she pressed the phone between her ear and the couch so she could use both hands on her body.

"Jesse?" she gasped.

"Yeah, babe?"

"I'm about to come."

She was. The tension had her back arching as she dug her heels into the leather couch, her pelvis thrust high in the air. She wished he were there to watch her. She imagined him standing at the end of the couch, his eyes hot on her body as she showed him how wet she was.

"Me, too," he admitted in a low voice. "But first I want to know how you like the taste of me. Imagine me in your mouth, Audra. Imagine me as you come."

The image of Jesse's face as she pleasured him exploded in her mind at the same time the orgasm ripped through her body.

From a distance, she heard his groan, and knew he'd found his own pleasure. A ghost of a smile flitted over her lips.

So much for him not having a wild imagination.

Audra felt too good to even care about her emotional warning alarm's scream of caution.

Because if the guy could make her feel this good over the telephone, there was no way she was running away until she had his body inside hers. Until she'd had the whole package.

Even if she was in mortal danger of falling in love.

9

AUDRA SMILED her goodbye to the last customer of the day and flipped the sign to Closed. She didn't lock the door, since Jesse was supposed to pick her up here instead of at her apartment, but she did pull the blinds.

Stress rippled across her weary shoulders as she turned off the display lights. What a hellish week. She'd had less than twenty hours of sleep in the last four days. For a woman who deemed anything less than nine hours a night roughing it, this had been pure torture.

The only thing that was going right was Jesse. Oh. My. God. The man was incredible. He'd sent her flying with his chocolate fantasy, then proceeded to make her come three more times as he'd shared his shower fantasy, then listened to a few of her hot thoughts.

She couldn't wait to try them all out with him for real.

Of course, who knew when she'd find the time? Even though she'd refused to give up her date tonight, she'd be busting her ass as soon as Jesse dropped her off.

She'd managed to ship the completed design boards to China. They should have arrived by now. She was dying to know what Natasha thought about the slick little leather number she'd slipped in.

Audra wasn't sure what was hurting more. Her fingers from the fine detail of the designs. Her eyes from strain. Or the crick in her neck from having to work while Natasha yammered in her ear to the tune of a hefty long-distance phone bill.

Like the call of the devil, the phone rang. She didn't even have to look at the caller ID screen to know it was her evening China call.

"Hey, Tasha," she said in lieu of hello.

"Audra, I received the couriered designs today. I have to say, you really outdid yourself this time."

Audra wanted to grin at the words, but the tone made her hesitate.

"You don't sound too thrilled," she said.

"I'm pleased with most of them," Natasha said, speaking slowly, as if she were choosing her words with extra care. "I'm a little confused why you'd send me this one, though. Leather? I thought we'd discussed this already and agreed to keep the designs in the tone Simply Sensual is known for."

Audra made a face at the phone. "It was just a fun idea I'd come up with. Remember we'd discussed that butt-ugly tie and how it might inspire a design? Well that's what I came up with, something a little kinky and a little crazy. You know, like the kind of person would have to be to wear that tie?"

She waited for Natasha to laugh.

She was met with dead silence.

Her own amusement faded, replaced by irritation. Damned if she wasn't tired of justifying her tastes, her choices and her hopes. It was a great design. Natasha should be excited her head designer had such insight. Not pissy because it wasn't covered in pink roses and foofy lace.

"What's the problem?" she asked. "It was just an idea. I didn't send it to get your knickers in a twist. It was something I thought you'd enjoy seeing. It's not like I mass-produced it and set up a display here in the boutique."

"No. But the designs arrived as I was on my way into the meeting. I didn't have time to check them first, since I was running late. I had no idea you'd have a surprise in there for me."

Audra snickered. "You presented that leather do-me teddy to the Chinese distributors?"

She tried to stifle her laugh as she imagined the faces of a bunch of guys ready for bridal wear and presented with wrist cuffs.

"Let's just say I don't think we'll be getting that particular account," Natasha said with a stiff laugh. "I guess it isn't that big a deal, since I didn't feel comfortable with them anyhow."

Audra winced, all laughter dying away.

She hadn't intended to embarrass her sister-in-law or do anything to jeopardize the account.

"Natasha—"

"Look, I know you didn't mean it. It's just, you know, one of those impulsive things you tend to do. And it's not a major loss. This was that impromptu presentation we snagged after I got over here. I hadn't even had a chance to check into the company," Natasha interrupted. Her words were obviously meant to reassure, but the underlying disappointment in her tone cut Audra deep. "I realize this design is probably a lot closer to your true style, Audra. But I thought you could balance that natural naughty bent with the kind of designs I need for Simply Sensual. Was I wrong?"

Audra started to deny it. But then she stopped.

After all, the naughtier designs *were* her preference. They were a natural expression of her bad girl side. They were who she was. But that didn't mean she could just shrug off Simply Sensual or what it offered her. Natasha had given her a shot, a career. Head designer, with her own lingerie line debuting in the fall.

Tension pounded a beat at Audra's temples. She had no idea what the right direction for her career was anymore. Hell, she didn't even know what the right direction for *her* was at this point. Ever-so-naughty Wicked Chick? Responsible businesswoman? Creative lingerie designer? None of them meshed; they were all in conflict.

No wonder her head felt as if it were going to explode.

"Natasha—"

"Just think things through," her sister-in-law suggested softly. "We'll talk when I get back, okay?"

"Yeah," Audra agreed. "But—"

"How's business been in the boutique?" Natasha asked in an obvious change of subject.

Audra considered refusing to follow her lead. But knowing Natasha, she wouldn't get anywhere pushing the confrontation. Even though it went against her personal preference, she sighed and let it go. Besides, she honestly didn't know what she'd have said.

"We've been really busy, actually," Audra replied finally. A lot busier than she would have preferred, given that Sharon was sick, leaving Audra to work the boutique alone while trying to get the last batch of designs done. "I'm guessing there will be just enough profit to cover your long-distance bill."

"Seriously, is it going okay?"

Depended on what the day's definition of okay was. Audra looked around the shop, unvacuumed, slightly disheveled and looking like a classy dame who'd partied a little too hard.

"Has it really been that busy?" Natasha persisted. "How's the inventory holding up? Do we need to reorder anything? You know Wednesdays are the deadline to order paper supplies."

Audra winced and averted her eyes from the empty hangers. She spied random threads strewn over the burgundy carpet and the empty boxes where the stock of gift bags were supposed to be.

Maybe she should do a little housekeeping before her date? She opened the storage cabinet and saw there were no more gift bags to stock. Maybe she should completely cancel her date?

If nothing else, this was a good distraction from the identity crisis throbbing in her head.

"Audra?"

"It's all good. Don't worry. The boutique will be exactly as you left it when you get back."

"I knew I could count on you."

Feeling sick to her stomach, Audra pressed her lips together. She spent a whole five seconds trying to tell herself to let it go and keep her mouth shut. Then she gave up.

"Look, Natasha, I'm sorry you were embarrassed by the design," Audra said. "I didn't send it to hurt you. I'm proud of that concept and wanted to share it, you know?"

"I know." There was a muffled conversation on the other end, then Audra heard her brother's raised voice. She rolled her eyes. She grabbed a piece of paper and pen, trying futilely to figure out which stock needed replenishing. She'd do better to list what she had on the racks, instead. It'd take less time.

"We'll talk when I get home, okay? But for now, your brother wants to talk to you."

"Drew? Why?" Audra asked, puzzled. She and Drew had a nice enough relationship going on. They weren't super tight, though, and she could count on one hand the number of phone conversations they'd had in her lifetime. Why waste money for a long-distance one now? Especially when he couldn't be pleased she'd embarrassed his wife.

Oh, man, he better not be planning to lecture her. Just what she needed, a kick in the butt to make life decisions via long distance. Audra's tension shot up another notch, this time slipping into anger.

"Why…" she trailed off as her brother's voice came over the line.

"Hey, Audra. How's it going?"

"Peachy. What's up, Drew?" Her tone was probably more defensive than he deserved, but she couldn't imagine this was going to be fun. She made her way to the stockroom and stared at the neatly labeled shelves of inventory. *Inventory?* Natasha was always boasting how easy stocking was thanks to her computer program. Maybe that'd help.

"I need your help," Drew said.

"You in the market for some sexy undies?"

Audra booted up the computer and glared at the inventory program Natasha was so proud of. She'd never tried to figure it out before. Then she remembered the carefully detailed instruction list, complete with color-coded bullet points. With a quick glance, she was actually able to punch a couple keys and get a list of what stock they'd sold that week and what they had in-house that she could restock on the sales floor. Neat trick.

Drew's laugh made some of Audra's irritation slip away. He sounded just like their late father when he did that. She heaved a sigh at the familial tug at her heart. She really needed to change her brand of water or something; she was getting all mushy lately.

"No thanks, I need a favor. Tash said it'd be a pain in your butt, but it's important to me."

"Sure, whatever you need." Even wallowing in her guilt over disappointing his wife, Drew was likely the only person on earth she'd give that open agreement to.

"Thanks. This is important. Remember old Joe? A regular at the Sports Bar? I think he used to buy you Shirley Temples and play Go Fish with you for pretzels?"

Audra grinned as the memory of the old guy flashed through her mind. "Looks like Popeye, right? Old sailor dude, tattoo of an anchor on his arm, always smelled like peppermints?"

"Yeah, that's him. Perfect, I'm glad you remember. He'll be glad, too."

"Will he? Why?" She took the computer printout into the stockroom and started gathering inventory to put out.

"Tonight's his birthday. It's been like a tradition since he started coming into the bar, back when Dad first bought it, that he comes in on his birthday for a drink. On the house."

"Okay? So what? You want me to call your manager and make sure she remembers his drink?"

"Nah, it's on the calendar. That's not the problem. The thing is, he always makes a fuss about how he's been served his birthday drink for the last twenty years by a Walker in the Home Run Sports Bar."

Audra paused in the act of restocking satin chemises on their padded hangers. "Twenty years? How old is the guy? He seemed ancient when I was a kid."

"I think he's in his eighties. So you see why this is so important to him?"

Audra squinted from the list in her hand to the phone. "I guess, sure. It sounds like this drink might be the highlight of the old guy's year."

"Exactly. So you'll do it?"

"Do what? I'm not following you, Drew."

"You'll go to the Home Run and serve him his drink?"

"Tonight?" No way. The only thing getting her through this hellish week was the fact that she had a date tonight to look forward to. She had to get the first of three dates with Jesse out of the way so she could get to the main event.

"Yeah, tonight. What? It's not like you can ask a guy in

his eighties to hold off a week or so, right? I mean, he might not last, you know?"

Her already tapped-out guilt meter flashing red, Audra's lower lip poked out and she dropped the silky midnight blue nightie she'd been hanging. Not last? Now that wasn't a pretty thought. Poor old Joe.

"Will you do it? You don't have to do much more than be at the bar around eight. The bartender will get his drink ready, you serve it with a rousing chorus of 'Happy Birthday,' maybe give him a kiss on the cheek if his heart's up to the excitement."

Shit. As if she could refuse that? Not only was Drew directly responsible for any successes she'd achieved, but he never asked anything of her. And old Joe? He'd taught her to bluff. She'd be a heartless bitch to say no to handing the old guy a drink and singing to him.

But what about her date?

"So? Will you do it?"

"Of course," she said with a sigh as she rehung the blue nightie.

Maybe Jesse was into sports bars?

JESSE STOOD outside the gilt-trimmed door of the boutique and ground his teeth. This was the last place he should be. On a date with a suspect he was in imminent danger of falling for.

A suspect, for that matter, whose worst crime to date had been flirting with a known criminal. Because other than the flirting, and Dave's conversation afterward, Jesse had nothing on Audra. At least, nothing illegal.

Especially now that they'd found out her sister-in-law had blown off the lingerie company in China that sidelined as a money-laundering front. Reports said the woman had barely kept the appointment. Whether it was because they were backing away from dealing with the triad, or because the women really weren't involved, Jesse couldn't tell.

Nowhere in the communiqués, the e-mails or the chats he'd hacked from Davey's computer was there any reference to Audra by name or by any description other than "hot babe." Without more, the only involvement he could pin on her on was whatever Dave had passed to her in the club. That, and the large sum of money conveniently deposited into the boutique's account.

Neither of which, so far, was enough to convict her. Which meant there was a remote chance she could be innocent.

Jesse should be focusing on the case. He'd finally made a breakthrough on Davey's computer system. The guy had accessed an off-site storage unit to transfer a large sum of cash. Jesse hadn't been able to break into the system yet. But the way his fingers tingled when he worked at it assured him it'd be the key he needed to blow this case out of the water. A little deep excavation and he'd have enough to nail Davey boy. And, if the strings he was pulling led where he thought they would, enough to take down the *Du Bing Li* triad too.

He should be working on that now instead of going through with this date. He was a lousy actor. There was no way he'd be able to pull off the smitten suitor bit.

But the captain had other ideas. Shale had as much as promised Jesse his coveted promotion if he nailed this case with no loose ends. A promotion that would prove, to Jesse at least, that he'd succeeded by doing things *his* way. Using his brains and those computer skills his father had so often disparaged. His family would finally accept that his brainiac tendencies were just as valuable as his father's flash.

So he squared his shoulders, reached for the door handle and prepared to reel in his last loose end.

Audra was bent at the waist talking on the phone. Her

back was to him so he had a mouthwateringly sweet rear view. Her short skirt hiked up to show the seams running up the back of her black stockings. Jesse swore he felt his heart stop. Other parts of his body, however, raced to full alert.

Damn, she had to be the sexiest thing he'd ever seen. When she straightened and turned, a glowing smile on her face as she saw him, he wanted to groan. She looked that good.

"So he's that good, huh?" she said into the phone as she blew Jesse a kiss. "You're definitely welcome."

With a quick goodbye, Audra clicked off the phone and leaned across the counter to set it in its cradle.

"That was my friend, Isabel, calling to thank me," she said with a wicked look on her face as she turned back to face him.

"For?"

"Bringing her over to the naughty side." She winked. "We have all the good sex over on this side."

Jesse's body stiffened in reaction. He wasn't going to give in to the naughty. He had a job to do, loose ends to tie up. And arrests to make.

"It sounds like she appreciates your bad influence."

"Definitely," she said, coming toward him. Those delicious, stocking-clad legs seemed to go on forever, from the edge of her short skirt to feet encased in gladiator-style spiked heels. Her hair was a solid black, giving her an oddly conservative look after her fuchsia-tipped ends of the previous week.

Audra reached him and, without hesitation, put both hands on his chest to lean up and press her lips to his. Against the soft pressure of her kiss, he opened his mouth without thought and met the sweet dance of her tongue.

Jesse's hands curved over her slender hips, and he pulled her flush against him. His body welcomed the feel of hers like a homecoming. It was all he could do to break away and end the kiss.

"I missed you," she said in her husky tone. That voice had haunted his dreams. In those dreams, he'd imagined her doing all sorts of decadent things to his body, describing each one as she did it. "I haven't been able to think of anything but you and our phone conversation since last night. How soon can we do it for real?"

"I missed you, too," he admitted. And he had. Not just because his body had been rock-hard every time her image popped into his brain. But he'd missed her sweetness, her fun outlook on life.

Then he shook his head and gave her a rueful look.

"I'm really not trying to be a tease or whatever you'd call it. But I do want to spend more time with you before we actually, you know…"

"You know? Last night, you told me how delicious I tasted, and today you can't say sex?" she teased with a laugh.

"Go figure." Jesse grimaced, then gave a laugh and a stiff shrug. Last night he hadn't been looking for evidence to arrest her. He'd do well to keep that fact front and center in his brain tonight. He had to get the goods to nail her, or cut her loose. "You ready to go? I thought we could get something to eat, spend some time talking."

"Sure. I just need to grab my jacket and shut down the computer first. Dinner sounds great. I need to make one stop first, if that's okay with you."

He followed her down the hall to the office and stopped in shock at the sight of the once immaculate room.

"Whoa. What happened here?" It looked as if someone had tossed the place. Maybe in search of missing or stolen information? "Did you call the cops?"

"Cops? Why on earth would I want to bring some busybody cop in here?" Audra followed his gaze around the room. As if seeing the mess for the first time, she winced.

"Ooooh, you mean the mess? If I claim a tornado set down in here, do you think Natasha will believe me?"

"You did this yourself?"

"It's been a hellish week. I guess I kind of let housekeeping duties slide." Audra's shoulders sagged and she ran her hand through her hair. "I don't suppose you'd care to have a seat and flip through some lingerie magazines while I tidy this up a bit?"

She eyed what was probably still a shell-shocked look on his face and wrinkled her nose. She looked around the mess of papers, piles of fabric and lacy things, and the half-buried computer. Then she grinned.

"I know, you're a computer geek, right? Want to play online or something? I won't be more than a quarter, maybe a half hour at the most. And I'll treat you to a drink afterward?"

Could it get any better? If she *was* crooked, she really needed to take lessons. The first rule of being a good criminal is not to trust anyone. Audra was practically inviting him to invade her privacy. Then again, she'd welcomed his fingers into much more private places than her computer keyboard.

Which didn't prove she was innocent, Jesse forced himself to remember. But, maybe a few quick strokes on that keyboard and he could at least figure out how guilty she was. Then he could find a way to make her a deal, get her to roll over on Larson. She'd be in minimal trouble, and he'd be there to set her on the straight and narrow.

"You can cruise the Net, play games or something. Whatever floats your boat."

Resolved and comfortable that it was for her own good, Jesse smiled back and flexed his fingers.

"What computer geek can say no to an offer like that?"

Audra laughed. "I wonder what would get you more

excited? A fully loaded, up-to-the-minute, technologically advanced computer? Or me, naked?"

Jesse let the images flash through his mind and heaved a delighted sigh. "How about both? You, naked, on my lap while I use the computer?"

"Kinky. I like that." She cleared a couple bolts of silky-looking fabrics in jewel tones off the rolling computer chair and, after looking around, stacked them in a corner by the door. "Here, get comfy. I'll run in and get you a soda. Then it'll only take me a little bit to tidy things here and we can go."

"Sounds great," Jesse said absently, his butt already in the chair and fingers hovering over the keys. He waited until she left the room before hitting her programs option to see what bookkeeping software they used. He'd opened it, minimized and was playing Tetris online when she came back.

"Cola, right?" She leaned over his shoulder to set in on the desk, her breast brushing his forearm. Distracted, Jesse saw the bars stack up on his screen through blurred eyes. A vision of her, naked on his lap while he worked some complex computer program, flashed through his mind.

Damn, he wanted her. And if he connected her to the crime, she'd be so off-limits, he might as well lust after a cover model as Audra. He'd have no chance with her. Who knew regret could hurt so bad?

Unable to help himself, Jesse pulled her around so she sat across his lap, her back cradled in the crook of his arm. Her eyes sparkled as she smiled up at him and she curled both her hands around the back of his neck and raised one brow in tempting dare. She felt right in his arms. Sexy, but comfortable at the same time.

"I like this," she said.

"You'll like this better," he assured her before his mouth

descended. They went from tinder to flames in an instant. She met his tongue with hers, challenged him to keep up with her demand for more. Audra would accept no less than complete passion, breaking down all inhibitions and hesitations. For once, Jesse knew he held a woman who'd not only meet any and all of his sexual needs, but she'd encourage him to explore his limits.

As their mouths continued their sensual dance, Audra slid one hand down his chest, teasing his belly before those talented fingers moved to play with the snap of his jeans. Sensual anticipation grabbed hold of him. He wanted to feel those clever hands everywhere, to experience the intense pleasure he knew they'd bring.

Jesse wanted her to feel the same exquisite wanting, the same desperate need he felt. Oddly enough, he wasn't intimidated by Audra's experience or her grasp on the art of sexual pleasure. But he *was* determined to make one hell of an impression himself.

With that in mind, using the lightest of touches, he brushed his fingers over the tip of her breast. He felt the intake of her breath against his mouth and, taking it as a good sign, continued his barely-there teasing. After ten seconds, she gave the slightest squirm on his lap and Jesse wanted to groan himself. He palmed her nipple until it pebbled beneath his hand. She left off playing with his snap to scrape her fingernails down the zipper of his jeans, making his already straining flesh burgeon with need.

Unable to deny the rushing intensity of desire any longer, Jesse tweaked her nipple. Audra's fingers convulsed on his dick, making him groan aloud and pull away from her mouth.

Jesse buried his face in her throat and tried to gather some control. Damn, she was incredible. He was about ready to come in his jeans, from just the simple pressure of her fingers.

He hadn't seen the woman undressed yet, but he'd dedicated so many orgasms to her, he felt as if they were in a long-term relationship.

But they weren't. And they couldn't be. He needed to remember that. To remember why he was here, what his purpose in her life was. To save her, not to screw her. Maybe if he had it tattooed somewhere, he'd be able to remember that.

With a deep breath, Jesse pulled back and brushed a kiss over her forehead. He forced himself to meet her eyes as he tried to come up with an excuse to not go any further.

But when he looked into those wide, brown depths, there was no demand or expectation. All he saw was happy pleasure.

"Nice," she murmured.

"Same to you."

She grinned and patted his cheek before sliding off his lap.

"Play away, I'll just be a few minutes. Then we'll go, okay? I do have to be at this thing by eightish, so I'll hurry."

Jesse refrained from asking what kind of thing, since he'd be there to find out himself. Besides, the sooner she got to cleaning, the sooner he could peek at her books.

"Are you one of those people who can't concentrate if someone is talking to you?" she asked as she started gathering bolts of fabric from around the room to stack by the door with the others. "Or are you a social computer geek?"

"In between," he admitted, keeping one eye on her as he pulled up her bookkeeping program. He frowned. It wasn't even password protected? She was such an innocent. That'd go in her favor when he was trying to plea-bargain a good deal for her.

"If I'm doing anything intense, programming or something, I'm better without conversation. But for games, most computer work, talking doesn't bother me."

After that, Audra kept up a steady stream of chitchat. None of which required much response, but was fun to listen to all the same. She had a quirky way of relating a story, of describing clients and salespeople. It told him a lot about how much she liked the people she dealt with. This lingerie business was definitely a labor of love.

Jesse looked over to see her sorting beads and things into a plastic container and clicked on the recent list of deposits. And there it was. Ten thousand, cash. With the initials "S.S." and a notation of *China loan* next to it.

S.S.? Jesse flipped through the files in his brain, but couldn't connect any names—or even nicknames—to S.S. What was the deal? Loan? Not payoff? Could it be to cover their criminal activities? That didn't makes sense. Not when there was a payment schedule outlined, complete with terms.

"Hey, what d'ya know? Natasha really does have a desk. I just had to clear enough stuff to find it," Audra said with a laugh.

Jesse hit the Close button and laughed too, albeit a little stiffly. His mind was going in a dozen directions, and none of them made sense.

"You about ready to go?" she asked.

"Sure. You want me to shut this down?"

"Thanks, yeah. I'll just grab my jacket and I'm ready."

Jesse used the time she took to do that, turn off the lights and lock up the boutique to puzzle through what he'd found. By the time they'd reached their cars, he still hadn't figured it out. He'd have to do some further computer investigation after their date. Good thing he'd given her that good boy excuse; at least she wouldn't be expecting him to spend the night. Not that he wouldn't want to, but it was a hell of a lot easier to fight one person's wants than two.

"Do you mind if I drive?" she asked. She gave a little shrug and glanced at her watch. "You can follow me to my place and drop off your truck. It's on the way. We're running a little late and it'd be faster if I didn't have to give directions and all."

"Um, sure," he agreed. Jesse tried to hide his frown. It wasn't that he was uncomfortable with a woman driving. Just with a suspect driving him to a possible crime scene.

"Where are we going?" he asked after he'd followed her three blocks over to her apartment complex and dropped off his truck. He settled into the passenger seat, gripping the door as she zoomed out of the parking lot with barely a glance for traffic.

The woman drove like she did everything else. Wildly.

"There's this little place in Auburn I need to go to. I have to be there by eight, eight-fifteen."

"Sure, no problem. Are we meeting someone?" he asked as they sped toward the freeway. Was it some kind of handoff? He flipped through his mental files, but nothing in Auburn sounded familiar. The triad tended to meet in clubs, Larson in nudie bars. But always in Sacramento. At least, not so far.

She took the on-ramp at high speed, zooming in and out of slower traffic with an ease that had the tension in Jesse's neck unknotting just a little. For all her wildness, she seemed to be in complete control.

"It's a nice place, a little bar I know. We'll be in and out before you know it. Call it a quickie." Audra laughed and glanced over at him. Her scent, that sensual, musky rich perfume, filled the car's interior and Jesse's senses. His mouth watered, because he knew the scent was stronger right along her collarbone.

"Bar, huh? Not a club? That doesn't sound much like your speed."

"You'd be surprised how much time I've spent in this particular bar," she said.

She paused, and Jesse glanced over. Sadness tugged at the

corners of her eyes and she sighed. Then, catching his gaze, she pasted her sexy smile on and winked.

"But it is a nice place, and the people are great."

"Okay. But there are plenty of nice places with great people here in Sacramento," he teased.

"Sure there are, but not like this. Besides, I promised I'd be there. It's a matter of life or death, babe. I can't blow off a promise."

Jesse raised a brow. He wasn't sure why the Auburn location, but something big must be going down. After all, it was *life or death*.

Fifteen minutes later, brows drawn together, Jesse watched Audra park in the reserved parking spot in front of the Home Run Sports Bar. This was, just like she had said, a nice place.

This was her brother's place. Jesse recognized the name from her files. Did she use it often for illegal activities? He'd have to check into it.

A middle-income neighborhood in the suburbs, there was a restaurant on one side of the bar and a flower shop on the other. Both looked to be frequented by families. The cars parked along the street and in the shared lot all looked middle- to upper-class. It didn't look like he'd need to worry about calling for backup.

Not a strip joint in sight, so it was unlikely the person they met inside would be Dave Larson. Which left any of a dozen others, Jesse reminded himself as he came around the car.

"Nice neighborhood," he commented as he opened Audra's door for her.

"It's picked up the last five years. The neighborhood was a little rougher, a little seedier before. But, yeah," she gazed around with a fond, indulgent look on her face, "it is nice, isn't it?"

"It sounds like you're really familiar with the area," he commented as he grabbed the metal door handle to let her enter the bar before him.

She didn't have to respond. It was like something out of that Eighties TV sitcom, *Cheers*. Except, instead of everyone yelling out "Norm," they all yelled "Audra." Jesse blinked, taken aback at the warm welcome she received. Not that he didn't expect people to be excited to see her. But because they simply weren't the *kind* of people he expected to be excited to see her.

With most of the patrons in their mid-thirties, it was definitely not a party kind of place. Beer seemed to be the drink of choice, if the sea of frosty mugs was anything to go by. Instead of a guys' hangout, the bar appeared to cater to couples and groups. A dartboard, pool table and bank of television sets tuned to different sports completed the setting.

The green and blue interior showed a bit of age, as did the scarred hardwood floors. The tables and chairs all looked new, and the plants and flowers on each table were well cared for. Overall, it was friendly and welcoming.

And Audra fit right in. As she made her way to the bar, she greeted a few people by name, responded to questions here and there and fielded congratulations on her recent graduation. And, in typical Audra fashion, patted a few guys on the butt.

"Audra, sweetie, I'm so glad you came," the bartender cried out. The tall blonde looked as if she should be home baking cookies, not manning a bar. "I was worrying, what with Drew being off gallivanting like a wild man."

"So tell me, how often does Drew call in? Seeing as he's the owner and all into running the place himself?" Audra asked. She sounded a little persnickety, enough to make the bartender raise her carefully manicured brows.

"Let's see, he's been gone a little more than a week, right? He's called three, maybe four times."

"Total?" Audra leaned her elbows on the bar and shook her head. "I get more calls than that in a day from Natasha."

"Ahhh, being left in charge is fun, huh? Congratulations on the promotion, by the way. We're all proud of you."

If he hadn't been gawking at her, Jesse would have missed the faint blush that swept over Audra's high cheekbones.

"Thanks," she murmured. Then she turned to gesture to Jesse in an obvious change of subject, "This is my friend, Jesse. Treat him right, huh? He's a hell of a kisser."

Now it was Jesse who was probably blushing. He muttered a hello to the laughing woman behind the bar and slid onto the empty stool.

Why were they here? Old home week? Was this a kinky twist on Audra's bad-girl-style dating? Something illegal? If her sister-in-law was involved, it stood to reason that her brother was, too.

"So," Audra said, sliding onto a barstool and spinning so she faced the room. "Have you got it ready? Is he here yet?"

There must be a pickup or drop-off scheduled tonight. Jesse looked around at the middle-class clientele and frowned. It simply didn't compute.

The bartender tapped Audra's shoulder and nodded over to a gaggle of old guys huddled together around a small table with a cup of dice. Then the woman set a drink of what looked like scotch on the bar next to Audra's elbow.

"There ya go, tiger."

Audra grinned and slid off her stool. She leaned over and brushed a kiss over Jesse's cheek and gave him a wink.

"I'll just be a second, okay? Go ahead and order a drink. It's on the house."

With a kicky swing in her hips, Audra took the single drink, placed it on the serving tray and swayed across the room to a table where the trio of octogenarians held court.

The guy in the center had a smile as long as the Golden Gate. His wizened face showed delight beneath his sailor's cap.

"If it isn't sweet little Audra."

"Sure enough. Nothing but the best for your birthday, Joe."

And with that, she proceeded to sing the old guy "Happy Birthday" in perfect tune as the entire bar watched, then chimed in after the first line.

Jesse stared. This was her important task? Life or death? He absently thanked the bartender when she set a beer in front of him.

"Old Joe's been coming in here for years," she explained, her arms crossed over her chest and a wide grin on her face. "Back when Aaron was alive—back before he got so sick and let everything fall apart—he was the first to serve up Joe's drink and sing to him for his birthday. His son, or now his daughter, have carried on that tradition for over twenty years. He'd be proud."

From what little he'd gleaned from his investigation, Aaron Walker had been a hard-ass who'd died after a long, rough bout with cancer. Before he'd gotten sick, the man had single-handedly raised his children in this bar. Audra had gone to live with her estranged mother, but she'd obviously retained a strong affection for her onetime home and what it represented.

Ironic that they were both so strongly influenced by their fathers.

Jesse gulped down a swig of beer. He'd always looked down on his father for blurring the lines on a case. And now? Now he was falling in love with a suspect who was, if connected with the crimes he was investigating, guilty enough to be serve time in prison.

When had he turned into a conjugal visit kind of guy?

10

"THAT WAS sweet," Jesse said as he escorted Audra from the bar to her car.

Audra snorted, but didn't deny the observation. Not that there was much to deny. They'd stayed for a drink and shared a basket of nachos while the patrons had regaled him with stories of Audra's younger years.

Instead of being embarrassed, as he would have been, she'd just grinned. He'd never met anyone so comfortable with herself as she was. All aspects of her, not just the social mask she presented. Sure, occasionally she'd corrected someone's story. But only if they were making her sound too nice or goody-goody. Not that there had been too much of that. From the sound of the stories, Audra'd been a handful from infancy.

"They're a good bunch of people. I don't get over here too often, but it's always nice. I'm glad you had fun," she said. They reached her car and she gave him a considering look, then dangled the keys from her finger. "Wanna drive?"

"You don't mind other people driving your car?" Jesse frowned.

"Nah. Besides, we've already established we'd take turns leading. I led us here, you're in charge of the rest of our date."

His frown faded and he caught the keys she tossed to him. He unlocked her door and settled her into the passenger seat before going around to the driver's side. Her car was a lot sportier than his old truck. Eight horse-power, it'd be a pleasure to handle.

Much like its owner.

Jesse slid into the car. He started the ignition and glanced over at her.

"It sounds like you were a hellion growing up." Which was in keeping with the reputation he'd uncovered in his investigation. "And yet they all seem to love you."

Which wasn't in keeping with that rep. For a woman who'd grown up with juvenile delinquent tendencies, a neglectful father and a drunken mother, she had some amazingly well-developed people skills.

"Hey, I'm a lovable kind of gal. Hadn't you noticed?" she said with a laugh and a vampy look.

"So you grew up in the bar?" Jesse headed toward the freeway, determined to solve this puzzle, or at least a portion of it, before they got back to Sacramento.

"Over it, really. Dad's apartment was upstairs. My brother lived there off and on for a while, too. Mostly off. Then my dad got sick and my mom was forced to take custody."

Her tone was so matter-of-fact, Jesse almost misunderstood the words. A quick glanced showed no evidence of emotion on her face.

"Forced? You mean she won custody, right?"

"Nope. My parents weren't much for nurturing, if you know what I mean. My dad was a good guy, but he didn't know diddly about raising a kid, let alone a female kid. He'd had enough trouble with Drew, then I came along. He'd have preferred my mother raise me. You know, females belong together and all that jazz."

He slid her another glance. Like her words, her face showed no trace of bitterness. Her easy acceptance was a surprise. Especially since he was used to criminals who blamed their misdeeds on parents who'd denied them video games and candy.

"And your mom?"

"She's cool. We had some pretty wild parties. My place was the hangout, which gave me ready access to a lot of hot guys," she said in a teasing tone.

Parties. Jesse mentally reviewed Audra's file. She'd lived with her mom between the ages of fourteen and seventeen, including the time of her arrest at sixteen. Somehow he didn't think those parties included soda pop and spin the bottle.

"What about your brother?"

"My dad died when I was sixteen. Drew took it hard. He had the bar to run then, and was pretty busy. I hardly saw him again until I was an adult."

She shrugged as if it didn't mean much, but Jesse'd learned to look to her lips for a true reaction. Audra would be a hell of a poker player with that bland face and go-to-hell eyes. But when she talked about her father's death, the slight tremble in her lower lip gave her away.

Those years with her mother must have been hell. If he remembered right, it had been her brother who bailed her out of jail and had signed the court papers when she'd been arrested. Interesting.

"How about you?" she asked, turning the tables. "Tell me about your family.

Jesse gave a laugh. "My family? They're about as average a family as you can get, I guess."

"C'mon, that's a copout. You mentioned sisters before. How many? Are you older or younger? Where'd you grow up, what're your parents like?"

He shot her a shocked look. "All that?"

"Yes, all that. Now that you know just about everything

there is to know about me, it's only fair to share the knowledge. Besides, you are the one who wanted to do this dating thing to get to know each other. If you don't want to talk, I'm perfectly content to have sex."

His blood went south, instant reaction stirring at her words. Damned if his body wouldn't be perfectly content to have sex, too. But as long as she was a suspect, he'd keep his pants on.

"Fair's fair," he agreed. "I have four sisters. Bossy, interfering know-it-alls, every one of them. We grew up in Grass Valley, an ancient house with more leaks and problems than money to fix them. One bathroom, four primping girls. It's a wonder I managed to shower at all in my teens."

"You love them a lot, huh?"

He glanced over, expecting to see mild disdain at best, all-out derision at worst. Instead, her eyes were filled with warmth and interest, her lips tilted in an encouraging smile.

"They're good people," he finally said, borrowing her earlier words. "All four are married now, which makes my mother happy. She's on the warpath for grandkids, but nobody is in a hurry to accommodate the demand."

"Aren't you her main target? I'd think there would be that whole 'family name' thing to live up to."

Jesse bit back a sigh. She didn't know the half of it. Of course, in his family's mind, his being a cop meant he was living up to the family name. Thankfully, no one but him knew the truth behind his father's reputation as a cop. Or how hard Jesse worked to make sure he didn't follow suit.

"Nope, her ticking grandma clock seems focused on the females. She's had a hard time since my dad died two years ago," he heard himself admitting. "I mean, I know she'd like to see me settled down and all. But she's old-fashioned, I guess. It's okay to nag at her daughters, but once dad was gone, I became the man of the family. To her mind, that means I'm above questioning and nagging."

Like his father had been.

"A get-out-of-nagging free pass?" she joked. "It sounds like she's a cool mom. Tough but loving. Like those old-fashioned moms you see on TV Land."

He gave a little laugh. Then as he thought of just how old-fashioned she was, his laughter died and bitterness coated his tongue.

"As much as I love my mother, that old-fashioned system might work for bringing up a decent pack of kids. But sometimes I wish to hell she'd been less subservient to her husband. Maybe if she'd laid down the law with him as well as she had with her kids, he might have shown more loyalty."

Jesse glanced at Audra, curled in the seat next to him. Faint shadows of exhaustion rimmed her eyes, but she still managed to look hot, sexy and sweet, all at the same time. Her gaze was locked on his face, a look of compassion in those eyes.

"He strayed, huh?"

"Yeah. She never let on like she knew, though. So maybe he kept it from her." Jesse had only found out after joining the P.D. His father's exploits were stuff of legend at the cop shop.

"She knew," Audra said softly. "A woman intuitive enough to successfully raise five kids, not a screwup in the bunch? She'd know."

"She never let on," he repeated.

"Like you said, she's strong. And it sounds like her family was number one. Some women believe it's more important to keep the family intact than open those closet doors and clean out the skeletons."

He considered that, then nodded. "Would you?"

"Keep the door closed?" she clarified. At his nod, she grimaced and shook her head. "Nope. Then again, I'm selfish and greedy. If I ever end up married, he'll be loyal or I'll castrate his sorry ass."

Even though he felt the same way, Jesse couldn't keep from clenching his thighs in protest.

"After all," she continued, "if I ever loved someone enough to promise him forever, that means my body as well as my heart, right?"

Jesse tried to shove aside the sudden, overwhelming urge to pummel this imaginary guy who would be lucky enough to have Audra's heart.

"So," she said in a bright tone, "it sounds like your family is still close, though?"

"Yeah, I guess we are," he agreed. "How about you? Are you close with your brother now?"

"I guess we are, yeah. Once Drew and I hooked back up, I even lived with him for a while. Until he got married, actually." Audra leaned her head against the seat and laughed. It was a sweetly sentimental sound that made Jesse grin. "Drew even bailed my sorry butt out of jail once."

Feeling her gaze on him, Jesse feigned a surprised look as he shot her a glance. "Jail? What did you do to land there?"

"I broke a friend out of death row," she said quietly. This time, Jesse didn't have to fake the look of shock on his face. Not at her words, but at the pain in her tone.

"Death row? That's pretty serious."

"Definitely. Jack, my dad's dog, was scheduled to be put down. He was a mean, nasty thing. The only way to keep him from snarling and biting was to give him booze. But he didn't deserve an ugly death. He'd got out one day and the pound wouldn't release him to me. Drew was out of town. I didn't have a choice…"

Her words trailed off, then she sucked in a breath and gave him a big smile. "It was sexy as hell. Middle of the night, clandestine behavior. Too bad the cops were such jerks. Even after I explained why I was breaking Jack loose, they threw the book at me. I'm a suspicious character, apparently."

"You mean you were then?"

"Nah, it's never changed. Cops don't trust me. They take one look, see bad girl, file me under guilty." The frustration in her tone was so subtle he almost missed it. Jesse knew he shouldn't feel like a total jerk, but he did. Then she flashed her usual smile and shrugged. "It's too bad, 'cause one of them was really cute. I mean, usually I have no use for the police, but you gotta admire a man who carries his own handcuffs."

Jesse gave a surprised laugh. He wondered if his having handcuffs might outweigh his being a cop in her eyes? Probably not.

Which brought him full circle back to the sister-in-law and the trip to China funded by *S.S.*

"You've come a long way from then, huh?"

"To say the least," Audra replied with a roll of her eyes.

"So, you seemed a little frazzled when I picked you up. Is work always this crazy for you?" he asked, changing the subject. He needed to nail down those initials. It was better to focus on the case than on the fact that Audra was the sweetest woman he knew wrapped up in the sexiest packaging he'd ever seen. Damned if this wasn't a confusing night.

"This is way overboard on the crazy times. Things are definitely not business as usual for me," Audra told him. "With Natasha in China and all the complications we've run into, I've been stuck with a lot more responsibility for the boutique than normal. I'd like to say I'm handling it well, but that'd be a total lie."

Perfect opening to grill her on the China connection.

"I'm sure you're doing great," Jesse heard himself saying instead. She seemed so assured in most things, it was weird to hear her sound less than confident.

"No. Not great. Barely decent. If it was just the boutique, I'd be fine. Or just the fall deadline. But now there are custom designs, and my own special project."

Special project? As in the triad?

"What kind of project?"

She shot him a look and pursed her lips as if she were trying to decide if she was going to share or not. He tried to look trustworthy and encouraging.

"It's kind of, well, personal."

"Audra, I've had my hand down your panties. I think we can share personal information, don't you?"

She laughed, but he could tell she was surprised at the analogy. What? She didn't think sex was personal? Special?

Jesse vowed then, when they had sex—and once he helped her straighten out her life, they damned well would be having sex—he'd make sure it felt both personal *and* special.

"Well," she said, for the first time since he'd known her, her tone shy, "I've been sketching up some new designs. I call this line *Twisted Knickers*, mostly because that's what will happen when Natasha sees it, get her panties all twisted."

"I don't get it? You're the designer, right? So that's your job."

"Technically, my job is to design lingerie in keeping with Simply Sensual's target market," Audra said, her dry tone making him laugh. "In case you didn't notice, the boutique caters to the sweeter side of sex. These designs are anything but sweet."

"Is that a problem?"

He caught Audra's shrug from the corner of his eye.

"It could be. I mean, it's reaching a point that I have to make a choice. I love working with Natasha, and she gave me my start. But the more I work on these, the more I want...need to see them realized. If she won't go for them, I'm going to have to find another outlet."

From the sound of it, that was a bad thing.

Jesse tried to figure where this might fit in with the triad and his case. No matter how he replayed her words, they didn't seem to have any deeper meaning.

Her voice, normally so upbeat and sensual, drooped with exhaustion. Jesse looked over to see her leaning her head against the window with her eyes at half-mast.

"You must be worn out. Not just worrying about the designs, but all the rest of the boutique business. Tiring, huh?"

"Yeah. I wish Sharon could have come in to help more, but she hasn't been feeling good. Add keeping that from Natasha to my list of irritating duties."

"Why would you be hiding this person's illness from your boss?"

"Sharon is her aunt. She's a total sweetie, a great lady. She'd actually sold Natasha the boutique and Simply Sensual a couple years back when she was diagnosed with M.S. She usually clerks in the boutique a few days a week."

Audra went on to explain about the health issues Sharon was dealing with and how crazy the work week had been as a result, but Jesse barely heard her.

Sharon? Natasha's aunt, as in *Sharon Stover?* S.S.? Jesse reviewed all the information he'd amassed on Simply Sensual and Audra, and had a giant *aha* moment.

That money wasn't connected to the Larson/*Du Bing Li* case. Not at all. It was simple coincidence. There was absolutely nothing to connect Audra to this case, other than the fact that Dave Larson had supposedly given her something in the club and that large sum of money in her account. Now that he knew the money was clean, that meant Audra was, too. He felt like yelling his triumph out the window of the car. He felt like pulling off to the side of the road, getting out and dancing on the hood. More than anything else, he felt like grabbing Audra to hug her close and kiss her.

She was innocent. Oh, sure, there were still a few *i*'s to dot and *t*'s to cross, but this information, along with his gut instinct, was enough to assure him she was one hundred percent innocent.

Of any crimes, at least.

AUDRA relaxed in the passenger seat of her car and watched Jesse navigate the streets to her apartment.

This had been one interesting date. Not one thing they'd done had fit into her realm of experience. First, she'd taken him to her childhood home. He'd watched her give in to sentiment and sing to an old man. Then she'd spilled her guts, not just about her childhood, but her design dreams.

Then? If that all hadn't been weird enough, they'd gone to the movies. A romantic comedy, complete with an extra large buttered popcorn, soda and, of all things, M&M's.

"You know," she told him in a contemplative tone, "I don't think I've gone to the movies with a guy since I was ten years old."

"Your dad?"

"Nah, a date. But that's the last one that took me to the movies." She laughed at the mock glare he sent her.

"After your barside serenade, I couldn't think of a lot of options," he said defensively.

"Really? I can think of a bunch. Clubbing. Sex. A fast drive to the ocean. Sex. Music at one of the jazz clubs. Sex."

"I think I'm seeing a theme there."

"Oh, yeah?"

"Yeah. They're all things that would keep us up late."

Audra snorted. "Especially the sex."

"That's an all-nighter for sure," he agreed.

His husky tone sent shivers down her back. Audra could picture them, wrapped around each other's naked bodies as they tore up the sheets. From his clenched jaw, so could Jesse.

"So what's wrong with an all-nighter?" she asked.

"Besides the good boy thing?" he asked, reminding her of his stupid getting-to-know-her plan. "You're exhausted and we both have to work tomorrow."

Audra gaped.

"You'd put work before sex?" The concept simply boggled the mind.

Jesse started to say something, then shot her a glance. He shrugged and pulled into her apartment complex's parking lot.

"Yeah," he admitted quietly as he parked in the slot she'd pointed out. "I mean, in some cases, work has to come first."

Audra shook her head. Maybe it was the stress of the week, or the unfamiliar sexual frustration, but she had to force herself to hold back her snarky retort.

What the hell was she doing with a guy who put work before sex? A good boy who was more into having dialogue than getting horizontal? A guy who didn't think relationships were something to bullshit his way out of?

"Look," she began, about to let her remark fly.

Jesse shot her a surprisingly effective look, making her shift back in the seat and shut her mouth.

"Sometimes you have to do what's right," Jesse said. "Like your designs. Even though you have a sweet job, a nice title, you're willing to take a risk with something you value. You're ready to risk that to be true to yourself. To your vision and what you believe in."

All she could do was stare. Snarky retort forgotten, Audra tried to calm her suddenly racing pulse. Had anyone ever seen her so clearly, understood her so well? And still wanted to be with her? Not that she had some poor-misunderstood-me thing going. Quite the opposite. She was an open book. But people tended to only be interested in reading certain chapters. In connecting with certain aspects of her. Her friends were the perfect example, wanting her to fit their vision, rather than accepting that she was too much to fit in some easy definition. Natasha wanted her to fit her version, too.

But Jesse looked at her as if she were his every sexual fantasy just waiting to come true. And he listened. Not just to her, but he'd sat for hours this evening listening to stories *about* her. As if he couldn't get enough.

Audra had to swallow twice to get past the lump in her throat.

"You say that like it's a good thing," she joked, trying to distract herself from the unfamiliar feeling of vulnerability.

At his raised brow, she shrugged. "I suppose it is, although this is exactly the kind of thing my friend, Isabel, lectures me on. I mean, who is crazy enough to finally grab their dream, only to throw it away because it's not all that *and* fries on the side?"

"A woman who believes in herself enough to fight to make sure that dream is exactly what she wants it to be. A woman strong enough to hold out for what she's worth," he suggested.

Never one to doubt her self-worth on the surface, his suggestion still made her frown. Was that why she was hesitating? Did she really believe in herself? She believed in her sexuality. Her body. Her ability to bring a man to his knees and have him beg. And she believed in her talent as a designer.

Didn't she?

Jesse shut off the ignition and turned to face her. He traced the back of a finger down her chin and leaned closer. Close enough that she could feel his breath on her cheek. She could see the banked heat in his eyes.

Yum. An answering fire sparked in her belly. He presented the perfect distraction from her neurotic soul-searching.

Not willing to wait and see if he'd move on the desire so clear in his eyes, she did it herself. With a little growl, Audra leaned forward and took Jesse's mouth with hers.

She slid her tongue over his lower lip, then nibbled at the delicious pillow of flesh. She felt him relax, the surprised tension leaving his body as she massaged his shoulder.

Hmm, relaxation was never her goal in a kiss. As sweet as this was, Audra decided she was gonna have to kick it up a notch.

With that in mind, she turned up the heat. An all-out sexual assault of tongue, teeth and lips, she used every skill at her disposal as a self-professed kissing expert.

Damned if his body didn't tense right back up again. She grinned against his mouth in satisfaction, then gave herself over to the kiss.

His moan of appreciation was muffled by the sound of blood rushing through her head. Maybe it was the pent-up anticipation. Maybe it was the edgy attraction that'd been building for the last week, or the dreams. Or even the phone sex. Whatever it was, just the touch of Jesse's lips beneath hers had Audra primed, wet and ready to explode.

"We seem to be making a habit of getting naughty in my car," she said with a breathless laugh as he trailed his lips down her throat.

"It's that voyeurism factor combined with a safety net," he murmured, his lips tracing a delicious pattern down to her collarbone.

"Safety?"

"Yeah." He pulled back to grin at her. His hair was all finger-mussed so that a long black strand trailed down his forehead in a way that made her heart melt. "After all, this damned car is too small to really get carried away."

"Oh, I don't know. I'll bet you do pretty well in tight spaces," Audra purred. Then she laughed and leaned back. Detecting weakness, she scanned his face. He was turned on, for sure. But he still had that good boy glint in his eyes.

Could her bad girl self overcome his good boy reticence? She'd put money on it.

Audra leaned forward to brush that sexy strand of hair off his forehead and gave Jesse a long look from under her lashes.

"I suppose you're right. It's probably time for both of us to be getting into bed."

She watched his throat move as he swallowed and hid her grin. Excitement warred with relief. She wanted Jesse like crazy, but there was more to her excitement than simple wanting. She was grateful to know she hadn't lost her sexual mojo, but there was more to her relief than simple ego.

Bottom line? She wanted Jesse like she'd never wanted any man before. And since she didn't know what to do about it, she'd go with her fallback answer. Seduce him into a puddle of lust, and have her wicked way with him.

"I'll walk you to your door," he offered.

Smiling her agreement, Audra waited for him to come around and open the door before she slid from the car. As she stood, she made sure her breasts brushed his chest. Her breath caught at the delicious sensation. The dark desire in his eyes was gratifying thanks for her effort.

She led the way to her apartment, sexual energy zinging between them like an electrical arc. She had it all figured out.

She'd open the door, give him enough time to clear the threshold, then slam the door shut and pin him up against the wall.

Hot, wall-banging sex. What better way to see how high he rated on the orgasm scale?

11

JESSE TRIED TO FOCUS on something other than the hypnotic sway of Audra's hips as she led the way to her front door. Even though he knew, both instinctively and with the new evidence, she was innocent—at least of the involvement with the triad—she was still off-limits. Until he'd come clean, told her the truth, he couldn't give in to his raging desire.

Nope. Like he'd told Audra, he was a good boy. He had control. He wasn't ruled by lust.

Audra reached her door and pulled keys out of a tiny purse. The look she tossed over her shoulder, pure temptation combined with the promise that she could make his every dream come true, sent all the blood in his brain south. So much for control.

Clearly reading his struggle, Audra giggled. The sound was both sultry and sweet, filled with heat and delight. It summed her up perfectly.

Jesse realized, in that moment, he was lost. Body, heart and soul, he was hers.

Without a word, she pushed the door open and took his hand. Other than an impression of flash and color, he barely noticed the interior. His attention completely focused on Audra.

In a smooth move, she pulled him inside and shut the door behind him. One step, then two, and he was trapped against the door. She didn't touch, instead letting the promised heat of her body, the heady scent of her perfume, seduce.

"I decided to take your advice," she told him with a sultry smile as she tapped her finger against his lips.

"Huh?"

"I know what I want and know I'm worth having it."

She took a small step, just enough for him to feel the brush of her breasts against his chest. Jesse's head spun.

"I'm strong enough to take it, too," she informed him softly. "But I'd rather take turns."

The images flashed in fast-forward through his head. All hot, all naked, all intense. Each of them taking turns giving the other the ultimate pleasure.

Jesse tried to reel himself back. Tried to get control.

"Taking turns, huh? Maybe I'm not that kind of guy," he said.

"That's okay. I'm enough of that kind of woman for both of us."

His heart skipped a beat at the naughty promise in Audra's smile. Even the cocky arch of her brow excited him. She was a fantasy come true, with that slightly wicked, dark edge to her. The kind that came without guarantees or safety nets.

The kind of woman that forced a man to ask himself if he was sure he had what it took to handle her. To satisfy her. A warning voice screamed in his head to watch out. She was involved in his case, even if she was no longer a suspect. He stifled the voice with a reminder that he wasn't using her for information or to forward his investigation.

Jesse swallowed. She tilted her head to one side, obviously giving him a last shot at running. Instead, Jesse took that last emotional step and, throwing caution and good sense aside, slid his hands over her lush hips and pulled her against his straining body.

With that one move, he risked it all. His reputation, his self-image and his job ethics. And most of all, his shot at a real relationship with Audra after this was all over.

All hesitation took a fast dive down a sheer cliff when their lips met. One hand on the sweet curve of her waist, Jesse ran his fingers over the delicious length of her silk-encased thigh. His hand slid easily under her flirty skirt to cup her bare butt, realizing as he did that rather than panty hose, she wore stockings and a garter.

Their mouths battled for control. Neither of them tried to dominate the other; instead, they were both doing their damndest to drive the other crazy. Jesse traced the lace edge of the garter, running his fingers under the elastic to feel her warm skin. Skin he needed to see, ached to taste.

With a low growl, he pulled his lips from hers and stared down into her passion-clouded eyes. She stared back, challenge clear in the set of her chin.

"Not bad," she murmured in a teasing tone. "A kiss like that's a nice start toward at least a six on the orgasm scale."

"Six, my ass," he promised. "I'll have you seeing stars and crying my name before you can count that high."

"Big talk."

Jesse didn't bother answering. Instead, he dropped to his knees in front of her. Audra's grin was pure dare. She cocked her brow, then shifted so she leaned against the wall. In a deliberate move, she placed one foot on either side of his knees.

Her gaze holding his, she trailed the back of her hand over her cheek. He thought of their sexy phone call, heat intensified low in his belly. His gut clenched at the remembered intensity of their words, their shared fantasy.

Using the backs of her hands, Audra caressed her throat in a slow, sensuous slide until she reached her cleavage. Like a generous offering, she slid her hands down to cup her breasts, holding them in obvious pleasure.

Jesse swallowed hard as her thumbs flicked over the tips, just a couple swipes, and he could see the beaded nipples pressing against her silky blouse. He wanted to take those peaks between his teeth, suck them until she screamed.

But first, he had a six to beat.

His gaze still holding hers, he reached out to embrace her calves. His fingers smoothed over the fine seam of her stockings, climbing up the back of her knees, up her thighs until he reached the lacy top. Again, he smoothed over the elastic garter.

He groaned in protest when her hands left her breasts. Then she winked, reached down and lifted her skirt for him. She took the hem, tucked it into the waistband, baring herself to his hungry gaze.

"Just thought I'd make it a little easier for you," she said with a naughty laugh. Jesse didn't bother responding. He wasn't sure he could speak if he'd tried. He eyed the tiny magenta triangle between him and heaven. His hands left her garter and cupped the smooth, tight skin of her bare ass. One finger snagged the string of her thong and pulled. With a wiggle, she helped him release her femininity from its tiny bit of modesty.

"Should I start counting?" she challenged in a tone husky with desire.

Jesse cupped the feminine treasure she'd bared for his worship, the other still kneading her cheek. He slipped a finger into her folds, loving the wet heat that greeted him. The scent of her desire intensified the pressure against his zipper. Enough of the slow buildup; he was ready to hear her scream his name.

"Go for it," he instructed just before he took the slick folds into his mouth.

AUDRA'S BREATH shuddered out as Jesse worked his magical mouth over her. His tongue traced along her swollen lips while his finger slipped in and out, in and out. The tempo slowly increased, her breathing along with it.

Damn, he just might make a seven. She'd have bet that was impossible with clothes still on.

He sucked at her clitoris at the same time he shifted the tempo. All feeling, all of her focus, centered on those ever-so-sensitive nerve endings he was so expertly coaxing. Her slick heat coated his fingers as he moved faster. The pressure wound tighter, her breath came in gasps now as her body climbed.

Her eyes closed, and Audra grasped Jesse's head. Her fingers curled into the silky softness of his hair. She let her own head fall back against the wall, her hips undulating against his talented mouth. When his hand left her butt, she almost moaned in protest.

Then he reached up to cup her breast. He tweaked her stiff nipple at the same time he scraped his teeth over the swollen bud of her clitoris. That combination, with the swift pumping of his finger, sent her over the shuddering edge.

Audra panted, hanging on to the orgasm with all her might. Her body tense with the intensity of the sensations ripping through her, she finally gave in and rode the wave of pleasure to its crest.

Her head too heavy to lift from the wall, she couldn't even open her eyes when she felt Jesse move from between her legs. She heard a rustle, the metallic slide of a zipper, then the sound of ripping foil, telling her he was tearing open a condom package. Before it all registered, though, Jesse's hands tore the fragile fabric of her blouse from her with a loud rip.

Audra gasped and her eyes flew open just in time to see the almost feral look on his face as he stared down at her now naked chest. He met her eyes and gave her a tight grin before he cupped both breasts in his hands. He held her stiff nipples between his middle and index fingers, pinching them as he squeezed her breasts together with just enough pressure to make her catch her breath.

"It's going to feel so good you're going to scream," he promised just before he took one of those aching nipples into his mouth.

Desire swirled higher and higher, building and tightening until she was ready to scream for him to hurry. Audra felt as if she were running a race against her own body, rushing toward the promise of a pleasure so fine she'd never forget it.

She clutched at his shoulders, loving the feel of muscle rippling beneath her fingers.

With one large hand, he wrapped her leg around his waist and thrust into her. Audra whimpered at the delicious length of him as he embedded himself fully in her welcoming body.

When she grasped his shoulders, Jesse pulled away, his dick slick with her juices. She made a sound of protest and he grinned. Someone was getting a kick out of his power over her body. She'd have issue with it if it weren't for the fact that he was doing such a good job, he deserved all the jollies he wanted. In fact, she intended to make sure he got his jollies off like never before.

With that in mind, she trailed her hand down his chest, scraping her fingernail over his nipple. Jesse's eyes narrowed, and Audra could see the pulse at the base of his neck beat a little harder. Good. Time to show him a little of her power.

She wasn't sure why, was almost afraid to find out, but she'd never wanted to make a guy as crazy for her as she did with Jesse. Crazy for her body. For what she could do to his. For what they could do together. It was like a deep-seated need, more powerful than anything she'd ever felt before.

She smoothed her palm down his flat belly, her fingers tingling as they trailed over the crisp path of hair leading to his stiff dick. She curled her hand over his straining flesh, her fingers sliding easily over the wet, latex-covered silk.

Jesse growled and grabbed her hand. He raised it to his mouth, licking the damp evidence of her pleasure from her fingers. The desire, so tightly wound in her belly, speared out at the move, need spiking through her system.

Her hand still in his, he grabbed the other one, too. He raised her arms over her head, bracketing her wrists in one hand to hold her captive as he slowly, ever so incredibly slowly, slid back into her waiting flesh. His eyes holding hers captive, he pumped in and out. Audra pressed forward to meet each thrust.

It was the look in those eyes, that ever-narrowing look of hunger, that seduced her as much as the delicious things he was doing to her body.

The curling heat in her system climbed again. Her lower lip tight between her teeth, she watched his eyes for the signal of his own loss of control. Jesse's movements came faster, his breath harsher. Audra struggled to hold on, to keep control. She wanted his mouth against hers, but couldn't bear to release his gaze.

He thrust, held. His gaze flickered. Her entire body so tense she felt she was going to rip apart, she started to lose her grip. Audra's lids fluttered as the climax started deep in her belly, its power ripping through her in a vicious rush of pleasure so intense it bordered on pain.

Not willing to go over alone, she met his next thrust with a grinding motion, her leg wrapped around his waist so she used her foot to press him deeper. To hold him tight as she undulated against him.

Jesse's guttural cry of release was the last straw. Audra exploded with a panting cry of pleasure. The orgasm was like a wild storm, ripping through her with devastating ferociousness.

She'd finally met a guy good enough for her bad self. That

was her last thought before she lost all awareness of anything but the pleasure.

IT WAS at least five minutes before Jesse could even consider raising his head from Audra's shoulder and trying to breathe again.

"Damn," he muttered against Audra's hair. "I can't feel my legs."

Audra's foot did a long, slow slide down his ass and over the back of his thigh. Her spiked heel caught in the jeans pooled around his ankles. He winced at the reminder of his tacky haste. What kind of guy took a woman against the wall with his pants still halfway on?

Shame tap-danced its way over his conscience. What a jerk. He should be shot. Oh, sure, he'd made her scream as promised. But where was finesse? Gentleness?

Dread filled him as he forced himself to pull back.

An apology on his tongue, Jesse got a good look at Audra's face. Her head still against the wall, her features were slack with pleasure. A faint smile played around her lips like a naughty secret just waiting to be shared.

Sensing his stare, she opened her eyes to meet his gaze. After a couple seconds, she cocked a brow and tilted her head in a considering way.

"Well, well…"

Jesse's ego swelled at the considerable pleasure in her voice. He tried to keep the grin from taking over his face, but doubted his success.

"Look at you, all satisfied and smug," she teased.

"As long as you're satisfied and smug, too," he returned, sliding away from her with regret. "Never let it be said I'm the kind of guy to hog smug satisfaction all to myself."

Audra laughed with delight. Then, in a move that sealed

his heart's devotion to her forever, she stood on tiptoe to brush a sweet kiss over his lips. The act, pure affectionate joy, was even more emotionally intense than their lovemaking.

Jesse had to swallow his declaration of devotion. He was sure nothing could be more guaranteed to get his ass kicked out of her apartment and her life. And he planned to do everything in his power to stay in both.

Instead, he pulled away to dispose of the condom. He watched as she slipped off what was left of her ripped blouse. She eyed it, then him, and winked.

"I'm proud and humbled to say you, my amazing man, scored a sweet eight on the 'O' scale." She glanced at the shredded fabric again, then grinned. "Actually, I swear just the memory of that little session gives me a mini-orgasm. That has to kick you up to an eight and a half."

Pride and affection mingled as Jesse returned her smile. He brushed his finger over her bare breast, just above the nipple. Her body gave a satisfying response, the dark coral bud tightening.

"What do you say we try for a nine?" he suggested.

She rolled her eyes, but her smile told him she was pleased. "I have to warn you, if you stay you won't get any sleep. I doubt I'll be able to keep my hands off you."

"I still don't want to leave," he admitted.

"I thought you were a good boy?"

"I'm good enough to score that nine," he promised.

"I like a man with a goal," she said with a laugh. Then she unsnapped her rumpled skirt and pushed it off her hips.

With a wink, she stood before him in a garter belt, black stockings, those wicked gladiator-style sandals and a glittery belly button ring. Jesse's body, so recently satisfied, stirred with interest.

"Let's try it horizontal this time," she suggested. Then she turned and led the way to her bedroom. She shot him a wicked glance over her shoulder. "Don't forget, it's my turn to take advantage."

His eyes glued to the hypnotic sway of her bare-except-for-the-garter-belt hips, he realized he couldn't wait.

A FAINT CHIME sounded from somewhere far away, tugging Audra from her deep sleep. She felt Jesse pull away from her, immediately missing the comfort of his warmth.

That thought pulled her the rest of the way out of sleep. With a frown, she watched Jesse's sweet butt as he bent over to tug the chiming cell phone from the pocket of his discarded jeans.

When had a man's body in her bed brought comfort? Pleasure? Often.

Satisfaction? Mandatory.

But this sweet sense of comfort and sappy emotions? Audra wrinkled her nose. What was up with this? Not that the sight of Jesse's naked body in the soft morning light wasn't a total turn-on. But to want to cuddle just as much as she wanted to make him arch his body in gasping pleasure beneath her mouth?

Panic overwhelmed the desire in her stomach, taking control and making her pulse skitter.

She understood sex. But emotions? What did she know about emotions? If she wasn't careful, she'd start thinking crazy. Start considering futures and having hopes and depending on someone other than herself.

Since the entire concept was impossible, and she knew it, she'd have to nip this in the bud. Send Jesse on his way with a thanks and a kiss, like she'd done so many guys before.

And if her heart spasmed at the concept, well, all the more reason to do it.

Audra caught sight of herself in the wall-to-ceiling mirrored closet doors. Her hair was spiked in bad girl wildness, and her chest was red with whisker burns. Swollen lips and heavy eyes greeted her inspection. She looked well-loved, satisfied and damned smug.

Exactly as she should after a night of incredible sex. Hell, Jesse had even scored the mythical nine. Maybe nine and a half, but she'd passed out, so it was hard to tell.

This wasn't gooey emotional crap, she assured herself. It was sexual satisfaction. No reason to kick the guy out of her bed for that.

Happy now that she'd settled that in her head, she raised her arms overhead, pointing her toes to the foot of the bed, and stretched the stiffness from her body. Thoroughly satisfied, she slid her hands over her breasts in pleasure. Maybe they had time for another go-round before work?

"I'm a little busy," Jesse said in a low whisper. "No, you handle it. I'll be in later. Right now I'm…" Jesse glanced over and winced when he caught Audra staring at him. "I'm busy," he finished.

With his sleepy eyes, tousled hair and guilty look, he was like a naughty little boy caught with his hand in the cookie jar.

It made a woman glad to be a cookie.

Audra gave him a wink.

He blushed.

She ignored the melting feeling in her heart and shifted to her side, letting the sheet fall away.

His gaze slid from her face to her bare breasts. The heat in his eyes was enough to make her wet.

Then the person on the phone said something, Jesse's eyes got huge and he ripped his gaze from her body as if he'd been slapped on the back of the head.

She giggled and opened her mouth to tease him, but he gave her a frantic hand motion to hush. One brow raised, she leaned across the bed to grab one of the pillows from the floor. Sliding back to a sitting position, she was glad to see Jesse's gaze back on her body. His glazed look promised she'd be starting the day quite nicely.

Audra grinned and plumped the pillow behind her back, then settled against it to listen to his conversation. And, of course, enjoy the view of his nude body and its gratifying reaction to her nakedness.

"Sorry," Jesse said as he pushed the Off button with look of relief. He tossed his cell phone back on his jeans and shrugged. "That was the office. There's a job they need me to take care of this morning."

"Isn't it awfully early in the morning to have to deal with business calls? That's what voice mail is for."

"I can't ignore the phone when I hear it. I guess it's a good boy thing," he said with a grin.

Then he curved his large, warm hand over her bare hip, and Audra shoved the curiosity aside and focused on the here and now. Tingles of awareness shivered through her. Desire, never far from the surface when she was around Jesse, flamed higher. Audra reached out and pressed her palm against his chest, combing her fingers through the smooth hair. She glanced at the clock. Six-thirty. Plenty of time for breakfast.

"You know," she said, leaning forward to run her tongue around his nipple, "I seem to have developed a serious yen for good boys."

"Oh, yeah?" Jesse's smile turned her on almost as much as the hand that was now caressing her butt.

"Yeah. So, seeing as I'm feeling generous, I think you should be rewarded."

"For being a good boy?"

"Well, that and the level nine orgasm you so awesomely

rocked my world with last night," she said with a delighted shiver of remembrance.

Jesse took her mouth with his. She leaned into his kiss with a purr. The taste of him filled her senses, his tongue dragging her deeper and deeper into passion. His scent enveloped her and Audra just wanted to grab his broad shoulders and never let go.

He slowly eased back, the kiss tapering from passion to soft, sweet nibbled kisses on her lower lip. When Jesse pulled completely away, Audra's lashes fluttered open. She met his rich brown gaze with a passion-glazed one of her own.

"That'd be a nine and a half, thank you very much," he corrected.

She blinked twice, then burst out laughing. "Can't forget that half, can we?"

"Would you want to?"

"Definitely not. And," she said, pulling away and giving him a pat on the cheek, "I'd say such a grand accomplishment definitely deserves a reward."

"What? A T-shirt proclaiming me the best sex you've ever had?"

"Your ego is no little thing there, is it?" she said with a roll of her eyes as she slid from the bed.

Jesse glanced down at his dick, then back at her with both brows raised. Audra got his point and couldn't keep from laughing.

"Okay, so you probably deserve a little stroking. Your ego, too. For now, though, will you settle for breakfast?"

Jesse's mouth dropped open. "Breakfast? As in you'd make me food? To eat?"

"You say that like it's such a crazy concept that I can cook." Audra tugged a T-shirt over her head, its hem brushing the top of her thighs. The bunny on the front proclaimed her Cute But Psycho.

Jesse swung his legs over the side of the bed and stared at her in puzzlement as he pulled his jeans on. "I can imagine you doing just about anything. Hell, I *have* imagined you doing any number of things. It's just that cooking isn't anywhere on the list."

"Ye of little faith."

With a heavy dose of body English in her hips, she led the way to the kitchen. She gestured for him to have a seat at the tiny bistro table.

He watched avidly as she sauntered to the pantry. Audra shot him a naughty look over her shoulder, then reached in and pulled out an octagonal-shaped jar with a gold foil label.

Jesse's eyes lit up like fireworks at the sight of the chocolate fudge topping.

"You went out and bought that?" he asked in delight.

"Nope. I've had it a while. It's actually my favorite ice cream topping. Among other things."

"Breakfast?" he asked.

"Breakfast in bed," she corrected as she dipped her finger in chocolate, then rubbed it over his bottom lip.

12

HE WASN'T REALLY a spiritual man, but Jesse had to admit if there was a heaven, this was his idea of it. An incredible night, out-of-this-world sex and the perfect woman. He vowed to make damned sure not to lose any of them.

He lay back on the cool sheets of Audra's bed, the scent of their lovemaking mingling with the exotic vanilla aroma of the candles she had all over the place. Morning light filtered through the filmy curtains, giving the room a soft glow.

Of course, the woman standing at the foot of the bed, her nude body a work of art in the golden light, could never be termed an angel.

Thank God.

"How hot do you like it?" she asked with a teasing grin. She used her index finger to stir the chocolate sauce still in its glass jar. The rich scent of chocolate overlaid the other scents in the air.

Jesse's body stirred, realizing this woman was about to make one of his wildest fantasies come true. Could life get any better?

"I'll take it as hot as you can get it," he assured her, folding his hands behind his head as he leaned back against the headboard.

Audra peered at him, then shook her head and tut-tutted.
"What?"

"You look much too comfortable there. Like you're a despotic king about to enjoy being serviced."

Jesse burst out laughing. Had he ever had so much fun with a woman? Sure, the sex was the best in his life. But just the fun? Even more than sexy, Audra was quirky and sweet. The woman, he realized with sudden, absolute conviction, he wanted to spend the rest of his life with.

The realization didn't even bother him. It just felt good. Felt right. He probably best keep it to himself, though. Or she'd kick him out of bed without chocolate.

"Despotic?" he asked instead.

"Yeah. Like you're so sure you know what's coming next and it's all about you."

"All about us," he corrected with a grin. Because no matter who did what, he'd be getting pleasure beyond belief. *That* he knew. And there was no way he'd be stopping until her pleasure was ripped from her while she screamed with ecstasy.

With a roll of her eyes, Audra slowly shook her head.

"Never get too comfortable," she warned. "The last thing I'll ever be is predictable."

With that, she pulled her fingers out of the chocolate and lifted them to her mouth. Holding his gaze, she sucked first one, then both fingers into her mouth. Her tongue slid down the length of her hand, sipping up the chocolate that had dripped down to her wrist.

Jesse swallowed, trying to wet his suddenly parched throat. More than anything, he wanted to taste that chocolate. But only if it was off her body.

Eyes narrowed, he watched her dip her fingers back in the jar, coming up with a scoop of the rich brown liquid. He held his breath and waited to see where she'd put it. And wished with all his might it was somewhere he could lick it off.

"We're gonna play a little game," she informed him.

Her words seemed to be coming from a distance through the blood roaring in his ears. She lifted her chocolate-drenched fingers to her breast, the deep brown confection a vivid contrast to her pearly white skin and coral nipples. All his concentration was focused on the sight of those fingers swirling the sweet syrup over her nipple.

Jesse leaned forward and grabbed her by the waist. Audra knelt on the mattress between his spread legs, but that was as close as she came. He sat forward, trying to get a taste, but she leaned back, limbo style.

"Nope," she said. "It's my game."

"Are you going to tell me the rules?" he asked.

"Of course not," she said with a light laugh.

He'd have objected, but she was now spreading chocolate over *his* nipples.

"I'll give you a hint, though. The first round—"

"Round?" he interrupted. His dick was already so hard it could drive nails and she planned to go *rounds?* The woman was crazy.

"The first round," she said again with a raised brow, "is follow the leader. You have to do what I do, match for match."

Jesse grinned. Given the directions were already painted in chocolate, this would be a definite pleasure. Anticipation making him cocky, Jesse reached out and flicked his finger over her chocolate-covered nipple.

"But," she said as he stuck his finger in his mouth and sucked at the bittersweet flavor, "I'm the leader. Which means you can *only* do what I do. No improvising."

"No…"

"None." She tilted her head to the side and, watching him through hooded eyes, cupped her hand under her breast as if offering it up for his pleasure. "Can you follow the rules?"

"As long as I get to set them for round two."

"Deal," she agreed.

Then she leaned forward and used that amazing tongue of hers to drive him insane.

His head spinning with sensations, Jesse gave in to the game. He followed her lead, reveling in the sensations as she tormented his body with her mouth, her hands and her own sweet body.

On his turn, he gave equal measure. Jesse wasn't sure which was more exciting—the satisfaction of Audra's body writhing with pleasure beneath his mouth, or how incredible she felt and tasted. Jesse's mind was a fog of sharp, edgy need. All he could think of was the woman in bed with him, even as his body screamed for release.

With slitted eyes, he watched Audra lean back and scoop in another fingerful of chocolate. Sitting forward, she took his mouth in deep, biting kisses. He was so into it that it wasn't until he felt her grip his dick in her slick fingers that he realized they'd moved on to the pinnacle of round one.

She scooted down to kneel between his legs, and Jesse knew this was heaven. Barely holding on to control, he watched as she licked away the chocolate and knew he wasn't going to last much longer.

With a groan, he pulled her up to meet his mouth.

"My turn," he said against her lips. "This time, we'll see who can make the other scream first."

AUDRA'S BREATH shuddered at the look in Jesse's eyes. His face tight with desire, he slipped around so they both lay on their sides facing one another with his feet toward the foot of the bed, hers toward the top, their mouths within easy kissing distance of each others.

"More follow the leader?" she asked after he brushed a soft, sweet kiss over her mouth.

"Follow my lead," he said, trailing his lips over her jaw, then down her throat. Since he was essentially upside down, his chest was now in front of her face.

Nice.

Audra took advantage of the delicious expanse of well-muscled flesh. Gliding her hands over the smooth plane of his chest, she used her teeth and tongue to tease his nipples.

She wanted to focus on making him scream. Proving her own sexual prowess by driving him wilder than he'd ever been before. But he had his mouth on one breast, nibbling little kisses in an ever-tightening circle. And all she could think was *Please hurry.* She had to feel his mouth on her nipple, his teeth. Something.

As if he'd heard her silent plea, Jesse took one stiff bud in his mouth at the same time he tweaked the other with his fingers. Already dripping with desire, Audra squirmed.

Gentleman that he was, Jesse released her breast and slid his open palm down her body until he reached her aching core. Audra gasped when his fingers flicked her throbbing center. She was ready to explode. And damned if she'd go alone.

She pulled away and slid down so his hard length was in front of her face. Jesse shifted so he was on his back, she on her knees over him.

Audra took him into her mouth at the same time he licked his tongue along her swollen lips. She pressed herself to him and used every bit of talent she had with her mouth and hands to send him higher and higher.

Her breath coming in gasps, Audra lost her focus. Forgotten was her intent to drive Jesse crazy. She couldn't find the energy to care about proving her prowess. She sucked his delicious flesh into her mouth, her hands cupping his jewels and giving him a gentle squeeze.

She felt the tension in his body, the involuntary pumping of his hips and knew Jesse was right there…so close.

And with a swirl of her tongue and the lightest scrape of her teeth along his head, she sent him moaning over the edge. She swallowed deep, taking in his essence.

With barely enough energy to grin at her triumph, Audra focused on the feelings surging through her body. The sensations reached that painful edge between pleasure and pain, winding tighter and tighter. Then, like an overwound spring, the desire suddenly snapped.

The orgasm ripped through her in a wild torrent. Like freefalling over a cliff, Audra could only feel. She lost herself in the incredible power of her climax, vaguely aware of Jesse's hand smoothing the small of her back. Grounding her body to reality while the rest of her floated somewhere in a wild never-never land of pleasure.

Audra wasn't aware of whether Jesse moved or if she did. But when she finally became conscious of anything other than the aftershocks of pleasure surging through her, she realized Jesse was holding her against him, her head tucked against his shoulder.

Audra sighed and cuddled in the warmth of his arms. This was good. The best sex of her life, and the greatest guy she'd ever met. Love didn't suck as bad as she'd thought it would.

With a start, Audra's eyes flew open and she replayed the discovery. Her body was too worn out from a long night of deliciously decadent sex, but her mind was suddenly wide-awake.

And totally freaked-out.

This couldn't be love. Could it?

Unlike the guy she'd thought she loved when she was seventeen, Jesse appreciated her. He'd never ask her to drop out of school to join him on a cross-country trip, only to leave her stranded in Nebraska.

Instead, Jesse seemed to accept every aspect of Audra's personality, including her odd little quirks and weird habits. He had more faith in her designs that even she did. And that was saying a lot. He made her feel good inside. A kind of good she'd never experienced before. The kind that lasted through fights, sexual dry spells, old age.

The scary kind.

She wasn't ready for love. Hell, she didn't know who she was anymore. How could she share her heart with another person when she was in the middle of an identity crisis? The last thing she needed was a guy—even a guy as hot, sexy and sweet as Jesse—confusing the issues even more.

Besides, it was too soon. They'd only just had sex. There was no way to know if a physical relationship this intense had any shot at lasting more than a few orgasms.

Audra ignored the little voice in the back of her head mocking her fancy steps around the issue. She had enough to deal with already. She'd worry about finding an acceptable definition for what she felt for Jesse later.

After a few more of those orgasms.

She groaned as he moved against her. He had to be kidding. She'd just had a mind-blowing orgasm, followed by several very sweet smaller trips over pleasure hill. He couldn't want to do it again?

"Shower?" he murmured against her hair.

"That way," she said, half-heartedly pointing toward the bathroom.

"Join me?"

Audra pulled back to see his face.

A night's growth covered his cheeks, giving him a tousled pirate look. His eyes gleamed with satisfaction and something else she was afraid to try to identify. She was too tired and worn out to even worry, though. The man had just experienced the best sex of his life. He had a right to look a little smug.

"As many times as you rose to the occasion, so to speak," Audra teased, "I doubt you'd be able to do justice to a dual shower."

"Wanna bet?" he challenged.

She wasn't sure if she had enough energy to actually walk to the bathroom, let alone go another round of sexual gymnastics.

But she'd be damned if she'd back down.

So Audra winked and reached around to pat his ass.

"Babe, I'm all yours. Let's see what you've got."

THERE WAS NOTHING like good chocolate to top off a night of excellent sex. Audra popped an M&M into her mouth and savored the delicious taste. She hummed a little as she slid her leg into the silky welcome of her stocking. With a practiced move, she hooked the garter and stood, shaking out her skirt.

Music pounded through the living room speakers, giving a nice downbeat for her impromptu dance of joy. She felt great. Sexy, satisfied and unstoppable.

With a shudder of remembered delight, Audra glanced at the bed. Nine and a half. Jesse was definitely a keeper.

One last look in the mirror assured her she was ready for her date, even though Jesse wasn't due for another fifteen minutes.

Which was a testament to her feelings for him, since Audra's policy was never to hurry date preparation. But she couldn't wait to see him. And not just for the sex, although the thought of that had kept her juices stirred all day long.

Just as her thoughts were heating up, her cell phone rang. "When You Wish Upon a Star" chimed out.

"Speaking of good sex," Audra said with a grin as she answered her phone. "Hey, Isabel."

The only thing more satisfying than a night of the best sex of your life was knowing your friends were getting their own. It made gloating so much easier. Audra bit her lip, hoping Isabel hurried with her greeting so she could share the awesomeness of her nine-and-a-half night.

"Don't mention sex to me," her friend growled.

"What?"

"Live a little, you said. Go ahead and let loose, enjoy. Great advice, Audra."

With a frown for the hurt beneath the snippy words, Audra sank to her bed. "What happened?"

Isabel hiccuped, then sniffed. Audra's heart dropped. *Damn. It was bad.*

Her mind raced. Kinky sex? That'd freak Isabel out for sure. Even years of Audra's influence hadn't prepared the woman for fur-lined handcuffs. Bad grooming? That wasn't so bad, but Isabel wouldn't have gone for the guy if he were a slob. How bad could it be?

"Randy's married."

Shit. That *was* bad.

"You're sure?" Audra asked quietly.

A rare sense of guilt felt like a lead weight in her belly as Audra listened to Isabel.

"He says he's separated. That's why he has his own apartment. He claims they're getting divorced, but have to work out the details first."

Audra grimaced. Those excuses wouldn't matter to Isabel. Hell, they wouldn't matter to Audra, either. Separated meant still married. While that might be a fine distinction, it was an important one. It put him off-limits until he'd dealt with his issues. The only thing worse than a man who cheated on his wife was a man who was still tied up in a marriage he claimed was over. Those strings were usually ugly and painful.

"Isabel, I'm sorry. I shouldn't have encouraged you to let go and get wild. At least, not without warning you to do a status check first."

"It's not your fault," Isabel said with a sigh and another hiccup. "I've listened to you advising those status checks often enough, I should know better. I just never thought it'd happen to me, you know?"

"I know." Audra glanced at the clock. Jesse was due any second. "Look, do you want me to come over? I can pick up some ice cream, grab a couple DVDs. We'll eat junk food and dish dirt."

"Nah. I'd rather be alone."

After a few more minutes of bad-mouthing the worthless Randy and assuring herself that Isabel would be okay, Audra finally hung up. Just as she did, the doorbell rang.

Even as she moved to open the door for Jesse and their hot date, she couldn't help but wonder if her bad girl ways were to blame for her friend's heartbreak. How ironic that she was turning into such a goody-goody over Jesse, and yet she still managed to be a bad influence.

DAVE LARSON shielded the apartment door with his shoulders as he worked a long piece of metal in the lock. Piece of cake. He'd go in, look around for his tie, be back out in fifteen minutes flat. And since this Audra chick was such a good friend of his Bea, he wouldn't even lift anything. Well, unless it was cash. Cash always came in handy. Once he'd snipped this nagging little thread, he'd be on his way to easy street. With the second half of his payment, he'd be *on* easy street. The perfect life. Riches, high-powered connections and the woman of his dreams.

Watch out, world, Dave Larson was about to make his mark. And for once, he was making it in style, with a hot chickie by his side. The luscious Bea, woman enough to inspire him to even give up his porn. He'd shower her with jewels, buy her way onto the cover of any magazine she wanted.

All he had to do was retrieve that chip and make sure his ass was covered with the triad.

He could barely keep from patting himself on the back. Tracking down the Walker chick had been easy. A few questions to Bea while she'd serviced him, a few clicks of the computer mouse. That's all it had taken to get the name, home and work address of the only person who might block his road to success.

With a quiet snick of the lock, he swung her front door open and sneered. He was as good at breaking into buildings as he was hacking computers.

Wiping a bead of sweat from his chin, Davey scanned the sparsely furnished apartment. It was like pictures he'd seen of Mardi Gras. Bright colors, a lot of shimmer and shine. Dave eyed the wide purple couch. He'd bet it saw a lot of action. Other than the couch and a pile of oversized throw pillows, some big, fancy dresser with doors holding a TV and stereo and a few plants, it was empty.

He took a quick look around and then headed for the bedroom. Fifteen minutes later, Davey was sweating up a storm. Nothing. No tie. No evidence of any triad connections on her computer, either. He had found sex toys, plenty of leather and enough lingerie to dress the entire cast of his favorite weekly porn series. But that was it. Could she have thrown it away? Probably. This was a waste of his time.

He checked out the other bedroom. It was small, almost claustrophobic. The sketch-covered walls didn't help the suffocating effect. Ignoring the deficiency of air, he took a minute to appreciate those, given they were of women in lingerie. Fabric was stacked on the corners, piled on the floor.

A rope hung from one wall to the next, fancy strings, beads and trim stuff draped over it. He rifled through them. No tie there. A quick glance over the large drafting table didn't reveal any fabric. No tie there. Just as he was turning to leave, though, something caught his eye.

Dave grabbed the paper with a frown. The words, written in a loopy scrawl, made his gut churn.

A list of names and addresses. All in China. He recognized one as a money-laundering front for the *Wo Shing Wo* triad.

Son of a bitch. Sweat slid down the back of his neck as Dave tried to catch a breath. This Walker chick had obviously duped him. She had connections in China. Crime connections that were going to end his life. Dave didn't recognize the address on the paper, but it was all the proof he needed that he'd been double-crossed.

Rage surged through him, a black film coating his vision as his ears rang. Nobody, especially not some damned woman, screwed over Dave Larson.

Giving in to the fury, he shoved the table across the room. He grabbed the rope, yanking it from the wall. Beads clattered against the window, their loud pings sounding out like shots. He kicked a few piles of fabric, then started to punch his fist into the wall. Just inches from it, though, he remembered how much he didn't like pain, and how valuable his hands were. Instead, he kicked it a couple times, then stormed out of the room.

He glanced at the clock. Ten on a Friday night. God knew when she'd be home. With a breath, he shoved the address in his pocket to look into later and rocked back on his heels. Did he wait for her in here or not?

He could hang out, but she might not be alone. Given the state of her apartment, she'd probably be whining to the cops before he could get back in here and deal with her.

He'd deal with her later.

On his way out of the apartment, Dave glared at the mess. He had planned to keep his visit secret as a favor to Bea. He knew she wouldn't want her friend upset. Just break in, grab the tie and maybe a souvenir or two, then leave.

But he wasn't the kind of man to let a little thing like lust stand between him and someone who screwed him over. Rage, still simmering, stirred an idea in Dave's head.

He stormed back into the trashed office and grabbed one of the sketches he'd ripped from the wall. He snatched up a pen and with strokes so deep they ripped the paper, he left a message. One he was sure would get the two-timing bitch's attention.

Nobody ruined Dave Larson's dreams and got away with it. She'd get him that tie, or she'd pay. Dave Larson wasn't going down alone.

IT'D TAKEN Audra a few hours and two phone calls to get over her worry about Isabel. One more point in Jesse's favor was how understanding he'd been of her need to check up on her friend.

"Thanks for the fun night," she said, leaning into Jesse's side as he walked with her to her apartment door. "I had no idea miniature golf could be such a turn-on."

"It's all in how you use your putter," he assured her with a straight face. "If you nail those balls just right, it can be the hottest game in town."

Audra rolled her eyes at the lame joke, but couldn't hold back her smile. Even though he'd acted as if he had something serious to discuss with her when he'd picked her up, as soon as he found out how stressed she was over Isabel, Jesse had been pure entertainment.

Between the jokes, a delicious dinner and the sexual sparks Jesse kept stoked to a low flame, Audra was finally relaxed. Now for the best part of the evening. Jesse, naked, in her bed.

Anticipating an eight, maybe an eight-point-five, given that they were both tired after last night's lack of sleep, she slid her key into the lock and swung open the door.

It stuck.

Audra shoved. "What the…"

She slapped at the switch on the wall next to her. As light filled the room, her stomach pitched.

Jesse's broad shoulders crowded behind her. She felt their warmth as she gaped at the mess strewn over her apartment.

"I take it this wasn't a visit by your cleaning service?" he teased. But under his light words was a cold, clinical tone she'd never heard. It both comforted and made the tiny hairs on the back of her neck stand up.

"Someone trashed my place?" She felt tears well in her eyes, but blinked fast. Wicked Chicks didn't cry. With a deep breath, she shoved aside the pain and lifted her chin.

"Well, we might want to delay our hot sex," she joked stiffly. "I think I'd better tidy up first."

Not meeting his eyes, she stepped over the bolt of cloth that'd been blocking the door and made her way into the room. At second look, it wasn't as bad as she'd originally thought. It was a mess, and someone had obviously invaded her space. But nothing looked broken. Her TV was still in the armoire, as was the stereo. So why were her hands trembling?

Audra took a shaky breath and tried to calm the pained emotions swirling through her system. It was just stuff. Just an apartment. Maybe if she told herself that often enough, the devastating pain would subside.

She bent down to pick up a few paperback romances that looked as if they'd been kicked around. Jesse grabbed her arm.

Startled, she looked up at him. He was shaking his head,

even as he pulled his cell phone from his pocket. He punched a couple of keys and held it to his ear.

"I'd like to report a break-in," he said into it. His eyes held hers as he gently pulled her to him. He wrapped an arm around her shoulders and, despite her stiffness, rubbed his hand over her back. She should pull away. She didn't need soothing. But she couldn't bring herself to leave the haven of Jesse's arms.

The tension slowly left her body and she let herself lean into him. His strength enfolded her as Audra tuned out his words and closed her eyes to the devastation of her home.

And, for the first time in her life, she lowered her guard, and her heart, enough to let herself be comforted.

13

JESSE WAVERED between amusement and irritation as he watched Audra lead the investigating officer around by the…nose.

"She's not much into cops, is she?" Rob Dutton asked, a scowl creasing his freckled forehead. Jesse's partner leaned against a doorframe, tapping his pen against his blank notebook.

Jesse just shrugged, trying to ignore the sick knot in his belly. He'd had no idea Audra's warm, sexy charm could take on such a sharp edge. Her mood didn't bode well for him. How would she take his eventual confession?

"You think it was Larson?" he murmured, indicating the trashed office.

"Pretty sure," Rob agreed. He glanced at the nasty missive he'd pulled from Audra's wall, the angry words glaring through the clear plastic of the evidence bag. "Even though the guy's a notorious wimp, I'll put an APB out on him. Walk me out, huh?"

Jesse frowned.

Ignoring Audra's questioning glance, he followed Rob out of the apartment. A soft evening breeze stirred the dark night. The two men were silent until they reached Rob's car, lit by the streetlights.

Jesse frowned again at the note, sealed in an evidence bag. *You're not getting away with it. Give it back, bitch. Or you'll pay, and pay big.* Apparently Davey was getting desperate.

"We picked up a bimbette tonight," Rob said without preamble. "While she was shoveling dirt to get her ass out of trouble, she tossed a few clumps at the triad. She also said she was stiffed on a deal. She was supposed to pick up a handoff of goods a week or so ago at The Wild Thing from ole Davey boy."

Ahh. Last piece of the puzzle. Jesse nodded his satisfaction. Audra was clear. A few knots he hadn't even realized he had loosened in his shoulders.

"You don't seem surprised." Rob took the evidence bag and tossed it into the backseat before leaning against the car and crossing his arms.

"I'm not. You weren't in the office this morning, but last night I'd discovered where the cash came from. As far as I'm concerned, Audra's clean. Nothing ties her to the triad or Larson except an accidental meeting."

"And the goods he passed off in the bar," Rob reminded him as he got in his car and started the ignition. "You might want to keep that in mind. Especially since whoever tossed the place obviously has a hard-on for your girlfriend."

Jesse winced at the reference to Audra. But there was no condemnation in Rob's eyes, just sympathy and a hint of worry.

"Don't wait to break the case against the triad," Jesse ordered. "Larson's a threat to Audra. Pick him up, maybe we can get him to roll on the them."

"You're kissing your promotion goodbye if you don't pull down the big boys. You know that, right?"

With a nod, Jesse shrugged. He wordlessly watched Rob drive away. The promotion had been important. Proof that he was as good a cop as his father. But it wasn't worth Audra's safety. Nothing was.

Between the bimbette's confession and the break-in, Audra was pretty much cleared. But, unfortunately for Jesse, it moved her cleanly from suspect to target.

And shoved her right back to the off-limits list. If he thought sleeping with a suspect was dirty, sleeping with someone under his protection was simply taking advantage.

Five minutes later, Jesse confirmed the drive-by schedule with the uniformed officers before closing the door behind them. Then he eyed the sexy woman across the room from him.

"Well, that wasn't quite how I planned to start off our wild night of hot loving," Audra said. Her tone was joking. But the stiffness of her smile and the stress bracketing her eyes gave away her turmoil. Even so, she stood in her usual, hip-cocked sexy stance and gave him a wink.

Was it any wonder he was crazy about her?

"Crime has a way of ruining the mood," Jesse shot back, figuring she'd appreciate the joke more than his observation of her emotional state. "I'll help you clean this up, huh?"

She looked around silently and then gave a sigh and a shrug. From where they stood, they could see the barely touched living room and bedroom, and the very trashed room that served as her office. Other than Davey's mess, her place was sexy as hell. Much like Audra herself.

"Did you want to come home with me?" he asked as they gathered CDs and books to put back on the teak shelving unit between the bedrooms. "Is there someplace else you'd rather stay tonight?"

"Stay? What are you talking about? I'm staying here."

"Here? You heard what the cop said. You should find someplace to stay until they catch that dirtbag who did this."

"Cops say lots of things. Most of them irritate me, so I rarely listen." At his frown, she shoved the last handful of books on the shelf, the red paperback spines willy-nilly and teetering precariously, then stood.

"Look, I'm sure he had good intentions. Serve and protect, and all that jazz. But this is my home. No lowlife is going to drive me out of it. Like I told the cop, I have no idea why someone would threaten me and definitely have no clue what that note was blathering about. Besides, that one guy in the jeans, the one you were so chummy with?" She shot him a look that made Jesse's shoulders twitch. It was a combination suspicion, curiosity and underlying trust. "He said they'd be doing drive-bys and keeping watch on my place."

Jesse rose and stood over her. Trying to throw off his guilt over ignoring the question in her eyes, he offered his fiercest frown. "Drive-bys are all well and good, but they are no guarantee of safety. Are you willing to take that chance? Willing to go climb into your bed and hope he won't be back?"

Rather than turning pale, stuttering or even looking thoughtful, Audra lifted her chin and gave a chilly smile.

"Let him try."

"Fine. Then I'm staying with you."

Her cold smile turned to steam and she gave him a look hot enough to melt his shorts. Beneath it, though, was a vulnerability he'd never imagined in Audra.

If he'd had any illusions of keeping his hands off her until after the case was closed, that look shot them straight to hell. But not tonight. That'd just be wrong. His body was putting up a fierce argument, but Jesse tried to convince himself he wasn't led by his dick.

"Look, you've had a rough night. The break-in, the threat. You're probably emotionally overwhelmed right now." He ignored her wide-eyed stare and gestured to the now tidy hallway. "I'll stay the night, but on the couch. I'm not going to take advantage of you in a vulnerable state."

Audra's jaw dropped, a look of blank shock on her face. After five excruciatingly long seconds, she burst into laughter. He wasn't sure if he was relieved to see she wasn't overwrought, or offended.

At the sight of her delighted grin, he settled for relief.

"I can't remember the last time anyone took advantage of me. It sounds fun, though. Wanna take turns?"

She took a step toward him and her foot hit a string of beads, sending them flying across the room with a reverberating rattle. They watched as the string hit the wall, bright red orbs flying every which way on impact.

Jesse grimaced at the mess and glanced back at Audra to ask her where she kept her vacuum. His heart clenched at the sight of her face, silent tears swimming in her huge eyes.

With a barely audible groan, Jesse stepped forward and pulled her into his arms. Her scent, the heady richness of it, wrapped around his senses. Jesse rubbed her shoulders and murmured comforting nothings as she pulled in a shaky breath.

"You okay, babe?" he asked.

"Yeah," she said against his shoulder. "I'm just pissed. And a little freaked that someone would hate me enough to break into my home and mess it up so bad. It's hard to fight someone when you have no idea who they are or how you pissed them off, you know?"

Jesse winced. He had to tell her. As much as he'd like to put it off, to protect her—and, if he was honest with himself, protect his place in her life—he had to clue her in.

Somewhere in the back of his mind, Jesse realized once he'd arrested Dave Larson and kicked his ass for breaking into Audra's apartment, he'd likely thank the guy for bringing her into his life.

That was, if there was a chance she'd still have anything to do with him after she learned the truth.

With a heartsick sigh, Jesse knew he didn't have a choice. It was time to confess. Both for her own good, and to find out if she had any idea what Dave had been trying to hand off that night.

But damned if he wasn't positive his admission was going to screw him but good with her. And not in the way he'd enjoyed last night.

FEELING LIKE a wimpy idiot, Audra sucked in a deep breath and tried to tamp down the fear whispering in her head. That note had been so angry.

Audra shuddered. Then she frowned. How dare someone come into her home and threaten her. As she'd told Jesse, she'd be damned if some dirtbag was going to mess with her or scare her out of her own place.

Or worse, screw with her sex life.

With that in mind, she took a deep breath and cleared her face. To push back the fear, she pictured Jesse naked, his hard body poised over hers just before he took that wild plunge of pleasure.

She pulled back and gave him her *let's-get-dirty* look.

"Since you're staying the night, why don't we go in the bedroom and get comfortable? I can deal with this mess tomorrow. I had other plans tonight, and I'll be damned if some loser is going to keep us from having fun."

Audra watched the expressions chase across Jesse's face. Maybe it was stress overload, but she was definitely getting a weird vibe off him. It had started when he'd been all chummy with that cop. And now he had a guarded look in his eyes. It was as if all emotion had been wiped away, giving him a blank, official kind of look. The kind Child Protective Services had always worn when they'd come to check on her mother.

She tried to brush off the sick feeling in her stomach. But the tiny hairs on the back of her neck wouldn't lie down, and she suddenly felt like hurling.

Audra had never fallen apart in front of a guy before. Never let her rarely admitted vulnerability show. She'd never felt an emotional connection with a guy that made her feel safe enough to even consider it. Until tonight. Until Jesse.

And now? Now he was pulling away, distanced and cold. With that closed look on his face.

All bad signs.

"What's up?" she asked.

"I have a confession to make. Something I need to tell you." His casual tone sounded forced, as if he didn't want to scare her off.

Audra bit her lip. From his tone and the look on his face, she didn't think she was gonna be giddy with delight over whatever it was he wanted to share.

Since it didn't look like she could put off the conversation until she'd regained a solid emotional footing, Audra gestured that he go ahead. Jesse swallowed uncomfortably and winced. Then he gave a shrug and took her hands.

"Okay. Here goes… I'm not just a computer geek. I'm a cop. With the Cyber Crimes division of the Sacramento P.D."

She blinked.

Huh? A cop?

Son of a bitch. The longtime bad girl in Audra pulled back a few inches. Her entire body tensed up, her defenses going to automatic full alert. That would explain his ease with the cops who'd tramped through her house. His private powwow with the one in charge.

"Okay," she said slowly, trying to figure out if the anger building inside her was because he was a cop, or because he'd lied to her. "Why didn't you tell me this before? I thought you worked with computers."

"I do. Work with computers, that is. Cyber crimes are just that, computer crimes. I spend most of my time working with a keyboard."

"Oh." Should she be relieved? Had he actually lied? Maybe

not, but it sure as hell felt like it. Audra forced herself to unclench her teeth and smooth out the furrows digging into her brow. "That would explain why you were so chummy with that dude tonight. The cop in jeans."

"He's my partner," he confessed with a grimace.

"Partner? Why…? What's going on, Jesse."

Needing to be away from him, Audra stepped back. Still able to breathe in the spicy scent of his cologne, she took another step back. She needed all the distance she could get to clear her head and get a freaking clue as to what was going on.

"I was in the club the night we met because I was on a case," he confessed.

"I thought you just said you worked behind a computer?"

"Usually, I do. But I went undercover. It was a dare, of sorts."

Of sorts. Audra winced at the memory of that night and her own dare. Of how and why she'd hooked up with Jesse.

"I was there tailing the dork. That guy you'd had the 'sort of' dare date with. Remember him?"

Audra nodded slowly.

"Dave Larson, that's his name. He was there to make a connection. To pass off a chip of stolen IDs. He's involved on the fringes of a Chinatown-based crime ring and was selling the information to them. My plan was to identify his connection, trail her back to the crime ring."

"Her?" It was finally all clicking together. Audra's stomach had stopped swirling, now it was clenched like an angry fist. "If I remember right, the only woman that geek hooked up with at the club was me."

"Well…yeah."

It didn't take her long to connect the dots. Betrayal slapped her with a stinging blow.

"You think I'm a criminal?" Shock made her tone sharp enough to cut glass. She'd thought he was different. Someone who looked at her and, yeah, recognized she was a bad girl, but realized that didn't mean she was a bad person. But no. Jesse was just like all the other jerks in her life. He'd not only had low expectations of her, he'd pegged her for a criminal.

"Look, that's not the point right now. What matters is that I'm sure it was Larson who broke in here and threatened you. You have something he wants, Audra. I need to find out what it is and get it so I can protect you."

Audra swore she felt her heart actually crack. Pain like she'd never felt, even during her father's prolonged illness and death, poured through her. Her breath caught at the intensity of Jesse's betrayal. At the misery of realizing he not only didn't return her feelings of love, he'd used her.

This was one hell of a time to find out that whole stupid cliché was rooted in reality. A red film of betrayed anger glazed her eyes, and Audra glared to clear her vision. She grabbed on to the fury, glad to have it there to shield her from the misery tearing at her heart.

"Not the point?" she hissed over the pain. "You think I'm dirty of some crime and that's not the point? You used me. You slept with me, all the while thinking I was a…what? A criminal? An accessory to something?"

"Don't make this into more than it is. There was a lot of evidence against you."

"Why? Because I talked to some geek? How the hell does that make me look guilty of anything except bad taste?"

"It was the money in your company's account. The trip to China. A lot of little things," he said in a stiff tone, misery clear in his eyes.

Audra didn't care how bad he felt. He deserved it. After all, he'd done the unforgivable. He'd made her open her heart. And for what? A police investigation? She pressed her hand against her stomach.

"You checked me out? You poked into Simply Sensual's finances and investigated our business?" Outrage made her words shrill. She thought back to that night, the club. Then the parking lot. How could she have been so stupid? She'd been worrying about forgetting a damned condom and the whole time she should have been worried about her blind trust. What Wicked Chick worth her stilettos didn't sense a setup?

To hide her heartache, Audra sneered. "I suppose that invasion of privacy was a piece of cake, though. After all, you had your hand in my panties first, didn't you. Your job sounds like so much fun."

Jesse stiffened. "Look, I cleared you. You might be a little grateful instead of nasty."

"Grateful? For what? I wasn't guilty of anything. Except believing your bullshit."

He wasn't in love with her. Hell, he probably wasn't even in like with her. He'd slept with her in the name of the job. She, her heart, they didn't count. Only her connections to his nasty little crime. And she'd thought he was a good boy?

Audra gulped back the tears clogging her throat and stiffened her lower lip before it could quiver. No way in hell she'd give him the satisfaction of knowing what he'd meant to her. To know she'd fallen in love with him.

"Look, Audra, it's not like that. I mean, yes, I didn't tell you everything, but I couldn't."

"Nope, can't tell the criminals you're on to them, right? Or should that be *on* them? Under them? In them?" Jesse made a sharp gesture for her to stop, but Audra just glared and raised one sardonic brow. Anger was the only thing keeping her from falling to pieces. "Behind them? That was nice, huh?"

"Stop it," he snapped. The way he cringed assured her

she'd hit a tender spot. Good. Now that she knew where to strike, she could get him the hell out of her face.

"You're good at giving orders, Jesse. What rank are you? Bet you're high up there, a man like you, willing to do anything to get the job done. Or is that do anyone?"

"Audra, quit. Stop demeaning what we have."

"Had." Forcing herself into action, she sauntered over to the front door, making sure she put enough body English into her hips to make a blind man drool. "What we had. We have nothing now. We're through."

"You can't do that. Don't end it like this." Jesse followed her. He put a beseeching hand on her shoulder. She gave his hand a look, then met his eyes. He let go.

"This, whatever it is, is over." She wanted him out before she started crying.

"Audra—" he started.

"No," she interrupted. "I want you to go. We're nothing. We never were. All I was to you was a suspect, then a means to an end. And all you ever were to me was a dare," she lied.

"A what?"

She took grim satisfaction in the look of confusion on his face. Good, let him feel betrayed, too.

"A dare," she said with relish. "I told you that night in the club about dares, remember? Well, you were mine. All I had to do to keep my Wicked Chick status was sleep with you. I guess I should thank you for the extra credit points. You were pretty good, too."

"I thought that was a blind date."

"Hardly," Audra said with a sneer. "That was a dare. That's why I went up to your creepy criminal that night in the club. The girls dared me to do the first guy to come through the door. You were close, but he was first."

"Do?"

"Do. Screw. Down and dirty. Sex, Jesse. You remember sex, don't you? You were pretty good at it in there." Audra made a sharp gesture toward the bedroom. "I'd never have pegged you for a cop, being as you came off as such a good boy. But then, you were undercover, weren't you."

"You went after Larson for sex?"

"You got it." She gave him an evil smirk, then raised a brow. "Or got me, if you prefer. He was my dare, but his little chicken ass ran out. You, by default, were my backup dare."

Brows furrowed, Jesse tilted his head as if he didn't understand. "Are you trying to claim you only had sex with me for a dare?"

"Exactly."

The anger suffusing his face didn't even come close to the level burning in her gut, but Audra blinked anyway. For the first time, she felt intimidated by Jesse.

All the more reason for him to leave.

"I don't believe you." Fists clenched at his hips, Jesse glared at her. "There's too much between us to be some stupid game."

"What? Your crime? Get real. There's nothing between us. After all, I just remembered there's a good reason I don't do good boys. And I especially don't do cops."

Audra had to swallow to get past the lump in her throat. Knowing she couldn't keep herself together much longer, she gestured to the door.

"Go. I don't want to do this anymore."

"We need to settle this between us, Audra. And I need to find out about that night, ask you some questions about what Larson said to you, if he gave you anything." At Audra's vicious look, he frowned, then shrugged. "If you can't do this now, fine. We'll wait until tomorrow. But we have to talk, Audra. Soon."

Fear pounded in her head as she shook it in denial.

She couldn't talk to him again. Couldn't stand to see him and know there was nothing there but a case. It already hurt too much. Not knowing any other way to get him to leave before she completely lost it, she did the only thing she knew how. She pulled her hard-ass attitude around her like a shield and lashed out.

"You try to say another word to me, and I'll turn you in for sexual harassment. I'm sure there are some rules in your good boy book against lying to and sleeping with a suspect."

Jesse gave her a long look, then shook his head. "We need to discuss this. But if I've learned anything from my sisters, it's that it's pointless to push when a woman is so pissed she looks like she's ready to rip my head off. I'll call you later, we'll get together and talk."

"Don't bother. I only had to do you once, and since we're already well over that quota, I don't have any further use for you."

He shot her an indecipherable look. One that scared Audra to her very soul. Then with a shake of his head, he opened the door. Once through, his hand still on the knob, he looked back.

"You don't reach a nine and a half on just a physical level, Audra. That's about emotions. That's a connection that goes beyond two bodies and sex. It's about love."

He shut the door behind him with a quiet snick. She stood and stared at the white expanse of wood until it blurred.

It wasn't until she moved to slide the dead bolt into place that she realized everything was blurry because of the tears streaming down her face.

It looked as if she'd finally found the answer to the identity crisis that had been plaguing her the last couple of weeks. Dare achieved or not, she'd lost her bad girl status. Because Wicked Chicks didn't cry. Especially over men.

14

"HE'S A COP and he slept with you while you were under investigation?" Bea asked, her breathy voice tinged with shock. "That's terrible."

"Men suck," Isabel claimed in a rigid tone. Her pale face, hair pulled back in a punishing ponytail and baggy sweats were all clear signs of man trouble. Given her discovery that her first-time fling was a lying cheat, Audra figured the fact that she wasn't burning a well-endowed male effigy and spitting on the flames was a miracle.

"Be fair," Suzi said with her usual logic, "Audra did a number on him, same as he did her."

"There's a difference," Bea insisted.

Suzi just laughed. A cynical, mocking sound that played on Audra's already raw nerves.

After she'd kicked Jesse out, she'd thrown a nice little temper tantrum. Two hours at the gym trying to exhaust her body and a carton of Heath Bar Crunch had only made her angrier. She'd come home and ripped the sheets from the bed to remove all traces of her night with Jesse. Then, when that hadn't made her feel any better, she'd waited until dawn, and called for reinforcements.

She hadn't really felt up to company, but she'd known being around her friends would force her to put on her game face and suck up the hurt. And true friends that they were,

Isabel, Bea and Suzi had jumped right out of bed—in Suzi's case, someone else's—and come right over.

She sat with the other women on the floor of her office, sorting through the mess of designs, trim and beading. With a sigh, she scooped up the shredded pieces of her fall design boards. Like her love life, her career was sucking hard.

"I know," Bea offered, "Let's spend the day pampering ourselves, then tonight we'll get dressed up, hit a few clubs and see how many hot dudes we can reel in."

"I thought you were seeing that photographer guy?"

"That wasn't going anywhere," Bea said. She jingled her wrist, the pale morning sunlight glinting off the diamonds in her bracelet. "I mean, he was just too clingy and weird. I guess I should let him know it's over, huh?"

Audra groaned. "Jeez, Bea. You haven't told the guy it's over yet?"

"Nah. I hate hurt feelings. I keep hoping he'll clue in when I don't call him back."

"That's not fair. If you're going to end it, do it clean."

"He's a man," Isabel said with a roll of her eyes. "It probably serves him right."

"You're a little on the bitter side, don't ya think?" Suzi asked with a surprised stare.

"I just don't think this guy had any right to let the relationship go as far as the bed," Isabel insisted, ignoring Suzi's question. "Men are pigs. Lying left and right just to get a woman into bed."

"Sure guys lie. So do women, it's not like truth is exclusive to one sex or the other," Suzi said dismissively. "The bottom line is, Audra did her dare. It wasn't like she fell for the guy or anything. Right?"

She peered at Audra, her face looking oddly young and almost sweet without its usual polished makeup. Blue eyes

Audra knew as well as her own were filled with questions. I
wasn't the curiosity that worried Audra, though. It was the
sympathy.

"It was good sex," Audra retorted with a shrug. As long as
she forced herself to treat it like any other encounter, she
could keep away the pain. "A little practice and he'd have hi
the fabled ten on the orgasm scale."

"That good, huh?"

"Yup."

"It'd be a shame to let go of someone who could toast your
buns so perfectly."

"Let him go? I never had him." Maybe if she said it enough
she'd believe it, too.

"Maybe you should report him," Isabel mused.

"Why? Do they give medals for sexual prowess? He deserves
one, sure, but I don't usually go in for ego strokes, you know?"

"Stop it. You're as bad as Suzi." Isabel quit straightening and
stacking a pile of designs to glare. "Don't blow this off. No
only did he take advantage of you, you were—are—in danger.'

Done sifting beads, Audra closed the lid of the plastic
case. She stared down at the rainbow of glass shapes until they
blurred into a kaleidoscope of running colors. She tried to
shove the pain back down, but it was like the lid she'd kep
on her emotions for so long, once peeled open, refused to shut

Finally, she looked up and met Isabel's outraged gaze, her
own eyes sheened with tears.

"He didn't take advantage. You know that. Sure, I was a
suspect, but he was a dare. Which of us took advantage of
the other?"

Isabel pressed her lips together as she considered, then she
shook her head.

"But he hurt you," she said softly. Her own eyes were
liquid with sympathy.

"Yeah." Audra drew in a shuddering breath and tried to shrug. But as hard as she wanted to ignore the pain, it wouldn't go away. "But it wasn't like he owed me anything. We didn't make any promises, you know?"

"Oh, my God, will you stop being so damned fair," Suzi snapped in an abrupt about-face. "Quit it. I don't give a rat's ass how he was a nice guy, how he was doing his job or how good in bed he is. Isabel's right. None of that excuses him hurting you."

Walls crumbling, Audra's lip trembled for a brief second before the dam burst and tears poured free. Damn Jesse, he'd totally ruined her Wicked Chick vow to never cry over a man.

When her friends' faces crumbled too, Audra knew she was done. The tears poured free. The other women sniffed, rubbed her back and gave each other helpless looks. Audra still couldn't stop.

Finally, Isabel got up and went to the kitchen. She came back with a grocery bag. She pulled out sour cream and onion potato chips, pretzels and Doritos, along with a four-pack of wine coolers and a big bag of jelly beans.

"Breakfast of champions," Bea pointed out.

Even through her misery, Audra had to giggle.

"What? No chocolate?" Suzi asked with a watery laugh of her own.

"No," Isabel said quietly with a sympathetic look at Audra. "I'm pretty sure Audra's had enough chocolate."

Audra eyed the fattening feast spread over the tattered remnants of her designs. "So much for my Wicked Chick status, huh?"

"What are you talking about?" Bea asked, tearing into the chips.

"This heartbreak over some guy," Audra specified. "It's so totally against all the rules. Next thing you know, I'll be

whining in an Internet self-help group while eating a pint of
Chunky Monkey in my flannel jammies."

Suzi snorted, but Isabel just stared.

"Since when do Wicked Chicks follow rules?"

Audra frowned, but couldn't think of an answer so she
shrugged instead.

"You of all people should know being a bad girl is all
about attitude," Suzi pointed out as she handed Audra the bag
of Doritos. "This crappy one of yours sucks right now. But
that's not a permanent thing. More like a temporary break-
down. We're all entitled to those."

"Even you?" Isabel teased.

"Sure. But if it were me, I'd lose the flannel. Hell, all I own
in the sleepwear department is Audra's stuff anyway. Even if
most of it is sweet and fluffy."

They all laughed, but Audra had to blink a few times to
keep the tears from starting again. For a badass friend, Suzi
was pretty damned wonderful.

"So what are you going to do?" Bea asked around a
mouthful of jelly beans.

"Yeah, are you going to go after this guy? Or are you
going to trade him in for three guys and a bag of Doritos?"

"I don't want three guys," Audra said as she shoved a
nacho chip into her mouth.

"Then what *do* you want?"

Good question. Audra licked the orange powder from her
thumb and considered. She remembered how good it'd been
with Jesse. The laughter and the jokes, the simple enjoyment
of his company. Who knew it'd be those things, instead of the
wild sex, that would send her head over heels for a guy?

He was a cop. A cop who'd used her. Lied to her and suspected the worst of her.

And he was a dare. One she'd used to prove herself.

Which made them even, in her mind.

She knew what she wanted. The real question was, could she handle it? The Wicked Chick and the cop? It was so far-fetched, what were the odds?

Then again…she was a Wicked Chick. Damned if she couldn't play those odds and win.

"I want Jesse," Audra admitted.

Bea took the bag of chips from Audra's hands and pointed to the door. "Then fix your crappy attitude, take your bad girl self and go get him."

LATER THAT MORNING, after a cold compress and a change into her sexiest lingerie and a leather skirt, Audra sauntered into the Good Times Sports Bar. Attitude at full throttle, she was ready to deal with the first of her tiny problems.

Once she'd confronted Natasha, she'd either be out of a job, or have the creative freedom she needed to do her current one.

Then she'd go tackle her other problem.

Jesse Martinez, good boy cop.

The bar was empty, as she'd figured it would be at eleven in the morning. She waved to the daytime bartender, then made her way to the back stairs that led to the second-floor apartment where her brother lived.

Since they were expecting her and because she was in the mood to seize the upper hand, Audra knocked once, then walked right in.

"Hey, Audra," Drew said from the couch. He aimed the remote at the TV, hit Off and tossed the wand on the coffee table. With a grin, he rose and gave her a hug.

Audra let herself lean into him for a whole five seconds. There was something comforting about Drew. Maybe his re-semblance to their father, maybe his easygoing manner.

Either way, she figured she might as well snag her hug

while she could. Who knew how he'd feel about her once she'd had her say.

"Hey, you look like China agreed with you," she said when she pulled away. And it was true. With his red hair mussed and his face the most relaxed she'd seen in a while, he looked like a guy who'd had a great vacation.

Natasha walked in, her face a study of cool, composed breeding. Audra wondered, not for the first time, how the hell such an uptown lady had ever hooked up with Drew.

"It was a good trip," he was saying. "We've got pictures. I'll put you to sleep with them later, huh?"

"Vacation pics?" Audra asked in mock horror. "Ack, no."

"There are a few you'll really like," Natasha assured her as she offered a hesitant smile.

Audra's stomach clenched at the reserved look. It didn't bode well for her long-term job prospects.

She lifted her chin. So what? She wasn't sidelining her beliefs anymore. Like Jesse had said, she believed in herself enough to fight, to hold out for what she felt she was worth.

"You don't mind me stopping in, do you?" she asked them. "I figured this was a better place to talk than the boutique with all its distractions."

"No, this is perfect. I wanted to talk to you before we settled into the work week anyhow, and weekends are always so crazy." Natasha gestured to a chair. "Have a seat, I have to get something. I'll be right back."

Audra raised an inquiring brow at her brother, but he'd slapped on his poker face. He pointed to the chair, then sat himself back on the couch.

"So," Natasha said as she joined Drew on the couch, a large folder on her lap, "let's talk design."

"Let's," Audra agreed. Natasha opened the file, and there on top was the naughty little design with the wrist ties. Audra looked at it and felt a surge of mingled pride and excitement. It was one of her best pieces. Innovative, sexy and unique.

She lifted her chin and met her sister-in-law's gaze with her own level stare.

"I didn't intend for that to be shown in China, but I did intend for you to see it," she admitted. "I realize you want to wait until later, if at all, to introduce any changes to Simply Sensual product focus. But as much as I enjoy designing for you, I need to be able to expand my portfolio. Creatively, I can't keep stifling the naughtier, wild designs that come to me."

In a totally bullshit show of calm, Audra leaned back in the chair and gave a little shrug. She was sure the nerves jangling through her system didn't show on her face.

Unfortunately, she couldn't read anything from Natasha or Drew's expressions, either. They glanced at one another, then Drew got up and headed for the kitchen.

Chickenshit. He probably didn't want to have to watch his wife fire his sister.

"I'd hate to be responsible for stifling creative expression," Natasha said slowly. She lifted the design and gave a little laugh. "And leave it to you to find inspiration in that buttugly tie. Keeping your designs from the world would be an absolute shame. You're talented and deserve to make the most of your gifts."

Audra pursed her lips. Nothing like a few pats on the ass before you got booted.

"So, I'd like to offer you full creative control of Simply Sensual's new line. Since it's your designs, and you'd come up with such a clever name, I thought we'd call it Twisted Knickers. And, if you'll take it, partnership in the company."

Stunned, Audra stared. She gave a little shake of her head, the only sound in the room the tinkle of her dangling earrings.

"You're kidding, right? This is a joke to get me back for embarrassing you in front of the distributors?"

"Why would I do that?"

"You were pissed."

Natasha grimaced, then shrugged. "Yes, I suppose I was. I'm used to being in control of my business. And, I guess, feeling that I know what's best."

"What changed, then?"

"Drew."

"Huh?" Audra squinted at her, totally lost.

"While I was having a meltdown over how much more interested the distributors were in your naughtier design than what I'd brought to present, Drew looked at it." With a glance, she passed the board to Audra. "He pointed out that this was likely your best work yet, and after I got over the urge to throw something at him, I had to admit he was right."

Her brother had stood up for her? Audra's heart did a little happy dance.

"What about Simply Sensual? What about the money constraints and marketing and all that other stuff?"

Natasha lifted one shoulder. "The spicier line will be marketed under the Twisted Knickers label and distributed separately. I've worked up the specs, and it's all doable. As for money," she glanced over as Drew returned with a bottle of champagne and three glasses, "the Chinese distributors are placing much higher than expected orders, based on your naughty design. And if we need more financial backing, Drew's offered to bankroll Twisted Knickers."

Her brother had that much faith in her succeeding? Tears sprang to Audra's eyes. Oh, God. She was turning into a total wimp. She tried to take it all in. Not just what was being said, but what was going unsaid.

Her brother's faith in her. Natasha's willingness to take a chance on her. The fact that they were offering her the world.

Excitement dueled with joy in her belly, doing a happy little cancan. Jesse had been right. Her dreams were worth standing up for.

And now that one was being handed to her, wrapped up in a black leather bow?

She didn't want to take it.

"Don't be pissed," she said slowly, "but I'm going to say no."

"What?" Drew yelped, the champagne slopping as he poured.

"Why?" Natasha asked, her tone a lot calmer.

"I'd suck as a partner, Natasha. I mean, the design aspect, well, that's a dream come true. I'd love it. But running the boutique, well… I blew it. Things got messy, the store isn't as well stocked as it should be."

Audra sucked in a deep breath and kissed the best business offer of her life goodbye. Then she grabbed the half-full glass of champagne from her brother and downed it.

"It's just not my gig," she admitted. "If I've learned anything the last couple weeks, it's that I've got to be true to what works for me. And that boss thing, well, that isn't it."

Feeling sick and a little miserable, Audra held out her glass for a refill. Drew, though, was staring at Natasha. The two of them were doing that whole silent communication thing.

Then Natasha nodded. With a smile, she rose and came around the coffee table to pull Audra out of the chair and give her a big hug.

"How about the design offer, then? They aren't a package deal."

Like the sun had come out on a bitterly rainy day, hope shone again. Audra grinned. Then for the first time ever, she grabbed her brother and sister-in-law both in a huge hug.

JESSE WATCHED Shale peruse the case file. He wished he felt even half the level of triumph the gloating grin on the captain's face indicated.

"You're sure of this?" Shale asked.

Jesse nodded.

"You did it, Martinez. You nailed them. Not only Larson, but the whole *Du Bing Li* triad as well. You've tied them to China and gave us the connection's name."

Jesse tried to smile, but he was sure it looked more like a pained grimace.

"Once Larson accessed his off-site computer storage unit, I was able to trace his connection. Hacking into it was easy at that point. He's a tidy thief. Everything was neatly labeled, ready to download. I'd bet the triad warned him to ditch the IDs once he'd handed them over, but a guy like Davey likes to have backup."

"Have you physically located his off-site unit?"

"No, not yet. He's smooth. Without the chip he was reputed to hand off, this won't be as easily admissible in court, but we can make it stick. Especially since I was able to access the list of IDs. The triad's moving human cargo from China and already assigned at least a dozen of those IDs to their people. It's not all tied up with a bow, but it's a solid case."

"Too bad we didn't have that chip, or we'd blow it wide open. Even so, this is more than the chief had hoped for. Good work, Martinez. It'll go far toward that promotion. I gotta say, you have a lot of your father in you."

"Yes, sir," Jesse agreed with a grimace.

Yup, he was one righteous bastard, just like his father. Here he was, justifying sleeping with a woman involved in his case. Good ole dad couldn't have done any better.

"Although, if you don't mind me being honest with you, as much as I admired Diego, he didn't have your knack for tying up loose ends. Or your care to make sure the bystanders and victims in your cases are taken care of. To be honest, his methods were sometimes a cause for concern."

"Sir?" Jesse stared across the desk and wondered if he'd heard right. Didn't everyone universally adore his father's methods?

"Don't get me wrong, Diego had a sterling rep and a solid arrest record. You take that extra care, though. People are more than just names and means to ends for you, Martinez. I appreciate that, and I'm proud to have you on my team."

Jesse wasn't sure what to say to that. Shale didn't think he was like his father? Not in the ways Jesse was worried about. Sure, he'd let his emotions get the better of his common sense with Audra, but maybe that wasn't the same. He'd been with Audra despite the case, not because of it. Which meant maybe, unlike his father, he wasn't destined to lousy relationships. He thought back to Audra's parting shot, her anger and swaggering attitude. And now that he was remembering it without the cloud of guilt, he felt the faint stirring of hope.

All he had to do was convince her to give them a chance.

For the first time in fourteen hours, Jesse smiled. Hell, yeah, he'd convince her. Audra was meant to be his, and he'd show her exactly why. Jesse knew her—appreciated her—like nobody else in the world. And he'd use that knowledge to court her, to lure her back. Then he'd marry her and tie her to him for the rest of their lives.

AUDRA SLID into her car, the grin still plastered to her face. Rock on. She'd shown up ready to be fired and ended up with her own line of lingerie. Better yet, she'd realized that she really did know what was right for her and what wasn't.

Now to do something about the man who was right for her.

Audra would be damned if she'd give up a guy who not only got her, but got what made her *her*. What made her special.

She fingered the design Natasha had returned to her, eyeing the scrap of that ugly tie. She remembered Jesse's words about being true to herself. How clearly did he see her? More clearly than she saw herself, apparently.

So what was she going to do about it? Did Jesse really care, or was his interest in her based on his good boy genes trying to justify his naughty foray into down and dirty sex? Could he handle the real her?

Audra thought back over her time with him the last two weeks. He'd never shown any hesitation in accepting her, even when she hadn't been able to do the same.

Maybe she'd underestimated herself. As crazy a concept as it was for a woman who'd always been sure of her own strengths, Audra thought back over her brother's words.

Drew gave her credit when she didn't herself. He was willing to stand up and fight for her when she'd settled for being shuffled aside. Nobody had ever done that before, she realized.

Like Jesse, Drew believed in Audra's talent. In her vision and her ability to make her dreams a reality.

Audra stroked the ugly material she'd hacked off the end of the tie. The cheap, poorly constructed polyester felt slick beneath her fingers. Then she came to the tip, and winced. It really did feel as if someone had left a needle or something in the fabric.

With a frown, she tugged the tie free of its staple and tore at the material. A small chip, about the size of her thumb and encased in plastic, fell into her lap.

Well, well. It looked as if Jesse had been right. She was guilty, if unknowingly.

Audra pressed the tiny chip between her fingers and considered her options.

She'd always been proud to be unique, to march to her own drumbeat. All of this worry about who she was and soul-searching were a waste of energy. She was who she was. A bad girl with a soft spot for good boys. One hell of a designer with a knack for the naughty. A wild woman who was strong enough to make her dreams come true.

And a woman in love.

Which brought her to the real question.

Was Jesse man enough to accept her? The whole her, totally?

She rubbed the chip again.

Maybe it was time to find out.

15

JESSE LEFT Shale's office and tried to keep his triumphant grin from splitting his face. He'd nailed it. The case, and his internal struggle over his choices and work methods. And damned if he didn't feel good.

Now to get Audra to talk to him again, find a way to work things out with her, and he'd be great.

"You look like a happy man," Rob said as Jesse approached. Feet up on his desk, the redhead looked like he was about to fall asleep. Jesse raised a brow.

"The case is pretty much nailed," Jesse said with a frown. "What's up?"

"You had a phone call."

"Informant?" Jesse dropped into his chair and booted up his files. He wanted to make sure his case against the triad was as solid as possible. No loose ends, no easy walks.

"Nah. Girlfriend."

Jesse's fingers froze on the keyboard. "Audra called?"

"Yup. Said she had something you might be interested in."

He was interested in everything she had. That didn't narrow things down much. He squinted at his partner.

"She didn't leave details. Just said she had something you might want to check out."

Jesse was already out of his chair and halfway to the door when he thought to ask, "Did she say where she'd be?"

"Nope. But she mentioned a leather couch."

AUDRA TURNED the sign on the boutique door to Closed, but didn't lock up. Just in case Jesse decided to drop in. Would he? She was pretty sure he would, despite her nasty slams the other night. After all, his parting comment had made it clear he was either emotionally invested or the best damned actor this side of George Clooney.

Of course, he had a major investment in retrieving the tiny computer chip she had tucked away in the pocket of her mini-skirt, too.

But she'd ignore that possibility until she saw him face-to-face.

Audra checked her appearance in the gilt-framed mirror on one wall. A tweak here, a shimmy there, and her leather skirt and chiffon blouse were just right. The glint of her rhine-stone belly-button ring showed through the sheer top. She fluffed her hair, liking the redone magenta tips, and grabbed her purse to find her gloss and add more shine to her lips.

Shoulders squared, Audra took a long, hard look. Damned if she didn't like what she saw. A Wicked Chick with an attitude, but a solid grasp on her future. Not bad.

Not bad at all.

The front door rang a gentle chime as it opened. Anticipa-tion swirled a whirlwind through her belly and she lifted her chin. Showtime.

She gave her reflection a wink, a seductive grin curving her lips as she turned.

"Hey, big boy."

Oops. It wasn't Jesse.

Instead of her sexy hunk, some geeky guy sauntered into the shop. Short, dark and unimpressive.

Audra squinted. He looked familiar, but in the designer sunglasses, it was hard to tell.

"Can I help you?"

"Since you owe me, I'd say you're definitely going to help me now."

"I beg your…"

The guy whipped off his sunglasses at the same time he pulled out a nasty-looking knife.

"What the…"

"Game's over, hot stuff" he snarled, his tone pure anger. "You've screwed me over and now it's time to pay."

"Screwed you over? I have no freaking clue who *you* are," Audra explained, taking an automatic step backward. This was a joke, right?

Except the knife in the geek's hand was anything but funny.

Geek.

Oh, my God.

"Dave Larson?" she whispered, her mouth suddenly as dry as the Mojave. His laugh sent chills down her spine.

"I'm glad you're not playing dumb," he said with a friendly smile. That smile worried Audra more a lot more than the shiny knife in his hand. It was pure ice, with an edgy anger that made it clear he was a man with nothing to lose. "I'd hate to think I'd have to educate you. This way, we're on the same page and can help each other out, hmm?"

"Just because I know your name doesn't mean we're on the same page," Audra told him.

His icy smile melted. Apparently, she should have kept her mouth shut.

"Thanks to you, I'm screwed. Not only did you sell me out to the triad, you ruined my love life. Because of you, I've lost everything."

Audra tried to make sense of his words. Sell him out? He must mean something to do with the chip she had in her pocket. That part she got. But his love life?

"Dude, you can't pin a lousy love life on me. I gave you a

chance for a wild time once already. You're the one who ran away."

Like the mercury in a thermometer on a hot day, she watched the color climb Dave's cheeks in slow heat.

"Bea was mine," he claimed in a low, empty tone. "She was totally into me. Then I find out you're dirty, that you double-crossed me to the triad. And suddenly she's not returning my calls. She's too busy to see me. I know a kiss-off when I get one. It's your fault. It has to be. You ruined things. Every-thing."

This guy was Bea's photographer? God, that girl had rotten taste. Audra tried to swallow, but her throat felt as if it had closed up. She drew in long breaths, trying to push back the black haze from her vision. She'd never passed out before and she'd be damned if she'd do it now. Not over some geek with a grudge.

"Look, let's talk about this," she said, gesturing to the high-backed velvet chairs. "I'm sure we can figure some-thing out."

"I've already figured it out. You screwed me over, you'll pay." The knife held low at his side, he took a measured step toward her.

Audra sucked in a shaky breath, and the geek's gaze dropped to her breasts. The heat that flared in his beady eyes turned her stomach. Then it sparked an idea.

Jesse would come. She had to believe in him, believe that he'd really meant it when he'd said what they had was all about love. She'd never believed in love before. Not enough to trust it. Not enough to trust anyone to believe enough in the emotion to actually be there when she needed them.

But she believed in Jesse. He'd be here. And she'd be damned if he'd find her cowering from some geeky loser. Still scared, but determined, Audra racked her brain to figure a way out of this mess.

She gave Dave a long look up and down. The guy had a good sixty pounds on her. While he didn't look very muscular, she'd bet anger gave him more strength behind that knife than she wanted aimed at her.

At her look, he preened a little. Shoulders pulled back and he visibly sucked in his belly. Audra narrowed her eyes, assessing the signs. She knew men. More importantly, she knew how to read the male species. Dave wasn't immune to her charms. He'd run from her once. Could she do it again? It was worth a shot.

"Look, we can work this out," she said in a smooth, husky tone. Audra pulled out all the stops, giving him her sultriest look and running the tip of her tongue over her bottom lip. With a little extra swing in her hips, she slowly stepped toward him.

His eyes glazed over.

Audra pulled her shaky courage around her like a paper-thin chemise and sauntered closer to Dave. She fluttered her lashes and gave him her best *do me* look.

Dave swallowed audibly.

"We don't have to have all this tension between us, you know. I'd be happy to work things out so you're completely…satisfied."

A bead of sweat trailed down Dave's face.

"You get me back that chip," he demanded, trying to sound tough. "You do that, I'll make a deal with the competition. I can even cut you in," he offered with a leer.

"Cut me in, hmm? Sounds like you'd take good care of me. But what about Bea?"

"She was just a passing thing, you know? To get to you, track down my chip."

Audra was so glad Bea had dumped the jerk.

Triumph surged as he closed the blade of the knife and

dropped it into his pocket. Now they were on a more even footing.

"I'm confused," she admitted. "When you came in here, you accused me of sending that chip to China. What makes you think I can get it back? Or even if I could, that we'd get away with it? I'd think whoever has it would have already used the information, wouldn't you?"

"This chip is password protected. Your contacts in China won't be able to open it. They'll either be contacting you soon for instructions, or sending it back. A smart man always has a backup plan. And I'm one helluva smart man. That chip is worth a fortune, and only I know how to use it," he said, his hands shaking as they ran over her shoulders.

Audra had to force herself not to throw up at his touch. Thinking fast, she eyed the filmy pink robe on the hanger by the dressing room.

"Why don't we make ourselves a little more comfortable and discuss this, hmm?" Taking his hand in hers, she had to hold tight to his fingers to keep the sweaty appendages from slipping away. She led him to the public dressing room and gestured to the open door with her chin.

"So tell me," she asked as he eyed the narrow room and its plush red velvet chair, "do you like it better on top? Or on bottom?"

His hand shook so hard at that point, she gladly let it go. Audra reached over and pulled the sash from the robe, holding it taut as she pressed it against Dave's chest to push him backward. His legs hit the chair, and he fell into the seat with a clumsy thump.

Audra mentally rolled her eyes and pasted what she hoped was a simpering look on her face.

"All this intrigue talk has me all turned on." Audra licked her lips and, with a slight wince, straddled the geek in the chair. "When I'm this turned on, I just want to be kinky. Wild." She leaned close, as if to give him a wet, openmouthed kiss. She pulled back before she made contact, though. "A smart guy like you, one who takes such huge risks, I'll bet you're good at the kinky stuff."

Sweat flew from his forehead as Dave nodded so hard, he should have had whiplash.

Audra reached down to take his hand and, holding it inches from her breast, she wrapped one end of the rosebud-pink sash around it. He frowned. She grabbed his other hand and wrapped the sash around it, too.

"I'm not into pain, but I'm huge on dominance," she said, reading his arousal clearly. She swallowed as nausea rose at the image, but kept bluffing. "I want to tie you to this chair. While you watch, I'll strip off all my clothes, then all yours. Then I'll run feathers, so soft and light, over your body."

She swore there was drool on the guy's chin.

With a tight square knot, Audra secured each end of the sash to the arms of the chair. Then, sucking in a shaky breath, she rose. Crossing her arms in front of her, she gave Dave a seductive look and grasped the hem of her blouse. Hopefully seeing her bra would be enough to keep him giddy until she could run out on the pretext of finding those feathers.

"Audra? You here?"

"What the…" Dave started, pulling at the scarf.

Panic and relief surged in equal doses at the sound of Jesse's voice. She hadn't even let herself consider what she'd do if he hadn't shown up. And now that he had? Were the knots tight enough? Had she put him in danger?

Her vision blurred with anxiety, Audra had to swallow twice to find her voice.

"In the front dressing room," she called out. "I've got company, though. You might want to be careful."

"Hey," Dave protested with a yelp. He started to get up. Worried he might escape, Audra moved fast to plant herself on his lap. She knew she couldn't hold him down, but between her body weight and his tied hands, she could keep him at a disadvantage.

Jesse stepped into view, and she drank in the sight of him. His hair brushed the collar of his black T-shirt and worn jeans curved over hard thighs. His face was blank, although his eyes flashed what was either irritation or surprise at the sight of Audra on Dave's lap.

She winced. Maybe not a smart move, but if it kept Jesse safe, it didn't matter.

"This is a private party," Dave said, his tone pure male posturing. "Get lost, dude."

"I got your message," Jesse told her. "I'm going to hazard a guess this," he indicated Dave, "isn't what you had for me?"

"Hardly. This was an unfortunate surprise," she replied.

With a relieved sigh, Audra slid from the geek's lap. His hands still tied in front of him, Dave glared at them. So glad to have Jesse there, and safe, Audra just winked back. Dave's glare turned to acid, then he got a rat-like look on his face.

"I don't know where you get off, buddy, but we're busy here. We don't need an audience, so you can get lost."

"Pink's a good color on you, dude. You always let yourself be tied up for public sex?" Jesse asked snidely.

"Hey, she likes it kinky, if you know what I mean."

"Right," Jesse said with a roll of his eyes. He reached behind him and pulled a set of handcuffs from a tiny leather pouch on his belt. "You'll have plenty of time to imagine kinky sex in jail, I'm thinking. Although they might restrict your access to porn, Davey boy. Bet that'll be rough."

The geek stiffened. His eyes narrowed, first on the handcuffs, then on Jesse's face.

"Jail? You can't lock me up for dirty sex, dude. This one," he pointed to Audra with his chin, "will vouch for me. We're doing the sex thing. She seduced me, tied me up and now we're going to play with feathers. It's a two-person game, so you're not welcome."

"Actually," Audra said, gesturing toward Jesse with a sigh of relief, "I'd much rather do sex things with him. I've had him already and he's—" she gave Dave a wicked look and a slight shudder of delight "—incredible."

Dave narrowed his eyes, then his face tightened in fury.

"You wanted me. You were so hot, you couldn't stop yourself from climbing all over my body. Hell, you even came up with the kinky idea to tie me up…" As his words trailed off as he caught a clue. As he realized just how well she'd played him, his anger was a visible thing.

Now that Jesse was here, though, it didn't scare Audra in the least. She wiggled her brows and flicked the pink bow at Dave's wrists.

"To be honest," she told him, "you're really not my type. I'm not much into criminal lowlifes with teensy little… knives."

Dave lunged for her, ripping one of his hands free of the scarf. Audra skipped back a few steps.

"You go ahead and say that for your boyfriend, here," Dave said with a sneer. "But you're the one that came on to me, remember? You are the one who wanted me so bad in the club that you were practically in my lap begging."

Audra rolled her eyes. What an idiot. "All three of us were in the club that night, *dude*. And two of us watched you run like a scared little virgin when I flirted with you."

"Regardless," Jesse said, obviously fighting a laugh, "your sexual prowess—or lack thereof—isn't the issue here, Larson. You're under arrest for identity theft, conspiring with known criminals and breaking and entering. And that's just the appetizer."

Obviously realizing this was bigger than he'd thought, Larson turned pale. He shook his head, then got a crafty look in his eye.

"You won't make it stick," he claimed. "Besides, what kind of guy arrests his own girlfriend?"

Audra gasped.

"What are you talking about?" Jesse asked.

"You take me down for this, you're gonna have to take this little bitch, too. She's in as deep as I am. As a matter of fact, she was my handoff that night. She's a smart one, though. She bypassed the local triad and hooked herself up with the big boys in China."

Audra growled low in her throat at the blatant lies. She'd been plenty bad in her time and had no problem owning up to her naughty ways. But she'd be damned if she'd have some geek wrapped in a pink ribbon spout lies about her.

Before she could call him on it, though, Jesse made a low humming sound.

"She's dirty, is she? Want to give me a few details?"

Eyes huge, she stared. Jesse didn't meet her eyes, focusing solely on Dave as the guy babbled details that meant nothing to Audra.

Her breath hitched, her stomach was tied in knots. What was Jesse thinking? Did he actually believe the jerk? She couldn't tell from the bland look on his face. Was her trust misplaced? Was all that stuff he'd said about level nine needing an emotional connection just fluffy emotional crap?

Or did he actually care, but he'd arrest her anyway?

Because, as any bad girl knew, the naughtier she looked, the naughtier she was. And Audra was one of the naughtiest.

"So you're telling me Audra was your handoff to the *Du Bing Li* triad? And that tie you gave her had a chip, right? But she didn't give it to the locals, she sent it direct to the Chinese contingent?"

"Yup," Dave said, leaning back against the velvet cushion with a look of smug satisfaction. He obviously didn't mind going down as long as he took someone else with him. "She's the handoff. She's got ties with both triads."

Jesse gave a slow nod. He didn't even glance at her. The room was silent. Audra wondered if her brother would be willing to shift his funding from her new lingerie line to her criminal defense. Obviously, there was enough circumstantial evidence here to make Dave's claims believable.

Most people would accept them as true. The question was...what did Jesse think? She tucked her hand into her pocket, fingering the tiny chip. She could hand it over now, prove Dave wrong. But she needed to see what Jesse did. What he said.

After years of people believing the worst about her, she had to know what he believed.

He pursed his lips, then smiled.

"Dude, you just admitted to your crimes. Thanks, you made my job a little easier."

"I didn't... I mean, I... Sure, I was involved, but just on the very outermost circle. This bitch is guiltier than I am. Hell, she's probably cheating on you, going down on the leaders. Look, you want dirt, I'll give it to you. You give me a deal. I'll give you enough evidence to nail this double-crossing bitch to the wall, along with the triad."

Anger flamed on Jesse's face. He reached down, grabbed Dave by the pink sash still tying one hand to the chair, and yanked. The cloth ripped free as Dave flew to his feet. "I think you might want to apologize to the lady, Larson. On top of everything else, you probably don't want her to press charges, do you?"

"Screw her. She's guilty and she knows it."

Jesse's face darkened with a rage like Audra had never seen. She hurried to his side and placed a hand on his shoulder.

"He's not worth the trouble," she murmured. "Besides, I have something for you."

Jesse held Dave's frightened gaze for another solid ten seconds before slowly sliding a look toward Audra. She held the chip between her fingers, the metal catching the gleam of the overhead lights.

Jesse reached out and took the chip without comment. Then, for the first time since he'd busted in, his gaze met Audra's. There in those chocolate-brown depths, she saw love. And complete acceptance.

Audra couldn't hold back her relieved grin. "You're not buying his claim?"

"That you're involved? Nah. I told you already, I knew you were innocent." At her raised brow, he laughed and corrected, "Innocent of any crime."

Like a warm blanket on a chilly day, his love settled around her. Unlike their sexual games, this wasn't edgy and wild. Rather, it was both empowering and comforting at the same time.

Audra realized then Jesse knew her to the depths of her soul. And he not only accepted all of her, he appreciated her.

It was enough to turn a girl to mush.

"MARTINEZ?" called out a voice from the boutique.

"Back here," Jesse called out, glad to have reinforcements here. He'd had enough of Larson's bullshit. All he wanted was to get the guy out of his sight so he could hold Audra. Leaving the frilly bow in place, he slapped the cuffs on Larson's wrists and pushed him through the door at a waiting uniformed officer.

Audra's eyes widened as she looked into the shop. He followed her gaze. It probably looked as if cops had overrun the entire boutique.

"I see you brought the cavalry?" she said softly.

"I called it in when I saw his car out front," Jesse said. He shot her a glance, then winced. She was as pale as the white walls behind her. As if her usual tough shell had been peeled away, she looked vulnerable and unsure. He wanted to think it was because of his emotional declaration. But being threatened by a desperate criminal at knifepoint probably had a little something to do with it.

Jesse gave a few orders to the gathered cops. Within thirty seconds, they'd cleared the boutique. Audra visibly relaxed when they heard the front door close.

"I found the chip this afternoon. I'd totally forgot about the tie the geek had tossed at me that night in the club. I didn't mean to ruin your case, but I had no idea that chip was in the tie when I cut the tip off and sent it to my sister-in-law," Audra explained. She obviously realized she was babbling, because she abruptly stopped talking and pressed her lips together. He watched the adrenaline fade and her hands start to shake.

"You didn't ruin the case. We nailed Larson and the triad. That chip will help us make sure the case is rock-solid, though. Thanks to you."

At his words, she threw herself into his arms. Jesse buried his face in her hair and inhaled the musky rich scent with a groan of pleasure. She fit perfectly against him. He wanted to make sure she stayed there.

"I'm sorry," she murmured against his chest.

"No," he said. Jesse pulled back to see her face and lifted her chin. "I'm sorry. I'm sorry I kept things from you. I wasn't using you, I swear. I can see why you thought so, but honest to God, Audra, I wouldn't have slept with you if I wasn't sure you were innocent."

She gave a watery laugh. "I've been a bad girl so long, I'm almost used to being guilty. Or at least naughty. But to have a cop declare my innocence like that is strangely gratifying."

"Despite the previous evidence to the contrary, I hope you finally believe I'm totally on your side. I've wanted you from the first moment I saw you," he vowed. Then he gave her a teasing wink. "Even if it took a do-me dare to get you interested in me."

"You gonna do me now?" she asked with that smile he loved. The one that promised sex, but hinted at the humor and fun that went with it.

"I'll do you anytime," he vowed. "I hope you keep all those do-me dares just for me from now on, though."

Vulnerability like he'd never seen was clear in her eyes as Audra stared up at him.

"You're looking for an exclusive?" she asked hesitantly.

Jesse took a deep breath, the adrenaline quieting in his system, just leaving pure nerves. What if he'd misread her? What if they were just about sex to her?

Damned if he'd let a *what-if* get in his way, Jesse kissed her. When they finally came up for air, he looked into Audra's eyes.

"I love you," he said simply. "I guess you'd say I'm definitely angling for an exclusive. How about you?"

Her eyes went huge and her mouth moved, but no sound came out. Then she gave him that slow, sexy smile that sent his heart reeling and his body into overdrive.

"Yes," she said.

"Yes?"

"I want you," she admitted. With a deep sigh, she curved her hands over his biceps and pressed against him. "I'd blame it on all that leftover adrenaline, but that'd be a lie. I want you, Jesse. Always."

He frowned, looked around the dressing room, then out the door to where cops were probably waiting.

"Here? Now? Um, can it wait a bit?"

"I'll wait as long as you want," she admitted. Then, with a deep breath and in typical bad girl fashion, she laid it all on the line. "I want you for more than just sex, even though you've achieved immortal status with that nine and a half."

Jesse knew his smile was pure smug male satisfaction. But he didn't care. Obviously, she didn't, either, since Audra grinned back and shrugged.

"I want you for your humor and your sweetness. For all those good boy traits that make you so strong, so special. I want you for the way you make me feel. Sexually and emotionally." She took a deep breath. "I love you, Jesse. I want you for good."

Jesse's heart did a flip. He'd followed his conscience and stuck to his beliefs in this case. And look what it got him. Every possible dream he'd ever had, right here in his arms.

Life didn't get much better than this. He'd bet his father would be proud of him.

"For good, huh?" He leaned down to brush a kiss over Audra's mouth. He'd intended it to be a sweet gesture but, as did most things with Audra, it quickly turned hot and wild. Their tongues dueled, her hands gripping his shoulders. Desire, always close to the surface when he was with her, surged. A sound in the boutique reminded him they weren't alone.

Jesse pulled back just a little and caught his breath. "For good sounds perfect," he said. "Especially since I'd planned to tell you the same."

"You're sure you can handle me? All of me?"

Could she doubt it? He tugged her hips tighter to his, letting her know just how much he wanted her.

Her roll of the eyes made him laugh.

"Always," he answered. "In every way."

Her smile lit up the small dressing room.

"Shall we commemorate it?"

"Let me take that loser down and book him, tie up a few loose ends, then we'll celebrate."

"Celebrate?"

"I'm thinking something with whipped cream, chocolate syrup and jar of cherries."

A burst of happy laughter escaped Audra, and she hugged him again. She winked. "Bring those handcuffs, huh?"

"I'll bring them," he agreed, "but you don't need them to keep me with you for the rest of our lives."

Who knew? A Wicked Chick and a cop…forever.

His own personal fantasy.

* * * * *

MILLS & BOON®

Want to get more from Mills & Boon?

Here's what's available to you if you join the exclusive **Mills & Boon eBook Club** today:

✦ *Convenience – choose your books each month*
✦ *Exclusive – receive your books a month before anywhere else*
✦ *Flexibility – change your subscription at any time*
✦ *Variety – gain access to eBook-only series*
✦ *Value – subscriptions from just £3.99 a month*

So visit **www.millsandboon.co.uk/esubs** today to be a part of this exclusive eBook Club!

MILLS & BOON®
By Request

RELIVE THE ROMANCE WITH THE BEST OF THE BEST

A sneak peek at next month's titles...

In stores from 18th September 2015:

- **His After-Hours Mistress** – Margaret Mayo, Trish Wylie & Tina Duncan

- **Rich, Rugged and Royal** – Catherine Mann

In stores from 2nd October 2015:

- **Scandal in Sydney** – Marion Lennox, Alison Roberts & Amy Andrews

- **His Girl Next Door** – Soraya Lane, Trish Wylie & Jessica Steele

---